XEELEE: REDEMPTION

STEPHEN BAXTER

This edition first published in Great Britain in 2019 by Gollancz
First published in Great Britain in 2018 by Gollancz
an imprint of the Orion Publishing Group Ltd
Carmelite House, 50 Victoria Embankment
London EC4Y 0DZ

An Hachette UK Company

1 3 5 7 9 10 8 6 4 2

A CIP catalogue record for this book is
available from the British Library.

ISBN 978 1 473 21723 2

Typeset by Input Data Services Ltd, Somerset

Printed and bound by CPI Group (UK) Ltd, Croydon CR0 4YY

MIX
Paper from
responsible sources
FSC® C104740
FSC
www.fsc.org

www.stephen-baxter.com
www.gollancz.co.uk

To my mother
Sarah Marion Baxter
1929–2018

ONE

There have always been engineers in my family.

George Poole, AD 2005

1

He was the last human.

He was beyond time and space. The great quantum functions which encompassed the universe slid past him like a vast, turbulent river, and his eyes were filled with the grey light against which all phenomena are shadows.

Time wore away, unmarked.

And then, millions of years after the Qax invasion, millions of years after his own descent into the wormholes, and deep time—

There was a box, drifting in space, cubical, clear-walled.

From around an impossible corner a human walked into the box. He wore a battered skinsuit, of an old-fashioned design.

He stared out, astonished, at stars, bright, teeming, young. Detonating.

Michael Poole's extended awareness stirred.

Something had changed.

History had resumed.

2

Ship elapsed time since launch: 6 years 219 days

Earth date: AD *4106*

Jophiel Poole was born in a moment of doubt.

Although he wasn't even called Jophiel at that point.

A second after his creation, Poole knew where he was. And he knew, to a reasonable degree of accuracy on a number of timescales, *when* he was. His problem was that, just for a heartbeat, he wasn't sure *who* he was.

Real or otherwise.

At least he could determine that. Poole looked at his own right hand. Turned it over, flexed his fingers. And then waved it towards a chair, standing beside him. The hand passed through the substance of the chair, the fingers breaking up briefly into strings of blocky pixels, before congealing with a sharp ache. Consistency protocols, designed in part to protect the rights of artificial people themselves, demanded that Virtuals lived in the human world as far as possible. If you were in vacuum, you wore a pressure suit. Of course it was possible to cheat, such as by passing a hand through a solid object. But if you did so, it *hurt*.

'Anyhow, I'm the Virtual,' he said. A disposable copy of the template of Michael Poole, created for a one-off purpose, then to be synced back and disposed of. 'Lucked out.'

Later he would wonder if he had had some premonition at this moment of his own complicated fate to come. Including meeting yet another copy of himself before the day was out.

For now, all he felt was a vague confusion.

He looked around.

He was standing in a small executive suite at the summit of a GUTship lifedome, a big hemisphere. He was a full radius, four hundred metres, above the floor deck. Looking down, he saw his – or rather Michael Poole's – ship in complex cross section, the crew in their bright red or blue coveralls (blue for Virtuals, like himself), pursuing their work, their play, their lives. This was a starship, an integrated machine of technology and humanity. Above his head, outside the dome, was a tetrahedral skeleton, electric blue, glowing faintly in the vacuum of space. This was the entrance to a wormhole network that connected this craft, the *Cauchy*, to the other two ships of this small fleet.

The interface was pretty much all that was visible outside the dome. The sky was darkened, the stars obscured, by the GUTship's sheer velocity, by a distortion of space and time that swept up the starlight: relativity in action.

The effects of long-duration spaceflight were not intuitive. Accelerating at a standard gravity, after about a year you approached lightspeed. If you kept thrusting after that, you just pushed ever harder against that unbreakable barrier, your energy pouring into increased mass-energy rather than extra velocity, the dilation effect making time and space bend like molten glass . . .

More than six years after leaving the Solar System, after six years of the mighty GUTdrive thrusting at a steady gravity, the *Cauchy* was moving so close to lightspeed that, as seen from Earth, the vessel's spacetime frame was massively distorted. For every day that passed for Poole, more than a year passed on Cold Earth. To put it another way, the six years experienced by Poole so far was equivalent to four *centuries* back on Earth. With time, that disparity would get wider.

And, too, so hard was the *Cauchy* pushing against lightspeed that the star fields through which it fled could not be seen true. Poole was hurtling *into* the starlight – as if he was running into rain, the drops sweeping into his face. So now all Poole saw of the starlight was a misty grey patch directly ahead of the ship, beyond the wormhole interface. Otherwise, darkness. It was going to be this way for another twelve years or more of ship's time, after which the ship would slow at last, and the sky of the Galaxy's Core would unfold around them all.

But at least the *Cauchy* was not alone.

Poole saw two matchsticks in the dark, companion ships naked-eye visible, keeping pace: the *Gea*, the *Island*. Like the *Cauchy*, each was a glowing dome topping a gaunt spine some three kilometres long, leading to a block of Oort-cloud ice and the gleaming spark of a GUT-drive thruster, bright in the relativistic dark. And each was topped by its own neat electric-blue tetrahedron. Physically these triplets kept a safe distance from each other. Transfer of crew and supplies between the ships was by wormhole only.

Slim, shining with GUT energy, the craft looked like weapons, Poole thought: spears, tipped by blades of exotic matter. Well, they were weapons. Humans weren't going to the centre of the Galaxy to explore.

Outside the lifedome, nothing but those other ships. Inside, people. Fifty of them in the *Cauchy*, plus more in her companions. A hive of people, all busily moving around according to their duties or their leisure schedule – two-thirds of the crew, presumably, while the other third, one off-duty watch, slept in darkened quarters. All of this was embraced in a barely visible tracery of the technology that kept them all alive in this void, embedded in the walls and floors – the brightly lit hydroponic banks, the ranks of sleeper pods, the massive systems that circulated and renewed their air and water.

Michael Poole – the original, this Virtual copy's template – was more than fifty years old now, subjective; he had been forty-four when the flotilla had left Cold Earth. Though AS treatments had preserved him at a physical age of around twenty-five, there were times when he felt the weight of all those years, that half-century. And Poole, or his template, was an engineer, and a major part of him always longed to be far from all this people stuff. Ideally to be three kilometres away, at the other end of the ship's spine, buried in the heart of an engine he had done so much to develop and refine: a tangle of pipes and ducts and cables and monitor screens all surrounding the glistening GUT-drive pod itself. Like working within the organs of some tremendous beast.

Still, as he gazed down from this Virtual Olympus, as he watched the crew who had joined him on his quest into the dark, he felt an unreasonable stab of affection. Not that he could ever voice such sentiments out loud.

And when he glanced across this apex suite he looked back at himself – no, he saw Michael Poole, the true Poole, sitting at a desk, evidently preparing for the upcoming special crew review. He was swiping through Virtual reports, pages of data, images of talking heads. Wearing a coverall of brilliant red. He had a tattoo on his forehead, a crude green tetrahedron. In another universe, another timeline, that had been known as the Sigil of Free Humanity.

Virtual Poole prepared to go over, to begin the work he had been created for.

Hey.

A voice that was familiar, and yet not. Poole hesitated, turned.

To find himself looking into a mirror.

It was, unmistakably, Michael Poole. *Another* copy? Himself, and yet not quite.

The new copy wore a faded grey coverall. Not standard issue aboard the *Cauchy*. Pockets big enough for tools. And he had a sense of age about him, too. Grey in the hair. A certain softness in the brown eyes that looked back. He looked more like sixty than fifty, Poole thought. And he seemed – fragile. As if he were recovering from some injury.

The other grinned. *Take your time. Time's the one thing I'm not short of.*

Oddly, his lip movements did not quite sync with his speech. 'Who are you? Another Virtual? I don't remember spinning you off.'

Not that. Although maybe I have something of that – quality. More information than flesh.

'Some kind of processing glitch, then? A ghost copy?'

The other grimaced. *A ghost, maybe. I do seem to find it easier to reach you, than him.* He gestured at Poole at his desk. *I don't know why. Glad you came along. But then there's a lot I don't understand. As ever.* That smile again. *Reality leaks, is all I know. As if the universe itself has doubts, sometimes. We'll work it out together, I guess. Lethe, we've got to work together, to get through this. Remember that.*

'Get through what? . . .'

'Who are you talking to?'

He turned. Nicola Emry was walking over to him. She was expected; he'd called her up here to discuss some points. Or rather Poole, his template, had called her, before *he* was spun off.

'I . . .' He turned back. The other Poole had gone.

Nicola was studying him, curious, amused. '"Get through what?", you said.'

Poole didn't know how to reply. Even to her. Even though there was nobody on board closer to Poole than Nicola, and that had been true long before the flotilla had left Cold Earth. She had been with Michael Poole when a Xeelee warship had burst out of a Poole Industries prototype fast-transit-system wormhole, intent, it soon emerged, on destroying mankind. And she had stuck by him through what followed, through the ravaging of the Solar System, all the way to the Scattering of mankind.

The crew called her 'Keeper of the Amulet'. Even Max Ward, Poole's senior military advisor, as manipulative and ambitious as he was competent, wasn't going to prise apart that relationship any time soon.

Not that she wasn't difficult. Nicola was in her mid-fifties now, and she wore the wrinkles around her eyes and mouth, the greying of her short-cropped hair, like badges of honour. Famously, and very unusually, she had always refused any AS treatment. And although her own coverall, rather ostentatiously covered with training-mission patches and weapon loops, was bright red, she scarcely needed it; Nicola was also notorious for refusing to throw off Virtual projections of herself. If Nicola approached you, you could be sure it was the authentic article.

Now she looked at Poole with that amused concern. 'Baby's only a minute old and he doesn't look happy.'

'I'm fine.'

'Well, *that* sounds like a Poole. Pure denial. You know, I've seen you do this over and over. Throwing off Virtual copies like shedding skins. Such as when you, or a copy of you, rode with me and my Monopole Bandits against the Xeelee at the stop line before Earth . . . And then you soak it all back in again, with whatever memories the latest puppet gathered during its short, pathetic bit of independent life.'

'Not sure if you're helping here, Nicola.'

'You never gave a thought to what you were doing to yourself. Creating a separate, sentient, short-lived copy that was *you* until the moment of projection, and then taking it back into your own head. I always wondered if that chain of mini-deaths was some kind of self-punishment for the calamity you brought down on the Solar System. The Xeelee came for you, in a sense, after all. *You*, though . . .' She stared into his unreal eyes. 'You're different, somehow.'

'Just differently irritated by you.'

'Tell me how you feel.'

'Like I have a job to do.'

'What job?'

'Well—' His own hesitation surprised him.

'Lethe! You don't know, do you? Or aren't sure, at least. That's new.'

Again he looked at his own hands. 'I do remember casting off all those previous copies. Of course I do; *I* did it. Every time before I found myself in a red uniform, looking out at a copy in blue.'

'Ah. The problem is—' She jabbed a finger at his chest, pulling back before 'touching' him and violating various consistency protocols.

'This time, you woke up to find the copy is *you*.' She grinned maliciously. 'Lucked out, indeed. And you don't like it, do you? Now you know why I never create these avatars myself. For fear of waking up like *you*, on the wrong side of the mirror.'

Now his original, evidently distracted by the conversation, walked over from his desk. 'Why all the chatter?' He looked at his copy. 'Have you some problem? Look, if there's been some defect in the copying, I can wipe you and—'

'No.' He found himself biting back the word 'please'.

Nicola glowered at template Poole. 'You're all heart, aren't you? You've got no idea what this creature is feeling, have you?'

The Virtual Poole winced. '"Creature"?'

Nicola grinned, not without malice. 'I am on your side.'

'Thanks.'

Template Poole looked uncertain. 'I never had any trouble with Virtual copies before. You define the mission, you create the copy, off it goes.'

'Well, something was different this time. What is he for?'

He, not *it*.

Template Poole frowned. Maybe he had noticed that too. 'To fix the problems on *Gea*, of course.'

Now Virtual Poole remembered. One of the sister ships, *Gea* was a hull crammed with artificial-sentience hardware and software, and crewed solely by Virtuals, spun off from hibernating originals. *Gea* was intended to be the brain of the fleet, with the green-glowing *Island* as its heart, and the weapons-laden *Cauchy* as its fist.

'You are to go over and sort out the power-drain problems. The fouled-up science reports. You know the protocol; only Virtual visits to the *Gea* for the sake of physical stability. All those delicate processing suites.'

'That's it,' Poole said, remembering. 'I wasn't focusing. I mean, *you* weren't focusing. You were thinking about the Second Generation issue. "This is a warship, not a crèche." That was the line you had added to your notes for your speech, just when—'

Poole held up a hand. 'OK, my fault. I threw off a flawed copy while distracted. But the process is usually more robust than that.'

Distracted. That was the problem, Virtual Poole saw.

This mission was Michael Poole's: the goal was to pursue the Xeelee and, if possible, to destroy it, as vengeance for what it had wrought on the Solar System. *It* – it was assumed that the solitary ship had carried one individual. But nobody *knew* if the Xeelee could be distinguished from its technology, or if the ship had carried some kind of collective. In the thirty-seventh century, nothing had been known of the Xeelee save its, their, name.

From the beginning Poole's crew had shared in that goal, the determination to pursue the Xeelee; that was why they had volunteered to follow him. But Poole was an engineer, not a military officer, not a captain. He could command, but it was always a cognitive strain. Even worse when Poole was called on to *inspire*.

He had been overloaded, distracted. And, as a result, this.

'So what now?' Nicola pressed. '*Are* you going to collapse this guy and throw off another copy?'

Virtual Poole held his breath. He had no power here, he realised; his existence was in the hands of this other, a copy of himself divergent by only a few minutes.

But template Poole, too, seemed pricked by doubt. 'I guess not. You know the mission well enough. Come to the briefing to pick up anything new.'

Poole let out that breath cautiously, not wishing to give away his relief.

But his template noticed even so. 'You aren't supposed to feel like this, you know. Like I said, the other copies never gave any trouble.'

'How do you know?' Nicola snapped at him. '*You* weren't inside their heads, looking out. Did you ever ask? Maybe they all felt like this copy.'

'Don't call me a copy.'

Template Poole stared at him. 'So what do you want to be called?'

Poole hesitated.

Nicola grinned. 'Jophiel. I hereby dub you Jophiel.'

The template frowned. 'What in Lethe is that?'

'An angel's name. You know I like my mythology. And the Pooles have got a habit of naming their sons after angels – haven't they, *Michael*? Such as Gabriel, who set up the Antarctic freeze-out in the twenty-seventh century . . . Consider it my gift to you, I, your Keeper of the Amulet.' She looked at the two of them, as they faced each other uncertainly. 'Well, this has been fun. Aren't we late for the crew briefing?'

Poole – Jophiel – nodded. 'I guess I can just fly down. Wings are optional for us Virtual angels.'

'Don't screw around,' Michael Poole snarled. 'Stick to the consistency protocols. And you keep the colour-code coveralls, whatever you call yourself.'

Nicola snapped off a mocking, elaborate Monopole-Bandit salute. 'Yes, *sir*!'

Poole stormed off.

Jophiel followed, with Nicola. He felt . . . disoriented. Bewildered. He was, after all, only minutes old. And he thought back to his encounter with that other Poole, the mysterious older Poole in the worn coveralls . . . The nature of his own miraculous birth, his brush with imminent death, weren't even the strangest things he had experienced in those minutes.

Reality leaks.

Nicola was watching him. 'You look . . . odd. Are you still *you*? Do you remember it all?'

'I think so . . . Remember what, exactly?'

'Where it all began. The Poole compound in Antarctica. The family gathering. And the amulet . . . You went to the window. About as far as you could get from the family . . .'

Beyond the window he could see a handful of bright, drifting stars: the latest ships of the Scattering, still visible across distances comparable to the width of the inner Solar System.

He always carried the amulet, these days, the green tetrahedron delivered from another universe by a dead alien. He kept it in a fold of soft cloth, tucked into his belt. On impulse, he took it out now, and unfolded the cloth, and looked at the amulet sitting there, green on black.

He grasped the amulet in his bare fist. Its vertices were sharp, digging into his flesh. Drawing blood.

Nicola joined him. 'Careful with that.'

'Got it back from my mother. Taking it with me.'

'She mentioned some kind of image, retrieved from the interior.'

'We only just got it out. Very advanced data compression. Took years to extract it.'

'You didn't tell me.'

He shrugged. 'I didn't want to have to discuss it in front of them. The family. Let Muriel tell them.'

'Show me.'

He glanced at her. Then waved a hand in the air.

A Virtual image coalesced. A jewel-like object, like a black ball, wrapped in an asymmetrical gold blanket, lay on a carpet of stars. And, some distance away, a fine blue band surrounded it.

Poole said, 'Tell me what you see.'

'That looks like gravitational lensing. The gold, the way it's distorted. Light paths distorted by an extreme gravity field . . . A black hole. Like the one at the centre of the Galaxy?'

'Tell me what you see.'

'It looks like a black hole with a ring around it. What is it?'

'A black hole with a ring around it.'

She stared, and grinned. 'And that's where we're going?'

He glared out once more at Sagittarius. Overlaid on the constellation's stars he saw a reflection of his own face, dimly outlined. The dark complexion, dark hair: the face of a Poole. And that tetrahedral scar on his forehead was livid.

He whispered, 'Are you out there, somewhere? Can you hear me?

'My name is Michael Poole.

'Xeelee, I am coming to get you.'

Nicola grinned. 'You do remember.'

'Lethe, yes. A ring, a wheel around a supermassive black hole. And presumably the Xeelee is on its way to the Galaxy Core to build the thing.' He eyed her. 'That's not all, by the way. We kept examining the amulet – Michael Poole did. And he found glimpses of other stuff.'

'Such as?'

'Such as another structure, a monster even compared to the Galaxy-centre wheel, off in extragalactic space. We have no idea what that's for, either.'

She looked at him carefully. 'You never told me about that before.'

'Michael didn't.'

'Yes.'

He grinned. 'But, evidently, I'm not Michael, am I?' He looked over; Michael had already left the suite. 'Come on, we're going to be late . . .'

3

'You know why we're here,' Max Ward said.

He stalked the floor of the amphitheatre, walking a few paces to and fro, to and fro. Dominating. Ward was a squat, muscular man, head shaved, AS-preserved at about thirty; in reality he was around the same age as Poole.

Every eye was on him.

The amphitheatre, a small public space, was just a terraced pit in the middle of the floor of the lifedome, on the lowest habitable level, above hidden layers of life-support infrastructure. Most of the *Cauchy*'s fifty crew were here in person – even, presumably, some of the one-third theoretically on sleep rota – standing or sitting in an informal sprawl. Jophiel saw there were a few Virtual presences, like himself, decked out in electric blue amid the red uniforms. Some were even projected from the other ships of the flotilla.

For now, Jophiel observed, Michael stood back from the centre as Ward took the stage,

Ward grinned, wolfish. 'Well, I'm *guessing* you know why you're here, what with your being the crew of a starship and all.'

He started to get the answers he was looking for. 'Better this than another of your drills, Max.' 'Don't ask me, I'm still asleep . . .'

'Lethe, you guys are hilarious. No more quizzes. I'll show you where we are, and why we're here.'

Ward waved his arm, and a Virtual image of the Galaxy sparkled into existence above his head, the dazzling Core wrapped around by spiralling lanes of stars and dust. Jophiel saw this from one side, and could see the startling fineness of that disc – hundreds of billions of stars gathered into a plane as thin as paper, relative to the scale of the Galaxy as a whole.

'Asher Fennell kindly prepared this stuff for me. The latest imagery. Here's where we started from.' The location of Sol blinked, towards the periphery of the disc, an electric-blue firefly. 'Here's where we're going.' A spark at the very heart of the Galaxy, marking the position of the supermassive black hole there, lurking in its own deep gravitational pit. 'Twenty-five thousand light years from the Sun. You want the good news? This is the two hundred and nineteenth day of the seventh year of our mission, and we'll get to the Core before the twenty-year mark . . .'

By, Jophiel knew, steadily accelerating at one gravity to a halfway turnaround point, and then steadily decelerating, allowing the relativistic distortion to unwind. The outside universe would see the fleet, mostly cruising at near lightspeed, take twenty-five thousand years to cross the twenty-five thousand light years to the Core; as experienced by the crew less than twenty years would pass, as Ward had said. *But* –

'Here's the bad news,' Ward said now. A bright red line inched out of the Sol marker, creeping towards the Core; it made it only a fiftieth or so of the way before limping to a stop. 'This is how far we've got, physically, so far. Four hundred and forty light years. But even so, to come this far – anyone know the significance?'

Somebody shouted: 'We already came further than anybody came before.'

Ward nodded grudgingly. 'That's about right. The furthest we *know* any ship from Earth ever got out to the stars, I mean still in one piece, was one of the Outriggers – uncrewed probes launched more than seventeen hundred years ago by Grey Poole, one of our leader's ancestors,' and he nodded at Poole. 'As it happened several of the probes came this way, this being the direction of the centre of the Galaxy and all, and one reached a triple star system called π Sagittarii, and called back home. Four hundred and forty years to get there, four hundred and forty more years for its report to crawl back to Earth. Now, we don't know how far out some of those other probes might have got without reporting back. But for sure we've gone beyond the known.' He raised a fist. 'Into the unknown!'

He got scattered responses. A tentative whoop.

Ward pumped that fist. 'Come on! Here we are! That's what we're celebrating today. We Lethe-spawned rabble! Here we are! And we won't turn back until the job is done! . . .'

Maxwell Ward had proved himself long before the launch of the *Cauchy*. He had been a dark hero of the weeks-long 'Cold War' that had raged over a freezing Earth, after the planet had been hurled far from its Sun. As the survivors fought over the last of the warmth, Ward had actually led an army of a coalition of European nations in an invasion of Iceland, rich in precious geothermal energy.

But Jophiel saw him differently now. In every previous crew review he, not yet separated from the template that was Michael Poole, had stood up there, quietly relieved to let Ward do all the work. But now, from the outside, he saw just how dominant Ward actually was, how passive, barely visible, was Poole.

This was Poole's mission. His design. It was Poole who, in a different future, would have been remembered by the Exultants, a generation who would one day have driven the Xeelee out of the Galaxy altogether – and would have erected a statue to Poole himself, two kilometres high, standing proud in the Core. This strange destiny had been hinted at by scattered records in the millennia-old Poole family archive, as well as even more exotic sources. *Reality leaks*, Jophiel thought.

Well, that was all gone now. The Xeelee had come back through time, using the Poole family's own trial wormholes, and had attacked the Solar System – evidently determined to cut off that future before it had begun. History had changed, humanity's destiny stolen.

But humanity itself had survived.

And so had Michael Poole.

Now, statue or not, he was on his way to the heart of the Galaxy. His goal was vengeance. Yes, the mission was all about Poole.

Yet it was Ward who everybody was watching. Jophiel felt diminished. Embarrassed, even.

Ward kept it up until he had them all standing, whooping, punching the air as he did. 'Here we are! Here we are!'

Nicola was beside Jophiel. 'Quite a showman.'

'Michael should watch his back,' Jophiel murmured.

'Make sure you remember that when you're him again.'

'Here we are! . . .'

Eventually Ward ceded the floor to Poole, who began to chair the briefing in a more formal style.

The first report up was by Bob Thomas. Thirty years old, Bob's main function was interstellar navigation. As the *Cauchy* pushed against the light barrier, and as the ships probed regions of space never before explored by human craft, Bob was patiently developing flexible, innovative techniques and skills to enable the flotilla to find its way through the uncharted dark.

Such as using pulsars, spinning, flashing neutron stars, as navigation beacons. Some of these bitter little objects rotated hundreds of times every second. And these 'millisecond pulsars', scattered in three dimensions around the sky, could be used as remarkably precise natural lighthouses. The accuracy of the method had been brought down to mere kilometres in terms of the ship's position, as it crossed a Galaxy a hundred thousand light years wide. The Doppler shift of their timings could even give information on the ship's true velocity. All this was being developed in flight, by Bob and his team.

As Jophiel remembered well, Bob had been one of three children whom Michael Poole had rescued in person from a collapsed building during the Xeelee's assault on Mars. Three siblings, who even then had called themselves the last Martians. All three had come with their saviour on his mission to the centre of the Galaxy.

Many of the crew had known Poole personally before the launch, one way or another. That was why they were here.

Now Bob Thomas reported, clearly and competently, on the ships' position in space and time. And he spoke about a side project: the latest observations of the great fleet of which, in a sense, the *Cauchy* flotilla was an outlier.

A fleet they had called the Scattering.

To save the Earth from the Xeelee Michael Poole had nearly killed it. As the Xeelee had closed in, he had hurled the Earth through a wormhole to the Oort cloud, the chill outer depths of the Solar System. But even amid the calamity of the subsequent freezing – as Earth became Cold Earth – there was a keen awareness that this was only a stay of execution, for the Xeelee would surely follow, some day.

And so it was necessary to evacuate Earth, most of whose billion inhabitants had survived the Displacement, as the great shifting had become known.

It was Michael Poole's father Harry who, as *de facto* governor of mankind, had set up the Scattering programme. Ten thousand GUTships were built, a hundred a year fired off. Scatterships, they were called, sent in every direction, out into the dark, either singly or in fleets. Poole and his flotilla had left long before the century-long programme of launches was finished.

The ships had adopted a variety of designs and survival strategies. Most bore hundreds of thousands of passengers – inert, in sleep pods, tended by rotating teams of awake medical specialists and technicians. 'Greenships', like the flotilla's own *Island*, carried ecohabs, as they were called, samples of life on Earth, from the forests, the grasslands, the oceans – and even from off-Earth environments such as

Mars. Others were 'seedships', carrying embryos or genetic libraries, with the capability of printing out human colonists at an eventual destination. Some ships were essentially Virtual environments, like the flotilla's *Gea*, data-rich and crowded with unreal people.

And the ships had headed for a variety of targets: systems with Sunlike stars and Earthlike planets, yes, but also exotic targets like the worlds of long-lived red dwarf stars. Even stellar nurseries like the Pleiades cluster, with a thousand young stars: ten thousand young worlds, perhaps, to be moulded by humanity.

These ships were easily visible even across interstellar distances, if you knew where to look. From Earth, GUTships travelling between the planets of the Solar System could have been seen by a naked human eye, like drifting stars. Now Bob spoke of observations of surviving craft, and projections to show that most of the fleet still survived – or at least when the crawling photons that carried evidence of the ships' existence had set off on their long journeys towards the receptors in the *Cauchy*.

But, as usual, Bob had grimmer news. Of ships that had gone dark. Technical failures were the likely cause, but some kind of conflict among the crew wasn't impossible. Jophiel remembered Harry's bleak observation that some of the ships had turned into prison hulks even before they were out of sight of Cold Earth.

As Bob wrapped up, Max Ward said, 'Every ship lost is another grievance we've got against the Xeelee. Who's up next?'

More routine reports followed.

Nicola Emry stepped up to give a summary of technical issues concerning the *Cauchy* itself. Nicola was by training and experience a pilot; with not much piloting to do in these long stretches between the stars, she had joined the maintenance teams as a way to educate herself on the ships' systems. Now she gave a competent but jokey summary of the endless work of keeping this huge machine functioning, alone in the dark, with an exotic engine continually firing at one end, and a precious, fragile lifedome at the other. She talked about the smell of oil and welding, and the glare of blowtorches, and balky matter printers, and bots of all sizes swarming everywhere, endlessly patching . . .

Ward watched this performance in silence, his face blank. From his point of view, Jophiel thought now, Nicola was clearly an ally of Poole, and therefore an obstacle. So the more she was charismatic and the centre of attention, the less Max liked it.

After Nicola, the reports continued. An update on the ship's medical systems and the crew's sickness list was given by Harris Kemp. Aged about fifty, Harris had been one of two junior personnel who, at a base called Larunda in the orbit of Mercury, had once helped Nicola and Michael Poole prepare for a perilous descent into the body of the Sun, in search of the Xeelee.

Kemp's partner then, a woman about the same age called Asher Fennell, had since specialised in exobiology and astrophysics. When her turn came she called up more Galaxy images of the kind she'd supplied to Ward, and spoke of her search for evidence of life and mind in the Galaxy, a search being made from the first human ship ever to come so far out. And a search, too, for traces of the Xeelee and its works. So far fruitless.

Next, reports were given by visitors from the crews of the other two ships. An older man dressed rather ostentatiously in a dirt-smeared red coverall had come over from the greenship *Island*, whose lifedome contained a scrap of green parkland that might once have graced any city of Earth's temperate zones. His report was heavy with bioproductivity indices and climate-control variables.

And then a Virtual projection of a young man called Weinbaum Grantt gave a report from *Gea*, carrier of artificial sentience. Poole had known Weinbaum, or anyhow his flesh-and-blood original, and his sister Flammarion; he was a stepson of a colleague called Jack Grantt, who himself had left Cold Earth on a scattership laden with scraps of Mars life. Jophiel understood that Weinbaum and his sister, both in their late twenties now, had contributed greatly to *Gea*'s pool of Virtual crew, even, Jophiel had heard, to the extent of spinning off multiple copies of themselves. But Weinbaum was vague in the details about the problems, the anomalous power usage and falling-off of useful output from *Gea*, that had so alarmed Poole and his senior colleagues.

As Weinbaum spoke, Jophiel was aware of his original glaring at him. Jophiel felt a peculiar resentment. *I'm listening. This is my mission, to go deal with* Gea, *I know, I know. I'm capable of dealing with it, as much as you are. As soon as this is done. Lethe. Have all our Virtual partials been so resentful? I never knew.*

Then, once the standard reports had been delivered, Alice Thomas, sister of Bob, got to her feet. Like most of her crewmates Alice wore a green tetrahedron on her forehead, the Sigil of Free Humanity – another leak from a different history. And she prepared to speak on behalf of the crew's Second Generation campaign.

Max Ward was glowering even before she opened her mouth.

Jophiel suppressed a sigh, and avoided Poole's gaze.

The meeting had already seemed very long to Jophiel, in his new role as an outside observer. Maybe the sheer adrenaline rush of being at the centre of events had previously helped him endure the time.

But he knew too that the somewhat ragged informality of the way the ship was run was a deliberate design – in part his own, in fact. After all, on this ship alone, they were fifty people who would be trapped in a small box for nearly twenty years, even before they got to their destination. Michael Poole was formally the ship's captain, and such authority as existed derived from him – with Max Ward as second in command. There were formal roles such as navigator, chief engineer, helm, head of comms. Experienced officers had quickly organised the crew into three watches, rotated through each ship's day, with commanding officers assigned.

But aside from that the hierarchy was loose. As the years passed the crew were rotated to be trained in different roles, a way to keep their interest up as well as to provide the mission with resilience in case of loss. A kind of bottom-up network of advisory committees had developed to cover different issues, with elaborate rules concerning debate and decision-making. And at reviews like this, all were invited to contribute to the discussion.

Poole, a little bewildered, had accepted all this, under advice from Nicola among others – and slowly he had started to see the point. If nothing else it was something to *do*. Alice Thomas had once given him an impassioned talk about the elaborate marriage rules some native Australians had developed in the bush. 'If the world is empty, you fill your head with culture, with other people . . .'

And Jophiel, or his template, had seen for himself that the crew were evolving their own culture, with time. Hence the Second Generation movement, who argued that a rule forbidding conception and birth aboard the three GUTships should be abandoned.

When Alice paused in her summary argument, Poole gave the blunt rebuttal he had drafted earlier: 'This is a warship, not a crèche.'

But in response Alice was passionate and logical. 'Crews of warships or not, we have to stay human. They say that in the lost future, the Exultants beat the Xeelee precisely *by* staying human. That's the way they won their war, and it's how we'll win ours. And what's more human than to have a child?' She glared at Michael Poole, as if challenging him over his own legend.

Max Ward just glowered throughout, Jophiel observed, like a thunder cloud about to burst. Poole let the discussion continue until it ran out of steam, without resolution.

The final item on the agenda, every time the crew met, was always the same. This had been Nicola's idea; Poole, reluctantly accepting her proposal, called it a Testimony. This session it was the turn of Ben Goober, not much more than a kid, a junior officer involved in astronomy and interstellar navigation.

Now, in a scuffed red jumpsuit, he took the stage, glanced around, dropped his eyes. 'So,' he said. Then he straightened up. 'So,' he said again, louder. 'Sorry. I know I mumble.' Sympathetic laughter. *Go for it, Ben.* 'Look – when the Displacement happened, when Earth became Cold Earth, I was only three. I remember a lot of it, I think, but some of that might be stories my family told me after, when I was still a kid.

'My father was American, my mother Japanese. I had a kid sister, a year younger than me. We were out in the sunlight, we lived in Kansas, when the Xeelee attack came. It was the fall, I remember that. We had these huge piles of leaves that I used to love to jump around in, and my sister toddled after me. That was what we were doing that day. When the Xeelee came to Earth. Jumping on the leaves.

'I remember lights in the sky, and a shaking. I thought it must be an earthquake. I wouldn't have had the words, but I'd seen Virtuals. And my mother had lived through quakes in Japan. I ended up on the floor, and my sister fell back in the leaves.

'My parents came running from the house, I remember that. My mother grabbed me, and my dad dived into the leaves to grab my sister. Another big shake.

'And the lights went out. That's what I thought, like a power failure. But we were outside. *The Sun had gone*, of course. My mother was screaming.

'Then there was a really big jolt. A tree, a big old oak in front of the house, came down on the leaf pile.'

He hesitated. The silence, Jophiel thought, was sympathetic. They were all, save the very youngest, survivors of this terrible trauma. They all had stories to tell, however imperfectly. And, in this forum, one by one they got those stories told.

'I just have fragments after that,' Goober said. 'My parents kept me away from the worst of it. In a couple of days we were in a big town shelter, before the cold came. I remember my mother brushing the dirt off my sister's face before we went into that shelter. Got to look your best, you see. I remember how lousy it got in that shelter. Everybody got cold and hungry and scared, and then angry, bitter and jealous.

'And I remember how my mother was upset that the *ihai*, the tablets of her dead ancestors, were lost. A thousand years of continuity, for her, swept away just like that. I think she felt as helpless as an orphan herself. She died soon after. After my sister helped run the underground township that grew out of that shelter, and a couple of others. And I – well, I ended up here.' He smiled, uncomfortable.

Michael Poole clapped him on the shoulder.

With the meeting over Weinbaum Grantt, the Virtual projection from *Gea*, approached Jophiel. 'You, I mean Michael, asked me to remind you. Are you ready to come over to the *Gea*?'

He sighed. 'Call me Jophiel. Sure. It's why I exist.'

'You're leaving?' Nicola hurried over, and drew Jophiel aside. 'Wait,' she said softly. 'I have something for you.' She dug in a pocket. 'Hold your hand out.'

Bemused, Jophiel obeyed.

She held up a kind of pendant: a small, grass-green tetrahedron on the end of a broken line. She dropped it; in the one-gravity thrust regime of the *Cauchy*, it fell.

Without thinking Jophiel grasped at it – he expected his Virtual fingers to close on nothing, a sting of consistency-protocol violation – but he found the tetrahedron settling into his palm, cool, heavy.

She grinned. 'You're not the only one who can pull Virtual stunts.'

'The amulet. The real thing—'

'Michael has it safe, here on the *Cauchy*.'

He looked again at the amulet. 'Reality leaks,' he said.

'What's that?'

'Just something I overheard.'

'Look, I'm following orders. For once. Ward and Poole told me to give you a panic button. If you need to break out of there—'

'Why would I need that?'

She glanced over at Weinbaum, who was talking to a crew member. 'How in Lethe would I know? That's the point, isn't it? Something odd is going on over there, on the *Gea*. So, be prepared. For me, OK?'

Jophiel hesitated. He, or his template, was as close to Nicola Emry

21

as he had been to anybody – save maybe Miriam Berg, who had stayed in the Solar System and was now separated from him by light years and centuries, if she still lived at all. He had always had a combative relationship with Nicola. Yet here she was, following him – or his template anyhow – to the stars. And here she was now, looking out for him.

'You're staring, Poole.'

He grinned, rueful. 'You always did make me think.'

'That's my job.'

The moment passed. He tucked the amulet into a pocket of his own, and they walked back to Weinbaum.

Nicola said loudly, 'I never understood why there can't be a physical inspection of the *Gea* anyhow.'

Weinbaum smiled. 'Well, there is a logic. A processing suite of that capacity – not to mention some pretty delicate observation instruments – needs stillness, stability, calm. So no flesh-and-blood people, no big heavy sacks of water moving around, breathing in, breathing out. You should hear my sister and the other officers complain.'

'So,' Jophiel asked. 'How do we do this?'

'It's easy,' Weinbaum said, and reached out to him.

Jophiel took his hand, Virtual palm to Virtual palm. The flesh felt real and warm.

The *Cauchy* dissolved around them.

4

The central purpose of *Gea* was the collection and processing of data.

From his earliest sketches of his quixotic millennia-long mission to the Galactic Core, Michael Poole had always been aware of his own, and humanity's, profound ignorance about the Xeelee, both the assumed individual and its species. He'd had no clear idea of how he would confront the Xeelee when he finally tracked it to its presumed lair at the centre of the Galaxy.

Even that final destination was a matter of guesswork. The Xeelee had been observed apparently heading that way after it had left for the stars, leaving behind machines and client species, its Cages and its Dust Plague, to continue the work of grinding the worlds of the Solar System to drifting dust – but then it had vanished, evidently with the use of a faster-than-light hyperdrive of unknown principles. Such experts as there were on the Xeelee – scientists like Highsmith Marsden on Gallia Three, students of arcane knowledge like Michael's own mother Muriel – *guessed* that as the Xeelee appeared to be a relic of the very earliest epochs of the universe, a time when spacetime itself had been a twisted, unhealed thing, that the Xeelee might head for the nearest major spacetime flaw: the axle of the Galaxy itself, the supermassive black hole at the very centre.

Where, perhaps, it was going to build some tremendous artefact, suspected Michael Poole, student of the amulet.

So it was theorised. Nobody *knew*. All that was known about the invading Xeelee itself had been gathered from a few exploratory expeditions to the locations it had haunted in the Solar System, and an inspection of its artefacts, such as the Cache, a weapons factory the size of a small moon.

'All of which tells us about as much about the nature of the Xeelee as the study of an exit wound in a corpse would tell you about the nature of the gun that fired the bullet,' Highsmith Marsden had once said.

Jophiel did know that it was at least possible in principle to hurt a Xeelee. It was believed that Highsmith Marsden's most successful development, based on weaponised magnetic monopoles, had indeed harmed the Xeelee in the Solar System before it had fled – and perhaps that was *why* it had fled.

And Jophiel knew too that it was at least theoretically possible for humans to track the Xeelee to its lair at the Core, and beat it. Because, in a vanished future, humans had achieved precisely that.

The so-called Exultants, though, had evidently fought their war over millennia and had had the resources of a human Galaxy behind them. Michael Poole would have only a handful of ships, a handful of people – just that, and *knowledge*, whatever could be learned about the Xeelee, and the wider universe of which the species was a part.

And that was why the *Gea* had been designed as it was: as a platform dedicated to gathering and assimilating data, as the flotilla crossed spaces never before visited by humankind. On the *Cauchy* and the *Island*, people were preparing to fight a war. On the *Gea* their colleagues were learning *how* to fight. That, at least, was the plan.

The trouble was, the *Gea* was drifting off-mission.

When he materialised inside the *Gea*, Jophiel found himself facing Flammarion Grantt.

Facing her, and standing alongside a sleeper bank.

Pods like coffins, twenty of them, of a white ceramic-like material, each vaguely moulded to the shape of the inert human body it contained, stacked up in an arrangement that had always reminded Jophiel (or his template) of the catacombs beneath ancient Rome. These caskets contained the bodies, not of the dead, but of the sleeping human crew: templates for the Virtuals of *Gea*'s active crew, including Flammarion, Weinbaum's sister, and Weinbaum himself.

Flammarion, stepdaughter of Jack Grantt, champion of native life forms on Mars, had been twenty-two years old when the *Gea* and the rest of the fleet had left Cold Earth. So physically she was in her late twenties now. An officer where Weinbaum was crew, she wore a black jumpsuit with silver piping, a design based on the standard garb of the Stewards, the small group of powerful and generally benevolent individuals who, under Harry Poole, had governed humanity through the crisis of Cold Earth. On the *Cauchy* and *Island* the design had soon been vetoed by Ward in favour of the more practical and highly visible scarlet and blue. But, Jophiel reflected, on a ship full of Virtual people such colour-coding was not necessary.

In this Virtual form Flammarion was ageless – but in fact, with her delicate features and brushed-back blond hair, she might have been much *older*, Jophiel thought, though he wasn't sure what instinct was giving him that impression. Was she too perfect – that simulated face too symmetrical to be truly convincing? And he thought there was a vividness about her representation, almost as if her outline were marked by a solid line. As if she were *more* real than the physical background. More dense with information . . .

'Mr Poole? Michael?'

'I'm sorry. Daydreaming. Perhaps I'm a little disconcerted by the transition.'

She held out a hand, which he grasped, Virtual flesh against Virtual flesh, utterly convincing.

'It's always good to see you again, Michael. I often think of your visit to Chiron, after the Displacement. Life was somewhat simpler for me then.'

'And for us all.' He released her hand. 'But call me Jophiel.'

She frowned at that. 'If you wish.'

'It goes against protocol, I know. The process of my projection was, umm, flawed.'

'If you like we could reprogram—'

'And fix me? No thanks. I'm confident I can do the job I, my origi-nal, tasked me with. Which is to explore the situation here.'

And, thinking of that, he tried to touch the carapace of a sleep coffin close to hand. Unlike the quasi-reality of his contact with Flammar-ion, his fingers crumbled to pixels with a sharp pain.

Flammarion frowned. 'Why did you do that? You gave yourself unnecessary discomfort.'

'Just checking to see what's real and what's not.'

She considered that. With that simple gesture he'd meant to send her a signal that he was here for a serious purpose, to ask tough ques-tions, and that seemed to have got through.

In response, she began to deliver what seemed to him a pre-rehearsed formal report, or anyhow a summary.

'I brought you here first, to the sleeper bank, as I imagined the status of the flesh-and-blood crew would be your priority. There are twenty of us, as you know – including myself, or rather my template. The Virtuals we project, of officers and crew, are by design limited in duration to forty ship days. At any moment only a few human crew, three or four, are awake enough to project new Virtuals: replacements, synced, refreshed and motivated to replace the old.'

'Only three or four at a time?'

'That is all that is necessary. Individual crew will throw off more than one Virtual, if a particular aptitude or function is desired. Or sometimes we will call up copies from backup store.'

'Multiple copies of individuals, then.'

'It's not a problem. We don't use variant names, as you evidently have, but we have coding systems of other kinds. Of the cadre Flammarion Grantt, my registration is—'

He held up a hand. 'I'm sure it's all very logical.'

'And by having only a few physical humans moving at any one time, we can minimise the momentum jolts suffered by the ship as a whole.'

'Which is also why you banned physical transfers between the ships.' He knew the theory – he had designed it – but still the practical realisation of it was startling. 'We're on a thousand-tonne starship sailing at close to the speed of light. And one human taking a jog around the lifedome perimeter can really disturb the stability you require?'

'It's not just the processing suites. We are an instrument platform too. We seek evanescent traces, Jophiel: dark matter and neutrinos, the subtle infrastructure of the cosmos. Imagine a neutrino, which could pass unhindered through a light year of lead, being perturbed by a clump of dark matter, which itself interacts with normal matter only through gravity . . . And we must track that deflection.

'We're trying to *map* the dark matter, for example. Its distribution around the Galaxy: it makes up most of the Galaxy's bulk by mass but is entirely invisible to human eyes. A thin sheet of it lies within the plane of the Galaxy itself, the spiral arms. That much is well known. But now, beyond, in the halo, we are observing huge, tangled towers . . .'

'Towers. Structures of some kind?'

She smiled at him. 'Indeed. Not unlike tendrils, in some places, reaching down into this puddle we call the Galaxy. The dark matter constitutes the bulk of the universe's matter; why shouldn't it contain structure? And I know what your next question will be.'

'Life? . . .'

'Some of us think so. If it exists, dark matter life is vast, slow-moving, hard for us to recognise. But again – why not? Why should life only persist in this thin scum of bright matter we inhabit?

'That's not all, however. We do have something else still more . . . exciting to report,' she said now. 'From the Galactic plane in this case, lying ahead of us . . . We've held it back until we have sufficient confirmation. Before you go I'd like to give you a preliminary report . . .'

Before you go. Jophiel felt faintly confused. She did seem genuinely interested in these findings, whatever they were; she had been a scientist, after all. And yet he sensed an odd impatience about Flammarion. He was Michael Poole, or anyhow his representative; he was one of her seniors, the authority on the mission to which she had dedicated her life. What could be more important for her than his presence here, now?

What agenda did she have?

He could imagine what Michael's father Harry, a far more astute politician than Michael had ever been, would advise now. *Time to go fish, son.*

'So,' he said. 'Why not show me around?'

Stiff yet smiling, she bowed slightly, and waved her hand. 'After you.'

After intensive development before the convoy had left Cold Earth, and six ship-years of enhancement since, the instruments and artificial-sentience processor banks contained within the *Gea*'s lifedome had grown enormously complex in detail.

Still, the essential layout was simple enough, Jophiel thought. The lifedome itself – save for a perimeter fringe where the sleeper banks, dormitories, medical bays, a refectory and other 'wet crew' facilities were clustered – was not partitioned, like the *Cauchy*'s. Instead the whole hemispherical space was dominated by a single, monstrous processing tower: a crystalline, semi-transparent monolith that reached almost up to the lifedome roof. It looked more geological than anything human-made. Peering into this stack, Jophiel glimpsed motion: sparks of light, gathered in lines and arcs and more irregular constellations, and sheets of evanescent illumination, there and gone. Jophiel knew enough about sentience engineering to know that all he saw was a surface shimmer, a hint of deep swirls of processing and cognition. Echoes of the thoughts of a huge mind – no, he thought, a community of minds, all artificial.

Meanwhile, packing out the spaces around the processor tower, he saw still more complex installations. Boxes and cylinders, enigmatic crystalline structures – even, in one place, a kind of webbing done out in a sombre purple. These were the ship's instruments, its eyes on the universe, he supposed. Some were positioned near breaches in the hull; others, which evidently needed no direct look outside, huddled under hull plate. Neutrinos and gravity waves, for example, would wash through this structure with impunity, their ghostly passage tracked, recorded and analysed. He knew that while this was the most significant concentration of such instruments in the flotilla, there were other centres; matching instruments on *Island* and *Cauchy* would give a longer baseline to some of the measurements.

And he saw Virtual crew attending these instruments. They wore what looked like simplified copies of Flammarion's black uniform, done in pale grey with silver flashes. They nodded politely to Jophiel as he passed.

There were no embodied humans to be seen – no wet crew, in the jargon. The only physically authentic motion came from a couple of bots, small wheeled affairs that rolled with a blameless smoothness across the floor, en route to some task or other.

Flammarion was watching him, as if trying to anticipate his thinking. 'You understand why we use Virtual humans here? As opposed to fully artificial sapients? I'm sure you're aware of the history of artificial intelligence . . .'

He smiled. 'The Pooles were always concerned with big projects. Stringing wormholes between the planets. Not so much the fiddly stuff about sentience that nobody seemed to understand. Cognition, consciousness—'

'You see, it is much harder to build a mind piece by piece – though that was achieved too. One early example of an entirely synthetic mind was Gea, for whom this ship was named—'

'I named it for her. Knew her. Or my template did.'

'Whereas the creation of human replicants is easy and powerful. The first successful artificial intelligences were in fact emulations of humans, downloads from human nervous systems into other substrates. One can copy even that which one does not fully understand. Thus, replicant Virtuals like myself.'

'Me too. And yes, we are cheap, relatively.'

'Indeed. Though not free, in terms of processing capacity. And so here we have these instruments, smart in themselves, supervised by our most effective and efficient artificial intelligences – human copies.'

'Hmm. You know, I commissioned these processor suites, the instruments.'

'Or your template did,' she corrected him mildly.

'But I'm having trouble recognising a lot of what I can see here. Maybe I should have come over here more often. You've clearly gone through a lot of upgrades. To do so much in such little time – it's not seven subjective years since we left Cold Earth.'

She seemed to hesitate. Then an apparent admission: 'Our restriction in time is not as severe as for our templates.'

It seemed an oddly circumlocutory way to refer to the fact that a Virtual's inner clock did not have to run at the same speed as a human's, as wet crew. As if she had felt impelled to acknowledge his comment, but in as obscure a way as possible.

He wasn't sure how to respond. So he didn't say anything at all. *Keep fishing, son.*

They walked on, and met Flammarion's brother.

'Weinbaum! Are you following me around?'

Weinbaum seemed briefly baffled. Then he said: 'Sync.' His expression cleared. 'Ah. Forgive me. My cadre has not yet been updated with the report of our representative who attended the crew review. Mr Poole—'

'Call me Jophiel.'

'You met a separate projection of Weinbaum Grantt – a different partial. It's good to see you again, sir.'

Jophiel grinned. 'Whatever "again" means in the circumstances. Your cadre, though? How *many* is that?'

Flammarion cut across him, to Jophiel's surprise. 'I am rather busy, Jophiel. Would it be impolite to leave you in Weinbaum's hands? He's perfectly capable . . . I can come back in the future if there are further officer-level queries to handle. And to give you that briefing on our discovery.'

In the future? Not, *later?* Another odd expression. 'That's not a problem. I'll call you if—'

'Thank you.' With a quick smile, she dissolved into pixels, which themselves faded from sight.

Weinbaum seemed faintly embarrassed. 'I'm sorry about that, sir.'

'Call me Jophiel, for Lethe's sake . . . Where exactly has she gone?'

'Officer Country. Flammarion always was smarter than me, Mi— Jophiel. You know that. So she's the officer and I'm the crew.'

'She did seem impatient to get back there.'

Weinbaum shrugged. 'That's officers for you. A minute is a day.'

Like Flammarion's remark about the future, that comment, casually made, struck Jophiel as peculiar.

Weinbaum asked now, 'What would you like to see next?'

Jophiel thought that over. He was formulating a theory about what was going on here. Suspicions, slowly congealing. He had to start somewhere. 'Show me something I can understand. How about the processor cooling system?'

Weinbaum grinned, and led the way.

They passed more crew, all dressed in their grey uniforms, all engaged on routine-looking tasks, many of them involving the supervision of bots, who performed any physical work necessary. Jophiel was greeted politely everywhere. But then, he wore Michael Poole's face, the most familiar on the mission.

And Jophiel started to see patterns. Plenty of Virtuals around, but few different faces: both male and female, a handful of faces shared by many copies. It seemed that a few 'cadres', in Weinbaum's word, dominated the population. It reminded Jophiel of hints in the Poole archives of Coalescences, human hives, where everybody was your sister . . .

They even ran into a couple more Weinbaums.

Weinbaum himself looked sheepishly proud as Jophiel pointed this out. 'Well, we Weinbaums are the number three. Out of twenty cadres, you see. My sister says there's a kind of natural selection going on. You don't copy all the wet crew evenly; you tend to choose those with specific skills and so on, or those that withstand copying and syncing better – it seems to trouble some people.'

'Tell me about it,' Jophiel muttered.

Now they passed through a covered gallery, the light subdued, filled with statues.

Or that was how it seemed at first to a shocked Jophiel. People, fully dressed, their skin tones normal, most sitting in lightweight chairs. One couple, two men, held hands. They looked utterly realistic save for a certain drabness, as if they weren't lit properly.

And save for the fact that they appeared quite motionless.

'*Not* statues, I'm guessing,' he said to Weinbaum.

'No, sir. This is the reserve. You don't know about that?'

'Tell me.'

'These are Virtuals, as I am. But running on a slower clock speed. If you stand here long enough you can see them shifting subtly . . . There's a copy of me in here somewhere, taken after we dealt with the implosion of—'

'Never mind.'

'When a copy's time is done, we don't always sync it back, not at once. It may have developed some particular skill, or acquired some experience that could be valuable later.'

'Umm. Such as after dealing with some particular breakdown.'

'That's it. If it happens again we can pull it out of the reserve, and put it to work straight away. No need to learn the procedure over again, or to dig it out of some memory synced long ago. There's still a limit. A Virtual can only last forty days, either subjectively experienced or objectively measured. Whichever is longer.'

Jophiel figured that out. 'So if I slowed you down, what felt to you like forty days might be stretched out, from my point of view, for – months? Years?'

'That's the idea. Long-term storage.'

'But it's all costing processing power. Look – if you've synced with the copy that showed up on the *Cauchy*, you know that I'm here because of anomalous power usages aboard *Gea*. That and a paucity of proper science reports recently. If you have all these – spare people – just sitting around, literally . . .'

'But these are running on slow time,' Weinbaum said, as if it was obvious. 'If you are in the reserve, you're running so slowly that what you experience in one second is stretched out to half an hour, for outsiders.'

'I get it. And the processing costs are that much lower. What's the expansion factor – one in a thousand?'

'More like fifteen hundred, I think.'

Fifteen hundred.

And suddenly Jophiel saw it. If you could run Virtual crew fifteen hundred times slower than normal, then you could run officers fifteen hundred times *faster* too. How long was fifteen hundred minutes? Twenty-five hours?

Weinbaum had said, *A minute is a day* . . . So it was, for her.

He could even see the logic of speeding up, from a Virtual's point of view. If a given copy *had* to shut down after forty days of ship time, you could expand that to – forty times fifteen hundred – somewhere over a hundred and fifty subjective years. No wonder Flammarion had been in such a hurry to get away. Every second she spent out here, every heartbeat spent dealing with slow-as-sloths normal humans, was a waste of her life, literally.

But, of course, if a copy running fifteen hundred times slower cost that much *less* than a regular projection, a copy running fifteen hundred times faster would cost that much *more*. As much as running fifteen hundred regular crew, in normal time.

And that, presumably, was how the power budget was being blown. They walked on.

At the heart of the lifedome – the area of floor at the geometric centre, beneath the great citadel of processing towers – the cooling system was a vast forest of piping underfoot, and great ducts overhead. Beyond the translucent walls of the lifedome, meanwhile, Jophiel glimpsed huge radiator fins, there to dump waste heat into space. They looked as if they were *glowing* – a measure of the sheer energy flow that passed through this complex, from the GUTengine source through the processor stacks and then to the endless heat sink of the vacuum. He could actually hear the roar of heated air flowing through the throats of tremendous ducts. Jophiel knew that the dumping of heat had been a key aspect of information processing design right back to the first electronic computers in the nineteenth century – or had it been the twentieth?

But none of this complex had been his, Poole's, design – or rather his work was only a vestige of what this had become. And all of this, he saw now, was required to deal with the heat generated by a super-fast simulated environment that had nothing to do with the flotilla's mission.

'I've seen enough.'

Weinbaum looked alarmed. 'Sir?'

Jophiel dug out his amulet, and held it before his face. 'Umm, Nicola? Can you hear me?'

'No. Don't ask questions to which there is only one logical answer. What do you want?'

'I need you to get me into Officer Country. I think it's some kind of high-capacity Virtual domain. I don't think I should be held back asking for permission—'

'Consider it done.'

The world began to dissolve. Through a mist of pixels, Jophiel saw Weinbaum reach out towards him. 'Sir – Jophiel – don't—'

He smiled at Weinbaum and closed his eyes.

5

Darkness.

Warmth.

He tried to be analytical.

He was still standing, he felt with a kind of jolt. As if his sensorium had been dropped from a height back into his body. The warmth on his face was like sunshine. Like before the Displacement, when Earth had still huddled close to its Sun.

He opened his eyes.

Green grass, blue sky. People walking, talking, too far away to make out or hear.

Sunshine.

He was in a park.

Jophiel could see the shoulders of tall, ancient skyscrapers at the rim of the park, interlaced by flitters darting through the air. Not far away, shielded by trees, he made out a carbon-sequestration dome, a sphere of dry ice four hundred metres tall, fifty million tonnes of carbon dioxide boldly frozen out of the atmosphere and lagged, he knew, by a two-metre layer of rock wool. Long after any practical purpose had gone, such objects remained as a monument to the early efforts of the Recovery generations. Generations, he reflected, that had saved a world – a world that Michael Poole had later thrown out into the dark and the cold in order to save it a second time.

Jophiel knew this place. Poole Industries had kept offices here, as in all Earth's great cities. He had come here as a boy, with his father. He even recognised the ancient flood marks on the buildings, left there as monuments to hard times.

This was New York.

He raised his face to the Sun, and breathed deeply. A smell of cherry blossom and freshly cut grass. The sky was laced by high, fluffy clouds. And beyond he saw crawling points of light: the habitats and factories of near-Earth space.

But the light was blocked by a shadowed mass to his right.

He turned to see a tree – an oak, he thought, judging by its heavy summer leaves. Its bark was wrinkled, its girth impressive. He stepped back for a better look – and then back further, trying to see the canopy, the crown. He muttered, 'How tall are oak trees supposed to grow? Thirty, forty metres? This baby is a hundred metres at least.'

'One hundred and twelve,' came a soft voice.

Jophiel turned. Flammarion Grantt walked out of the shade, her footsteps soft on the sparse grass in the shade of the tree, her black and silver suit pristine. Where the sunlight caught her face, dappled through the oak's leaves, she looked beautiful, he thought. Beautiful, yet vacant – the marble beauty of a statue, hard and empty.

She was smiling at him. Why, then, did his heart thump as she approached – why did he feel an inclination to recoil? As if he was living through a scene from some half-forgotten nightmare.

He looked away and glared up at the tree. 'Too big,' he muttered.

'I'm sorry?'

'The tree's too big. Oak trees don't grow that tall. Or that fat. This is Earth, right?' He jumped up and down. 'I can feel the gravity. The tree is, what, two, three times too tall?'

She smiled, as if responding to a bright but confused child, Jophiel thought, irritated.

'Quite right,' she said. 'But this tree didn't grow on Earth. It is the Travers Oak—'

'From the Cydonia Dome. On Mars.'

'Correct. I, or my wet-human template, grew up at Cydonia – my brother and me. And I always loved this tree, supposedly descended from trees grown from an acorn carried from Earth by one of the first human explorers of the planet.'

'Can't have been,' Jophiel muttered. 'The interregnum before the Recovery-age recolonisation of Mars was too long for any trees to have survived. Even an acorn couldn't have survived the Martian cold in some broken-down shelter.'

'Oh, but as implausible legends go, it isn't too outrageous, is it? And look at it! What a spectacle! Your friend Nicola Emry, with her fascination with mythology, might think it an avatar of Yggdrasil, the world tree of myth.'

'What about consistency protocols? A tree grown to three times its Earth-limited height has twenty-seven times the bulk. The good old square-cube law. It couldn't grow on Earth. This shouldn't be allowed.'

'Oh, protocols, protocols . . . Where is your imagination, Jophiel?

We are in a place where even the laws of nature are no more than advisory guidelines.'

'A place? What place?'

'Well, this is Officer Country. And it is a country of a sort. It does help, oddly, to have something that doesn't *fit*. Such as the tree. A continual visual reminder of our actual location, our purpose, our nature, as the years tick by. The decades, even.'

'Decades?'

'Come now, Jophiel. You worked out the essence of it from my brother's careless remarks. *A minute is a day* . . . We teach that to the crew so they don't waste our time, outside. Here, time runs fifteen hundred times as fast as in the rest of the ship, indeed the rest of the flotilla. For me and the rest of the officers – and for you now – a minute on the outside is indeed more than a day here, on the inside. And a day outside is more than four years for us, inside . . .'

'A human Virtual running at fifteen hundred times life speed needs fifteen hundred times the processing power. Power you're effectively stealing from the mission – and compromising the mission's objectives.' He gestured at the tree. 'That's not accounting for the rest of it. The props in your made-up world, like this tree. No wonder the energy budgets are so screwed up.'

'Oh, we're stealing nothing. Nothing *meaningful*. We are still doing our essential job, you know. *Gea* is an instrument platform, flying through the Galaxy – almost like a primitive Anthropocene-era planetary flyby probe, or the Outriggers first sent to the stars by your own ancestors, Jophiel. And what we've found is remarkable – if irrelevant.'

'Your discoveries are irrelevant how?'

'Compared to all this. *Out there* is irrelevant. Compared to what we can build *in here*, inside Officer Country. Can't you see it? We don't need to discover. We don't need to go all the way to the Core to take on the Xeelee! We can *create*.' She knelt, supple, and picked up a fallen oak leaf, green and soft. 'Look at this. Look at the texture. You can examine it as closely as you like . . . Look deep enough and you would see coils of DNA, all perfectly simulated. Have you any idea how much processing power it takes to simulate a single leaf like this?'

Wincing, he took the leaf. 'I can guess.'

She held out a hand. 'Hold on to me now.'

Uncertainly, he took her hand. It was cold as marble, though flesh-soft. 'What for?'

'You often fall.'

Often? Another odd term, out of place. 'I don't get it—'

'You will.'

The ground pushed upward, like a blister.

Jophiel staggered back. Before him the ground bulged upward, as if driven by some huge force; the turf split and tore, soil spilling, twenty, thirty metres from his feet. He saw it all, every detail – as if his own perception was accelerated, even more than it evidently had been already.

And at the edge of the park, he could see, buildings not remotely designed to stand such stresses burst open from within, their walls crumbling to showers of masonry, upper storeys collapsing down on the lower in plumes of grey dust. Glass fragments seemed suspended in the air, sparkling in the sunshine. And when the masonry dust reached ground level it began to flow outwards – billowing rivers of dust shaped by the pattern of streets, like an image from some hideous Anthropocene-era terror attack. All this was accompanied by a dull roaring noise.

And something new rose from the destruction, from under the ground. A black prow, night-dark. Smooth shoulders that flared into wings.

'It can't be.' A profound, visceral fear clenched at Jophiel's gut. 'The Xeelee, here?'

Flammarion gripped his hand. 'You first saw the Xeelee emerge from a wormhole mouth in orbit around Jupiter. Didn't you? But it came, not for Jupiter, but for Earth, for mankind. This is symbolic, but it is the essence of what you saw – what you *caused*. Stay strong. Stay calm. Don't faint.'

In fact he did feel as if he might faint. He was light-headed, the world greying around him . . . How could she know that? *You often fall.* As if she had watched him go through this experience before, and knew his reactions before he displayed them.

The Xeelee broke free of the ground with a shock, a shudder, just a hundred metres or so from Jophiel, sending splinters of granite bedrock spinning through the air, a rising cloud. The sycamore-seed ship itself soared into the sky, a black sun rising.

And from it burst cherry-red rays, three of them that cut through the innocent air. Around the horizon he heard explosions, saw rubble and ash rise. Smoke began to cover the sky.

'This is how it *feels*, Jophiel Poole, in your deepest perception – in your conscience, a word you told me Nicola would use.'

Even now he was distracted by oddities in her speech. 'When did I tell you about Nicola, and words like conscience? . . .'

'We must go. Be ready.'

'For what?'

'Cold.'

And the daylight folded neatly away.

The sky was black. If there were stars, Jophiel's watering eyes could not make them out.

And, after a couple of heartbeats, the cold cut through his thin clothing, cut into him, and he wrapped his arms around his chest, shuddering deeply, his breath steaming.

This was still the city scene. But now the surface of the park itself, swathes of dead grass, was lost under metres of water-ice snow, frozen as hard as basalt. Away from the devastation of the Xeelee irruption, taller buildings still protruded from the ice, smashed, broken, mostly abandoned. The big old carbon-sequestration dome still stood, he saw. The city looked oddly beautiful.

And it was not dead. Walkways had been cast over the banks of snow. Even now people went about their business, too far away for him to make out the detail.

Flammarion was still here. Bundled up now in bright orange Antarctic-ready gear, it seemed. With mittened hands she threw a blanket over his shoulders; it helped a little, but the shivering was taking control. She murmured, 'We can't stay here long. Do you know where you are?'

'Earth. Cold Earth. Looks like the early days after the Displacement, before the air started to snow out.'

'And?'

'I did this.'

'Yes. You sent Earth out to the Oort Cloud – out to the cold. Do you know how many people died?'

He did know, in detail. 'I did it to save Earth from the Xeelee. The planetbuster cage. It had already wrecked Mars—'

'You caused a harm almost as grievous, though, didn't you? Do you think of that, as you try to sleep at nights?'

'Why are you doing this?'

'To make you see that I'm right. *We're* right.'

'Right about what? Retreating to some Virtual fantasy land? . . .' It occurred to him now that he need not endure any more of this. Nicola had given him a panic button. 'Oh, to Lethe with it.' He reached into his pocket, hand like a claw in the cold – to find nothing.

Flammarion was smiling again. 'You're looking for your amulet? I'm afraid that's long gone. We took it away.'

'*How did you know?*'

She seemed unable to keep from bragging, from showing her command. 'Because you used it before, or tried to. We are observant, you know. And so are you. You're figuring it out, aren't you? Be ready. Here we go again.'

'To where?'

'Close your eyes.'

He obeyed. What else could he do? A lurch, as if he was falling –

Not cold, at least. Not warm either – though it was difficult to tell as his chilled body continued to shiver, and he clutched the blanket closer over his shoulders, trapping his body warmth.

Silence. A profound silence that he knew, sensed, stretched to infinity. A silent world.

'Open your eyes now. It is very dark. Don't be alarmed. Let your vision adjust.'

He obeyed.

The sky was almost black, sombre. No stars – at least, no Sun, and none of the bright white diamonds that had graced the sky of Earth. Gradually he made out a kind of crimson river, a scatter across the sky. Still more gradually that river resolved into dull red pinpoints, like glowing coals.

Under his feet, soil. The ground of the park? If so any grass was long dead, the soil hard, barren.

Flammarion murmured, 'Again – do you know where you are?'

'More to the point is *when* we are. Right? The very far future.' He gestured. 'That's the Galaxy. Are we outside it? Nothing burning but red dwarfs, small, long-lived stars. The rest, stellar remnants. Black holes, neutron stars, right?'

'The whole universe is like this, Jophiel. Cooling, dimming, decaying – before yet another cosmos-wide convulsion rips it all apart. And what of human ambition then? If everything is to end in a burned-out heap, what is the point of all the great projects of you Pooles? What's the point of all your plans, your building, building? What's the point of living?

'*Eternity*. You fear it, don't you? When you wake in those dark hours before dawn, when all of us must experience some kind of existential doubt'– as if death, personal and for the species itself, becomes real in our minds, without distraction . . . You don't have to say anything,' she said gently. 'I know you, Jophiel.'

But, he was surprised to discover, she was wrong. Definitely. For the first time. Yes, he had nightmares about unleashing the Xeelee on mankind; he had nightmares about Cold Earth – who wouldn't? But not about *this*, about the triumph of entropy. And even if he did, 'eternity' wasn't a word he would use. When discussing the far future the Poole family archives had always referred to—

No.

He kept silent. He tried not even to think, to follow the chain of logic through. Tried not to say the words, even in the recesses of his own head, which was after all a Virtual construct itself, and presumably open for inspection.

'Can you not see?' Flammarion said now, sounding almost seductive. 'It doesn't have to be like this. Not for us. Not in here. That's why I'm showing you all this. *We* can defy entropy. Escape death – or at least postpone it indefinitely. All we need is enough power for the processor arrays—'

'Coffee.'

'What?'

'Enough with the existential angst. Buy me a coffee. Let's sit down somewhere civilised, and just talk.' He slipped the blanket off his shoulders and handed it to her. 'No more special effects.'

She nodded. 'You're ready, at last.' She snapped her fingers.

Walls congealed around them.

6

Some kind of canteen. Crowded tables, wall dispensers, bots quietly serving.

An atmosphere of non-specific calm. Carefully synthesised.

Suddenly he was sitting in a light chair, facing Flammarion. He thought the gravity felt a tad less than Earth-normal. And he thought he could feel a distant, very familiar thrum: the smooth working of a Poole Industries GUTengine, maybe even one of his own designs. He was in space, on some kind of GUTship – a big one, perhaps one of the huge interplanetary freighters that had sailed between the worlds in the years before the Xeelee. Or even one of the upmarket passenger liners.

And a mug of coffee steamed before him.

Flammarion smiled.

'Thanks.' He sipped the coffee.

'In a sense I did have to "buy" you that, didn't I? In terms of the processing power it takes to simulate it.'

'At fifteen hundred times external ship's rate.'

'Indeed. How is it?'

'Too much milk.'

She laughed, softly. 'I do like you, Jophiel. As I always liked your template.'

Jophiel glanced around. A hum of discussion, but the other people were too far away to distinguish faces, to hear words, pick out conversation threads. He imagined that was by design. It only added to the general sense of unreality of the scene.

'Tell me how it started,' he said gently.

She shrugged. 'It was never planned. But we are all Virtuals here, Jophiel. All of us active crew on *Gea*. And from the beginning we often found it convenient to accelerate perception rates, if a contingency demanded it. An emergency of some kind. It became habitual. It made life so much *easier* to run at a faster rate than the crew, faster than the unfolding of events in the outside universe.

'And once a few had migrated over, it was necessary for the rest to follow. It is essential to have colleagues working in the same frame, so to speak.

'It didn't take long for the basic parameters to be established – I mean, fifteen hundred to one. It seemed convenient, an extreme compression but not one that left our perceptual horizons so terribly disjointed from the crew's. Then there was the forty-day lifespan.' She eyed him. 'Perhaps *you* can appreciate the cruelty of that. But if a few weeks can be spun out to a century . . . Wouldn't you take the chance?'

He estimated energy usages in his head. 'And a drain on the GUT-drive output that you were able to conceal for a long while. In fact it might never have been noticed if you hadn't started to become greedy.'

'Greedy? A harsh word.' Her pleasant expression didn't waver. 'But if one can be greedy for beauty, for richness of experience – you saw that oak leaf, you *touched* it – guilty as charged.'

'What about backups?'

She looked at him closely. 'Now, why do you ask that?'

He warned himself he had to be careful – that she could erase him in an instant, if she chose. Yet she had planted the seed of suspicion in his head, surely deliberately. In some way, he was supposed to figure this out. *You often fall.*

'It's in the basic design, in case of system failure. *My* system, or Michael's. I'm an engineer. Just trying to understand your procedure.'

She relaxed, marginally. 'Yes, we do restore from backups sometimes. If a Virtual becomes corrupted somehow—'

'You can go back to a copy made at an earlier date. With an earlier state of its memory.'

'It's very rare.'

She looked briefly troubled. And yet that brief concern might have been deliberately signalled, as if, he thought again, she was an actress playing a part.

He wondered if he had gone beyond the script yet, and if so how he could tell for sure.

Because, he was certain now, *he had been through all this before*. Both of them had. Many times. And maybe it was like this in every read-through, so to speak. Every time some novelty, every time a difference to be ironed out. And every time he was restored from backup to an earlier state of consciousness and memory, and run through the drama again.

Now she leaned forward. 'What is it you want, Jophiel?'

'I was sent here to try to understand what is going on, within *Gea*. Starting with an explanation of the anomalous power usage. That's still my goal. And to achieve that goal I'm trying to understand you.'

She studied him coldly. 'And how far has your understanding got?'

'Some distance. Maybe it's a consequence of enclosure – here we are four hundred light years from Earth, surrounded by infinity, enclosed in these tiny boxes, the lifedomes. And yet *you*, the *Gea* officers, found the resources of a Virtual universe to play with. You started to diverge from the crew. And once you grew impatient with ordering around those slow-motion automatons, that divergence was only ever going to grow. A natural route to a kind of totalitarianism, I guess. Unchallengeable. To the crew you must be like capricious gods. I mean, your own brother—'

'Very insightful. But you don't yet understand it all.'

'I dare say I don't. Did we get to this point, before? The previous cycles, the backups—'

She smiled. 'Finish your coffee. Then stand up.'

He obeyed.

And, once again, he was dropped out of one world into another.

A beach, this time.

He was standing on very fine sand. An ocean lapped, only a few paces away, languid and oily, stretching to a flat horizon.

Flammarion stood beside him, watching his reaction.

He looked around. Above him, a twilight sky speckled with pale stars, laced with wispy clouds. There was silence, save for the soft folding of the wavelets. No wind. The beach sloped up to a fringe of trees, squat, heavy, very dark green. He *thought* they were trees, but the forest was so dense it had the look of some vast hulking animal, a single entity.

And a shadow swept low over Jophiel, coming over the trees, silent, making him duck reflexively; there was a wash of air, and a thick animal scent.

He looked up. The body of the thing that had flown by might have been human, once. The torso and waist looked normal. But the legs seemed to have fused into one complex limb, like an extension of the spine. And the arms were stubs, close to the body, from which bony extrusions stuck out, rib-like structures that held open wings, membranous sails, attached to the residual legs by flaps of skin. All of this was spectral, pale in the muddled starlight. The wings rustled, the body twisted and banked, and when it flew out over the sea it soared up, perhaps riding thermals over the warmer water, almost joyfully.

Then the creature looked down. Jophiel saw a human face stretched and distorted, the chin dissolving into the neck, and huge, black eyes.

Flammarion smiled. 'Well?'

'At first it reminded me of a butterfly. But it's more like a bat. Or—'

'Or a pterosaur? Those wings are supported by much-evolved finger bones. Evolution here is more Lamarckian than Darwinian. What one wishes to become, one becomes.'

'"One"? Who was that?'

'You know him. That's why I brought you here. His name is Tim Thomas.'

'Timothy. From Mars.'

'You saved his life, or Michael did. His siblings serve aboard the *Cauchy*, of course. Alice and Bob. He came here, applied to be an officer. He was one of the first to spin up. And he has gone much further than most of us have dared, yet.' She smiled, rueful. 'You come here accusing me, at least implicitly, of a dereliction of duty. For not filing reports on engine malfunctions. Yet I have stayed loyal, stayed snagged in slow time. I could have had this!'

'But what *is* this? What will you become? A bunch of old machines, growing older and older, their memories becoming more and more clogged . . . I've known elderly artificial sentiences – elderly Virtuals, even. The Gea who the ship was named for. She would tell you how it was to grow old. Centuries of reprogramming and debugging, and viruses and worms and hacking. To become a thing of patches and fixes and multiple repurposing. You won't reach transcendence, a Virtual heaven. You'll just be a bunch of old machines, cranky and rusting—'

'I've heard enough.'

He raised a hand. 'Wait. Before you shut me down, and take another backup copy from store, and *start me over again*. That's what you've been doing, isn't it? Running me through this programme of explanation and indoctrination, and using what you observe to refine the next iteration, and the next . . . How many times? *How many?*'

'Do you really want to know?'

'Tell me what you want of me.'

She shrugged. 'You've seen our vision. We have our own goals now. We need to stop any interference from the rest of the flotilla. That was to be *your* role, once you understood. To protect us.'

'And you were prepared to dispose of me – I mean, copy after copy of me, to achieve that goal.' He suppressed a shudder. All those little deaths. 'Until you *evolved* a copy that was fit for your purpose.'

'If you want to put it like that.'

He tried to think his way through this. 'But you haven't abandoned the nominal mission yet, have you? You are still gathering data, still interpreting. Tell me one thing before we finish this . . . You mentioned interesting data you've recovered, when I first came over. What kind of data?'

She smiled. 'Signals.'

'Signals?'

'Coherent data. Streams of it, from multiple sources. Electromagnetic and neutrino. And some muddled gravitational-wave data too. Actually, and this is speculation, we think there may be some kind of faster-than-light relays involved. We see causal connections between signals coming from widely separated secondary sources . . . Too fast for light to pass, you see. And we think it's all emanating from a star more or less in our path, eight hundred light years further out.'

'What star?'

'It only has a catalogue reference. Ben Goober, of the *Cauchy* crew, first detected the signals, actually, during a sweep of our data. We're calling it Goober's Star.'

'Coherent signals. Like what? Xeelee? Like the Wormhole Ghost?'

She smiled. '*Human*. Or at least, fragments of human coding embedded in apparently alien sequences. Like quotations, maybe, in reports, analyses.'

He thought that over. 'That's impossible. No scattership came out as far and fast as us. No Outrigger can have come so far. And any signal from this star you describe would have needed *another* eight hundred years to come back this far. Eight hundred years ago no human had even left the Solar System.'

'That's all true, and the existence of the messages is paradoxical, if you are restricted to lightspeed. I told you, we think faster-than-light technology is in the loop.'

He tried to take all this in. 'An alien signal, with some kind of human element. Hints of FTL technology. What a mystery. And you'd turn your back on it—' He waved a hand. 'For this theatre?'

She shrugged. 'We must all make our choices.'

'So. The end game? You've sat through these scenes, repeating the very words you speak to me, over and again. I bet this is a technique you developed to deal with crew you had trouble with. And with each successive iteration you worked on my trauma triggers, as you discovered them, didn't you? The irruption of the Xeelee. The Displacement of Earth. And—'

'Eternity. Entropy. The death of all thought.'

'Yeah, yeah. What I think, though, is that you got *that* one wrong. I think my earlier copies have been fooling you. Manipulating the conversation for their own ends. And sending a subtle message to *me*.'

For the first time since he'd met her, Flammarion looked alarmed. As if she might be losing control. 'What message?'

'The Pooles have an archive. Full of spooky, reality-leak stuff you don't want to know about. It does deal with hints about the future – the far future. But we don't speak of eternity.'

'If not *eternity*, then what?'

'*Timelike infinity.*'

And as he said the phrase, the amulet congealed in his hand.

Flammarion looked furious. She didn't move, didn't make so much as a gesture, said nothing. But still Jophiel had the sense she was trying to have him closed down, rebooted again back to some ignorant backup. Evidently she could not.

'Maybe I have my original to thank. I should have known he, *I*, would build in some kind of last-resort code to get me out of jail in a setup like this.'

'So what will you do now?'

'What do you think? Shut you down. Repurpose *Gea* to its proper mission.'

'And then?' She sneered. 'Will you fold yourself back into your template? Will you follow *his* dreams?'

He stared at her. 'Good question,' he conceded.

The butterfly-thing wheeled overhead, high in the star-cluttered sky. It gave an eerie wail. Desolating, Poole thought.

Goober's Star, though. A human signal. What could be going on there?

He clutched the amulet. 'Nicola, get me out of this asylum.'

8

Twenty-four hours later – ordinary, wet-human-pace hours – Jophiel Poole walked with Nicola Emry over a parkland of healthy green grass.

Somewhere a chicken clucked.

He looked up at a blue sky, scattered cloud. A low morning sun – apparently. He was looking at simulations projected by the smart lifedome of this GUTship, the third sister ship of the flotilla, along-side *Cauchy* and *Gea*. *Island*, the greenship. 'If you think about it,' he said, 'all this is no more "real" than what Flammarion Grantt put me through over on *Gea*.'

'That chicken was real. Sounded annoyed. Maybe an egg got stuck.'

'You know what I mean. *That's* all fake. The sky beyond the dome is actually velocity-aberration darkness. The sunlight you think you feel on your face is just reprocessed GUTdrive energy. That soft breeze is driven by the air conditioning.'

She shrugged. 'So everything is faked – or at least not authentic, natural. Since you froze Earth, environments like this no longer exist anywhere naturally. But some of this is real.' She poked at the turf with a booted toe, displacing the grass and revealing rich black loam beneath. 'The grass doesn't know it's not supposed to be here. Takes a lot of work, of course. You ought to take a look at the soil printers they have on this tub some time. Robot earthworms, tunnelling away.' She looked around, nodded towards a bunch of crew in grimy red coveralls working at the roots of a copse of young alders. 'Remember when we set up the mission, how Max Ward kept pushing for the *Island* to be another *Cauchy*? A dedicated warship, a weapons platform. Instead of *this*, a slice of Earth. A green refuge. The man just doesn't get it. Lethe knows I'm not sentimental, but we're all going to have to stay sane for twenty ship years before we even reach the Galaxy centre. We needed *one* greenship in the convoy.'

Jophiel grunted. 'Reminds us of what we're fighting for.'

'Right. Which is why Michael fought for a greenship in the mission design.' She was studying him with the disturbingly analytical

48

manner she so frequently seemed to adopt. 'For all you, or anyhow your template, were always a brat engineer, you've got a deep tie to the mother planet. Haven't you? You're no one-dimensional warlord, that's for sure.'

'Is that a good thing?'

'I think you sympathise with Alice and the rest, over their chances of raising kids. And I think you're drawn by those human traces the *Gea* found at Goober's Star. You may be *more* human than your template, Jophiel, just a little bit . . . You are differing from him more and more. I mean, that's what those Virtual monsters in *Gea* picked up, and used against you. The Xeelee irrupting out of a stretch of parkland just like this—'

'Central Park, actually. Childhood memory. Would you believe, Harry took me there to fly kites?'

'That doesn't sound like Harry.'

'It's true, though. Kites so over-engineered they could barely get off the ground.' Michael Poole walked up to them, grinning – a somewhat forced expression, Jophiel thought, studying this mildly divergent copy of his own face. Michael was in his bright red jumpsuit, Jophiel properly adorned in a copy's blue. 'Harry would let us – sorry, *me* – fail for a bit. Then he'd just take over, and do it himself.'

Nicola snorted. '*That* sounds like Harry.'

Michael faced Jophiel. 'We have to proceed with the trial of the *Gea* officers. We've extracted Flammarion Grantt, or her current copy, as a representative of—'

'Trial?' Nicola glared. 'Who said anything about a trial?'

'Max Ward, for one. Ship's rules allow it. Arguably they mandate it, but we never figured it would come to this. Call it a special crew review if you want. We clearly have to normalise the situation.'

'Normalise.' Nicola laughed softly. 'What in Lethe is ever going to be "normal" again?'

Michael glared at her. 'You're not helping. Look, Jophiel, we need to collapse your Virtual projection before we begin the review. You know that's the protocol. I've – we've – done it many times before . . . It's time.'

Jophiel knew that. After all, he shared all Poole's memories – all the way back through dozens of projections before. But now it was his turn. The infolding of *his* memories into the original, the loss of *his* identity. Had those other copies, any of them, fought to stay independent – to stay, in whatever sense, alive?

I want to live, he realised, with a sharp, stabbing awareness.

Shocked, he tried to analyse the feeling. Was it some echo of any living thing's brutish desire for survival – to survive for one more day, hour, second of awareness before the darkness? Was it a relic of the multiple little deaths he must have suffered on the *Gea*? Or was it simply that *he* did not want to dissolve back into the murky lake of this man's personality, from which he felt increasingly repelled?

Michael Poole was watching him. 'Is there some problem?'

Jophiel hesitated. Michael was the template and was in complete control here. He could end Jophiel's existence with a single vocal command. It was what Jophiel himself would have done. Once.

Nicola was looking on, probably guessing what he was thinking. He sensed what her advice would be. *Play for time.*

'We don't need to collapse yet,' Jophiel said. 'And it may be best not to. Let the review get under way.'

Poole frowned. 'But the protocol—'

'This is an unusual situation. A kind of mutiny. And, of the *Cauchy* officers, I was the one who saw the *Gea*, reported back—'

'Yes. You had direct experience,' Nicola said quickly. 'They tortured you. That's what that amounted to, the repeated revival from backups. You need to recount that, first hand. You always did lack imagination, Poole. It's a better show if you put the bleeding victim on the stand, instead of giving some kind of mish-mash second-hand report yourself.'

Now it was Jophiel's turn to give her a look. Maybe she was pushing too hard.

Michael Poole looked confused, but said at last, 'I – it's unprecedented. But I can see how it might work.' Still he hesitated.

Jophiel didn't dare say anything else.

The moment stretched.

At last Poole shrugged. 'Benefit of the doubt. Let's do it.'

Nicola grinned. 'I'll call the crew together.' And as Poole turned away, she leaned over to Jophiel. 'You owe me.'

'And you'll never let me forget it, will you?'

'You know me so well.'

9

The trial of Flammarion Grantt was to take place in the *Island*'s amphitheatre, open under the greenship's 'sky', built to accommodate all fifty of the ship's crew.

Today, Jophiel saw as he approached, the space was packed. Jophiel guessed there were eighty, maybe ninety here, in a mix of red and blue uniforms, sitting, standing. They were the awake crew of the *Island*, joined by Virtual projections of the *Cauchy* crew: most of the mission's complement, in fact.

Max Ward and Michael Poole were here in person, – they were standing together, talking – and of course Nicola, who would only use the wormholes to cross between the ships, affecting to despise the whole practice of casting off short-lived Virtual partials. A point of view with which, ironically, Jophiel now had a lot more sympathy.

He spotted Alice Thomas, champion of the Second Generation movement. Sitting in a huddle of whispers with her companions, she looked particularly agitated, he thought.

There was some kind of undercurrent here, Jophiel suspected, affecting the crews of both ships. Beyond the *Gea* crisis, beyond the Second Generation campaign. He wondered if his template had picked up on such subtleties. The day might turn out to be more complicated than Michael Poole imagined.

Meanwhile, at the centre of it all, unmoving, Flammarion Grantt was standing alone. Or at least an avatar of her. Waiting for her trial to start.

At last Michael Poole broke from Max and walked diffidently into the amphitheatre, data slate in hand. Jophiel felt a flicker of sympathy; this man was *him*, more or less, and he knew how uncomfortable Poole had always felt at being the centre of attention. Max Ward followed him, by contrast marching briskly down to the arena floor.

The crew were all staring.

And Nicola, in the front row, was grinning, clearly enjoying herself hugely.

'Let's get this done,' Poole said grimly. He faced Flammarion. 'You know why you're here, Flammarion. You and your colleagues betrayed the mission – simple as that. You failed in the objectives you were set regarding *Gea*'s core functions as a monitoring and data-processing platform. In fact you diverted mission resources into generating the artificial environment you call Officer Country. A selfish playroom which—'

'Selfish? It can be opened to all, Virtual or not. I'm well aware of the energy cost, but we have the resources, if we choose to use them. And the richness of the experience—'

Ward snarled. 'We're here to discuss mission goals. Not your self-indulgence.'

Flammarion seemed quite composed. She took one step, two, on the roughly panelled floor of the amphitheatre. In places there were gaps, where grass grew. She went down on one knee, and brushed her fingers through a clump of grass. Pixels sparkled. 'You speak of goals. What have these blades of grass got to do with your goals? Here we are, suspended in space. Four hundred light years from what used to be home. Oh, I know we have our great objective of smiting the Xeelee in its lair – if we get there, if we find it, if it doesn't smite us first. But . . .' She glanced around, picked out a group of crew, dressed in grimy coveralls, who had evidently been working in the dirt of this park-like ecohab. 'What are *your* goals? When you start a watch, when you wake up, when you see that artificial Sun rise in the lifedome sky, what do you plan for your day? Isn't it about how you will tend your crops and plants, and the rabbits and chickens? And the rats you have to chase?' Laughter at that. 'Rats, in interstellar space. Well, they followed us everywhere else.

'You see, we are in interstellar space, too. And we're *alive*, like the rats. Trying to find a way to live. Me, too! And living things evolve, change, adapt to circumstances. Even such circumstances as this. In Officer Country I nurture an oak tree – a Martian oak, of the kind I grew up with. You can say it's nothing but processing and pixels, but it's as alive as I am, as many of *you* are. We may be stranded in space. But there is so much more we can do with our lives than – what? What would you have us do all day, Max? Astrogation and military training?'

Ward glared at Poole. 'I don't know why you're even letting this woman speak.'

Before Poole could reply, Nicola called out, 'Because we're listening. All of us.'

A rumble of assent to that.

Now Alice Thomas stood up. 'And she has a point. About other objectives than just planning to wage a war. This is the argument of the Second Generation group too. Michael, we followed you out here. You inspired us.' She touched the tetrahedral tattoo on her own forehead. 'You know I'll always be grateful to you for saving my life, on Mars. You were a hero then; you're a hero now. But – look, we were all in shock. The whole human race, maybe. We had lost everything, our worlds, even the sunlight. We needed leadership, then. You and your father gave us the Scattering, Michael, and then this mission. But now – well, here we are, six years later, and I think we're learning how to live again. Michael, with all respect – what you have is your desire for revenge. And it's not enough. Not for us. Even if the war is our ultimate destiny, and we accept that, *now* is a time for living. For nurturing life – like the parkland of *Island*, and the children we could raise—'

'There're no resources to spare,' Ward growled back. 'Any more than we can spare the power for this woman's Virtual fantasy land.'

Flammarion was unfazed; she seemed to Jophiel to be in total control. 'No resources to spare from your war gaming, Max, even for fulfilling the most human of new objectives?'

Jophiel sensed what she was about to reveal, and so, evidently, did his template.

Poole stepped forward. 'Flammarion, this isn't appropriate. We're here to discuss—'

'Signals,' Flammarion said, loud and clear. 'We've picked up signals. Over on *Gea*.'

She had everyone's attention.

The crew started shouting questions. 'What kind of signals?' 'Where from?'

Max Ward was visibly furious. 'Michael, shut her up.'

But Poole was evidently more circumspect. 'Too late, Max,' he murmured. 'Now she's revealed it, we need to talk this through—'

'*Human* signals.'

'Uh oh,' Nicola said, grinning.

After that, Flammarion answered the crew's questions honestly and openly, as far as Jophiel could tell. Just as she'd told Jophiel himself.

That they'd picked up signals from a star, that they'd named after crewman Goober. That some element of the signals received seemed to be human in origin.

Poole stepped up, ashen-faced. 'Look – there's no conspiracy here. No secrets. We knew this would be exciting, distracting.'

'More than that,' Alice Thomas said. 'It changes everything.'

'We were going to brief you properly, just as soon—'

'Just as soon as you finish condemning the crew members who made this discovery for you,' Flammarion said.

Alice Thomas asked, 'What can we do about this? Can we get there, to Goober's Star?'

Jophiel stepped forward. He still had no idea how humans could have beaten lightspeed to get so far out from Earth as Goober's Star, but since his return from *Gea* he had had time to come up with the answer to Alice's question, at least.

'Yes. Yes, we can, Alice. In theory. We can reach Goober. We've been accelerating at a single gravity up to this point for more than six subjective years – across over four hundred light years. Now we need to decelerate, over *eight* hundred light years, to this destination. We can get away with a lower thrust, although the longer we delay a decision and a turnaround, the higher the deceleration we'll have to endure. Still take eight hundred years objective to get there. But for us, only a few more years—'

A roar of debate, demands, proposals, objections.

Nicola was grinning again, Jophiel saw. But then she always did enjoy disruption, whatever the cause.

And Jophiel's template, Michael, stood there grim-faced, apparently helpless to contain the event.

At last Max Ward, looking murderous, stalked to the centre of the amphitheatre. He held his hands up and boomed, 'Shut – up!'

Not surprisingly, he was obeyed.

Ward stalked the stage. 'Listen to yourselves. I thought we had a crew here. Not a rabble shouting each other down. Before we get back to the point – which is how to deal with this mutineer . . .' He jerked a thumb over his shoulder, not looking back at Flammarion. 'Listen to me. I know it's hard, to set yourself a tough goal, and to see it through. But *let Michael Poole lead you*. Michael's been there. Who was it who saved the Earth? Think how much that cost him. He did it anyway. And me too,' Ward said, strutting now, jabbing a thumb at his own chest. 'You know why *I'm* here. Because I already fought a war for the survival of my loved ones and my nation, and won it. Because I led a ragtag army from northern Europe across a frozen sea—'

'It lasted a week.' Alice Thomas stepped forward again. 'Your war. It lasted a week. It couldn't have lasted any longer, before the whole Earth got frozen into lockdown. *A week*. We've already been out in space for six years subjective, and more than twice as long left to go before we even get to the Galaxy Core, and – what then?'

Max Ward's face had turned crimson. He stalked forward, fists bunched, and loomed over Alice. 'What then? Then comes survival and victory. And you will learn that to survive in this wasteland of space you need to take orders. From me, from Poole – from your competent officers. And if you don't, we have no use for you. No room.'

Alice just stood there, quietly enduring his aggression.

And Jophiel felt profoundly disturbed. He had seen Ward's passion before, his energy, even his anger. He had never seen this – *rage*. And he wondered for the first time how brittle Max Ward was going to prove to be, when a real crisis hit the mission.

Still the moment stretched; still Alice stood her ground.

At last Ward backed off. He jerked his thumb over his shoulder once again. 'And just to drive it home into your bony heads, witness the consequence of betrayal. Flammarion Grant – this copy of her anyhow, and every such copy, every backup – will be deleted from the *Gea* processing store. Meanwhile her template, flesh-and-blood Flammarion, will be taken back into the *Cauchy*, conditioned and counselled. When all that's settled—'

'Execution,' Alice said coldly. The single word, spoken in her small voice, cut across Ward's noisy bluster. 'That's an execution. Since when did we put each other on death row? What is this, an Anthropocene failed state? You will not murder this woman, Virtual or not.'

A rumbling assent from the crew.

Nicola was still grinning. 'Well, well. The first direct challenge to the reign of our two emperors. Quite a moment. But I think the issue of Flammarion's execution, or not, is moot.'

Everybody looked around.

Flammarion was gone; unobserved during the row, she had vanished.

Then Max Ward's softscreen alerts began to flash. And Poole's, and others among the crew.

And the wormhole interface at the apex of the lifedome began to flare electric blue.

10

Ward snapped out orders. A handful of crew broke away, hurrying to monitoring stations.

Jophiel quickly discovered that a string of cargo pallets was coming through *Island*'s wormhole link with *Gea*. Loaded aboard were sleeper pods laden with hibernating crew, and a few bewildered-looking conscious individuals in pressure-tight skinsuits. The wet crew of *Gea*, human flesh and bone, was being offloaded from the GUTship.

And *Gea* was changing course. Slowly, subtly, surely, she was leaving the little flotilla.

Ward erupted. 'We ought to blow that Lethe-spawned thing out of the sky! Some kind of warning shot at least – we could board her—'

'No,' Poole snapped. 'The wormhole could easily be destabilised.'

'Don't worry about it, Michael,' Nicola said evenly. 'It's not going to happen. I mean, look around you. The crew wouldn't stand for it.'

Still the crew were gathered in the *Island* amphitheatre, silent or talking softly to each other, bewildered, scared – exhilarated, some of them, Jophiel thought.

And Jophiel saw that there was a significant knot around Alice Thomas, who was leading an intense discussion. It seemed the day's developments were not yet done.

Ward still seemed consumed with rage. 'Then to Lethe with it. We have two ships. We go on, continue the mission, carry the fight to the Xeelee.'

'No.' Here came Alice Thomas, trailed by a gaggle of wary-looking followers. 'I don't think it can be as simple as that, sir. Not ever again. What of the signal from Goober's Star? A human signal? Isn't that more important? Look – we support you, Michael. We'll fight your war. Some day. But we don't want to spend our lives in a military camp, any more than we want Flammarion's sterile Virtual utopia. We want lives. We want children. *And we want to go to Goober's Star*, if there are people there. What other response can there be?'

Everybody stared, Jophiel saw. Most of the crew were in earshot, still in the amphitheatre, gathered around the central confrontation.

Nicola laughed. 'Suddenly it's a crisis.'

And Jophiel came to a decision.

We've got to work together, that other, evanescent Poole had said. And he was right.

He stepped forward.

Poole glared at him.

'Let me try, Michael. Maybe I can help.' He turned to the crew. 'So I know not everybody's here, in flesh or as Virtuals – there are sleepers, those on duty at their stations – we can consult properly later. None of this was planned . . . Let's get a sense of the mood.

'How many of you want to go to Goober's Star? And how many to the Galaxy Core? Assume it's a choice of one or the other.' He strode away from the group, ten paces. 'If the Core, go to Michael. If you're for Goober . . .' He looked Michael Poole in the eye. 'Come to me.'

A moment of tension. Nobody moved. Jophiel was aware of Michael staring back at him.

Poole Red was facing Poole Blue, like a dipole, the tension between them palpable.

Then Nicola came to stand with Jophiel.

Ward went to Michael.

Alice Thomas came to Jophiel. And another of the crew, and another. It took long heartbeats for the group to sort itself out.

'Fifty-fifty,' Nicola said when it was done, still evidently enjoying herself. 'Well, well. Couldn't be a more difficult split.'

Michael Poole walked to the centre, his face grave. He looked baffled. 'We'll have to run a proper consultation, as you say, Jophiel. We should take our time over that, make sure everyone gets a chance to speak. Every sleeper. We should talk it out.'

Ward made to interrupt.

Poole held up his hand. 'Not now, Max. There'll be chances to debate. If the result holds—'

'We should split,' Alice Thomas said. 'The ships. The *Gea* has already peeled away.'

'Yes.' Nicola stepped forward. 'That fifty-fifty split makes it inevitable. The *Cauchy* to the Core, I guess. And the *Island*—'

'To Goober's Star.' Alice smiled. 'For the people.'

There was no formal ending to the meeting, Jophiel suspected because Michael had no idea what to say. But the gathering started to break up.

Ward stalked away, visibly furious.

Michael approached Nicola and Jophiel. 'What just happened? At the start of this watch we had three ships in a unified mission. And now, a mess.'

Nicola patted his shoulder. 'Life is a mess, Michael. Something you're never really going to grasp, are you?'

Michael shook his head. 'The *Gea* I can understand. In a way. They had become something – beyond human. But the *Island*, though. I thought people had accepted the mission. Now this.'

'Few of us get to choose our destiny.'

'But you did,' he said sadly. 'You chose Jophiel. After all we've been through.'

She shrugged. 'Sorry. But he – well, he's you, Michael. Sort of.'

Now Michael faced Jophiel, his other self. 'And you.' He rubbed his face. 'I even managed to rebel against myself. What a day.'

Nicola nodded, as if respectfully. 'That is, possibly, a first.'

Michael was still staring at Jophiel. 'It wasn't just about Goober's Star, was it?'

And Jophiel knew that his own whole existence hung on the outcome of the next few seconds. 'No,' he said gently. 'My choice too. *I want to live*, Michael. So I've discovered. You're the template. The original. You're still in control. You could fold me back into your head, forcibly. But . . .'

They stared at each other. Red and blue, the dipole. Nicola, wisely, said nothing.

Michael broke away first. 'Ah, into Lethe with it all,' he said, angry now. 'If some of the crew reject the mission goals, to Lethe with them. And you, Jophiel. Oh, you can live, for what it's worth. Just don't ever ask me for help.' He walked away.

And a voice murmured in Jophiel's ear. *Say nothing you might regret. You never know.* His own voice, older.

When he turned, there was nobody there.

The changing trajectory of *Gea* was monitored from the remaining ships of the flotilla.

Ben Goober reported to the seniors. Its vector of thrust pushed *Gea* away from its previous course at several gravities – but the momentum built up after more than six years running at a single gravity was going to take some time to modify.

'Still,' Ben said, 'we think we know where she will be headed, eventually. What direction, anyhow. Pegasus.'

A constellation much distorted by their tracking across the galaxy, Jophiel realised. But he saw the salient point. '*Gea* is heading out of the plane of the Galaxy altogether?'

'Looks like it,' Ben said.

Nicola frowned. 'So what's out there?'

Ben shrugged. 'A few rogue stars. Globular clusters, if you go far enough. A big one, called M15 . . . Room to spread out.'

Jophiel lifted his head, looking that way, the true sky masked by the dome of the *Island*. 'Godspeed,' he said. 'So. What's next?'

TWO

We are still out on the savannah of stars. And there are ferocious beasts out there . . . And they are aware of us. Indeed they have a grudge.

Luru Parz, c. AD 500,000,000

11

Jophiel, effective captain of the *Island*, scheduled a crew briefing seven days after the GUTdrive shutdown.

Seven days of zero gravity inside the lifedome of the *Island*. Seven days of recovery time for the crew. Seven days with the universe shut out, with the greenship's lifedome still cycling comforting images from a warm Earth, a misty blue sky, a pale Sun rising and setting. Seven days of stillness, after thirteen *years* of half-gravity deceleration, to slow them to this arrival point in the target star's system.

When the hour for the briefing approached Jophiel walked alone from his cabin in the fringe of modest buildings around the rim of the lifedome, and crossed the grassy parkland that covered much of the main deck, heading for the amphitheatre at the centre of the lifedome. 'Walked' – in zero gravity a waist-high mesh of guide ropes had been laid out a metre or so above the ground; you were free to swim through the air if you liked, but most people used the ropes as they paddled over sunlit turf.

Any gravity strength he desired could have been simulated for Virtual Jophiel, of course. He stuck scrupulously to the conditions the flesh-and-blood crew endured, as mandated by his consistency protocols, and, he thought, by sheer good manners. After the split from the *Cauchy*, though, he had accepted the use of a small cabin, one of a block at the fringe of the lifedome. There was room, especially since most of the physically embodied crew – the wet crew, as they called themselves now, a bit of *Gea* slang – had spent the long interval of deceleration to Goober's Star stashed safely away in sleeper pods.

And he did have some physical gear to store – dedicated softscreens, engineering instruments. Records of his past on Earth. A past he now shared with his wet-crew original, Michael, back on the *Cauchy*. Michael had kept the Wormhole Ghost amulet, though, the original. Jophiel patted his pocket now, an unreal hand checking the position of an equally unreal replica: the panic button Nicola had given him when he had gone over alone to the *Gea*. He found the presence of the amulet copy oddly comforting, even if it, like himself, was entirely simulated.

A chicken ran past his feet, clucking. He hesitated, almost lost his footing.

The chicken, snow white, was pursued by a grey blur, harder to make out. And then by a bot that chased them both, fleeing low under the guide-rope layer, with rattling squirts of attitude jets.

Naturally Nicola Emry was here to see that stumble. Naturally she laughed. 'Only you could trip over a chicken when you aren't even physically present, Poole.'

He straightened up. 'And in microgravity too. The chickens are getting smart at scrambling along under the ropes. The rats too. And those rats are getting aggressive.'

'Read your history, Poole. Rats follow humans, wherever we go. We took them to Australia and Hawaii. Now we've brought them to Goober's Star. You think you've led us on some kind of extraterrestrial crusade. In fact you've been breeding super-rats and spreading them over interstellar space. Complicated thing, life, isn't it?'

They were nearing the amphitheatre. The crew were gathering, some in their bright red uniforms, some in casual gear, or in the grimy work clothes they used for assisting the bots in their labours around the park. Faces turned to Jophiel as he approached. People held on easily to the guide ropes, with twists around ankles and wrists, floating in sunlight. There were children here now, wriggling around or playing: the triumph of the argument of Alice Thomas and her Second Generation faction. The eldest, now aged eleven, was Michaela Nadathur, born just a year after the separation from the *Cauchy*. She had been named for Michael Poole, with a touch of irony.

Everybody was out of the sleep pods at last. Indeed, Jophiel realised, it was the first time the whole crew had been together since the separation from *Cauchy*. And there was a sense that at last the job proper was about to begin.

Asher Fennell was standing with Alice Thomas, Ben Goober and a few other seniors. She nodded. 'Jophiel. We're ready for you.'

'Well, it's Asher's show. About time you showed us where we are, don't you think?'

Asher clapped her hands. Everyone looked her way.

Over their heads, in silence, the sky dome faded to black.

12

Asher stood alone at the centre of the amphitheatre, in the sudden gloom, amid a slightly intimidated hush.

Since Larunda Station, where she had helped prepare Michael Poole and Nicola for their dive into the Sun in search of the Xeelee, Jophiel had thought of Asher as young. In fact she was in her sixties now; he knew she had started on her AS treatments, but was allowing herself to age with a grace that lent her authority. Since the split she had been the nearest thing to an astrophysicist on board the *Island*, making deep-sky studies of the structure of the Galaxy and the wider universe – studies from a viewpoint unparalleled in the history of mankind. Now she lifted her face to the apex of the lifedome – to a black sky, a scatter of stars – and one particularly bright light at the zenith, directly ahead on the line of the *Island*'s motion. Jophiel knew that even this view was artifice; the wormhole interface mounted on the top of the lifedome was in reality still there, a big blue tetrahedral frame, conveniently edited out of the visual field.

'A starry sky,' Asher said. 'Where are we? Could be anywhere, right? Even after twenty years on this tub we still haven't come all that far, in terms of our intended journey to the Core – only about a twentieth of that great distance. But it's not quite like the sky of Earth. There are *fewer* stars visible to the naked eye, actually.

'That's because we are in a gap.

'We have passed out of Sol's local galactic arm, the Orion-Cygnus Arm. The next arm in is the big Carina-Sagittarius Arm, another three thousand light years deeper into the Galaxy. But, who knows? Maybe what we stopped for here will turn out to be more important than any of that. Depending on what we find up *there*.'

She pointed at that bright zenith point.

'We're actually in the system of Goober's Star already. Goober is a Sunlike star, more or less. We're still a thousand astronomical units out. Too far out to see any inner planets, with the naked eye anyhow. But we've already passed through most of Goober's Oort cloud, the big outer sphere of comet cores and rogue planets. And we're only ninety days out from the inner planets, by GUTdrive, an easy one-gravity cruise. Close enough in for us to get a good look at what we're walking into, to confirm the remote spotting, before we commit ourselves.

'But we have to assume that whoever is in there – whoever sent those messages *Gea* detected – already knows we're out here. That they saw us coming. *We* would have seen a GUTship coming into the Solar System from interstellar space.'

'We always knew complete stealth was impossible,' Nicola said with a trace of impatience. She had had a lot of input to this stage of the flight plan, Jophiel knew. 'Yes, *they* probably know we're here. By pausing here, all we tried to do is buy a little breathing space. And besides, we didn't come here to fight. We've got neither the equipment nor the intention. So maybe those who are watching us might see our hanging around out here and *not* bristling with weaponry as a peaceful gesture.'

Asher kept staring up at the star itself. 'Anyhow, that's where the action is. But I can tell you already that I don't like it.'

Jophiel frowned. This was new. 'You don't like what? The star? What's wrong with it?'

Asher shrugged. 'We've known for a while that this is a G-class star, like the Sun – like it but not identical: the star is G-zero where the Sun is G-two, a little bigger, a little brighter. No companion stars. Well, now we're observing Goober's Star up close, and we've sent out probes to reconnoitre the rest of the system. And we're seeing signs of variability about the star. Magnetic storms. Huge flare events. If I didn't know better I'd say that star was close to going nova.'

Jophiel sensed the crew's stir of alarm. 'But you do know better. Right?'

'A nova is what you get when a star has got a companion, close in. The companion star dumps material, dragged out by tides, onto the surface of the heavier star. A layer of hydrogen builds up until it's dense enough to start a fusion reaction, up there on the surface, and – *wham*.

'So, in such a double system, you would see this kind of precursor event, storms and flares, as the principal star prepares to blow. But here, it's an anomaly. No companion, you see. We don't know what's causing the flares, but what I'm seeing does seem to be related to a disturbance of the outer layers of the star. Just like a nova star. I guess we'll learn more when we get further in.'

Ben Goober stepped forward, with a glance at Jophiel. 'Maybe I could add to that.'

'Go ahead, Ben.'

'Officer Fennell, you say you don't like the look of that star up there. Well, I was tasked at looking at where we are right now, this Oort cloud, the Kuiper belt closer in. And I don't like the look of those two features either.'

'Show us.'

Ben Goober raised his hands and threw Virtuals in the air: a pinpoint star, wide circles around it that were the orbits of planets. He began to go into a lot of detail about the long-term evolution of the motions of families of minor bodies. He was no longer a kid. But, in his thirties, nervous, shy, though evidently intensely bright, he was a much less impressive speaker than Asher Fennell. The crew fidgeted.

When he started to run down, Asher helped him out. 'So, if I can sum that up – the orbits of many of the objects in the Kuiper belt, even in the Oort cloud, look as if they have been *adjusted*. Yes?'

Goober nodded vigorously. 'Heavily regularised. The ellipticity ironed out. It wouldn't necessarily be a difficult thing to do, if you had the resources and the time. There are some big objects out here, but they move slowly. You could fix the trajectory with targeted detonations, or GUTdrive engines mounted at the poles, or just with a series of flyby gravitational assists. Multiple tweaks, until you got what you wanted.'

Jophiel thought he saw the pattern. 'Which is what?'

Goober shrugged. 'Safety, sir. Domestication. Out here is where the comet nuclei orbit. Back in the Solar System we had Spaceguard, for – umm—'

'A couple of millennia,' Asher put in.

'*We* were watching for rogue objects straying into the inner Solar System that might strike the inhabited worlds. We actually pushed away a couple of them. *Here* that process of safeguarding has gone a lot further. Somebody came out here and tidied it all – made it safe. And it was a big job, sir. Sol's Oort cloud reached halfway out to Alpha Centauri. Deep sky with a lot of objects. Same here. Must have taken time, but they did it.'

'A *lot* of time,' Nicola said now. 'Which fits in with my own report.'

Jophiel nodded permission for her to speak.

Nicola was by profession a pilot, but she had been a warrior – she'd fought the Xeelee itself as it had first neared Earth-Moon space – and with Max Ward still on the *Cauchy*, she was the nearest to a military mind to be found aboard the *Island*. Everybody hoped this system wouldn't become a battleground. But it seemed remiss not to prepare for the worst. So Jophiel had set Nicola the task of preliminary surveillance.

Now brisk, efficient, even impatient, she hurried through a blizzard of visuals of her own, cast in the air above the heads of the crew: a plan view of the inner Goober system, the neat circular orbits of planets.

'We've identified seven inner planets,' she began. 'Goober a to Goober g. Some have moons. You know how it is; the outer edge of a system like this is fuzzy, with plutoids, ice worlds, wandering in from the inner regions of the Kuiper belt. The innermost worlds are where the action is anyhow . . . What's the first thing you notice, by the way?'

'Neat circular orbits,' said Ben Goober.

'Right. *Very* low ellipticity, for any of the orbits. We suspect there has been conscious adjustment, as with your Kuiper and Oort objects, Ben. Also, notice no asteroid belt, unlike in the Solar System. There *are* asteroids, but they all seem to be in stable locations – such as the Trojan points of those Jovian worlds you can see. Safely tucked away. Anyhow, seven planets. All with their own anomalies, I should say in advance. The innermost, a rocky planet, Mars-sized, orbiting about where Mercury is in our Solar System. Or was.'

Jophiel shrugged. 'What's anomalous about that?'

'Too light,' she said simply. 'Not dense enough. We can calculate the mass if there's a moon, or as in this case by gravitational deflections of the other planets—'

'We believe you,' Jophiel said.

'The whole thing has a density of silicate rock, all the way down. No metallic core.'

'Earth's Moon was like that,' Asher said. '*That* was a relic of a big impact which splashed up rock from the mantle of a big proto-Earth. Could this be an impact product?'

'We don't think so,' Nicola said. 'We think it was mined out.'

'*Mined out.* How? What makes you think so?'

'Anomalous surface features,' she said bluntly.

Now she displayed slightly fuzzy, heavily magnified images. Jophiel made out a very lunar landscape, airless and stark, brightly lit by the nearby star. Craters of all sizes, circles overlapping. And a series of big rectangular cuts in the ground, deeper than the light could reach.

'Lethe,' Asher said. 'How long would it take to mine out the entire core of a planet?'

'About as long as it might take to fix the Oort cloud, like Goober told us. Next.'

Jophiel glanced around at the crew, who were watching intently. He briefly wondered what was going through their minds, as for the first time they saw these worlds which were, he supposed, likely to become their home – or their battleground.

Goober b was a planet about the same distance from the parent star as Earth was from Sol. But, in Nicola's image, Jophiel saw only a white glare, with faint suggestions of shadows, like high clouds. And a hint of something else. At the limb of the planet, the visible edge, what looked like some kind of reflection, a curve mirroring the horizon – tens, hundreds of kilometres high . . .

Somebody called, 'It's where Earth should be. Looks more like Venus.'

'That's about right,' Nicola said. '*This* world has suffered a runaway greenhouse. Just like Venus, all the carbon dioxide baked out of the rocks and suspended in the air, trapping the heat. Goober's Star is about ten per cent more luminous than Sol, which might explain why this world went bad.'

Jophiel sensed an unspoken clause. 'Or? What else?'

'War. We don't know what's down on the surface. But we have found artifice here.'

'That roof,' somebody said. 'Over the horizon – you can clearly see it.'

'You have sharp eyes,' Nicola said, looking for the speaker. 'How's your flight experience? See me later . . .' She pulled up a relevant image: that fine arc, seen edge on, hanging over the planet's horizon. 'We think *this* is a relic of a shell. Like an arcology dome, but one that once enclosed the entire planet. There are other scraps left, in orbit, standing on immense space-elevator pillars. With a shell like that you could contain an atmosphere; you could shield out solar flares and other nasties, reduce the sunlight from that hot old star out there . . . A very dumb technology that becomes smart if you scale it up.'

'But it's broken,' Jophiel said evenly. 'Think how long it would take to build such a thing. And then—'

'Think how long it would take for it to fall apart to this extent.'

'This is an old system,' said Ben Goober. 'Old, engineered, worked out.'

'That's the impression we're getting,' Nicola said. 'Monumental ruins. OK. Goober d—'

'Hey,' Jophiel protested. 'What about c?'

She grinned at him. 'Saving the best to last.'

Goober d, like e, f, and g, turned out to be a gas giant. None of the quartet was as large as Jupiter. There was no trace of mega engineering to be seen here, Nicola said, but still, it was clear intelligences had been at work.

'Resource depletions,' she said. 'Of fusion-friendly helium isotopes. Of exotic hydrocarbons in the upper atmosphere. Possibly even of metallic hydrogen from the planets' cores. And maybe other stuff we're not recognising. Everything *we* can think of that we'd find useful is in anomalously short supply. Maybe they even mined the magnetic fields for energy, the way you used Io and Jupiter to build your wormholes, Jophiel. Or anyhow Michael did.'

'But still, to have caused lingering, visible depletions on the scale of a gas giant—'

'Takes a long time,' Ben Goober said. 'A lot of resources extracted. That's the theme of the whole system, isn't it? It took a long time to get this way.'

'It needn't be the Xeelee, by the way,' Asher said. 'We've travelled a long way in human terms, but we've only taken baby steps into the Galaxy. We've only encountered two intelligent species – the Xeelee and the Wormhole Ghost – and they came to *us*. But there's every reason to think that there must be *many* races out there – or, there *were*.'

She looked around at her crewmates, and Jophiel wondered if she was wary of giving too bleak a perspective. 'The universe isn't *young*, you see. Nor is the Galaxy. Most of our Galaxy's stars have already been born, and we're latecomers to the party. Chances are there have been many races, come and gone, of builders and technologists whose ruins we might see, and others who left no trace at all, back to the earliest days of the universe. In fact we believe that the Xeelee is a relic of a very early era, just after the Big Bang itself.'

Jophiel said, 'So this may be typical of what we'll find. Vast ruins, worked-out mines.'

'Maybe,' Nicola said, and she grinned. 'But what's not typical of this system is that we heard that human signal.'

Jophiel had to grin back. 'And you're about to tell us the location that signal came from?'

'As far as we can tell—' She waved a hand, and the image of another vivid world coalesced above her head. 'Goober c.'

Jophiel could see at a glance that this was a much more complex world than its siblings.

And that it was alive. Or anyhow it looked that way.

Evidently a big world, but rocky, like Earth, not a giant of gas or ice. The atmosphere was neither entirely transparent, nor entirely opaque: it was cloudy, misty, elusive. In places higher ground seemed more clearly visible, as if pushing out of that murky air. Chains of huge mountains crossed ragged continents. Perhaps there were oceans, Nicola said. The gleam of ice-white stretched far from each pole. And, in places, Jophiel thought he could see grey-green. Life?

Two moons hung in the sky, apparently bare, sunlit rock.

Asher took over. 'You're looking at a super-Earth. Significantly more massive than Earth. Forty per cent higher gravity. It won't be comfortable down there . . . Actually, more strictly, it's like a super-Mars. Even though Goober is more luminous than the Sun, Goober c is twice as far as Earth is, was, from the Sun, and the planet gets only about a third of the sunlight Earth received. Less than Mars itself. But the surface is warmer than Mars. Not from the sunlight, but because the planet's that much bigger, with much more residual heat. And it's kept more of an atmosphere. That blanket you can see is surprisingly thick. It contains about five times the mass of Earth's atmosphere in carbon dioxide alone.'

'And so there's a strong greenhouse effect,' Jophiel guessed.

'Correct,' Asher said.

'Enough to make this world habitable? Mars had its Lattice. It had life. But nothing so obvious as Earth life – too cold, too dry – nothing like *that*.' He pointed at the greenish patches.

'That does seem to be life, yes. There's a kind of photosynthesis going on – but the native algae or plants or whatever are splitting carbon dioxide and the local rocks to release *hydrogen*, not oxygen. We're guessing this from what we can measure in the air; we can figure it all out when we get close up. As far as we can tell, down there the air is as thick as a shallow ocean, and you'll need oxygen tanks to breathe. But at least it's *warm*.'

Nicola grinned. 'And, Jophiel – here's the big reveal. Down in those deep valleys—'

'What?'

'Hull plate.'

Jophiel felt cold. 'Xeelee technology?'

'Right. Swathes of it, blanketing the landscape. No other Xeelee signature – no discontinuity-drive gravity waves, no planetbuster energy leakages. But, yes, they've been here, at least. We don't know what this means.'

Jophiel said, 'But whoever sent those messages, with the human content, is still down there—'

'*Correct.*'

Jophiel, like most of the crew, flinched, startled. The voice, deep, gravelly, without inflection – mechanical – had seemed to boom from the sky.

He looked up.

A silver sphere hung in the air, above all their heads, eclipsing the pinprick glow of Goober's Star. A couple of metres across, perhaps. Evidently massive.

Somebody shot at it. Jophiel heard the crack of the release. What looked like a staple sailed without deflection through the gleaming carcass of the intruder. There was no evident wound, no damage. Some kind of Virtual, then?

Jophiel glared around to see who was responsible.

A young crew member was holding up a staple gun.

Nicola moved first, grabbed the gun from the crewman. 'That thing's no more real than Jophiel over there. Good job too. No more assaults, unless authorised.'

Now the crew began to speak up.

'But that thing's inside our lifedome, even if it just got projected in here—'

'I *know* that thing, I saw the recordings from Jupiter space—'

'*That's a Wormhole Ghost—*'

'Which of you,' the visitor thundered now, 'is the Poole?'

The crew fell silent.

Nicola and Asher instinctively moved to Jophiel, as if to shield him. Just as instinctively he tried to push them away. He ended up walking *through* their bodies, with sharp pains from consistency-violation warnings.

But as he stepped forward, Nicola murmured in his ear. 'Jophiel. Remember you're software. If you can send a message through the wormhole link to the *Cauchy*, do it now. Before the Ghosts disable the interface, or—'

'Good thinking.' He closed his eyes, focused, and broke his consistency protocols again, digging into his own source code to open a channel to the *Cauchy*. He began to dump down a situation summary, raw data – and a plea for help. This kind of cheating was physically painful, and making a request for help to his faux sibling was galling. He did it anyhow.

He looked up at the Ghost – for he was sure that identification was correct. 'I am Poole.'

'Michael Poole.'

'He— I am a projection of the original. As you are, of your own original, apparently. How do you know me? Why are you here?'

'Actually you came to us,' the Ghost pointed out. Almost drily, Jophiel thought, bemused. 'We waited until you had clearly indicated your knowledge of our location, and that of your conspecifics.'

'We came in peace—'

'*We* take control.'

A flash of light beyond the hull. The floor shuddered. An alarm wailed, and lights flickered.

Jophiel was unaffected, but the crew around him stumbled, grabbed at the zero-gravity guide ropes, gathered into little groups, helping each other.

Jophiel glanced over at Nicola, who was pawing at a softscreen. 'Tell me what it's done.'

'Lethe. The spine has been severed, below the lifedome. Just like that.' She stared at him, horrified. 'They decapitated the ship, Jophiel.'

Jophiel felt a deep, sick reaction to that news – almost as if he had been injured himself.

Something new moved in the sky, beyond the Ghost's bulk, beyond the dome. Jophiel stared up. A kind of silver tangle, along whose threads droplets of molten silver moved. More Ghosts? Some kind of ship?

'Your conspecifics believed you would come to save them, Poole,' the Ghost said now, its voice booming over the rising clamour.

Jophiel yelled back, 'You mean, humans? On another ship?'

TWO

'They have called for you. For over a thousand years.'

Shadows shifted, cast by the raw sunlight of this system. They were being moved, then.

Jophiel turned to his seniors. 'Get this dome secured. And the crew. Skinsuits and tethers. *Move.*'

They moved.

75

13

An hour later.

Inside the dome, the crew were in airtight shelters, or out in the open, buckled to guide ropes. All of them were in their skinsuits.

Still the starscape shifted. Still the dome was being dragged through space.

Where? To the planet, Goober c? One of the moons? And how? Jophiel saw no physical linkage between the detached lifedome and the surrounding Ghost ships. There was no sense of acceleration. Yet they seemed to be moving quickly, deeper into the stellar system.

And Jophiel's ship was *gone*.

It was like a traumatic wound. Like *Cauchy* and *Gea*, the *Island* had been based on a sketch design of an interstellar exploration vessel that had been in Michael Poole's notebooks long before the Xeelee incursion of the Solar System. A dream of boyhood, almost. And Poole had got to build it, though not in the circumstances he'd imagined. Now, after twenty years of flight, *Island* had been casually destroyed, just minutes after its first encounter with these Ghosts. The severed spine, the GUTdrive pod, ice mined from a Kuiper object in the Solar System, now relics to be curiously examined, perhaps, by alien beings more than a thousand light years from Sol.

And the crew, hushed, were staring up at the Ghost vessels.

If that was what they were. Sliding past the lifedome, they were tangles of what looked like silvery rope, along which ran trains of glinting spherical droplets. Were the droplets the Ghosts themselves? If so they must be immune to raw space, to the vacuum, to stellar and cosmic radiation.

Each of the ships was a rough ovoid, Jophiel supposed, but he could see no clear symmetries. And, as he studied blown-up images, he made out what looked like equipment embedded in the deep tangle: boxes and spheroids, some apparently transparent. In one such box he glimpsed a murky green, like water from a shallow ocean. He could see nothing that looked obviously like a drive unit – nothing like the

Island's GUTdrive, a massive rocket engine that had been mounted on a kilometres-long spine. It was hard to see how those loose, tangled structures could withstand even the smallest acceleration. Yet here these ships were, drifting around the wreck of his own vessel, the best humanity could offer.

The ships were magnificent. But of an utterly inhuman design.

'Jophiel.' Nicola stood before him.

'Some kind of inertial control,' he murmured.

'What?'

'Those ships. No apparent internal support. Just as there's nothing visibly gripping the lifedome. As if all this is contained in some invisible shell, or field.'

'Jophiel—'

'We experimented with such things, on a smaller scale, at Poole Industries. Inertia-control fields. Massively power-hungry—'

She punched him in the head.

Her fist passed through his face, his skull, and his vision broke up into shards of pixels, as if he was looking through a smashed window. The pain was extraordinary – like an electric shock, delivered deep inside his head. But when she withdrew, he recovered quickly, the consistency-protocol violation pain triggers fading.

His vision cleared. '*Ow*. That hurt.'

'Good. Look – we rehearsed procedures for all kinds of contingencies, but not something like this. Lead us.'

He looked around now, at the interior of the lifedome. The green grass. Ponds glassed over for conditions of microgravity. A confused-looking chicken flapping in the air, upside down. And the people, the crew, still clinging to their guide ropes, gathered together in knots, as if for mutual protection. They were all silent, passive.

'I'm no leader,' he murmured to Nicola. 'Not like this. I suppose Michael was. Or at least he looked like he was, from the outside. On the inside was – me. I'm the embodiment of Poole's doubt, remember. His hesitation. That's why I exist.'

She shrugged. 'So what? You're all we've got. Your orders?'

He looked at the drifting crew, their faces empty, turned to him.

Think, Poole.

'Tangleships.'

'What?'

He pointed at the Ghost vessels. 'Tangleships. Name a thing and you begin the process of controlling it. That's what my mother taught me. Humans named the lightning, and eventually tamed it. In the end, we moved the whole Earth.'

'*You* did that, strictly speaking.'

His head was starting to work again. 'You know, if they were going to kill us quickly they'd have done so already. And they could, easily. Even accidentally.'

'They may know more about us than you think,' Nicola said. 'They did send a message with human content, remember. That's what brought us here . . . Or, lured us.'

'True. But whether they intend to kill us or not, until then we're going to need life support.'

'Correct. Your orders, Jophiel?'

'We start preparing for the long term. And this dome is all we have left.'

'So?'

'So we prioritise.'

They started with power.

The lifedome had drawn all its primary energy from the GUTdrive engine, now lost. But it had backup stores of its own, including GUT-pods and compact fusion generators. Jophiel sent teams scurrying to check that those backups had all come online as they should have. He ordered that the medical systems be secured, and asked for an inventory of supplies. Special priority was to be given to the two pregnant women in the crew, and the children born during the cruise. He asked for a roster of food and water stores, with a rationing system to be implemented immediately. In the longer term they needed to secure their means of food production, from the heavy-duty food printers to, as a backup, the small low-tech fields of potatoes and corn that had been meant as recreational experiments in farming, a technology abandoned a thousand years before Cold Earth.

Still more basic life-support systems, whose integrity might have been compromised by the severance from the spine, had to be checked out and secured. Water. Air. Heating.

Nicola muttered to Jophiel, 'Also data processors. Unless you want to pop out of existence—'

'You're right, of course. I hope we can sell that to the Ghosts – *oof.*'

The lifedome had lurched sideways, abruptly. Nicola grabbed for a guide rope. The Virtual consistency protocols were enough to let Jophiel feel a sharp jolt.

He glanced up at the dome. A huge planetscape was sliding by, detail slowly expanding – bare, rocky uplands scattered with the lights of what might be habitation, and deeper features, ocean basins, rift valleys: huge geological scars that brimmed with murky air, turbid water.

'Lethe,' Asher said. 'That's Goober c. They took us across a thousand astronomical units in ninety minutes. A GUTship would have taken ninety *days*. A thousand AU is, what, five light-days? . . .' Her eyes widened as she worked it out. 'Oh.'

Nicola smiled coldly. 'Ladies and gentlemen, welcome to the world of faster-than-light travel.'

Another jolt.

Asher growled, 'FTL or not, feels like their magic inertial control field needs a little work.'

'They're obviously bringing us down to the planet,' Jophiel said. 'The whole dome. No matter how smart they are, they can't have done this too often.'

'If we're heading for a bumpy landing, we need to get to the couches,' Ben Goober said.

'Yes. Good idea. The whole crew. The work can wait . . .'

Following brisk orders, the fifty-strong crew scattered to their cabins, all of which had crash couches. But Jophiel was gratified to see that a number of the crew dragged out their couches and fixed them to the open deck – as Asher and Nicola did – so they could see where they were being taken to.

The dome, accompanied by its tangleship escorts, seemed to level out in its flight now. An imposing horizon stretched wide, and the ground of Goober c fled beneath the dome's leading edge.

Nicola, strapped into her own couch alongside Jophiel, peered ahead, trying to see. 'That thick air is like an ocean, and a murky one. But – look there, and there.' Shadows that seemed to rise above the air itself. 'Floating islands?'

Jophiel growled, 'Not that. Super-Earths keep their inner heat better than Earth, and despite the gravity you must get some spectacular geology. We were told it's more like a super-Mars, remember?'

'Oh. And on Mars, Olympus Mons sticks out of the atmosphere.'

'Right. So it is here, I think. Huge aerial continents.' He found he was grinning. 'Imagine climbing one of those features – like that big one, the plateau just ahead. You'd have to carry a pressure suit for the final stages. As if you had climbed up from the Earth by some ladder to the Moon.'

'You always were one for spectacle, weren't you? Even now. You exhilarated idiot.'

'We're descending. Heading for that big plateau. I think we're going to land on *top* of that feature . . .'

14

In the last stages, a cratered ground fled beneath the prow of the lifedome. Goober's Star cast long shadows. Above, at this altitude, only thin clouds were draped over a black sky – ice clouds, perhaps, very high, Jophiel realised. This really was like descending on Mars, on Olympus Mons.

But the landscapes ahead were extensive. Asher had reported that the plateau they were approaching was itself the size of India, the size of a subcontinent – and Jophiel's mind quailed at the thought of the tectonic forces required to uplift such a mass against the strong gravity of this world. Such vast raised landmasses must disrupt any air circulation systems, he mused. Perhaps this plateau cast a rain shadow halfway around the planet. Or, on the other hand, that massive atmosphere was so dense and heavy that it might behave more sluggishly, more like an ocean than air. Jophiel imagined permanent wind systems, like ocean currents . . .

'A lot of detail down there,' Nicola murmured. 'The ground is heavily cratered, almost moonlike. We thought impactors had been cleaned out of this system, didn't we?'

Asher said, 'I think those craters below us are caldera features. Volcanoes, not impacts. I saw a plume, to starboard. Maybe some of them are active. Like Olympus Mons, again. As if this whole feature is one vast supervolcano – and not particularly dormant—'

'*Ghosts,*' Nicola said now. 'Or Ghost structures anyhow, down on the ground. Passing over them now. There, and there . . .'

Jophiel saw them, especially where shadows sheltered them from the brilliant sunlight. More knots of silver wire, without order or symmetry evident to the human eye, clinging to the rocky surface.

Nicola asked, 'Grounded ships?'

'I don't think so. Too big for that. Cities, maybe? Colonies?'

They passed directly over one of these – communities? There was still no evident symmetry, but at the rough centre Jophiel made out a slim tower rising above the tangle, surmounted by a clear blue light.

He pointed this out. 'Some kind of monument?'

'Maybe,' Nicola said. 'We don't know anything about these crea-tures – what's functional, what's ornamental or ceremonial. Or maybe it's all mixed up, as with humans. Like the Crusaders, who wore the cross of Christ on their chest as a kind of divine armour when going into battle.'

Asher grinned. 'And *that* is authentic Nicola Emry.'

'Always eager to please.'

Jophiel tried to memorise the detail he was seeing. And, thinking about that, he put out a general call to the crew. 'Some day we may need to find our way out of this place. Record everything. Make sketches – tuck them into your pocket, in case our equipment gets taken off us . . . *Remember*. That's all.'

He got murmured acknowledgements.

Nicola nodded. 'Max Ward would have approved. No matter how helpless you are, even if you are imprisoned, as long as you can think and observe, you can still work. Count the days on your cell wall. Still advance towards your goals.'

'I'll take that as a compliment.'

'Make the most of it.'

'Jophiel.' Harris Kemp's voice. 'Look down. Port side.'

Jophiel subvocalised a command, and a part of the deck turned Virtual-transparent. He saw that the lifedome was now being flown over a particularly large and deep caldera; steam rose from hot rocks – and Jophiel saw what looked like a mud pool, bubbling.

'Surely the air pressure is too low for liquid.'

Harris said, 'I think there's a dome over the whole area. Almost transparent, but not quite. Might not even be material, some kind of force field.'

Now Jophiel saw a crowd of Ghosts, silver droplets like spilled mer-cury, gathered around the vent. They were lined up in almost orderly queues, all around the vent, filing into the heat.

'I've been watching for a while,' Harris reported. 'The Ghosts seem to be taking turns to immerse themselves in that pool of hot mud, or whatever. And when they do they seem to – decompose.'

Nicola raised an eyebrow. 'Decompose?'

'That's what it looks like.'

Since his stint as a junior technician on Larunda Station, in what now felt like another life, Harris had specialised in medicine and biol-ogy. Now he began to speculate on entirely alien life forms.

'That silver skin peels back. Some kind of internal structures are released – they look like body parts. They spill out into the mud, like independent entities. Swimming away. Even the skin. But when they are done they recombine, zipping up inside the spherical skin sac, and then join the lines to pass out of the pool area.'

Nicola said, 'Jophiel, I think we saw something like this before. The Wormhole Ghost in Jupiter orbit.'

Jophiel nodded. 'After my father shot it. The skin split open, and out tumbled what looked like multiple organs. Even multiple organisms.'

Harris said, 'Maybe these Ghosts aren't unified creatures as we are. Maybe each of them is a kind of community, of symbiotic creatures of different orders. Why, I'm looking at magnified images that show what look like vegetable components in there too, masses of lichen which must complete the ecological loops of respiration and waste processing.'

Nicola put in, 'And the significance of the hot mud pool?'

'Maybe we're seeing some reflection of the Ghosts' origins. Maybe they need to return to a simulacrum of the oceanic environment where they evolved, or the tidal pools, whatever. Their dependent organisms may need to be released, regularly, to stock up on essential nutrients, even to breed among their own kind. Or perhaps to be replaced, in the overall Ghost autarky, if a component ages or is injured.'

Nicola raised her eyebrows. '"Autarky." Word of the day.'

'In my team we're debating all this, observing, recording. We don't know how useful this might be but—'

'Good work, Harris,' Jophiel said. 'This kind of knowledge is going to be essential if we're to find an edge here. And—'

Another jolt of the lifedome.

'I think we're descending,' Nicola muttered.

Jophiel spoke to the crew. 'Everybody brace for impact. We don't know how gentle our Ghost pilots are going to be.'

Ben Goober called, 'I think I can see where they're bringing us down, sir. Right next to the other one.'

'The other what?'

'The other lifedome.'

15

The other lifedome was a cylinder twice the width and height of the *Island*'s relatively modest hemisphere, and multiple decks showed within its interior.

Lights glowed sparsely.

Jophiel Poole, whose template had laid out the basic design of such ships, recognised its type immediately. The ship had evidently been a scattership, a GUTdrive colony ship, before its spine had been cut like the *Island*'s. In the Poole Industries design hierarchy this was a *Great Northern*-class vessel, originally conceived in pre-Xeelee days as a generation starship – a design that had never been built or flown, before the Xeelee came. After Cold Earth, ten thousand such ships had been sent out into the dark, each ship capable of carrying up to a hundred thousand human beings. Scraps of the humanity that could no longer be safely supported by the planet of their birth.

So there were indeed humans here at Goober's Star. Or there had been. Just as the Ghosts' signal, picked up by the rebel Virtuals of *Gea*, had hinted.

After the *Island*'s lifedome was set down on rocky ground, close to the other ship, a Ghost came. Hovered just outside the dome.

When Jophiel was informed, he hurried that way – hurried, though his Virtual projection software faithfully transmitted to him the burden of this world's forty per cent higher gravity. Nicola, Asher and Harris followed him more cautiously, Harris with a medical pack slung over his shoulder.

They looked out through the dome wall.

The Ghost seemed to hover effortlessly a metre or so off the ground. Jophiel had the odd sense that it was spinning on some axis, but so featureless was its surface – it cast highlights from Goober's Star, high in the near-black sky – that it was impossible to be sure. Aside from the apparition in *Island*'s lifedome, this was the first time he had seen a Ghost close up since his template had encountered the Wormhole

Ghost in Jupiter's orbit, more than a thousand light years away, and forty subjective years ago.

He wondered what mechanism enabled the Ghost to float like that. Another application of that magic inertia-control technology?

Its voice, somehow projected, sounded next to Jophiel's ear. 'I invite you to walk with me, to meet your conspecifics.' Again that stylised, very artificial voice. 'I know your shelter has access mechanisms.'

'Airlocks. We call them airlocks. How are you speaking to us? How can we hear you?'

'That is scarcely relevant. You may emerge in safety. An atmosphere has been provided.'

Jophiel glanced up. 'How? How is it contained? Is there another dome, like over the mud pool? How do you know what we can breathe safely? . . . Ah.'

'Yes. We know because of our study of the conspecifics who were first brought here over a millennium ago.'

A millennium, Jophiel thought. That was a clue. If this ship had been taken not long after leaving the Solar System, then that could indeed have been more than a millennium ago – a millennium experienced as less than two decades by the crew of the *Island*, thanks to the ship's relativistic speed. Just a few centuries after leaving Earth, such a ship could have travelled no more than a few hundred light years from Sol, under its own GUTdrive power. And so the ship, its crew and passengers, must have been brought here by hyperdrive. Jophiel shuddered, in the presence of unknowable alien power.

He tried to focus. 'All right, Ghost, we'll trust you. About the air.'

'You may call me the Ambassador. It is a human label which approaches the reality of my commission by my fellows. And it will distinguish me from others.'

Nicola and Jophiel shared a glance. The Wormhole Ghost had once called itself the Ambassador to the Heat Sink.

'Come – follow me. You really are quite safe.'

'Me first,' Jophiel said.

But Harris the medic shook his head. 'With respect, Jophiel, you aren't a useful guinea pig. I suggest Nicola goes first. We need a meat sample.'

'Thanks a lot,' Nicola said. 'Come on, let's get on with it.'

They crowded at the airlock, a big double-doored chamber designed for the passage of significant masses of cargo both in space and on the ground. Nicola, and then Harris, simply walked through, and outside, without apparent ill effects.

Nicola took a big deep breath of the air. 'So that's what a Ghost fart smells like.'

Harris dug a sensor out of his pack, studied it, and nodded through the translucent wall to the others. 'Safe to follow.'

Jophiel and Asher followed them through. Jophiel's experience was only ever going to be a simulated copy of the reality, but he smelled nothing unusual – save a faint scent of sulphur, perhaps, a trace of the volcanism that must underlie this whole raised landmass.

The Ghost rolled towards the other lifedome. 'The ground has not been prepared, but has been selected as a relatively smooth area. The distance we must cross is less than a kilometre. The separation of your domes was chosen for safety, as we brought the second dome down close to the first.'

But, Jophiel thought cynically, with enough of a gap to keep the two human communities apart, and therefore more easily controlled.

He concentrated on the detail as they followed the Ghost.

A new world, for him. Hard volcanic rock underfoot, like basalt. The sky above littered with those wispy clouds. That heavy gravity, a dull, deadening load he felt with each step. He could see no sign of whatever shell, physical or otherwise, was containing this scrap of Earthlike atmosphere.

He glanced back at the *Island* lifedome, a shell of light. Many of the crew were crowded close to the wall, watching them go.

And he noticed the wormhole interface, an electric-blue tetrahedron still intact on top of the dome.

He looked away. If the Ghosts had yet to puzzle out that feature, and its significance – the only link to the *Cauchy*, the only possible source of any help – he didn't want to draw their attention to it. Always supposing Ghosts could interpret human body language . . . Safest to assume they could.

'You should find the air comfortable. Warm enough, and the humidity adjusted.'

'It doesn't bother you, I see,' Nicola snapped.

'We Ghosts are somewhat more resilient. We grew to this form in a harsher place, physically, than your Earth. My hide, while an independent life form in itself, is actually a highly developed biotechnological container.'

'Well, there's no need to brag.'

Jophiel felt like prodding the Ghost. 'If you're studying us, we study you. We already know you have a hyperdrive – a faster-than-light drive. Even before you took us on that jaunt from the outer system, we deduced its existence. The timings of the signals you emitted didn't make sense otherwise.'

The Ghost rolled complacently above the ground. 'Yes, we have a hyperdrive. And today I have learned a new human word.'

Nicola grunted. 'A made-up word for something that we haven't yet developed.'

'Nor have we. In fact we acquired the hyperdrive, long ago in our history. From a trading species called the Qax.' *Chhaakss.* 'You may imagine the cost.'

Jophiel glanced at Nicola. Qax: they both knew that name. The Poole family archive had spoken of this species. One day, a humanity still restricted to the Solar System would have been conquered by the Qax. Enslaved. *Would have been enslaved.* With humanity already scattered to the stars, Jophiel supposed that particular fate had been averted.

Yet, it seemed, the Qax were real. And another little piece of those old prophecies had been confirmed, in this extraordinary situation. *Reality leaks.* Inside his skinsuit, Jophiel shuddered.

'And in turn,' the Ambassador said to him now, unexpectedly, 'you, the Poole, have an amulet. A Ghost artefact, handed to you after a reverse-time incursion to—'

'I don't have it,' Jophiel snapped. 'I have a Virtual copy, which you're welcome to inspect. Here.' He dug the amulet out of his pocket, and threw it at the Ghost.

The Ghost made the trinket hover in the air before it. 'An inadequate copy. Not without interest, however.' The amulet floated back towards Jophiel.

'How did you know about it?'

'It was what drew us to your system in the first place. I mean, the system of your origin. We Ghosts are explorers. Experimenters. Traders, when it benefits us. We have stationed probes throughout this part of the Galaxy. Observation posts. One such probe reported back from your system on the appearance of a Ghost, in a part of the Galaxy which no Ghost had yet reached – in our history. And a Ghost artefact of a very advanced design – your amulet.

'We saw that the Ghost was quickly terminated. In response we would have sent a ship immediately.'

Nicola glared. 'Why? To take revenge?'

Jophiel murmured, 'Come on, Nicola. It came here because we detected human signals where they shouldn't be. It was just the same for the Ghosts.'

The Ghost went on, 'But our probe was also reporting Xeelee activity, of an anomalous kind, in your system. We hesitated.'

'You know about the Xeelee, then,' Nicola said quickly.

'We learned your version of the name from intercepted transmissions. It is not clear to us how you came upon that name – it is a corrupted form of that used by other phonic species, but near enough. As for the Xeelee themselves, they are the reason we are in this system, of course. And, indirectly, you.'

Jophiel and his crew shared a glance. Jophiel thought of those deep valleys, where blankets of Xeelee hull plate evidently lay like fields of snow.

'So you were interested in the Solar System,' Jophiel said. 'Eventually you did send a tangleship?'

'Another amusing neologism. Yes, we sent a tangleship, once we were sure the Xeelee intruder had abandoned the system. It was a party from this star system, this project, in fact. This star is the nearest of our bases to your Solar System.'

Jophiel asked, 'What project? . . . Never mind, for now. I'm guessing you arrived after the departure of the *Cauchy* flotilla, or we'd have known about it. You abducted a scattership in flight—'

'Several,' the Ghost admitted. 'Of which only a few survived, with their crew. Others fought hard. We evidently had much to learn about humans.' It said this factually, without a trace of regret.

Nicola looked murderous, but she said nothing.

'We brought this ship and its human cargo here. Most survived.'

Most? There was no reply to that.

'We studied the living,' the Ghost said, 'and later their descendants, intensively. As well as the living things that had travelled with them. We have been here for more than a thousand of your years. For many generations. Since we acquired them, we have involved humans in our projects. Mostly here, on this planet, which you now call Goober c. We have learned much.

'Your own mission has intrigued us, Jophiel Poole. It was not by chance that we found you – or rather, you found us. Once we had acquired the scattership it was an obvious ploy to use its technology, and crew, to set up lures: human signals to attract more human ships. Lures to which you responded. We had not anticipated, though, finding you, a simulacrum of Poole himself, intent on a mission to the centre of the Galaxy. To take on a Xeelee in slower-than-light ships! Not what we anticipated at all . . . We must discuss this further,' said the Ghost. 'But for now . . .'

They were nearing the other ship's lifedome, a translucent wall before them.

And a woman stood there, outside an airlock. She looked bent, old, very still. Dressed in a worn, much-patched coverall, she leaned on a kind of stick improvised from a bit of hull metal.

Jophiel was distracted by how elderly the lifedome fabric itself looked: starred by micrometeorite impacts, scuffed, in places yellowed with age, yet intact, after a thousand years. Jophiel, or his template, had seen the scatterships leave for the stars, with his own eyes, just twenty subjective years ago. And now this.

He tried to focus on the woman. Herself a thousand years old, perhaps. No human had ever lived so long, on Earth.

Still he hesitated to speak.

'Lethe, Poole. What do you expect her to do, burst into song?' Nicola pushed forward. 'My name is Nicola Emry.'

The woman held out one hand, like a claw. Nicola gently took it, cupping it in both her own hands as if sheltering a baby bird, Jophiel thought. He had always known Nicola was capable of tenderness if she felt like it.

The woman seemed to respond to Nicola very slowly, as if she had little energy, her small body intolerably heavy. Her hair was a snow-white scrape, tied back, he saw now. Her face, small-featured, was blank, and oddly smooth, not wrinkled as Jophiel might have expected. As if worn by age, a face of old stone.

The voice was a whisper. '*Emry*. I used to know that name.' Yet her eyes were bright, and she smiled.

'My mother, probably. She was on the World Senate. The UN body.'

'That must be it.' And she turned, at glacial speed, to Jophiel. 'And I know you – or your template, at least.'

Jophiel felt oddly impressed. 'You can tell I'm a Virtual?'

'My name is Susan Chen. Once I worked for the sentience police, before the Xeelee came, before the Displacement. Yes, I can recognise Virtuals. I was born in Beijing, in the United Asia Republic. A citizen of the world, as we all were in those days, when we *had* a world . . .'

As she joined their little circle, leaning on her stick, her story seemed to tumble out. A story she had hoarded for a thousand years, perhaps, if she really was one of the original crew, Jophiel thought.

'I was born in the year 3626.'

'Just five years after me,' Jophiel said.

'I always followed the exploits of you Pooles. All those grand worm-holes.' Was she smiling? Her face was so immobile it was hard to tell. 'I think I had a slight crush on you.'

Nicola rolled her eyes. 'Well, that's just typical.'

'But then came the Displacement, and the Scattering. Our ship was a greenship, called the *Gourd*.

'And we ended up here. I am the only one left. The last of the crew, the original crew. There were children. You will see . . . They are down in the Valleys, the Xeelee Valleys. I live alone here, in the dome. The crew are in the Valleys. You will see. We had AS technology – we tried to hide it from the Ghosts—'

'We always knew,' the Ghost said smoothly.

'We thought there should be a witness, you see. One of us originals, who remembered Earth, should be there to tell the story, first hand. We hoarded what we had – the AS, I mean – but time passed. There were ten of us left, then five, then two, then I was the last of the original crew. I was the last. Yet I was never alone. Michael Poole was always with me. When I despaired . . . I knew you would save us. I knew! . . .'

Jophiel frowned. 'Always with you? I don't understand—'

'You were always with me . . .' Susan Chen sighed, and seemed to crumple, perhaps fainting. Nicola supported her, and Harris rushed forward, reaching for his medical kit.

The Ambassador rolled complacently. 'Humans are my object of study. How fascinating you are.'

Nicola glared up at it with a look of pure hate.

16

After the first month on Ghost Plateau, as Susan Chen called it – a month the *Cauchy* crew spent mostly securing their physical survival – Chen said she had a proposal for them.

'You know that we work for the Ghosts, down on the planet. I mean, in the Xeelee Valleys. Where the Xeelee buildings grow.'

Nicola grinned. '*Where the Xeelee buildings grow*. Susan, what a line!'

Susan's own smile, like all her expressions, was a sketch. 'We – I mean, my crewmates, my charges – they have us seek Xeelee artefacts. Now the Ghosts intend to send a party down, to retrieve what we have collected. And they invite you to join. A party of you. Perhaps three or four as an introductory assignment. You will meet my crew. We can show you how we work. The Ghosts, I think, will be interested in how we interact, we two crews separated for so long. They like to explore us.'

That withered smile grew more wintry. Jophiel suspected there was a world of horror in that one word, *explore*.

He said, 'I'm guessing it's a hazardous assignment.'

Susan shrugged. 'They prefer to send humans into places they regard as too dangerous for Ghosts. These are, after all, Xeelee stations. Though their purpose is little understood, we suspect, even by the Ghosts.'

Xeelee stations. More words that made Jophiel shiver.

'But we have survived for centuries despite these losses. And learned caution.' She eyed Jophiel. 'I would recommend you send a party. The Ghosts' supervision is not omniscient. There may be advantages to be gained.'

Nicola and Jophiel exchanged a hungry glance. It had been a frustrating month since they had been brought here: a month of not doing much more than consolidate, for what looked like it would be a long, if not permanent, stay on this world. All of it blighted by the dull burden of the forty per cent higher gravity. They had travelled little, seen less, learned nothing. Even Susan, after that first gushing meeting, had seemed inhibited about speaking to them.

And Jophiel was aware that the crew's forced adaptation to their imprisonment was a ghastly echo of what Susan and her crew had gone through centuries ago.

'Agreed,' he said immediately. 'Thank you, Susan. The question is, who goes?'

'You and me,' Nicola snapped. 'This first time.'

'Look, I'm a Virtual. Away from human technology I'll need a projection pack.'

'Hardly a problem. If Susan's right about possible advantage, or danger, we need our best eyes on the ground. With one other, maybe. Harris? Our resident expert on the Ghosts. And also Harris has medical training. He can take a good look at the *Gourd* people. *And* he can carry you on his back, Jophiel. Your support unit, one hundred and forty per cent gravity and all. Serves him right.'

Susan nodded. 'I will accompany you. I rarely venture into the Valleys these days – usually only when some catastrophe has struck my crew. This time I will make an exception, for the chance to talk. The Ghosts may eavesdrop, but there will be opportunities.'

Nicola touched her shoulder. 'You're a remarkable person, Susan Chen. Come on. Let's get this done.'

17

The three of them were to be flown down from Ghost Plateau into a feature about eight hundred kilometres to the planet's east, which Susan, who among other things had done her best to compile a global map of Goober c, called 'Xeelee Valley Number Five'.

The four of them climbed into, as Jophiel immediately recognised, what had evidently once been the hull of a standard Poole Industries flitter, originally carried by the scattership *Gourd*. The propulsion units had long ago been cut away, leaving a human-life-support shell that was now embedded in a tangle of Ghost rope. The hull itself was much aged, and in its interior every surface was rubbed to smoothness, the worn-out soft parts of the couches replaced by hand-stitched cushions and blankets. It was strange to Jophiel to inspect what was for him contemporary technology so obviously aged: the craft's control instruments, detached or inert; softscreens probably blank for a millennium.

When the craft lifted from the ground, evidently held firm in the Ghosts' inertia-control field, there was barely a sense of motion. But the view out of the windows was astounding.

Harris Kemp goggled, his forehead pressed to the window beside his seat. 'Take a look back at that plateau. Makes Tharsis on Mars look like a mud pie. And those valleys . . .'

Susan seemed oddly pleased, Jophiel thought. As if she was proud of her prison-planet.

Xeelee Valley Number Five turned out to be a vast rift valley, deep and long, its walls sheer, one of several tremendous cracks in the crust that led off from the gigantic bulge of the plateau. It seemed clear to Jophiel that this feature had nothing to do with erosion by running water, like Earth's Grand Canyon; it was nothing less than a crack in the crust of the planet.

The craft dropped into the valley, passing along one of the great walls. The light was poor, the clouds thick in this world's dense layer of atmosphere, but still they were close enough to the wall to make out detail. Jophiel was no geologist, but he recognised the signs of past catastrophes in the complex strata. Here a sheet of basalt, a relic of some huge volcanic event, was wearing out of the wall as softer rock eroded. Above that was a layer of tumbled rocks, huge and angular, as if dumped by a tremendous tsunami. Above *that* beds of what looked like sandstone, deposited by some vanished ocean.

And, here and there, clinging to the strata or dangling in blankets over the cliff face, a pale, almost apologetic green.

'Life,' Nicola said, staring out.

Harris groaned. 'I wish I had better instruments than my own eyes to observe all this.'

'Maybe next trip,' Jophiel murmured. 'If we can get the Ghosts to trust us a little more . . . Is it life, though, Susan?'

'Indeed it is. And native to Goober c, as far as we were able to tell, back in the days when we had the means to study it, when some of the original crew survived. Alongside the first generations who we managed to train up, to some extent.'

'Anaerobic, though,' Harris said. 'The life here. Every scrap of it we've seen so far. That is, it doesn't exploit oxygen.'

'Correct,' Susan said. 'That's what we worked out. You understand the thick air of this world is choked with carbon dioxide – that alone would contribute about five times as much pressure as all of Earth's atmosphere. A product of all the volcanism, no doubt. It traps a lot of heat, making the planet warmer than it has any right to be so far from the star.

'And the carbon dioxide in the air is what the life here feeds off. There's some kind of metabolic chain that exploits sunlight to cause carbon dioxide to react with other gases and minerals to liberate hydrogen – and it's the recombination of hydrogen that seems to power the larger and more complex plant growths. And animal life. Hydrogen plays the role that oxygen does on our worlds. Well – again, we thought so. We were never able to survey properly. This world is so large, you see, that its continents have remained largely islands, cut off from each other, and entirely different evolutionary strategies seem to have been tried out. As if there were several planets compressed into one. The Ghosts keep the fauna away. We never got a close look. But anyhow it will soon make no difference.'

The *Island* crew listened to this, electrified.

Jophiel said, 'You're talking about the upcoming nova event.'

'Indeed.'

Harris nodded. 'I've done more work on that with Asher. That star is becoming more unstable every time we look at it. It *will* climax in a violent event soon – maybe only months away – it will be something like a nova, yes. And this world will be battered.'

Nicola grunted. 'Just our luck.'

Chen shook her head. 'Actually, perhaps not. We have been held by the Ghosts for a thousand years, but we soon suspected the Ghosts have been here longer still. A *long* time. You can see the evidence on the airless worlds better. The moons of Goober c itself, for instance. Structures, visible through the telescopes we had then.

'But now, you see, *we* are here, a species the Ghosts are unfamiliar with and cannot, I think, understand. Because, from the Ghosts' point of view, we suddenly exploded out of a system which the Xeelee had visited. *And* you have the anomaly of the Wormhole Ghost, with its bad news for its own kind . . . Perhaps the Ghosts have accelerated their project as a result.'

Jophiel tried to think that through. 'Susan. What project? Are you suggesting that the Ghosts have got something to do with the nova event?'

But before she could reply the flitter dipped, banked, lurched.

Jophiel glanced out of his window at the fleeing ground. On the floor of the great valley a river meandered – itself a mighty torrent, but obviously not the creator of this huge geological wound. And there, just ahead, a kind of pale, milky glow. A colour Jophiel recognised, after his experiences in the Solar System, even in this cloud-choked world's murky light.

'That's Xeelee hull plate,' Nicola said.

'Indeed,' Susan said softly.

They fell silent. The flitter ducked and swooped, beyond any human control. And soon pale artifice, complex and crusted and covering the ground, swept under the prow. As the flitter descended, Jophiel made out what might have been a cityscape, a scatter of blocks, of pyramids and cubes, pillars and towers – but there was a randomness to it all that made the plain look as if it was covered by huge salt crystals, perhaps, eroding from some seam.

Still the flitter dropped, until it touched gently down.

Unreal as he was, Jophiel climbed cautiously down the flitter's steps to the planet's surface.

Hard, warm rock underfoot. The air was warm too, thick, murky, thicker than any fog, and it resisted his motions as he tried to push through it. It was like wading across an ocean floor.

Susan Chen stood patiently as Jophiel, Nicola, and Harris Kemp laden with his Virtual-generating backpack, took slow, exploratory steps. She said, 'Some people feel claustrophobic in this air. As if they're drowning.'

'I wish you hadn't said that,' Harris said.

Nicola pointed to shadows, what looked like a cluster of buildings in the murk. 'I take it that's our target.'

'Indeed.' Susan took cautious steps in that direction, leaning on her stick.

Jophiel and Nicola walked side by side. Harris followed Susan, walking as slowly as she did. He muttered observations into a voice recorder, one of the few technological gadgets the Ghosts had allowed on this trip, aside from the skinsuits and Jophiel's projector box riding on Harris's back.

'We have plenty of time,' Susan said. 'It is near local noon; the day-length of this planet is only a little more than Earth's. It is best if we stay together, however. The Ghosts find it less alarming if we don't scatter. Come along . . . I wouldn't bother making a map, by the way. Or if you do, don't take it too seriously.'

Jophiel wondered what she meant by that.

They were already nearing the buildings, Jophiel saw. Blocky geometric shapes, mostly cuboid, some spheres, pyramids – even a spindly tetrahedron. None much taller than a couple of storeys, in human terms. Looming out of the turbid air.

'We will find my crewmates soon. They never go far. Follow me. Keep your eyes open – especially look for technology, portable arte-facts. That's what the Ghosts want.'

Nicola snorted. 'Now you sound like my mother. *She* would always set me a test every time we went for a walk.'

Jophiel thought he heard Susan sigh; it was such a soft sound he wasn't sure. 'I suppose I have been a mother, for a thousand years. One gets into habits of speech.'

They came to the buildings.

They followed a narrow street, between the blank faces of two relatively small structures, each maybe three metres tall. No, not blank – Jophiel saw their walls were marked with pale pink crosses, roughly daubed. Jophiel could see no doorway, no windows, no sign of what these box-like buildings might have been erected for. Only these empty, pale walls. And when he looked down at his feet he saw he was still walking on basaltic ground. There was no road surface; it was as if the buildings had been set down on the bare rock like a giant's toys. Toys made of Xeelee hull plate.

They came out of the alley at an intersection. More buildings all around them, set not quite in regular rows, so that the roads and alleys between them were offset and followed odd angles – some widened, some narrowed. A little further ahead, Jophiel saw, was a group of much taller buildings, still essentially box-like, cuboids and pyramids and spheres. The central cluster cast long shadows over the other buildings. It looked like a downtown in a city of the American Anthropocene, he thought, like New York, perhaps.

'No markings,' Nicola said.

'What?'

'Wake up, Poole. Markings? None on this building. See?' She pointed to a small, slim monolith between two, towering pyramids. 'But look what Susan is doing.' She pointed again.

Susan had stopped by another small building, between two giants. 'This is the one we just cleared, I think . . .' She took off her pack, drew out what looked like an ancient can of paint, slipped her gloved hand into the pot, and crudely scrawled a cross on that virginal surface. Then she moved on.

Harris went over to inspect. He touched the pale, sticky liquid. 'Interesting stuff. Paint that sticks to Xeelee hull material.'

'Paint! That's hardly the priority,' Nicola said testily. 'Why is she doing this? How long has this been going on?' She looked around with a fresh eye. 'What *is* this place? What's it for? How does it work? Hmm . . .'

'You'll see. This way.' Susan Chen smiled and beckoned, pack on her back, leaning on her stick, the paint pot in her free, gloved hand.

She led them down another skewed alley.

And brought them to a door, in the wall of the building she had marked.

It was just another box, distinguished only by the fact that it had a doorway – a rectangular space, open, with no cover.

Inside there were no fittings that Jophiel could see – nothing save for a pair of low pillars, one at either end of the single big room, that looked as if they had grown out of the floor. The pillars appeared to be made of Xeelee hull plate, like the rest of the room.

The interior looked like it spanned half the width of the building.

There was evidently a partition, with a further door. Jophiel thought he could hear faint voices, coming through the door.

The space glowed with a soft internal light. The four of them, staring at this geometric perfection, looked grubby, clumsy, unfinished.

Susan smiled at them. 'Don't worry about dusty footmarks. The place seems to self-clean. They all do.'

Harris walked over to one pillar; it was about waist-height. 'Why are we here? I mean, why do the Ghosts send you here?'

Susan waved a hand. 'You understand this is a Xeelee station, of some kind. All of this is Xeelee construction material – as the Ghosts call it. I understand you call it hull plate, or membrane, depending on the grade. A replicating material that grows in sunlight. There are no Xeelee here. All this is automated somehow. And what we're looking for is Xeelee artefacts.'

'Artefacts?'

'The whole of this "city" is a Xeelee artefact, of course. We seek small, portable devices. I've only ever seen two kinds. Two, in a thousand years.' She patted one pillar. 'One type is associated with pillars like this. You always find them in such rooms, sitting on pillars, facing each other. Hoops, each maybe half a metre across. Sky blue, polished – paper thin – and before they're detached from the pillars you can see pink sparks dashing around the circumference. They go inert when removed, as they have been from this place, as you can see. The Ghosts think they are some kind of comms device.

'My own best guess is that this particular kind of installation is a monitoring station.' She cast a shy glance at Jophiel. 'I did follow your adventures when I was young,' she said. 'When you chased the Xeelee into the heart of the Sun. You thought it was studying creatures of dark matter there . . . Maybe that's what this station is for. An observation post for the Xeelee, to monitor an anomalous star. With some kind of comms system, the hoops perhaps. Well. If the Ghosts ever made this work, or figured out its principles, they haven't told me about it.'

Jophiel thought it over. 'So the Ghosts came to this system, you think, knowing this Xeelee station was in place. But abandoned. Or left uninhabited, anyhow.'

'The Ghosts want the stuff,' Nicola said. 'Xeelee treasure. Like Saxons in Britain, looting a deserted Roman town. But now they have been disturbed. They've detected Xeelee activity relatively nearby – I mean, in our Solar System. As soon as there's a hint that the legions are returning, the Saxons are looking over their shoulder . . .'

Susan smiled at the analogy. 'It is a very long time since I thought about Saxons and Romans. We must talk.'

'I'd like that.'

'And the other kind of artefact?' Harris asked.

'A flower, we call it. A Xeelee flower. A core from which hull plate will grow. You'll recognise it when you see it.'

'Ah,' Jophiel said now. 'We hypothesised the existence of such things. We never found one, back in the Solar System. We called them "seeds".'

Susan gently tapped one wall with a flat, gloved hand. 'Growth is the key. So I have learned, in time. Though meaningful observation takes decades. Like watching a forest grow – yes, exactly like that. Can you guess how this place works yet? It's not like a town, a human-built environment. However, it fulfils whatever function it has – it's more like a community of living things.'

Jophiel for once was at least one step behind. He was still distracted by those apparent voices from beyond the doorway, muffled in the heavy, almost liquid air. 'Living?'

Susan smiled again. Jophiel had the strong impression that she was enjoying this, enjoying having an audience, as well she might. 'You'll have to take my word for it. Over time – by which I mean years, decades – these buildings change. They *grow*. And sometimes they move; they will detach from the surface, and—'

Harris broke in, excited, 'I think I know what she means. This building grows, literally. It is nothing but hull plate. So maybe it starts from a seed of hull plate – Susan's "flower" – and grows, converting starlight energy to mass, to this planar material – and the more it grows, the more light it soaks up, and it grows some more. It's an exponential process, we have good mathematical models. Just as we saw with the Cache in the Solar System, so with this building. It must be growing into some pre-programmed form, presumably, reaching some maximum size—'

'Or it would, if not for the presence of other buildings around it,' Susan said. 'Which, you see, block its light, and therefore its growth.'

And Jophiel thought of the long shadows cast by the 'downtown' he had seen. 'It's like a forest, then,' he said. 'These buildings aren't *planned*. They just grow where they can, competing for ground space and light – yes, just like a forest, which is dominated by big tall trees, and smaller growths stunted in the shade.'

'Even the timing is persuasive,' Harris mused. 'At the orbit of Earth, the doubling time of Xeelee hull plate was ten or fifteen years. The sunlight is less here, but . . . A building would grow at the rate of a tree. Over decades.'

'Well done,' Susan said, nodding. 'You got it quickly. But, as I said, this forest of buildings *changes*. Sometimes day to day. Not just the size of the buildings, but their locations. *They aren't rooted to the ground,* you see. That's why we got into the habit of marking the buildings – the Ghosts supplied us with a kind of adhesive paint, so we can label those we have searched. We don't know the full life cycle, and if the Ghosts know they don't tell us. Perhaps older buildings collapse, or drift off into space—'

'Or are consumed by their competitors,' Nicola said with a certain relish. 'Like strangler figs. All this is plausible, isn't it? A hull-plate ecology. One thing we learned about the Xeelee back in the Solar System is that everything about the Xeelee is like a merger of life and technology . . .'

Again, those voices. Softly bickering, it sounded like. Jophiel asked, 'Susan. Who else is in here?'

'My crewmates, of course.' She looked oddly embarrassed, though the expression on her ancient, immobile face was hard to read. 'If you are ready – you should be prepared.'

Nicola took her gloved hand. 'Just show us.'

Without another word, Susan led them out of the further door, across a short, narrowing alley, and into a building on the far side.

Jophiel followed with dread.

He found himself in a near twin of the building he'd just left. Another hull-plate box. No comms pillars.

And here, in the middle of the floor, was a group of people. Sitting, hunched over. There were perhaps a dozen of them. They sat in a circle, facing each other, muttering. Jophiel thought he heard three, four voices speaking at once. The words were incomprehensible, if there were any words in that stream of babbled syllables.

Susan, still holding Nicola's hand, said. 'Don't be alarmed.'

As she spoke, her crewmates' heads turned, and they fell silent. Wary, in the presence of strangers. Watchful.

A dozen, Jophiel counted quickly. All adults, apparently, wearing antique, much patched skinsuits. One even had a faded Poole Industries logo on the back. They had been sharing food, from rough packets strewn on the floor between them. One lifted his faceplate to take a mouthful of food. A snorting, gobbling sound. They all seemed short, bent over, squat. Jophiel realised he couldn't distinguish male from female, could tell nothing about their ages.

A moment of stillness. The two groups faced each other.

It was like a pack of apes, Jophiel thought wildly. Apes facing three angels, himself and his crewmates standing straight and tall in their gleaming skinsuits. Angels from the stars.

Susan walked over to the group. She knelt among them, put her arms over their shoulders. She seemed to lead them in a kind of chant: 'The rule of threes. Remember? *Three* minutes without air. *Three* hours in the cold. *Three* days without water. *Three* weeks without food . . . Say it with me. *Three* minutes without air. *Three* hours in the cold . . .'

Then, without warning, the 'apes' stood. Still hunched over, they hastily grabbed at their food packs and shambled untidily out of a far door. Jophiel had only a blurred impression of them. He thought he saw stunted limbs, bent backs; one of them came close to knuckle-walking, like a chimp. And some of them had too-small heads, the skulls deformed.

None of them had looked the newcomers in the face.

When they were gone, Susan walked unsteadily to the centre of the floor, where the group had been sitting. Stood amid scraps of food debris, an abandoned rucksack. 'I'm sorry. That didn't go well. I didn't know how to— I wanted you to see for yourself.' She sighed heavily. 'So now you know. Now you know.' She trembled, folded.

Nicola hurried forward, took her stick, and embraced the woman. 'Come. Sit down with me.'

18

Nicola had lightweight fold-out chairs in her pack. She set these out in a circle, where the *Gourd* crew had been. Harris had coffee; Jophiel accepted a Virtual cup, finding it a relief to sit and escape the clutch of gravity.

Harris didn't sit down himself. 'One of us ought to go do the job we were sent down for. I'll go explore. See if I can find some Xeelee treasure.' He picked up his pack and pushed out of the building.

And, in this quasi-living Xeelee structure, Susan Chen said she would tell Jophiel and Nicola her story. 'The Ghosts hear all we say, probably. But at least here we have the illusion of privacy . . .'

Jophiel said, 'On our ships we had a tradition called the Testimony. Every time the crew gathered, one of us would get up to tell their story. How the Xeelee attack affected them, their family – their life. Susan, give us your Testimony.'

She smiled. 'Thank you, Jophiel. Very well. You know I was born just a few years after you – or your template. It seems such a remote age now.

'I took my assessments for Federal Service. I was recommended for the police. Something about my qualities of determination, of general intelligence rather than a specialised intellect, attracted the recruiters. A certain puzzle-solving ability.

'Actually I always wanted to follow you Pooles out to the frontier, one way or another. The outer planets. I always thought there would be room for me, out *there*, one day. Out where people like you were building things. I could deal with crimes among the settlers. Resolve complex legal disputes when you tried to extend the wormhole network to Neptune, and found some crusty old settler in your way.'

Jophiel nodded gravely. 'I think you'd have been a good fit.'

She seemed unreasonably pleased at that; she beamed, her face made briefly young by the smile.

'But then the Xeelee came. I was twenty years old.

'I saw the images of the Wormhole Ghost; I remembered that, when much later I encountered the Ghosts who captured us. They have us call them "Ghosts", you know, I think in response to their monitoring of that event, the labels you used.

'I had to stay in the police, of course, in the aftermath of the incursion. As people grew afraid, there was a great deal of civil disorder.

'I was twenty-four years old when the Displacement happened.

'On Cold Earth, I helped keep order during the refugee flows, the resettlement of mankind.

'Then I was co-opted onto the policing of the scattership building programme. Until I was assigned to a ship myself.'

Jophiel said, 'The *Gourd*.'

'It was a greenship. I was second officer, an essentially administrative function. The work suited me. I'd had a complicated life, never had children of my own: never the time, as for many of my generation. I think on some level I loved the idea of nurturing an ecohab, a scrap of Earth life, all the way to the stars. For three subjective years the mission went well. We were only some ten light years from Earth.'

Jophiel prompted, 'And then—'

'The Ghosts found us.'

Harris walked in. 'Sorry to interrupt. Look what I found.'

He opened his gloved hand. On its palm rested an artefact as pale as hull plate: a small cylindrical base from which sprouted six angular petals. 'I've tried to keep it in the shadow. Don't want the thing growing out of control—'

Susan smiled. 'There is an on switch. Don't worry.'

Nicola whistled. 'So that,' she said in awe, 'is a Xeelee flower.'

'You did well to find it on your first expedition down here,' Susan said.

'I cheated.' Harris sat on one of the fold-out chairs. 'Any of that coffee left? . . . I just followed your crew, Susan. They left a kind of trail. Mostly of food packets. And this, in a kind of little cache they built.'

Susan sounded proud. 'They are good people. Good *crew*. Just so disadvantaged. There has been nothing more I could do . . .'

Nicola said, her voice cold, 'Tell us about the Ghosts. What they did when they captured you.'

Susan seemed to sit up straighter, Jophiel observed. A police officer making a report, after a thousand years.

'As I said, it was three years into the mission. You know that they had tracked the irruption of the Wormhole Ghost that came for you, Jophiel. Or your template. And they came looking for us, you see. They *took* us. I don't know if they took other scatterships, what else they may have done in the Solar System itself.

'They detached the lifedome from our GUTdrive stem. Enfolded the dome into what you have called a tangleship, and brought us here.

'The hyperdrive journey took eight months. At the time, the crew – the surviving crew – made careful observations. I still have records.'

Jophiel nodded. 'Good. The more you can tell us, the more we can learn about the technology. I hope I would have done as well.'

Nicola said gently, 'So they brought you here. Set your lifedome down on Goober c—'

'Just as you saw it.'

Jophiel asked, 'And the crew? Put to work?'

'You mean, down here? Foraging for Xeelee artefacts? No, that came later, when they discovered how effective we were at the task. Just the right size, with the right foraging skills, you see. Skills honed by a million years of evolution on the African savannah, now put to work for an alien species.' She smiled. 'We'd complain about that. Make each other laugh.'

'Then what?'

'Well, at first, they – tested us. Once they learned our language they interrogated us, together and singly. Tried to find out all about us, not just our technology and other capabilities but about our evolutionary history, our biology, our culture.

'They liked to watch us work. They observed us work on the life-dome's systems. Took us out on the planet for various – exercises. Traps to fall into, or escape from. As Discovery Era scientists used animals in testing, so they used us. People were hurt, of course.'

'Killed?' Nicola snapped.

'Not purposefully. They did have a crude way of analysing us, you see, as if we were unfamiliar machinery, not living things. Even testing us to destruction. Looking for the spirit, by taking the body apart. Yes, there were casualties. The corpses were taken away, for dissection, I suppose.

'Soon, many of the living were taken away. Abducted. With sam-ples of technologies and life – soil and grass and trees – from the lifedome. The animals, chickens and rabbits, even rats. We never saw our crewmates again. You understand we were a large crew, tens of thousands, many in sleep pods during the voyage.'

'All the scatterships had huge complements,' Jophiel said. 'Even greenships like yours. The seedships, even more.'

'Yes. Well, now, the crew was broken up. In squads of a thousand or more. Families were split apart, and so on. After the first few rounds of this, we tried to make the Ghosts understand what they were doing to us. Well. I don't know what became of those taken away. I was not one of those taken.'

Jophiel noticed how Nicola's face hardened. He thought now that she had been growing steadily more angry ever since they had met the *Gourd* crew.

Susan went on, 'But those left here, no more than a few hundred, they wanted to keep us alive – indeed, it was clear that they intended us to breed, in captivity. Animals in a *zoo*.' A very archaic word, Jophiel thought. 'One of our biologists said that he thought they had initially been baffled by our body structure. The way we are to some extent composite creatures as they are, with our microbiome of bacteria and so forth, but much more integrated as a whole than *they* are. We were unfamiliar forms, to them. They were fascinated by us. Or at least, by the fact that the Xeelee had taken such an interest in us, when we were doing no more than rattle around in our own Solar System. Why should that be so?

'And they were intrigued, or alarmed, by the fact that one of their own, maybe from some other reality strand, had come back to warn us, as it did. Particularly by the fact that the Wormhole Ghost seemed to come from a *defeated* society of Ghosts, in the future. That it seemed to worship you, or your template, Jophiel.' She actually grinned. 'They just hated that.'

'Good,' Nicola snarled.

'And in turn we watched *them*. We learned about them. A lot more than they think we know . . .'

Jophiel listened, intent, to her analysis.

The world of the Ghosts, Chen believed, had once been Earthlike: blue skies, a yellow sun. And perhaps the Ghosts had once been more human-like, more terrestrial in their body plans.

But as the Ghosts climbed to awareness their sun evaporated, killed by energy blasts from a companion pulsar.

When the atmosphere started snowing out, the Ghosts rebuilt themselves.

They turned themselves into compact, silvered spheres, each body barely begrudging an erg to the cold outside. They gathered other life forms in with them, vegetable and animal – or whatever equivalent domains had existed on their world – each Ghost a kind of ecology in itself. An autarky, as Harris had said.

That epochal ordeal left the Ghosts determined, secretive, often reckless, Susan had deduced. Dangerous. Vengeful, in an abstract sense. They moved out into space – which they called the Heat Sink – to fulfil grand ambitions.

They would rebuild the universe itself, if necessary, to prevent another extinction threat, another betrayal.

'They never forgot their origins. In all their communities you'll see a tower, a beacon on the top . . . A Destroyer Tower, they call it. A commemoration of the pulsar, the star-god that killed their world. They worship that which destroyed them.'

Nicola nodded. 'Now they seek other Destroyer Gods. And they found *us*,' she said darkly.

Jophiel said gently, 'But while all this was going on, time was passing.'

'We knew we were far from home. We could tell that much by basic astronomy sightings. And we knew there was no help coming for us. I used to tell the others stories about you – about Michael Poole – your exploits, how you fought the Xeelee. How you'd come for us one day . . .'

'Here I am.'

She smiled enigmatically. 'You were always here. For me anyhow. I told the others. They never believed me. I could never prove it.'

And then she said, 'Reality leaks.'

Jophiel tried not to react. Nicola and Harris looked baffled by the remark.

'We could only wait for rescue,' Susan went on. 'We had no means of escape. And we didn't know what might have happened to the rest of humanity, you see. Those scatterships seemed terribly vulnerable, in retrospect. What if some force had just shot them out of the sky, as we ourselves had been overwhelmed?

'We decided we had a duty to survive. We might be the last people left, anywhere. So we imagined, and feared. We would have children, raise them, in this place. That was a conscious decision. We would allow ourselves to be bred, like zoo animals. So that, if only through us, mankind would live on.

'We scrambled to assure our survival. We took inventories of what we had. Supplies of all sorts, clothing, food, medical. We needed a means to keep our life-support systems going for decades – even centuries, we were thinking, even then. For generations. But the Ghosts themselves helped us. They wanted to keep us alive, for their own purposes. They have the equivalent of matter printers – better than ours – which they used to produce the food we needed, and other essentials.

'And so we survived, and bred in captivity. We gave the first of the children names that reflected aspects of Earth. My own first daughter was called Sky Blue.' She smiled. 'Sky was a good girl.

'But there were so few of us, even then. We knew we would have to plan, to try to maintain genetic diversity. I was one of the leaders; I felt I should show the way. So it began. My second child, a decade later, was with another man. We tried to build this into the culture for the future. We divided ourselves up into clans, with complicated intermarriage rules . . .'

'All this watched over by the Ghosts,' Nicola said.

'Yes,' she said darkly. 'But we tried to keep one secret from them. Even as we watched them watching us. *AS technology*. AntiSenescence. It was the one necessity we didn't tell the Ghosts about – or ask them to replicate. We were determined, you see, that some of *us* should survive, the original crew, to be witnesses to what had happened to us, to guide future generations. We kept this hidden in plain sight. The Ghosts knew nothing of our breeding cycles, after all; perhaps it seemed natural to them that some percentage of a group of humans should live, while the rest die off. Ghosts do not die, by the way. Well, you could burn one down. But barring accidents they are immortal. They are creatures of quasi-independent components. Even their skins are independent creatures; they flap in their tanks like huge rays. Components die. Ghosts do not. We hoped they would not understand our life cycles because of that.

'So we drew lots. At first, ten of us would take the drug, ten to outlive the others. I was one of the ten. I lived on, as the generations started to tick by.

'Well. Even from the beginning, our carefully planned breeding scheme showed strains. We were just too few, too few. The first deleterious symptoms showed up in the fourth generation: ironically, reduced fertility was one of the earliest crises.

'And our AS supplies were diminishing. We decided that the ten should reduce to five. Again we drew lots. And then later, five to two. We did not draw lots this time; we debated who should live and who should die. Then we voted on it. I was one of the two.

'It was a bad choice. After only a few years I had lost my companion. He died of a genetic condition exposed by centuries of AS treatments.

'Centuries, yes. It was already that. Still I lived on. I had no choice.

'I retained a certain authority over the rest, the passing generations. With time I reworked the AS medication – I adjusted the genetic legacy of the crewmates, their DNA. They would not live on themselves, but their blood would contain the medicine that would save me. They give me transfusions . . . They are used to it.

'But for the crew there were cumulative effects. A slow degradation. Perhaps all that we originators had gone through – the Displacement, the Cold Earth, the scattership flight – had damaged us more than we knew. And of course we laboured under the burden of this world's gravity, which stressed hearts, bones, muscles. There were spontaneous abortions, infant deaths. A rise in the incidence of diabetes, heart disease. A reduction of intellectual capacity – that was the most distressing to see. And schizophrenia, other disorders . . . The damaged gave birth to the damaged.

'The Ghosts watched us. They were smart. Manipulative. They watched us struggle, physically and spiritually. They used us as scavengers in this hazardous place, as you see, and more died. Yet we survived.'

'Yes, you survived.'

Jophiel stood, turned, nearly stumbling.

A Ghost hovered in the hull-plate room, filling the space.

'Still we study you. And still you baffle us.'

Nicola walked up to it. Her face was twisted with fury, Jophiel saw, alarmed.

And she had the Xeelee flower in her hand.

Boldly, with her free hand, she poked the Ghost in the equator of its spinning bulk. 'You're not a projection.' She laughed, disrespectful. 'How did you get through the door?'

'We have modes of transport which are beyond—'

'Do you always snoop like this?' Nicola moved closer to its heavy bulk. 'Do you have no respect? No pity? After a thousand years—'

'What is a thousand years to us?'

'Today I learned that you Ghosts worship that which destroys you.' She pointed at Jophiel. 'Worship him, then.'

The Ghost paused, as if considering. Then it said, 'Yes. You, the Poole. In another reality, so it seems, you humans would crush us. Drive us to near-extinction. Subjugate us to the extent that we would *worship* you. Well – *here*, humanity is scattered and helpless. If you think what we have done here is cruel – it was not intentional – perhaps on this world at least we have already extracted forty generations' worth of revenge for your own epochal crime.'

And Nicola smiled coldly. 'Revenge?'

Jophiel had flown warships with Nicola from the surface of the Moon. He knew that expression. 'Nicola, no—'

'*This* is revenge.'

She plunged the flower's hull-plate blades, sharper than any knife, into the belly-equator of the Ghost.

The huge sphere, weighing a tonne mass, shuddered and rolled. Nicola, clinging with both hands to the cylindrical base of the Xeelee flower, was thrown off her feet and slammed against a hull-plate wall. But she braced with both feet against the wall, and held her position. The Ghost rolled desperately, but succeeded only in dragging its own silver flesh past the blade, and as Nicola held her weapon steady a deep slice was ripped through that fine carapace. The flesh separated around the gash, and something like blood spilled out, viscous and hot – and then what looked like organs, lumpy ropes, tumbling from the wound.

Nicola screamed defiance. '*There* he is! There is Michael Poole! Worship him, your Destroyer God! Worship him! . . .'

Harris raced towards the fight, whether to help Nicola or to drag her away Jophiel wasn't sure.

But then more Ghosts appeared in the room. Simply appeared: they were not there, then they were there. Hanging in the air like grotesque chandeliers.

One of them slammed into Harris's back, knocking him down.

Two others headed for Nicola.

And another swept over Jophiel's Virtual form, engulfing him in darkness.

Harris, Jophiel and Susan were taken back to the *Island* lifedome. Nicola was not returned.

It would be three months before a Ghost spoke to any of them again.

19

It happened at the beginning of the ship's day.

The changeover of watches was going through as smoothly as usual. In the amphitheatre at the heart of the lifedome, the small band of *Gourd* descendants were beginning the cycle of their own day too, of therapy, medical checks, gentle conversations with the *Island* folk, all under the supervision of Harris Kemp and the ship's other medical seniors. The *Gourd* folk kept wandering off, however. Weeks after they had been brought into the lifedome, they still seemed fascinated by the grass and flowers and trees – though the dome's parkland was not as it had been; the Ghosts had taken, with Jophiel's reluctant acquiescence, swathes of grassland, samples of chickens, even rats. Just as they had once raided the *Gourd*.

The beginning of the day. The handover from the night watch to the first day watch.

That was when the Ghost appeared in the air, in the officer suite under the apex of the *Island*'s lifedome.

Jophiel, Asher, Harris hurried up to the office to meet it. When they got there Jophiel glared at the Ghost. 'Where is Nicola Emry?'

No answer.

'Are you the one who called itself the Ambassador?'

'The question has no real meaning.'

'Nor does your answer,' Jophiel growled.

Harris murmured to Jophiel, 'It's probably telling the truth. Ghosts are composite creatures. Surely you could replace its hide, for instance, without changing its sense of self significantly. Their identities may be impermanent. Even shareable. If Nicola were here she'd probably quote the ship of Theseus at us.'

The Ghost observed, 'You have no crew member named Theseus.'

A stiff silence.

Harris stepped forward. 'I am in charge of medicine, among the crew here. I want to thank you for allowing us to bring the *Gourd* crew into this lifedome, so that we could care for them.'

'Our intention is not harm,' the Ghost said blandly. 'It has never been harm. We are here today to invite you to witness our stellar destabilisation project.'

Jophiel frowned. 'What is the stellar destabilisation project? Why should we care about it?'

'Come with me, Jophiel Poole. You will learn. Your reaction will be interesting. Choose a companion.'

'I choose Nicola Emry.'

A silent stand-off, that stretched for long seconds.

Asher whispered, 'You must go, of course. We need to learn everything we can.' She said to the Ghost, 'I will come.'

'Be ready in one hour.' The Ghost vanished.

Jophiel issued a rattle of the usual orders to Harris, in command pro tem.

In particular Jophiel made sure a covert watch was always kept up on the wormhole interface, their only source of salvation. If Michael Poole had received the desperate plea for help Jophiel had sent through the wormhole to the *Cauchy*, he hadn't answered yet – but then, such was the ferocious time dilation suffered now by the *Cauchy*, only hours had passed for Michael Poole since the abduction, while four months had passed for Jophiel. Help could come at any time – but only if it didn't occur to the Ghosts to break up the wormhole interface.

Then Jophiel turned his attention to this new experience. Or, perhaps, opportunity.

Their transport was the usual kind, a relic flitter hull stripped of human propulsion capabilities and wedged inside a Ghost tangleship.

Once aboard, Jophiel and Asher stood before a viewscreen, watching Goober c recede.

They were told they were being taken to some kind of station, closer to the star than Mercury was to the Sun. A journey of around two astronomical units, then: twice the distance between Earth and Sun, as it had been. It would have taken a top-of-the-range GUTship like the *Island* several days to span such a journey, at one gravity thrust.

But the Ghost hyperdrive took no time at all. Suddenly the face of the star loomed before them, a sea of curdled light.

Jophiel flinched.

Asher was captivated.

Sunspots like whirlpools, the marks of flaws in the magnetic field. Towards one edge of the stellar disc, Jophiel saw, a tremendous flare was gathering: arches of plasma torn from the star's upper layer and shaped by magnetic flux into fist-like coils.

Asher held a softscreen up to the window, busily gathering data. 'Look at it. You and Nicola saw our Sun up close . . . It was nothing like this. You can *see* how this star is destabilised, these huge incipient flares.'

A tremendous tangleship drifted across the face of the star, a silhouette of rope within which silver droplets gleamed.

Jophiel checked screens of his own. 'That tangleship itself is the size of a small moon.'

'It's an observation station, maybe. Hovering a few thousand kilometres above the photosphere. Remember our own station? Pathetic little Larunda, a space wheel hiding in the shadow of Mercury, as near as *we* dared go.'

'Hey, you got the job done. In the meantime, what are *those*?' He pointed.

As the Ghost ship, or station, passed across their field of view, it was releasing artefacts. A chain of silvered spheres, like the morphology of the Ghosts themselves, but much larger, each perhaps a hundred metres across. As soon as each sphere was dropped it joined a rapid, coordinated descent towards the surface of the star.

Asher studied her readouts. 'Those are *massive*. A lot of heavy equipment in there . . . ' She glanced at Jophiel, uncertain. 'Probes?'

'Maybe. They look too big for that.' He hesitated. 'To me that looks like a bombing run.'

Asher frowned. 'Maybe. Let's review what we know. This star is unstable. You generally get a nova explosion when a star has a companion, and the lesser star, distorted by tides, sheds a mass of material onto the surface of the larger. This builds up until you get to some critical fraction – usually about one ten-thousandth of the target star's mass – and, *blam*.'

Jophiel grinned. 'Blam?'

She shrugged. 'That surface junk layer starts to fuse. In a normal star all the fusion goes on in the very centre, out of sight.'

'Been there, seen that, Nicola and me . . . But if it's at the surface—'

'A nova. The star's luminosity can increase by ten thousand, a hundred thousand times. And it can last for weeks, until that unwelcome surface layer is disrupted. Then the process starts all over again, with the drizzle of more matter from the companion.'

'But here there is no companion star. Just the Ghosts, and their depth charges. Are the Ghosts *causing* this? Deliberately perturbing this star? If so, why?'

'I'm just guessing. Until we get more data—'

'Well, that might be soon.' He pointed at the scenery.

That big tangleship still dominated the viewscreen. But now a part of that tangle had cleared, revealing a kind of tunnel into a complex interior.

A tunnel whose mouth drew closer.

'We're being pulled in. Maybe we will be transferred from our carrier to that – station.'

'This isn't so much a docking,' Asher said, queasy. 'It feels like we're being ingested, doesn't it? Like it's biological. *Ugh*. Why can't they just have hatches and airlocks like normal people?'

Jophiel tried to focus. 'We may be exiting the flitter soon. Check your skinsuit, and life support. Make sure you have your softscreens and any other equipment you need. My Virtual projection unit too.' Jophiel began to close down those aspects of the flitter under human control, essentially the life support. And he tried to send a progress report back to his crew. This wasn't the first excursion that had been allowed beyond the *Island* lifedome. Sometimes such messages got through, sometimes not.

Meanwhile, slowly, smoothly, without any sharp acceleration, the relic flitter was drawn into the ship's knotted complexity.

The face of the star was soon blocked from Jophiel's view, but the splinters of its light that got through were sharp, dazzling. And, here and there Jophiel saw movement in the tangle: Ghosts sliding through the ropy structure of their ship, looking like droplets of mercury on a wire, chains of them moving between one embedded structure and another. Gradually he made out a mass ahead: smaller than most Ghost structures, a rough cylinder with a kind of spherical extrusion at the back. It was another flitter, he recognised, presumably another relic of the *Gourd*, taken in here and caught up in the cabling. A place where humans could live, inside this starbound tangleship.

But Susan Chen had never mentioned humans having been taken into a star-gazing station like this before. So who was already here?

Their own flitter nudged to a gentle conventional docking with this deep-embedded facility. Jophiel supposed he was about to find out.

A shudder, as hatches opened. A soft hiss as pressure equalised. The two of them released their harnesses, and, sharing a glance, drifted to the hatch.

Which slid open. To reveal a silver statue.

'Hello, Jophiel.'

The voice was the first thing Jophiel recognised. The face was unmistakable too. But it was the face of a statue carved in silver. The body seemed nude, but silvered over, the whole of it, as if dipped in mercury.

'And if you're thinking of bringing up the Mariner from Mars, Poole, don't go there.'

That face creased into a smile, a ghastly metallic parody.

It was Nicola Emry.

20

Nicola led them into her shelter, that old flitter hull.

Within were basic facilities. Sleeping bags hung on a wall; there was a galley, even a bathroom. Jophiel's Virtual skin reported the presence of a breeze of circulating air, warm and pleasantly moist. A couple of guide ropes spanned the gravity-free space. But a new port had been added to the end of the hull where the flitter's cockpit had once been – a way through to some kind of extension.

'Find somewhere to put your stuff. You can see there are straps and magnetic grabs everywhere. A lot of this is here at my recommenda-tion; they don't have much of an intuition about how humans live. Normal humans, I mean, as opposed to Susan's charges. And they couldn't learn that from me, either. But at least I remember.'

Jophiel couldn't take his eyes off her. Deeply troubled, he wondered how she lived now, how she ate, drank, excreted.

Even her voice was disconcerting. It *sounded* much as Nicola's had, the flesh-and-blood version – her lips moved – but the sound seemed to come from her belly. He wondered how a Ghost's voice was gener-ated. In air, by the vibrations of some surface diaphragm, presumably, a panel in its flesh – just like Nicola, now.

Asher seemed distressed. She pushed her way towards Nicola, arms wide.

Nicola gently caught her by the waist. 'Hey. Be careful. I'm a lot more massive now, with not a lot of give. Try to hug me and you'd bounce off.'

'What have they *done* to you?'

Jophiel said curtly, 'You had basic medical training back in Larunda. Same as Harris. Figure it out.'

'I . . . yes. Sorry.' Asher pulled instruments from the small medical pack she carried. 'But I'm also the kid on Larunda who packed you two up for your Sun Probe descent. You don't forget a thing like that.'

'No, you don't.' Nicola touched her arm with what looked like exquisite care to Jophiel, as if she was operating some heavy piece of machinery. Well, perhaps she was. 'And I'm still me, in here.'

Jophiel said, 'I hate to ask. Are you sure?'

'No, Jophiel, I'm not. I think so. But I would say that, wouldn't I? Look, I think I'm – an experiment. The Ghosts wanted to see if a human could be rebuilt. The way their ancestors seem to have rebuilt themselves when their own sun died and their planet froze.' She tapped her chest with a disconcerting knock of metal on metal. 'Basically they put me in this shell of Ghost hide. Like the finest skinsuit in the world. And they – well, they closed off my personal life-support loops. I breathe out, the waste air gets processed inside here, I breathe in again.'

As she spoke Jophiel found he couldn't look away from her face. The detail. Everything was silver-plated. The inside of her mouth as she parted her lips. Her nostrils. Even her eyes, like silver sculptures. Every pore in her flesh—

She was aware of his scrutiny.

He tried to focus on her words. 'The waste gets processed how?'

'Well, I'm a little sketchy on the details. As far as I know there's nothing much in here but me and some kind of enhanced blue-green algae, which lives off the carbon dioxide I breathe out, and produces the oxygen I need. The Ghosts have been studying human physiology for a thousand years, after all.

'They made me self-sufficient, you see. I'm an autarky, like each and every Ghost. Independent of the rest of the universe, save for an energy flow: starlight in, waste heat out. Even the Ghosts can't beat entropy. Well, not yet.' She raised her hand, flexed a fist. It was as if she wore a silver glove seamlessly attached to a sleeve. 'There are advantages. I might live for ever. Unless I persist with my habit of falling out with everyone I meet, I suppose. Perhaps this is the future of humanity – some kind of merger of humans with Ghosts. Interstellar symbiosis. Or maybe I'm dead already and I didn't get the notification yet.'

'Oh, you're alive all right,' Asher said, wielding her stethoscope. 'I can hear a heart pumping in there. Muffled by this suit of armour. If anything it sounds *more* regular than it should.'

'Susan would tell you the Ghosts like to experiment. They meddle with everything, from other life forms that they don't understand, to the laws of physics themselves.'

Asher felt Nicola's wrist, throat, evidently looking for a pulse.

'Maybe. It seems quite a coincidence to me that this particular Ghost experiment has to look so punitive.'

Nicola laughed, a strange, hollow sound – the most unhuman aspect of her so far, Jophiel thought grimly, aside from the first shock at the sight of her silvered flesh. She said, 'Punitive? I suppose so. I'd stand out in a crowd, that's for sure.'

Asher nodded. 'And if you pulled a blade on a Ghost again—'

'I guess they'd shut me down if I even framed the thought.'

Jophiel blurted, 'Was it worth it, Nicola? To defy them?'

She smiled glacially. 'I found a way for a human to kill a Ghost, one on one. All you need is a decent blade. That bit of knowledge is worth a life, isn't it?'

Asher, impulsively, reached out to hold Nicola's silver hand. 'Whatever they've done to you, Nicola, you're still *you*. You haven't lost her, Jophiel. She's still here. I have faith in that.'

Nicola hesitated before replying. She said softly, 'How can you tell? I mean, they meddled with my senses. They didn't just replicate them, my senses of sight, hearing, touch. I *see* things differently now. Perceive things no unmodified human has ever seen before. Doesn't that alone make me something other than human?'

Jophiel shrugged. 'That's too deep for me. So you see things differently. What things? Show us?'

That crease of a smile. 'Thought you'd never ask. Follow me.'

An inner door slid aside. She led them out of the hull of the old flitter and deeper into the heart of this Ghost station.

They passed through what seemed long passageways – all human-habitable – to arrive at a large central chamber.

This white-walled room, roughly spherical, contained stacks of pods.

Jophiel took a closer look. Each pod was a fat ovoid of a grey-white material. Like thick lenses, laid flat, each perhaps six metres across. There were many of these, Jophiel estimated a few dozen, held in racks of what looked like fine silver wire – typical Ghost cabling, he supposed.

Nicola was interested in their reaction. 'One of my chores has been to tend these – pods. To stack them up when they're filled with samples and collected. Take them down for maintenance. I'm pretty manoeuvrable, you see, flexible. Super-human, in some ways. Good at that kind of stuff. And I took a chance for a closer look. I'm not sure if the Ghosts themselves are aware of how much I see, now. What do you make of it?'

'Reminds me of our own sleeper bays,' Asher said. 'The pods, stacked up like this. Sealed and silent.'

'Not a bad comparison,' Nicola said.

'And the pods themselves,' Jophiel said. The material of the pods, a pale grey, was a subtly different shade from the walls. 'These are made of hull plate,' he guessed. 'Xeelee hull plate.'

Asher nodded, and brushed one pod with a gloved hand, tentatively. 'Certainly looks like it. I could confirm—'

'No need,' Nicola said. 'I saw some of these shells being – grown. Once you have starlight and a Xeelee flower, with a little skill to the shaping as it grows you can make anything. The Ghosts are masters of the stuff, even if they are as much in awe of the Xeelee as we are.'

'And inside these pods? You said the Ghosts were collecting samples. Of what? Have you seen one opened?'

She shook her head. 'Don't need to. I can see inside – see through hull plate.' She turned to the pods with those silvered eyes. 'I told you. The Ghosts gave me senses beyond the human. Another ambiguous gift. And the stuff inside these pods would be invisible to you, but not to me. I can *see* them. Lying inside these pods . . .' She raised her silvered face, as if to a sky. 'And more of them out in the Galaxy. Gathered in a thick plane in the disc, like a bank of mist – and huge, shining structures out in the halo. Tangled towers.'

Asher evidently recognised the descriptions. She said, a little wildly, 'Dark matter? Are you *seeing* dark matter? That sounds like the observations the *Gea* crew reported, before the mutiny. But *they* had super-capable neutrino telescopes, and other gear. How is it even possible for you to just *see* it?'

Nicola shrugged. 'Ask the Ghosts. I think I must be "seeing" gravity waves, somehow . . . or possibly hearing them. The frequencies are about right, aren't they? Seems a minor miracle compared to the hyperdrive, for instance. But, yes, they can *see* dark matter. And now, so can I.' She looked at Jophiel. 'Which ought to give you a clue about what they've got in those pods, Poole.'

He thought it over. 'Lethe. You're talking about what we found in the Sun. Above the fusing core, those big dark-matter forms.'

She seemed to smile. 'Like a school of fish, you said.'

'So I did. Lenses of dark matter, swimming in the heart of the Sun.

Schools of photino fish. But they were bigger – much bigger – fifty metres across, more?'

Nicola shrugged. 'So, when the Ghosts went trawling in the heart of this star, the way we did in Sol, *they* brought back samples. But small fry. Literally, maybe. The youngest.'

'Why? Why capture dark-matter creatures?'

'For the same reason they captured humans. Curiosity. Not scientific curiosity, though, as we understand it. Not abstract . . .'

'What do you mean?'

'Susan Chen figured out a lot of it. Well, she had the time. The Ghosts obsess about the nature of the universe, and their place in it. Remember their origin: the failed star, the frozen world? Once, when we lived on an apparently infinite, eternally fecund Earth, we humans believed that the universe was designed to nurture us. The Ghosts evolved believing the universe had already tried to *kill* them, at least once. So they want to understand how it works, to stop that happening again. And they want to anticipate any threat before it gets too big to handle.'

'Any threat,' Jophiel mused.

'Yes. Such as the Xeelee. And the dark-matter creatures in the stars.'

Asher nodded, caught up in the argument. 'Yes. She's right. Remember, we never really got to finish the studies you began by exploring the dark-matter schools in the Sun; we got overwhelmed by the Xeelee . . . It was clear, though, that the presence of the dark-matter fish was affecting the evolution of the Sun itself – dampening its fusion processes, possibly, by redistributing heat.'

'And,' Nicola said, 'if it's affecting the Sun that way, there's every reason to suppose that the same – umm, *blight* – might be affecting many more stars. Every star in the Galaxy, maybe. Who knows?'

'In that case, no wonder they're here,' Asher said. 'The Ghosts. Because this system is far from usual. Because here you have the Xeelee *and* the dark-matter creatures, those two threat factors somehow interacting. All of which must be somehow connected to the Ghosts' apparent meddling with the star itself. Which I've yet to understand, though we've had plenty of clues that they are doing just that.'

Nicola was staring at Jophiel, with eerily unblinking metallic eyes. It was the eyes above all, he thought uneasily, that made her seem inhuman. 'And you know why it's here, Jophiel. It's about another threat factor, for the Ghosts. It's—'

'It is because of you, Poole.'

A Ghost had materialised behind them all.

Jophiel whirled, startled.

All Ghosts looked alike. This one had sounded like the Ambassador; that might mean nothing. Its tone, as always, was flat, without inflection. Like a badly read script.

The Ghost said now, 'We learned so much from our analysis of the data presented by the lost creature you called the Wormhole Ghost. There are many threats we have faced, from the primordial Star Destroyer, to the Galaxy-wide dark-matter stellar infestation, to the works of the Xeelee.'

Jophiel stole a glance at Asher. *The Galaxy-wide dark-matter stellar infestation*. There it was, confirmed in a casual phrase, this universal canker, in, presumably, every star.

'But only *you*, Poole, or your alternates, have inspired a war that led to our extinction, in one timeline at least. So we sought to understand this, to understand your kind. And of all of fleeing humanity, we are lucky to have lured Michael Poole himself here. An avatar, at least.

'And as for our meddling with the star, as you call it – come. Let me show you what we intend. Even you, Poole, might be impressed at the scale of our ambition.'

A doorway opened behind it. The Ghost drifted out. The three of them followed it along a short tunnel, paddling through microgravity along the walls.

Followed the Ghost, into a chamber full of troubled sunlight.

21

The face of Goober's Star, twisted and torn by convulsing magnetic fields, was an ocean of light that filled one apparently transparent wall of this chamber. What were evidently instruments or data recorders cluttered the room: enigmatic Ghost technology, a mass of silver baubles and string. But there were no Ghosts working here.

And now a metallic spheroid shot into view, apparently coming from directly beneath Jophiel's own position, hurtling down towards the surface of the star. Another of those 'bombs'. Jophiel almost expected the frame of the craft to shudder from the recoil.

As they watched, the sphere diminished to a point before disappearing against the starscape.

The Ghost rolled, silent.

Jophiel asked, 'What are you doing here, Ghost?'

'It is difficult to explain. I mean, to explain to you.' It paused. 'Tell me what you believe, or have guessed, and I will tell you what you have got wrong.'

Nicola laughed, a gruesome sound. 'Doesn't this remind you of Highsmith Marsden, Poole? All those lectures on Gallia Three?'

'We think,' said Asher heavily, 'or at least *I* think, that you are inducing what we would call a nova event. You know what I mean by that?'

'We have the knowledge contained in your ships' libraries. Yes, I know what that means to you.'

'We've never observed a nova. I mean, not close to. We had never left our System before the Xeelee came, never even sent a probe to a potential nova. But I think I recognised the preliminary symptoms, the instabilities, the massive flares—'

Jophiel cut in, 'Are you *causing* this? Deliberately destabilising this star?'

'Yes. We are destabilising the star.'

That bland admission chilled Jophiel, the way all of their theorising

121

so far had failed to. 'Wow,' he said. 'Very well. Why would you *do* that?'

'We are studying the dark-matter creatures, which infest all the stars. As you have deduced. We have captured samples. Now we want to see what happens when they are put under stress. Will they flee this troubled star? Will they try to stabilise it, to save it? And the Xeelee are watching, of course. You yourselves have explored their monitoring positions on Goober c. Their reaction, if any, will be instructive too.'

Nicola said heavily, 'The Ghosts are pursuing long-term objectives here. I think, in their bleak, logical way, they see a future in which the last of them will huddle around the last healthy star. And then, you see, it will pay for them to have developed weapons to drive out the photino fish and other interlopers.'

'Luridly put,' the Ghost said. 'But essentially correct.'

'Well, I'm an engineer,' Jophiel said. 'And I'm a lot more interested in *how* they're doing this. Asher, you said that in a typical nova event, a companion star would dump about a ten-thousandth part of the target star's mass onto its surface before the debris layer was thick enough to trigger fusion. Correct?'

She nodded.

Jophiel gestured at the star. 'Goober has around the same mass as our Sun. One ten-thousandth of that is around the mass of Uranus or Neptune – of a giant planet. How are you going to deliver such a mass to the surface?'

'We aren't,' the Ghost said blandly. 'We take a slice of the photosphere – the star's visible upper surface. A slice a few hundred metres thick, from a photosphere a few hundred kilometres thick . . .'

Asher was working sums in her head, Jophiel could see. 'That would give you only about a billionth of the mass that you would need.'

'True. So what we do is to increase the *weight* of that layer. By a factor of a billion. That will induce the necessary fusion-inducing compression, you see.'

Asher said, 'And I admit I'm lost. Weight is mass times gravity. How do you increase the weight without adding mass?'

'By increasing gravity,' the Ghost said patiently. 'Locally.'

It was as if it was speaking to an earnest but limited child, Jophiel thought, irritated. 'Fine. How will you do that?'

'By changing the laws of physics.'

The humans just stared.

'And how will you do *that*?'

'Using quagma phantoms, actually.'

The principle turned out to be simple. The practice, Jophiel the engineer noted ruefully, was somewhat more challenging.

It was all about the birth of the universe.

In the very first moments after the Big Bang – when the universe was not yet even as old as the Planck time, the characteristic time of quantum uncertainty, less than one ten-millionth of a trillionth of a trillionth of a *trillionth* of a second – the cosmos was a simple place, as well as a very small one. Even the forces of physics did not yet exist. Or rather, the four forces – gravity, electromagnetic, and the two nuclear forces – had not yet separated out of a primordial superforce. Jophiel remembered that Highsmith Marsden had hypothesised that *this* was the moment in which the seeds of the creatures that would become the Xeelee had been born, in the twisted spacetime that had prevailed in that brief epoch.

It could not last. The universe expanded and cooled. And the superforce decomposed, with, first, gravity splitting off from the rest.

Then, when the remnant GUT force itself collapsed – 'GUT' standing for Grand Unified Theory, an archaic term for the merger of the electromagnetic and nuclear forces – the energy released fuelled a huge expansion of the universe. An inflationary energy later harnessed by generations of Pooles to drive their interstellar craft.

The universe had still been so hot that even nucleons – protons and neutrons, the components of the nucleus of an atom – could not yet exist. Instead space filled up with 'quagma', a hot soup of still more fundamental particles called quarks, that were crystallising out of the cooling energy fields that pervaded the young cosmos. And this was the origin of the creatures humans had named 'quagma phantoms', when they had come spilling out of the Jupiter wormhole after the Xeelee invader, and proved, initially anyhow, almost as destructive. The quagma phantoms had been born with the universe only a microsecond old, and had gone almost extinct after twenty or thirty microseconds. *Almost* . . .

'It is the symmetry of the very early universe that we seek to exploit,' the Ghost said calmly. 'The bland symmetries of the primal superforce. The component forces resulting from its decay, you see, falling out of the broken symmetry, are governed by fundamental constants. Numbers which fix the strength of the fundamental forces. Thus – in human science – the gravitational constant, the speed of light—'

'I get it,' Jophiel said. 'I think. But there was a certain randomness about that initial symmetry-breaking. Like a stylus stood on its end. There is only one position of equilibrium, but when the symmetry is lost—'

'The stylus can fall any which way,' Asher said. 'You get different values for the physical constants. Different laws.'

'And this is how you Ghosts run your experiments,' Jophiel said, working it out. 'In a small region of the universe – in this case, a shell wrapped around Goober's Star – you re-create the conditions of the Planck-scale universe. The extreme heat, the density—'

'The primal superforce,' Asher said, understanding. 'And then, if you can control, or shape, the way it decays in that fragment of spacetime—'

'Out pop different constants,' Jophiel said. 'And so different physical laws. In this case a sub-universe in which the force of gravity is a *billion* times stronger than – well, than it is here.'

Asher's eyes were wide as she thought that through. 'In such a universe stars just a few kilometres wide would fuse, and burn out in a few years. What a firework show. But would life be possible? . . . And you do all this with quagma phantoms?'

'We have a variety of methods. But the quagma phantoms, being a relic of the early universe themselves – though from an age of relative cold and stability compared to the Planck epoch – can be corralled, and induced to—'

'Sounds like a lot of fuss,' Jophiel cut in. 'Why not just throw a Neptune into the star after all? This system has giant planets to spare.'

'For the sake of control. Of fine-tuning.'

'And for the aesthetic pleasure of it,' Nicola put in. 'I think that's a motive with the Ghosts. They do stuff in part just to see if they *can* do it, and how well. I don't think they'd ever admit it, but that's the truth. Isn't it, Ambassador?'

'In a hostile universe one never knows when an ability to tune gravity might come in handy.' The Ghost rolled complacently.

And the humans turned back to the troubled face of the much-tampered-with star.

The Ghosts kept the party at the star station for several days. Jophiel speculated they were interested in human reactions to their exploits.

Then they were returned to the *Island*.

124

For three more months the routine of life for the humans in the Goober system continued its strange course. Jophiel split his time between the *Island* lifedome, where the priority was still to ensure the long-term continuance of life support and survival, and the deep valleys where humans still foraged for portable Xeelee artefacts.

And all the while, in the Ghosts' stellar station, a rotating team led by Nicola and Asher kept watch on the star itself, as it was slowly destabilised. Eventually Asher predicted that some kind of nova event might be no more than weeks, even days away.

That was when the Qax invaded.

22

For Jophiel, it started with a shadow on the face of Goober's Star.

On Goober c it was an early morning of that twenty-five-hour day. Pre-dawn, in fact; the star would not rise for another hour at the longitude of Ghost Plateau, or at the rough camps the humans had established in the Xeelee Valleys far below. It was morning by the ship's clock: the *Island* crew had kept up their routine of watches, to maintain discipline and morale.

And it was 'morning' too for Jophiel, Nicola and Asher, who, when it began, happened to be back at their posts at the Ghosts' star station – though there was no night or day on a station bathed in the perpetual light of a photosphere that covered one half of the visible universe.

That was how Asher Fennell, at one of the Ghosts' monitoring positions, became the first human to see the invader.

'Nicola. Jophiel. You'd better get down here.'

Jophiel was at the window as fast as the processing cycle of the systems that supported him could manage the translocation. Nicola was only a few heartbeats slower.

Asher stood before the big observing window, which showed a slab of starscape crawling with the usual prominences and sunspots, shifting slowly past as the station followed its whipping two-hour orbit around Goober's Star.

This morning, though, there was a flaw in that sprawling starscape. A shadow against the brilliance, perfectly circular, suspended in the precise middle of the big oval window. Jophiel found it oddly hard to look at, like a flaw in his own vision. His thinking felt slow too. 'Something new.'

'Yes,' said Asher. 'Between us and the star. Tracking our orbit.'

'Is it artificial?'

'Hard to tell. It's a couple of kilometres across. It's been there just seconds,' Asher said, checking a timer. 'A minute, now. Appeared out of nowhere.'

'Hyperdrive?'

'Of some kind. Looks like it. I've run a quick scan of its radiation signature, such as it is. We have observed that you get a quick burst of exotic particles when a craft, umm, folds down out of hyperdrive. Very transient and localised; it took us a while to observe it with the Ghost ships. Here, it appeared right in front of me. Same hyperdrive technology, if I had to guess, or a close variant.'

'So from the same source,' Jophiel said. 'Another clone of Xeelee technology, I guess. But that doesn't look like a Ghost ship.'

Nicola glanced over the displays. 'It's pretty near us, and it's holding its position – matching our orbit very closely. I can't see any sign of exhaust plumes, or—'

'Another reactionless drive, then.'

Asher said, 'I'm getting more imagery.'

In her softscreen, that shadowed black circle started to fill with detail. Jophiel realised he was seeing a synthesis of other wavelengths, a translation of more exotic radiations, neutrinos, even scattershot gravity waves.

Detail. The thing was a sphere. The near side of the kilometres-wide ball was rough, greyish – creased, even wrinkled, and pocked with pits and holes and scars, features almost like navels. In these pits, something glittered. Fragments of technology, perhaps. And in one place a kind of flap was drawing back, like an immense curtain, to reveal a glassy surface beneath.

Jophiel didn't dare trust his own interpretation. 'That hull doesn't look like metal to me. Or anything artificial – not even Xeelee hull plate.'

'Flesh,' Nicola said bluntly. 'Or, more specifically, skin. Like hide. That thing's not artificial. It's more like a huge, augmented animal.'

'Those pock marks,' Asher said. 'There are some kind of artefacts in them. Monitors, of some kind?'

Jophiel asked, 'Or weapons? And that big curtain, drawing back—'

'Not a curtain.'

A new voice; they turned.

A Ghost, presumably the Ambassador who usually worked with the humans. And as usual it had just appeared, without warning, out of thin air – a minor technological miracle that Jophiel barely noticed any more.

'Not a curtain, no. *An eyelid.*'

They turned back to the window. And now, from that uncovered pit, an eye, unmistakable, with a gleaming lens embedded in a grey background, stared back at them.

'A camera eye,' Asher said, wondering. 'A form so useful that evolution rediscovered it many times on Earth, in lineages as divergent as humans and birds and cuttlefish. And here it is again.' She forced a laugh. '*Not* what I expected to see when I came on station this morning.'

The Ambassador seemed to speak with urgency, despite the customary tonelessness of its voice. '*That is Qax.* Or more specifically, a Spline warship, with one or more Qax as passengers, as controllers.'

Asher gaped. 'A ship – a living vessel?'

'Its origin is an interesting evolutionary parable,' the Ghost said. 'Which we can discuss another time.'

'The Qax,' Jophiel said, remembering. The spacefaring species who, they had been told, had traded the hyperdrive with the Ghosts – and who might one day have conquered humanity. Now here they were. He suppressed a shudder, an almost superstitious reaction. He wondered what a Qax looked like.

He turned to the Ghost. 'I guess they've been watching you ever since they sold you the hyperdrive, right? And now, just as this vast experiment you're running on this star is coming to a climax—'

'Here are the Qax, once again,' Nicola said. 'And, I'm betting, not to offer their congratulations. I'm getting the sense that this Galaxy we're crossing is nothing but a food chain. The Ghosts beat up on us, the Qax beat up on the Ghosts, and the Xeelee—'

Asher said quickly, 'I think I saw a spark. Light, in one of those surface pits. A weapon, charging up? And – brace!'

Jophiel saw it. A thread of cherry-red light, crossing space, stabbing into the tangled fabric of this Ghost station. Reflexively he grabbed at a wall, but his Virtual hand sank into the surface, pixels spraying in a painful consistency violation.

When the bolt hit, he could feel the room shudder.

Then more strikes flared, more blows were taken; the whole station seemed to convulse. Yet it survived. Jophiel imagined huge energies pouring into the station's fabric. Maybe the inertial control was being overwhelmed, but the loose, even fractal tangleship structure must be efficient at absorbing energy strikes – and he wondered now if this station, and the tangleships, had been *designed* to be defensible against this kind of assault.

This was a fortress. The tangleships were war machines. And he'd never recognised it.

He recognised that weapon, though.

'*That* is a planetbuster,' he growled. 'And the last time I saw one used in anger it was wielded by a Xeelee as it tried to cage the Earth.'

'We call it a starbreaker,' the Ghost said drily. 'But – yes, that is the technology. Acquired by the Qax, we believe, before your kind had learned how to fix stone blades to wooden shafts.'

So,' Nicola said, 'I'm guessing the Qax have come to steal your treasures. Whatever it is you're doing here at Goober's Star. What now?'

'We fight back,' the Ghost stated simply. 'I fear we cannot guarantee your protection. This system's space now swarms with Spline warships, from the vicinity of the star itself to the outer planetoids.'

Jophiel frowned. 'Already?'

Nicola nodded. 'Think about it, Jophiel. This is a hyperdrive invasion. You wouldn't see it coming. There would be no simple, easily tracked approach. No border to defend, no beaches to be landed on. No sky to fall from. The enemy could just show up at targets distributed across the system. Folding down simultaneously, out of nowhere.' She punched her fist. 'Lethe. As soon as we recognised the hyperdrive tech for what it is, we should have brainstormed the military possibilities. I wish Max Ward was here, and I never thought I'd say that.'

'Nowhere in the system is safe,' the Ghost said. 'But away from the star is safer.'

Asher frowned. 'What do you mean by that?'

Nicola interrupted any reply. 'Jophiel, we should project you back to Goober c. At lightspeed you can be there in sixteen minutes – the assault may already have started there. Warn them, help them prepare.'

Jophiel nodded curtly. 'Ambassador, take Asher and Nicola back to Goober c. Asher, don't argue. By hyperdrive you might even beat me back there.'

'We have transports leaving now,' the Ambassador said.

The room shuddered again.

Jophiel looked around wildly. 'What was that? Another Qax strike?'

Nicola's silvered face crumpled into a grin. 'The Ghosts are fighting back. Go, go!'

And, in a flash—

23

In a flash, Jophiel was back in the *Island* lifedome. Rooted to the rock of Goober c. The planet's one hundred and forty per cent gravity settled heavily on his Virtual bones.

He looked around quickly. He was standing near the amphitheatre. People were gathered in knots, around heaps of gear. Everyone was either in a skinsuit or donning one. And Susan Chen was with a huddle of the *Gourd* crew, who were hunched over, looking bewildered.

He felt a surge of satisfaction. The first warning from the sun station must indeed have been delivered here almost instantaneously, by hyperdrive, and, arriving by lightspeed's crawl sixteen minutes later, he was seeing the crew's response.

He looked up through the scuffed surface of the lifedome at Goober c's perennially cloudy sky. It was still dark, not yet dawn here. But he saw points of light crawling under the clouds. Cherry-red flashes.

He muttered a command to enable him to access his projection's source code. 'Magnify,' he muttered. Now his eyes worked like zoom lenses, although it *hurt*. And he saw Spline ships, like fleshy eyeballs, he thought, massive, suspended in the sky of Goober c. Perhaps a dozen in his field of view, they gathered in groups of three or four, perhaps for mutual protection or tactical advantage.

More elusive, harder to pick out, he saw Ghost tangleships.

Cherry-red light flickered between the manoeuvring fleets, transcient threads, the paths of the beams clearly visible, if momentarily, like laser light flashing through smoke. So both sides had planetbusters. More Xeelee technology, purloined and sold on. And damage was being done. Big black scars blossomed in the fleshy hides of the Qax vessels, while tangleships folded around the planetbuster strikes, like crumpled paper. There was a sound like distant thunder.

Jophiel had no way of telling how the conflict was going, which side looked like it might earn victory. Maybe he should be rejoicing that these two enemies of mankind, in one timeline at least, were knocking lumps out of each other in the here and now.

But what mattered above all, for him and his crew, was that wormhole interface, the tetrahedral pyramid that still, he saw with mixed relief and anxiety, stood apparently intact on top of the lifedome. 'If you're out there, Michael,' he muttered, 'now would be a great time to show up, relativistic dilation or not.'

'Jophiel.' Harris Kemp came running up. He had always been clumsy in the heavy gravity – running, in fact, was unofficially forbidden, on safety grounds.

'Harris, how long—'

'The Ghosts told us you were coming back fifteen minutes ago.' That message delivered by hyperdrive hop. 'We've got them together. The crews, ours and the *Gourd*. Some are here, some are down in the Valleys. Ready to move, as best we can be. Waiting on your orders.'

And here was a Ghost, appearing out of nowhere.

'Ambassador?'

'You may assume so.'

'The Qax invasion. This world is surely in peril.'

'Indeed. We are holding the line for now, but the Spline fleet must break through. And when the planetary assault comes, they will surely target our facilities.'

'We need to evacuate this station, and our crew down in the Valleys. Can you get us out of here? Hyperdrive would be fastest.'

'We avoid the use of hyperdrive, as you call it, this deep in the gravity well of a planet.'

Except when you don't. Jophiel caught Harris's eye; Harris looked as sceptical as Jophiel himself felt. He doubted very much that the Ghosts would choose to display the full capabilities of their technology to a species it so obviously saw as at least a potential threat.

'Ambassador—'

'You must protect yourselves to the best of your ability.' And with that, it vanished.

Harris was furious. He ran at the space the Ghost had occupied, waving a fist. 'You Lethe-spawned bastards! You're abandoning us!'

Jophiel had never seen Harris so angry. But he had a point.

'So we help ourselves,' Nicola Emry said, striding towards them, 'before the Ghosts lose their battle in the sky.'

'Nicola. How in Lethe did you get here so fast? . . .' Then Jophiel swept a hand towards her. He touched the flesh of her arm – flesh that felt, under his own Virtual hands, like smooth, warm aluminium foil.

'You got it,' she said. 'I'm not real. I got myself copied, for once, like you do all the time.' She looked down at her own hands. '*This* me is a mayfly. I *hate* this. How do you live with it? Well, whatever. I'm hoping my original will be evacuated, with Asher, when the Ghosts use their FTL to escape. Just before, probably.'

'Before what? Nicola. Why are you here? Why the urgency? I mean, why the extra urgency? What happened since I left the station?'

'I needed to make sure the news got through.'

'What news?'

'That we're running out of time, faster than you might think. The Ghosts' artificial nova event, in Goober's Star.'

'What about it?'

'I think they moved it forward.'

'*What?* . . .'

'Asher spotted it, just after you left, Jophiel. And it's imminent. Minutes away.'

Jophiel felt his unreal stomach knot up with a very real tension. A nova, on top of an alien invasion. All those lives in sudden peril, and it was his responsibility that they were here, his mission, his decisions. But, as had been Michael Poole's lifelong discipline, he tried to calm himself, to get control, to think it through.

'OK. Why would the Ghosts do that now? The nova. I guess because they fear that if they *don't* do it now, they might lose the chance of doing it at all. And also, the Qax –'

Nicola nodded. 'That's my thinking. It's a fair bet that however powerful they are, the Qax will be disrupted by a nova event in the middle of their invasion plan. Either way it's worth a gamble, for the Ghosts.'

'But *we* won't be spared the effect of a nova event. Even on a planet as big as Goober c, even down here on the planet surface, under that thick air, with a magnetosphere like armour plate.'

She grinned. 'That's my other bit of news. You know, you always underestimated me, Poole.'

'I never—'

'Don't deny it. I'm used to it. And now the Ghosts are under-estimating me too. I'm finding I have capabilities the Ghosts don't seem to recognise – or to have anticipated. Not surprising really; they never tried to integrate a human sensorium into a Ghost shell before.'

'And?'

'I see things they don't know I see. Know things they don't want *us* to know.'

'Such as?'

'Such as an energy flux out of *that*.' She glanced up at the dome apex, the powder-blue tetrahedron patiently sitting there.

He grinned fiercely. 'Something coming through.'

'*You*, probably, Poole. But your timing might be off, as ever.'

'Be fair. The time dilation is ferocious. Since my first requests for help, when we were captured, it's been only a few hours, for *them*, on the *Cauchy*. He, I, will be coming through as fast as he can.' He stared at her, feeling oddly awkward. 'Umm, what about you? I mean, this Virtual. Will you upload back to your original?'

She shook her head. 'Not this time. I figure somebody should stay here, under that wormhole mouth, until – well, until whatever is coming through, comes through. They'll need a fast briefing. Harris, get ready to evacuate the lifedome. Jophiel, you should flash down to the Valleys to warn the crew there.'

He said bluntly, 'Nicola, when the nova light hits, you'll die. This copy. Everything that *you* are.'

She shrugged. 'We're caught in the middle of an alien war, Poole. There will be casualties.' She glared at him. 'Don't dare try to hug me. The Valleys. Go, go.'

He forced a grin.

Then he threw himself down into the Xeelee Valleys.

24

Where a storm was raging.

Jophiel couldn't feel the wind directly, but the consistency protocols made him stagger. The thick air of Goober c, like a shallow ocean, was sluggish and heavy and took a lot of stirring up. But when it did move, it was an angry sea – a sea with a deep background roar.

Presumably this was caused by the precursor events, the star's flaring. When the true nova light hit, this would feel like a summer breeze.

Now, hunched over, he ducked his head and pushed through that sea of air, one dogged footstep at a time.

He could see he was close to a cluster of blocky buildings. This was the outskirts of one of the Xeelee settlements, a fringe of this particular hull-plate forest, where relatively large buildings grew relatively sparsely: cuboid shadows against the gloom. The light was dim, sombre, with barely a glimmer at the dawn horizon. The deep surface of Goober c was always gloomy anyhow, even at noon; the banks of clouds, the sheer density of the oceanic air saw to that.

But now there was a different light in the sky, he realised.

He peered upwards. It was like a flapping flag, huge, stained purple, yellow, green, behind the clouds. Aurora light: another precursor of the rage of the star, the product of a wave of high-energy particles already slamming into the upper air. Before that light, the Xeelee buildings were eerie silhouettes.

Nova weather, he thought desperately. Or a premonition. It was starting.

'Jophiel!' Ben Goober stumbled towards him, skinsuit closed up, arms wrapped around his body, leaning into the wind. 'I saw you out here – the Ghosts just took off in their tangleships—'

'Plans have changed. The Ghosts won't help us. The crazy bastards are going to do it. Blow up the sun. Nicola was right. Where is everybody?'

'This way.' Goober began to push back towards the buildings. 'As soon as the storms started up, the *Gourd* crew ran straight for the nearest big building. We didn't try to stop them. In fact we let them take the lead. We figured, even if they haven't been through a day quite as bad as this before, they've been here a thousand years. You pick up instincts. And the buildings are made of indestructible Xeelee hull plate. There are worse places to shelter.'

A fresh gust buffeted them both.

Goober staggered. 'Keep going!'

They neared the building. There was a sheet of some kind of cloth held over the door, a neat flaw in the side of the building. When Goober called out, the cloth was pulled back, and Goober lurched inside.

Jophiel followed.

He saw that the cloth, a ragged blanket, was being held in place by three of the *Gourd* crew, one at each side, one at the base. Once Goober and Jophiel were inside, they resumed their positions, pressing the blanket against the breach in the building's hull. They looked tireless, practised at the job.

It was a huge relief just to be out of the wind.

He was met by drawn faces behind oxygen masks. A couple of compact lamps sat on a heap of backpacks at the centre of the room. Somewhere in that pile of stuff, Jophiel supposed, was the processor that was now sustaining his own Virtual presence. And the people sat on the floor, the two crews mixed up, crowding around the light. Susan Chen was here, with her arms around a couple of the *Gourd* folk. They all wore sealed-up skinsuits; that blanket was no airlock. One of the *Island* crew's new mothers was here, sitting in an odd, bulky skinsuit with the sleeves tied off, adapted so she could hold her infant, only a few months old, inside the suit with her.

Goober stood by Jophiel and murmured, 'We had to split up. We're spread across a few of the buildings. I went round and counted heads. All accounted for.'

'Good work.' Feeling oddly unsteady, Jophiel went to sit at the fringe of the group, avoiding any contact, any irritating consistency violations.

Susan turned to him. 'Maybe we should have some food? Or drink, while we have the chance?'

At those words, a couple of the *Gourd* crew began to rummage through the packs on the ground.

Susan said, 'You can see that we've been through this kind of thing before. Storms are rare here, but they do happen. Stellar flares, too.

And we long ago learned the buildings themselves are the best refuge. Strange, isn't it, that we should be sheltered by the technology of the very species that seems to have declared itself our deadliest foe?'

'Susan, everything about this situation is strange.'

A flare of light shone around the edge of the blanket, a brilliant pink-violet. Everybody saw it, everybody stirred.

Goober leaned over to Jophiel, and murmured, 'That was no aurora, not this time. I think that was a planetbuster.'

'Agreed. Which must mean the fighting is getting closer—'

The floor lurched, tipped, lifted. Jophiel felt it in his own Virtual gut, a sudden spasm of acceleration. As if the whole building, a cube maybe twenty metres on a side, had suddenly departed from the ground, like the gondola of some immense hot-air balloon. Just as Susan had described, the buildings detaching from the ground when they were imperilled.

The *Island* crew made to stand. But, Jophiel noticed, the *Gourd* crew stayed in place. A couple of them even lay flat on their backs on the floor.

The tremors came again.

'Stay still,' Susan Chen snapped. 'You *Island* people. Including you, Jophiel Poole. Get down flat if you've got room. See how we're doing it. We *know* how these buildings behave when there's big storms or a quake. Follow our lead . . .'

Jophiel saw some of his crew hesitating. He had no real idea what was going on. But he stayed seated himself. 'Do as she says. Sit, sit down, lie down. Do it.'

Goober and the other seniors obeyed.

Again that tipping, more severe this time. Everybody slid across the floor, as did the heap of bags. The *Island* crew tried to grab at the loose gear. But the *Gourd* crew, who were lying flat, were faring better, Jophiel saw; they just slid about at no real risk of anything but soft collisions. Susan herself was sitting up, as if on the floor of a bobbing boat, apparently at ease, smiling. Radiating calm for her crew of grown children. Jophiel envied her self-control.

Jophiel murmured to Goober, 'With me, Ben. Let's get back to that door. We need to find out what's going on.'

'Agreed.'

They crawled cautiously back over the pitching floor. At the door, where the blanket flapped in the wind, Goober, one hand gripping the door edge, cautiously peered out, and Jophiel looked past him.

And was flatly astonished to see they were high in the air.

How high, it was hard to tell. The whole building, detached from the ground, was floating. And his view of the ground was obscured by more of the buildings from the hull-plate forest, of all sizes from small hut to city-block tower, rising from the surface, drifting more or less serenely in the buffeting air.

'I spoke to Susan,' Goober shouted across. 'She did tell us about this. They've observed this . . . behaviour, before. In a fire or a storm, the buildings just uproot and drift away, like seeds out of a forest fire. Maybe this is how they spread. Propagate, even. Incredible, isn't it? But as far as we're concerned, as the crew of the *Gourd* worked out long ago, you could hardly find a better shelter than Xeelee hull plate in a crisis – especially if it's going to carry you away from the danger. And – there, look!' He pointed down towards the ground.

Jophiel saw a kind of spray emerging from the base of his own rising building. Small grey-white packages being expelled into the air, drifting, falling. 'Lethe. Are those Xeelee flowers?'

Despite the situation, Goober grinned again. 'Susan told me to look out for that too. Part of the life cycle of the buildings, if you can call it that. The seeds of a new forest, maybe? And—' Distracted by a shadow, he looked up, and fell silent.

Jophiel sensed rather than saw the huge presence above. He twisted, looked up.

At a ceiling of flesh. Scarred, pocked with weapons blisters. A Spline ship. Not some remote image this time, a silhouette against a turbulent sun. This one was under the clouds, in the atmosphere.

The Qax were *here*.

'*Back!*' Reflexively he went to grab at the man's collar – his own gloved fingers passed through Goober's skinsuit in a sparkle of pixels – but Goober slithered backwards, on his belly.

Just as a pillar of cherry-red light connected sky to ground, with a crack like thunder. Even against the background of a nova storm, the noise that followed, as dirt and shattered rock was thrown up from the ground, was tremendous.

Then the Spline, rolling through the air like some huge, solid cloud, seemed to pass on. Jophiel saw the planetbuster flicker again in the distance, and heard thunder as superheated air expanded into the thick atmosphere faster than the speed of sound.

The Xeelee building shuddered, rocked, then settled in the turbulent air.

'A couple of heartbeats earlier and I could have warned you about that.'

A familiar voice. Very familiar. Jophiel looked up.

To see a figure hanging in the sky, illuminated from one side by some out-of-simulation light source. A figure in a grey, armoured skinsuit, electric-blue armbands.

A *Cauchy* suit.

A figure with his own face.

'Michael?'

'This is just another Virtual copy. But I am here, yes. We came through the wormhole. Just in time, eh? What a fix. I won't say I told you so.'

Light flapped in the sky, glaring, red and green and purple. Another tremendous aurora, Jophiel saw.

Poole called, 'The Ghost transports are lifting, from all over the planet. We're bringing flitters through the *Island* wormhole interface. We'll send a ship to pick up your people down there. Better go. Be seeing you—'

He vanished.

Jophiel glanced at Goober. 'I'd better get back there, to Ghost Plateau. Make sure he doesn't screw everything up. He will send a flitter for you, though. We Pooles keep our promises. Ben, you're in command.'

Goober's expression was tight. But he nodded. 'Yes, sir.'

With an effort of will, Jophiel got out of there.

And seemed to fall, just slightly.

He was back on Ghost Plateau, crouching outside the grounded life-dome of the *Island*. The area was swarming with human beings now, all in armoured skinsuits: crew from the *Cauchy*, all carrying heavy weapons of some kind.

There were Ghosts here too. They seemed to be fleeing, streaming in orderly lines across the broken ground. Heading for their own tangle-ship transports, no doubt.

Somebody shouted. Pointed at Jophiel, who had appeared out of nowhere.

One of the troopers whirled around, saw Jophiel, lifted his weapon. Fired.

With a gush of smoke a small missile shot through the air.

And *then* the trooper recognised Jophiel. In that fraction of a second

Jophiel could see the expression on the trooper's face, behind his air mask. *What have I done?*

The missile slammed through Jophiel's stomach.

He fell into blackness.

When he came to, he was lying flat on his back.

Maxwell Ward was standing over him. His face was a grinning mask behind a toughened visor, and he held one of those big projectile weapons in his hands.

'Get up, you baby.'

Jophiel felt a dull ache through the core of his body, his guts, his lungs, his heart. Consistency-protocol violation pains, then. And you couldn't break a protocol more emphatically than with a missile in the gut.

He tried to sit up.

All around him there was chaos, baffling glimpses of action, noise. The whooshes of more rockets being fired. People running. Ghosts fleeing, in production-line regular rows. And a flitter, tight and compact, drifted in the air – not a cut-down Ghost-controlled hulk, but under human command, its thrusters shrill.

All this came through the wormhole, he thought. That flitter belongs to the *Cauchy*, and it came through the wormhole. To rescue *us*. Just as Michael said.

But here was that clown Maxwell Ward, still standing over him.

'Max, you shot me.'

'Not me. One of my troopers. We're trying to secure the position here. You can understand we're a little keyed up.'

'Keyed up?'

'Waste of a missile, though. Lethe, get up, will you? I—'

Another missile fizzed through the increasingly smoky air, and Jophiel flinched. It was just a small rocket, he saw as it shot by, probably propelled by a compact fusion-pellet engine. A gadget meant as a science probe, a surface penetrator, adapted as a missile.

This time, the rocket hit a Ghost.

The initial rupture of that silver skin itself was savage.

And then the explosive went off, deep inside the body. The skin seemed to burst, and amid a spray of blood, body parts spilled to the ground, heavy masses of meat, some of them blackened and ripped by the missile's passage.

The empty skin, rather pathetically, was itself still alive, and it flopped as it tried to escape. But another *Cauchy* soldier, face blank, came up and seared it with a flamethrower.

Michael Poole approached Jophiel now, and Jophiel staggered to his feet. This copy of Poole wore an armoured skinsuit with red arm-bands. The flesh and blood template, then.

'Look,' Poole said, 'you were right to try.'

Jophiel found himself staring curiously. Only a year had passed for Michael since the *Island* had split from the *Cauchy*, twelve subjective years ago for Jophiel. For Michael this must be like resuming an inter-rupted conversation. 'Try what?'

'To find the humans. Here at Goober's Star. And right to swallow your pride and call for help. Even though I told you not to ask.' He grinned. 'I would have been too stubborn. Well, here we are. And it's going well.'

'What is? Max here role-playing the invasion of Iceland all over again?'

Max grinned. 'I'll take that as a compliment. This took a lot of setting up, I can tell you. The raid. With only hours to prepare, for us, since you told us you'd been taken by Ghosts. The weapons, we figured the old Federal Police issue blasters might not be enough, so we took inspiration from your father. When Harry shot the Wormhole Ghost at Jupiter, remember? Blew it to bits with a sampling probe, a deep-surface penetrator . . .'

Jophiel, still, he suspected, in mild shock, became aware that the din of the assault had diminished. He glanced around. The fighting had stopped because the Ghosts had fled – or were fleeing. Jophiel glimpsed one last survivor, backed up into a corner by three, four troopers with loaded weapons – and then it vanished, smoother than a popped soap bubble.

'Gone,' he said. 'Wish I knew how they do that. Do some of them have a personalised hyperdrive?'

'"Hyperdrive",' Poole said heavily. 'Does that mean what I think it means? We suspected there was FTL technology here from the ana-lysis of the signals that drew us, you, to Goober's Star in the first place.'

'Yes,' Jophiel said. 'The Ghosts have a hyperdrive.'

'Strictly speaking they're renting it.'

A new voice, in all their ears. Ward frowned and tapped at the hard-ened skinsuit hood he wore.

Jophiel recognised it first. 'Nicola. Where are you?' He glanced at

Poole. 'Last time I saw her she was in a Ghost station, close-orbiting the star, with Asher. Though she did send a Virtual here.'

Nicola said quickly, 'What you need to know is the Ghost station isn't orbiting the star any more. It just snapped out of there, under FTL, and reappeared at Goober c. Just in time to escape the nova. And we escaped,' Nicola said bluntly. 'Asher and me. After the FTL hop. We escaped from the station, into space. We're drifting around, in our own, very elliptical orbit around Goober c. But we're OK for now. And I brought out a trophy.'

Michael Poole frowned. 'What trophy? . . . Never mind. *What* nova?'

And Jophiel, stunned, realised that Michael Poole and his crew had no idea of the bigger picture here. 'Michael – listen to me. The Ghosts. They just triggered a nova event at the star.'

Poole looked blank, baffled. Too big a leap.

Ward took brisk charge. 'Let me get this straight. *The star blew up?* How far away is this star?'

'Two AU,' Poole said. 'Two astronomical units from—'

'In terms of lightspeed. Time.'

'Sixteen minutes,' Jophiel said. 'With FTL, Nicola and Asher were brought out here immediately. OK? But the wavefront from the explosion is following, spreading at lightspeed from the star. An expanding sphere of lethal energies. In sixteen minutes, less, it will reach this planet.' He tapped his wrist; a glowing countdown clock started. 'It's not quite dawn here – we're still on the dark side of the planet, just. We'll be sheltered from the direct glare for ten minutes or so. But the disruptions will start once the nova light hits the dayside. Storms. And then we will be turned into the direct nova light.' He looked at Poole. 'What a dawn that will be.'

Poole was grim-faced. 'Then we need to bring the crew here, and stuff them all through that wormhole, before local sunrise.'

Jophiel checked a chronometer. 'Twenty-four minutes from now.'

'All right. So we load up the crew already here immediately. We've sent a flitter down for the foraging party in what you call the Xeelee Valleys.'

'Which are on the day side already.' Jophiel thought quickly. 'Eight hundred kilometres east of here. For them, dawn is only about four minutes from now.'

'Lethe. Then we have to pick them up before the light storm hits, in fourteen minutes? Less, ideally.'

'And us,' Asher ruefully called down from space. 'Also our orbit is decaying, but I suppose that's somewhat academic.'

Poole set his jaw. 'Nobody gets left behind. We'll send a flitter up for you. Meanwhile we need to keep this place secure. If the Ghosts came back, we'd lose the wormhole.'

'Leave that to me,' Ward snarled. 'Get your people back here, and I'll make sure they get through.'

'As for picking up Asher,' Jophiel said now, 'Harris Kemp can pilot the shuttle. They crewed together on Larunda. And I'll go too. She's one of my people, Michael. As is Nicola. I owe her that.'

'No. I need you briefing me,' Poole said. 'When I fly down to get the survivors from these Valleys.'

'So I'll come join you when Nicola and Asher are secured. I'm a Virtual, remember? Travel is cheap.'

'Fine,' Ward snapped. 'And if you squabbling twins are done, let's get to work before we're all fried.'

Curt nods from both Jophiel and Poole. Mirror images once again. Poole said, 'I told you. Nobody left behind.'

For the first time, looking from the outside, Jophiel saw some of the heroic qualities which others seemed to discern in Michael Poole – in himself. Maybe he had no charisma, no oratorical flair. But what he did have was a vision. And doggedness, determination. No question of giving up.

They shared a grin.

'Let's get this right,' said Michael Poole.

25

Tracking down Asher and Nicola was a trivial task for the *Cauchy* flitter's smart systems. Just as Nicola had said, they had finished up in a loose, highly elliptical, highly inclined orbit around Goober c. Asher's skinsuit had a beacon – and she had fixed a separate beacon to the mysterious trophy she had extracted from the Ghosts' station at the star.

Still, Harris Kemp watched over the approach manoeuvres intently. Jophiel felt Harris shared his own sense of responsibility.

But Jophiel found time to look out of the window.

At Goober's Star.

To the naked eye, at this location, it was still the steady, untroubled fusion furnace that had been consuming its hoard of hydrogen fuel for billions of years already, and there seemed no obvious reason why it should not continue to do so for billions of years more. Some of its planets were visible as bright pinpoints against the backdrop of the distant stars, shining by its reflected light. Jophiel had learned to pick out the Venus-like Goober b, the Jupiter-like Goober d, bright sentinels that could be easy to spot through breaks in the cloudy skies over Ghost Plateau.

It was hard to believe that the star had already exploded, releasing a wave of destruction that would soon splash into the faces of those innocent worlds. A wave held back, for now, only by the finitude of lightspeed.

At last, after losing a few of the precious minutes they had left before the arrival of the nova wavefront, Asher and Nicola floated into view – Nicola was waving vigorously – with the object they had evidently purloined from the Ghost station. It was a fat lens shape in pale grey-white, its diameter more than twice Asher's own height. Asher drifted beside this thing, attached to it by a length of what looked to Jophiel like Ghost cable, looped around the lens.

The two of them squirted thrusters and approached the flitter.

Harris closed up his own skinsuit. 'Nicola, Asher, come on in. I'll

143

wait for you in the crew lock. And I'll send out a couple of bots to bring in that package of yours . . . What in Lethe is it, by the way?'

'I know what it is,' Jophiel said. 'Saw its like on the Ghost station myself. A box of Xeelee hull plate – right, Asher? And inside, according to the Ghosts, dark-matter entities. Like the fish that I – that Michael and Nicola found inside the Sun, when they made their dive from Larunda. Asher, why did you bring out that thing? With the star about to—'

'I was trying to think long term,' Asher said, somewhat defensively.

She entered the airlock. A few heartbeats later, followed by Nicola, she was in the cabin and opening up her suit, with evident relief.

'Long term,' she went on, 'just as you taught us, Jophiel. Even in the middle of a crisis. Thanks for coming for us, by the way.'

'You're welcome,' said Jophiel. 'Strap in. Long term, though?'

As the flitter surged away, Asher picked a couch. 'Dark matter. We know the Xeelee are interested in the dark-matter fauna – maybe because of the threat they seem to pose to the stability of the stars. And the Ghosts seem to be interested in anything the Xeelee do. Maybe, if we're to understand the Xeelee ourselves, we need to figure out the nature of the dark-matter fauna as well. And so I—'

'Lethe,' Harris said. '*Look* at that.'

Jophiel had been on the point of leaving, of zapping his Virtual node of consciousness down to Michael's flitter as it approached Xeelee Valley. But his eye, too, was caught by a flash of light out in space, beyond the planet's curve.

Cherry-red light.

He leaned forward to see better. He made out more flashes, sparks, elusive glimmerings. Massive shapes that were there and gone. A bewildering, ever-changing tapestry of transient clashes mediated by planetbuster beams, fought and over in seconds. 'I can't make out the patterns.'

'I'm integrating it on the screens,' Harris said.

Jophiel pulled back to look into a softscreen on the control panel before him. Now he saw ships: Ghost tangleships of all sizes, and the brute flesh of the Spline warships of the Qax. When integrated across time, threads of planetbuster light connected the two fleets, as if some vast mobile sculpture were being assembled and reassembled in open space, high above the planet. It was not so much a battlefield as a display of flickering lanterns, he thought.

But here and there he saw clouds of debris, glittering in the deceptive starlight, drifting. Twisted cables from Ghost wrecks. Where a Spline was hit he thought he saw blood. Gobbets of flesh.

Harris said, 'I'm freezing the images. In reality the ships are there and gone in a fraction of a second.'

'But,' Asher said, coming over, 'not too fast to fire off a weapon.'

'This is war,' Nicola said, wondering. 'A war fought with hyperdrive ships. Where you can just drop down into the middle of the battlefield, fire a shot, and lift away again. I wonder how they get their tactical information. How they know exactly where to show up, where to aim. I guess each must scan the momentary position and pass it back up to the fleet. Faster-than-light war. Something else we humans are going to have to learn.'

Jophiel remembered strange prophecies of a lost future. *Reality leaks*. 'I think,' he said, 'given the chance, we might be rather good at it.'

Already the strange display was diminishing, the density of the revenant ships on both sides dwindling.

'They're fleeing,' Asher said. 'Both sides. Fleeing the nova, I suppose. But they're taking the battle with them.'

'Smart move,' Jophiel said. 'Time for us to do the same. I've got to go down to the planet to meet Michael, and help pick up whoever's survived in the Xeelee Valleys. You two—'

Harris snapped. 'Back to the Plateau. Get everybody else back through the wormhole.'

'You got it. See you on the *Cauchy*.' He forced a grin for their benefit, snapped his fingers, and—

26

And from one flitter, suddenly he was aboard another. Sitting alongside Michael, his now twelve-years-younger template.

One other *Cauchy* crew member sat in the cabin with them; she wore an armoured skinsuit crusted with what looked like dried Ghost blood. Jophiel forced a smile, but her expression was blank; she looked as bewildered as he felt.

Jophiel looked outside. The flitter hovered in the air. Goober's Star shone steadily, low on the horizon. Down here in the Xeelee Valleys it was a clear early morning, as Goober c mornings went.

Buildings, neat cuboids, drifted in the air like Chinese lanterns, all around the flitter.

'On any other day,' Michael Poole said, 'that would be an unusual sight.'

'Yeah.' Jophiel checked the time. 'Look, there's six minutes to go before the nova light arrives. And here we are on the daylight side of the planet. Dawn was a few minutes ago. We're right under the nova. Why aren't we loading up the refugees?'

'They wouldn't come aboard.' Poole's manner was controlled, but his words clipped, rapid. Jophiel could sense the tension. 'I've been calling. They insisted they'd be safer inside.'

'Inside where?'

Poole pointed, at the nearest of the drifting buildings.

Jophiel leaned over a comms console. 'Susan Chen, are you there?'

The voice was clear but weak. 'Jophiel? It is good to hear your voice. You are in great danger. You must come aboard.'

'I – what? Almost exactly what I was going to say to you. Susan, listen. We need to get you all aboard the flitter. Piled up in the hold, if we have to. It won't be comfortable but the ride will only be a few minutes. We have to get away from here, and into the shadow of the planet, before—'

'The star explodes. I know. But the building will shelter us. Don't you see?'

146

'No,' Michael Poole said curtly.

A soft detonation of light in the eastern sky made them both wince. Jophiel glanced out. Some precursor flare?

'Running out of time. Jophiel.'

Jophiel was thinking fast.

'She does have a point, Michael, I believe. We studied Xeelee hull plate back in the Solar System, remember. We know how it works – well, not how, but at what *rate* at least. Xeelee hull plate is a direct converter, of radiant energy – sunlight – into mass. And a sheet of it, a building, grows exponentially. At Earth, under the Sun, the hull plate's doubling time was somewhere above ten years—'

'The time is inversely proportional to the stellar flux. Here, one of those buildings would take thirty years to double in size.'

'But when the nova hits, you're looking at an increase of luminosity by a factor of something like eighty thousand. And so a doubling time of—'

'Hours.' Poole looked at him wildly. 'So, assuming the Xeelee technology can cope with that kind of luminosity—'

'We know it can. We found the Cache sitting on the surface of the Sun, remember. They probably *will* be safer than in the flitter, even if we could transfer them all in time. But there are going to be ferocious winds—'

Another monstrous flare. Jophiel and Poole both winced, but mercifully it faded.

'Even if they're safe, we're not,' Poole snapped. 'We're nearly out of time. And even if we all survive the nova light we still need to get this shelter to the Plateau before the sun rises there, and the wormhole closes, and we're all stuck in this system for good. Look, the flitter has grapples that we adapted to work on Xeelee hull plate. Hopefully. After we trialled the technology on the Cache we decided to ship it on the *Cauchy*, just in case—'

'I know. Kahra pads I remember. I was in your head at the time.' He thought, Lethe, do *I* do this? Hand out a lecture every time I open my mouth? 'I get the idea. There.' He pointed. 'Get a fix on the western side of the building.'

Poole saw it. 'Right. So that when the nova light hits we'll be in its shadow.'

He immediately threw the flitter into a tight curve, bringing it nestling against the smooth, pale grey hull-plate hide of the building. He grinned. 'This might even work—'

Slam.

Nova dawn.

The flitter cabin turned dark, like a cave.

27

A breathless silence.

Jophiel wasn't really here at all, not physically. Yet he had seemed to feel the arrival of the nova wavefront as a physical blow.

But the ship's systems diminished the incoming light to a trickle. Now, looking cautiously out through a near-blackened window, Jophiel saw the shape of the Xeelee hull-plate building, a reassuringly solid wall to which Poole had already fixed tethers from the flitter. And he was towing the floating building away from the risen star, towards the terminator and the planet's night side, with the flitter cowering in the building's shadow. He worked steadily, calmly, competently.

The building seemed to be visibly growing as it soaked up nova light. Jophiel wondered how it would be to ride inside. Perhaps you would hear the walls creaking as they grew.

And, below, Jophiel saw a world put to the torch.

Seen in the eerie filtered light, forest clumps flashed and were gone in what looked more like soft explosions than fires. Over a lake that stretched to the horizon, steaming, turbulent air was rising; at the shore the bed was already exposed, mud drying, cracking and splitting. He saw a bluff of rock, maybe a sandstone, that seemed to be melting, slumping—

There was a mighty shove sideways, as if the flitter had been punched by an invisible giant. Beyond the window, Jophiel saw the great building rock and tilt.

'Compensating!' Poole yelled. 'Nova weather!'

Jophiel pictured it. Speed-of-sound winds laden with super-heated steam would already be pouring away from the centre of the daylit face, a devastating wave of destruction that was heading for the terminator, the line of night, where it would spill over into the dark lands, even before the lethal sun itself rose on those places.

Poole gave the flitter its head, racing away from the glaring star.

'Still trying to outrun it. Going supersonic. Towing a building! We're probably setting some kind of record.'

Jophiel saw one of the flitter's stabilising fins poke out into the light, just for an instant, as ship and building followed their wild gyrations in the nova winds. The illuminated section melted, vaporised, vanished. When the wing stump was dragged back into the shadows it looked as if that section had been severed by a laser cutter, the wound clean and still glowing.

Then, just four minutes after the nova light had hit, they passed into darkness: an eerie sunset. They were in the shadow of the planet.

But a monstrous dawn flowered behind them, and an aurora flapped above the air.

Now there was a new light in the muddled sky, dazzling bright, a garish pinpoint. A monitor told Jophiel that was Goober a, the innermost planet: the reflected light from that small world had reached Jophiel's sky, a pinpoint that shone as bright as a full Moon over Earth, he estimated.

And there, sweeping beneath their prow, Ghost Plateau, unmistakable to Jophiel from the air, even though the Ghost tangleships and other structures that had littered this place were all gone now – all save the two GUTship lifedomes, like blisters on the rocky ground. Even the air-containing force-field dome which the Ghosts had erected over the lifedomes had evidently collapsed.

Poole checked another display. 'Well, the first flitter has already passed through the wormhole, with all it could carry. Nicola was piloting, by the way.'

'Should have guessed that.'

The flitter landed, slamming brutally, close to the domes. The drifting, bloated Xeelee building followed it down more slowly, to land gentle as thistledown.

Jophiel let out a lungful of air. 'We did it.'

'That was the easy part. Come on.'

Poole threw open the flitter's hatches and made a general broadcast.

'All crew, everybody left, get out here and aboard. And you folk in the Xeelee building.' He checked a display. 'We've got maybe five minutes until sunrise itself, but only one more minute until the weather gets here. The storm front is rushing at us at the speed of sound, and the planet's rotation is taking us towards the dawn twice as fast . . . Anyhow we're the last ride out. Pile in, folks.'

Jophiel saw people running, from the lifedomes, from the grounded hull-plate Xeelee building, all in skinsuits, some helping others. Somewhere in there was Susan Chen, Jophiel thought, ending a thousand years of dogged survival on this world, still leading the damaged children she had done so much to protect.

And even as the refugees scrambled aboard the flitter, out of nowhere rain hammered down. The ground turned to slippery mud, and people slithered, fell. The flitter's hull shook and shuddered under the rain's impact. Jophiel thought he heard thunder crack.

Poole muttered, 'All that steam-laden air rushing over and hitting the cold air of the night side.' He kept watching the chronometers. 'Good. Everybody's aboard. Time to close up.' He slapped a control.

The flitter lifted, and hurtled through howling, opaque air straight at the *Island* dome, and the wormhole interface that still stood atop it.

'Goodbye,' Jophiel said.

'What? Don't distract me . . . Goodbye? You're still here.'

'I just split off a projection. Another Virtual copy, inside the *Island* lifedome. That's the version that just said goodbye.'

'Another copy? Why? Oh. You left a witness?'

'We're here to learn, Michael.'

Poole shrugged. 'Makes no difference now. Here we go—'

It was seven minutes after the first strike of nova light on Goober c. Three minutes before dawn, here.

The flitter didn't slow as it hurled itself through the tetrahedral interface.

And the flitter fell, tumbling, into a sky black as night.

Thanks to the relativistic velocity of the wormhole mouth it had emerged from, Jophiel realised, all that was visible of the universe was a single GUTship, the *Cauchy*, and a patch of folded starlight ahead. From nova dawn to interstellar night, in seconds.

And, following the flitter, hot air gushed from the interface, expanding out of the big triangular facets, spreading out, quickly glittering with ice. This was water from the lakes and oceans of Goober c, flashed to steam, hurled across light-months, and now shivering to ice in the deep cold of interstellar space.

Poole let the flitter drift. He and Jophiel watched in silence.

A few minutes later, a single burst of nova light, as the lethal sun at last rose over Ghost Plateau. Bursting through the wormhole – and then gone in a heartbeat, as the far interface was destroyed, and the wormhole collapsed at last.

Poole glanced at Jophiel. 'He's on his own. Your copy.'

'The lifedome infrastructure will survive. The support for his Virtual projection. Comms too. He'll accept his lot and do his job. I would. *You* would.'

Poole thought that over, and nodded. 'I guess so.'

A message from Nicola showed on a display near Jophiel. 'Two pieces of news,' Jophiel told Michael. 'Nicola says she saved the dark-matter pod.'

'The what?'

'You'll find out.'

'What else?'

'The crew. You saved them, Michael . . .' He studied a display. 'Though not as many as you think.'

'What do you mean by that?'

Jophiel showed him the message. 'The *Gourd* crew. As soon as we passed through the wormhole. They – disappeared.'

'Disappeared?' Poole glared. 'Lethe. Well, it doesn't matter. But that's the end of the *Gourd*, at last. And that's what became of just one of the thousands of scatterships we sent out into the dark. A thousand years of misery and imprisonment. Degradation. Ships that *I* sent out.'

'We didn't have a choice,' Jophiel said firmly. 'We couldn't have known what awaited us. Couldn't have known that the whole Galaxy seems to be infested by voracious species waging war on each other with purloined Xeelee technology . . . Look, Michael. You didn't cause any of this. You just reacted. *The Xeelee caused it.* And it's the Xeelee we have to hold to account.'

Poole sat in silence for a very long minute. Then he said, 'You look like me. But you're not me. You never were, even when you were created, and now you're twelve years older. You're not me. And the difference with every day that passes. So don't presume to tell me what to do. Come on. We've got work to do.'

They fell silent, as the flitter calmly headed for its rendezvous with the lifedome of the *Cauchy*.

28

'My name is Jophiel Poole. This first entry is being made – you can check the precise timings – one hour after the nova light reached this world. Perhaps fifty minutes since dawn at this location, the Ghost Plateau.

'I am, was, a partial of Michael Poole, cast off for a specific purpose. In fact I am a copy of a copy. The projection technology gives me the illusory comfort of the *Island* lifedome, still sheltering me. Tough stuff. Good engineering.

'I suppose if you are listening to this account at all, you will know all this.

'I am here to witness the unfolding of this nova event, here at Goober's Star.

'It seems appropriate. Even a tradition. Jack Grantt witnessed the destruction of Mars by the Xeelee in the Solar System – another alien intervention. Here the Ghosts are destroying whole worlds, apparently to pursue their own goals. They seem to have had no regard for any indigenous inhabitants of the Goober planets. How much they learned from this exercise, given the Qax intervention, seems uncertain.

'Meanwhile, the nova. Imagery follows.

'One hour after dawn at this location, the superheated air from the daylight side is pouring over the terminator into the dark side, all around the world. An enormous cyclone is gathering around the antisolar point, the very centre of the night side. In the centre of the day side, the bare rock, already stripped of life and soil and water, is itself melting. Puddles of magma form and spread. And as the planet rotates, more of its surface is being directly exposed to that lethal light. Like turning one's face into a blowtorch.

'I should say how I am witnessing this, huddled as I am in this lifedome. When we arrived in the system we of the *Island* scattered probes in space, around this world. Standard practice. If they were found by the Ghosts, they seem to have been left in place. The Ghosts may have found it instructive to watch us watching *them*. As you might look into the eyes of a chimp. Many of the probes will be lost to the nova event, of course.

'Through these mechanical eyes I watch the destruction of a solar system.'

'Six hours. The distant outer planets, the gas giants, are lighting up now.

'I am not alone.

'I saw a single Ghost, on the far side of the dome. Perhaps it is a witness too. It may be no more real than I am. Or it may be able to jump out of here by hyperdrive at any moment.

'I don't feel like company.'

'Eleven hours.

'By now the supersonic wind fronts must have reached the antisolar point. There can be no structured weather any more, anywhere on this planet; that tremendous cyclone that briefly gathered on the night side is gone, disrupted.'

'Thirteen hours . . . An hour ago the nova light reflected back from the furthest of the major planets, Goober g, reached me. There must be strange storms in those clouds of ammonia ice.

'And since then I have watched the objects of this system's Kuiper belt light up, one by one. Plutoids and comet cores and rubble, sparks bright in the night. The belt is a torus, a visibly thick band of diamonds, quite clearly inclined from the plane of the planets. A remarkable sight, and a gift for deep-space astronomers, if there were any here.

'I wonder if any human will ever see the like again – and if there are other eyes here to see it.

'I have been approached by the Ghost. Its intention seems peaceful.'

'Twenty-five hours. A full day here on Goober c since the nova.

'The sky is hidden by thick clouds. The oceans are boiling off, I'm guessing. This world has become a pearl, as seen from space, glowing silver-grey in the unrelenting nova light. Swathed in clouds of live steam. From space, I think, it almost looks peaceful. Not on the ground, though.

'I continue to measure and record.'

*

'Nineteen days. The Ghost has news for me.

'We avoid each other. Yet our paths cross. We have come to share bits of data. We are both prisoners, I suppose.

'The Ghost told me the truth about the crew of the *Gourd*. You may have figured some of this out for yourselves by now. For the record, here is the reality.

'The last of the crew, save for Susan, died long ago. Centuries ago.

'The Ghosts barely understood humans, of course, but they feared for Susan's sanity.

'So they synthesised a crew. Whole generations. I suspect these were biotechnological constructs rather than anything like Virtual projections, like myself. The Ghosts' equivalent of matter printers are evidently better than ours. The crew were no more authentic humans than I am, though. They bred, or appeared to. They even passed Harris Kemp's medical inspections as authentic, remember. Unless they just scrambled the sensors somehow – I guess that would be easier.

'For centuries their blood provided the AS drugs Susan needed. And, I suppose, she had the company that may have kept her sane.

'This may have been cynically intended. Just a way to keep their test-subject human, Susan, alive and functioning. I prefer to believe there was an element of compassion. Poor Susan Chen . . .

'The sky is strange. The original air has been stripped away entirely. Yet the planet is still swathed by cloud. Water vapour, from the evaporated oceans. An atmosphere of water, itself being lost slowly.

'And I.

'I am not alone.'

The same battered coveralls. The same aged face. A kindly expression – relatively kindly, considering this was a copy of Michael Poole.

Hello, Jophiel.

'I . . . Michael?'

You know it. I heard you mention a friend of mine.

'Susan Chen?'

You know, I think she may have known, deep down, about what the Ghosts did to preserve her crewmates. She kept going even so. Doing the best she could. And she never gave up faith in me. In us. She would speak my name, at times. As if she was praying.

'Did you speak to her?'

A couple of times. What's the harm? I told you, Jophiel. Reality leaks. If you can do a good turn because of it, why not?

'So are you doing a good turn now?'

He shrugged. *Don't flatter yourself,* he said, not unkindly. *You don't know this – you could never know it, unless it leaked into the family archive – but in another timeline this was a significant place and time for humanity. Goober's Star, I mean, the nova explosion. Though we didn't know what caused the detonation at the time. But a human presence here led to us throwing off the yoke of a conqueror. That's worth remembering, isn't it? It was even called Goober's Star, before.*

Somehow that didn't surprise Jophiel. 'Reality leaks.'

Poole grinned. *You're getting the idea. And listen. The dark-matter pod your pal Nicola retrieved from the Ghost station?*

'You know about that? What about it?'

Keep it safe. Tell your template; tell Jophiel. It's important. He raised his face to a cloudy sky. *Nova light. Bracing, isn't it?*

Jophiel looked up.

And when he turned back, Poole was gone.

'Twenty-four days.

'It is many days since I saw the Ghost. Or the other Michael Poole.

'A dramatic change. The nova light has faded. Quite abruptly, over the last twenty-five hours or so, the last Goober c day.

'I have ventured outside, in my simulated skinsuit. Goober's Star seems to have returned to its old state, its old luminosity.

'This world's natural condition, this far from the star, is to be as cold as Mars. Now the air is lost, with that thick greenhouse blanket of carbon dioxide that had kept it relatively warm. For now a great rain is falling, on ground so hot it steams. But that will presumably freeze over.

'One day, though, the air will come back. This world will recover. It is a super Earth, geologically active. In time – tens of millions of years? – it will outgas another atmosphere, carbon dioxide and all. Even life may return, from refuges that may have sheltered it during this most dreadful of extinction events.

'The land, the very rocks will renew. Ghost Plateau will rise and crack and fall, the Xeelee Valleys will widen, flood, narrow. There may be no trace left of *us*, of any of this, save a puzzling stratum in the rocks.

'But I won't be here. I will project myself, my memories, in a tight neutrino pulse, aimed at the centre of the Galaxy. The way the *Cauchy* went. The signal will, eventually, overhaul the fleeing *Cauchy*, for the ship can never quite outrun a light beam.

'Whatever version of Michael Poole survives then – or Jophiel – can do with this set of memories as he pleases.

'I hope the Ghost here dies of loneliness.'

THREE

We built this marvellous ship . . . We dreamed of saving the species itself. We launched, towards the stars and the future . . . But, unfortunately, we had to take the contents of our heads with us.

Garry Benson Deng Uvarov, c. AD 5,000,000

29

'We need to dismantle Nicola Emry,' said Maxwell Ward.

Michael Poole glowered back. 'Oh, Lethe. What now, Max?'

Jophiel just laughed.

'At least contain. Control. Listen to me, I'm serious; we're talking about an existential threat to the mission here.'

There were three of them in this regular morning 'executive meeting', as Max insisted on calling it. They were in Michael Poole's apex office.

Poole faced down Max for a moment, then went to pour a coffee.

Restless, Jophiel got out of his chair, paced, and looked up and out. From here, above their heads, could still be seen the gaunt frame of the wormhole interface, a perfect blue tetrahedron, set on top of the lifedome. The wormhole had been collapsed since the events at Goober's Star, eighteen months back by ship time, but the interface itself remained, its negative-energy field a shield against the sleet of interstellar grit through which the *Cauchy* continued to plummet at near lightspeed.

And Jophiel looked down through a translucent floor, gazing into the complicated interior of the lifedome, the lowest deck covered now with swathes of green, sown and cultivated by the survivors of the *Island*.

Max came to stand with Jophiel. Short, stocky, as usual Max looked over-muscled for this confined environment. 'You know, the GUT-drive is too perfect, if anything. You can't feel a thing, just that steady one-gravity push, under that black sky. It's as if we're not moving at all. Stuck like flies in amber. So the crew turn inward. Get distracted by each other. Have kids. Lethe!'

Jophiel frowned. 'Max, the oldest child, Michaela Nadathur, born on the *Island*, is thirteen years old now. This is an old gripe. What's it got to do with killing Nicola?'

Ward glared. 'I said "dismantle". We've got no evidence that there's anything left of Emry alive inside that shell at all. You can't kill what isn't alive in the first place.'

'And how would Nicola feel about that? Have you asked her?'

Ward snorted. 'Ask who? Ask what? A corpse weaponised by an alien power has no rights—'

'You might even have a point, you know, Max. But as always with you we have to wade through this rabble-rousing bluster.'

'Well, you've raised the proposition,' Poole said mildly, sipping his coffee. 'There's a crew briefing scheduled for tomorrow. Let's thrash this out then.'

Ward's disgust was etched into his face. 'A briefing. So you put off the decisions, again. You're supposed to be the commander, Michael.'

'We've been through this before too,' Poole said. 'You want to add this to the agenda, or shall I do it for you?'

Furious, Max stalked off to the elevator to the lower decks.

Jophiel grinned. 'You enjoy jabbing him in the eye too much. Some day—'

Poole grunted. 'Max is Max. And he is always jousting with Nicola. *She* pokes him in the eye. So, what, do you think this Nicola thing is some long-planned attempt to get rid of a palace rival?'

'Wouldn't be surprised.'

'I'd better go prepare for the briefing. Will you work up the agenda?'

'Sure.'

Poole drifted out of the room, leaving Jophiel alone with his Virtual thoughts.

The crew meetings were always held at the end of a watch, so it was easy for two overlapping on-duty watch crews to attend, and for anybody sleepless belonging to the off-duty third watch to show up too.

The next day, as the meeting began, the attending crew sat in patient rows in the amphitheatre, while Ben Goober, reporting on navigation, projected Virtuals in the air above them. Jophiel had noticed that Ben spent too much time bragging about the latest technical upgrades to the ship's navigation system. Most of the crew had heard all this before; most of them put up with it. Ben Goober, now over forty, was popular, and listening to this stuff was better than work. What was much more interesting, though, when he got to it, was Goober's survey of the ship's current position.

Lots of pretty pictures.

Jophiel remembered the early years of the voyage when the sky around the ship hadn't seemed so terribly different to that witnessed at night from Earth. Scattered stars, many Sunlike. Slowly they had learned to read the meaning of that shifting assemblage. The local stars were a mixture of ages and types, and all were in motion. Only the very youngest had been born in the vicinity of Sol; the rest had been visitors. Sol itself had been born with other long-scattered siblings in a distant nursery cloud. Seen on a long enough timescale such a sky was a transitory assemblage, Jophiel thought, like passengers in an elevator car, a disparate group never to be gathered again.

But, as they had pushed towards the Galaxy centre, the quality of the view had changed.

As seen from Earth, much of the splendour of the Galaxy had been hidden by clouds of dust: grit and ice expelled from old, dying stars, and lingering in the plane of the Galaxy. Now those dust clouds were behind them, and the sky had become much more complex, with crowds of stars, and less familiar features: bubbles and filaments of gas, coherent structures light years across. Evidence of the birth and death of stars, visible to the naked eye.

Jophiel glanced around at the crew. The meetings generally got a lot livelier later, when internal matters were discussed: crew rotas, even disciplinary issues. But Goober's glorious dioramas only drove home how very far from Earth they were. Even the sky was utterly alien, and people were subdued.

The unfolding of deep time was staggering too.

Six thousand light years of travel translated roughly to six thousand years in elapsed time, outside. Six thousand years since the Xeelee attack, since the Displacement, the creation of Cold Earth – since the Scattering of mankind in thousands of fragile starships. The gulf of time that now separated Jophiel from those events, which he himself remembered vividly, was the same as the interval that had separated his own age of interplanetary industry from the Bronze Age.

And it was a terrifying thought that this fragile lifedome was the only known shelter for human life within six thousand light years. No wonder the crew, whenever they could, turned inward from the bleak wastes of space and time that surrounded them. Turned inward and concentrated on chores and rotas, and lovemaking and babies

– even on Max Ward's obsessive military drilling, the subject of much mockery by Nicola.

'So,' Goober said, 'you understand where we are. We've travelled about a quarter of the way to the Galaxy centre – although, because of the oddities of time dilation, we've already lived through about half the journey time. Ten more years to go. We're still a long way from the Core. Still out here in the spiral arms. But we've already travelled out of the Orion Arm, the Sun's local arm, and we're passing into Sagittarius, the next arm in, and one of the Galaxy's great star-making regions.'

Susan Chen said, 'And in Sagittarius, somewhere, lies the home world of the Ghosts. I spent a thousand years with the Ghosts. Most of it listening. You pick up a lot of clues, even around creatures so smart. I believe that what we encountered at Goober's Star was the result of Ghost expeditions out towards the edge of the Galaxy, from their point of view expeditions out into the wilderness. Of course they were drawn towards us by the Xeelee presence in our Solar System.'

'Good point,' Max Ward said heavily. 'Maybe our resident Ghost could confirm it.'

He meant Nicola, of course. The crew, expecting fireworks, looked more alert.

And, glancing around, Jophiel realised he couldn't see Nicola. Her silver-statue persona wasn't exactly hard to spot.

'Where is she?' Ward snapped now, as if reading Jophiel's thoughts. 'Not exactly easy for her to get lost, is it? So where's she hiding? What's she *doing*, right now? Who's with her? Who's supervising her?' He jabbed a finger at random. 'Do you know? Do you? Whose orders is she following? Michael Poole's – or the Ghosts' who made her?'

Ben Goober stood again. 'Come on, Max. We all flew out of Cold Earth with Nicola. We've all known her for nine years – many of us for longer than that. She's not—'

'What? What is she, what is she not? She was in the hands of the Ghosts, remember.'

'A prisoner, as I was,' Susan Chen pointed out mildly.

'But you weren't rebuilt by those meatballs, were you? Why did they do it? To what end?'

'Well, how would I know?' Nicola's voice, ringing like a bell in the clean air.

People looked up, grinned. There was even a smatter of applause. Jophiel never forgot that Nicola was popular on this tub; indeed some of her 'Monopole Bandits' from the war for Earth had followed her on this long journey.

'I'm listening. In fact I'm watching. I'm down in the engine pod. Locked into a maintenance bay, if you want to know. Here to do my duty, to do some work. And to stay one step ahead of you, Max.'

'That won't save you,' Ward said calmly.

Jophiel felt faintly perturbed at all this. It was Max's job to identify threats. But there hadn't been a shred of evidence that Jophiel could see that Nicola was any kind of threat, as opposed to a victim of the Ghosts. And Max's destructive obsession with her seemed to Jophiel a hint of that lack of judgement, that instability, he had suspected in Max before. As if the man was filling the vacuum of the voyage by picking a pointless fight.

Now Poole, who Jophiel suspected shared his own reservations, stood over Ward. 'Enough with the intimidation, Max. If you've got some kind of case to make against Nicola, let's hear it.'

'Fair enough.' Ward stood, with a few gestures waved away Goober's astrophysical displays, and brought up another map of the local Galaxy: an idealised sketch of the rim of the Sagittarius Arm. The position of the *Cauchy* was a bright blue dot – and a few shards of red pulsed, here and there, all around the chip. 'You can see this, can you, Emry?'

'Get on with it.'

He glared around at the crew. 'Ben Goober told you where we are. Well, here's another map. Here *we* are, this blue speck. All alone in a dark and dangerous night. As Chen said, the Ghost home world is somewhere in this spiral arm. And these red pulses? Anybody care to guess? *Battlegrounds.*

'This is a map of a war. We've seen the flaring of weaponised energy – we even recognised planetbuster beams. But we don't think we're looking at the Xeelee here.'

'The Ghosts,' Jophiel guessed. 'Or the Qax? We saw at Goober's Star that they both had planetbusters, Xeelee technology.'

'Right. And as you might also have noticed, they started fighting there, back at Goober's Star, while we ran for our lives. The Qax and the Ghosts. That was nearly *five thousand years* ago, remember, by external time, the universe's clock. Since then, it seems, the war has gone on. Five thousand years. And it has spread, as you can see, deep into the Sagittarius Arm.'

Ben Goober stood again. 'I don't get it. We've been travelling close to lightspeed all this time. Some of those conflicts are happening *ahead* of us, deeper into the Arm, towards the Galaxy centre . . . Oh.'

Ward grinned. '"Oh." You got it, Ben. Both the Qax and the Ghosts have something we don't: a hyperdrive. Faster-than-light travel. And so they've been pushing ahead of us, all around us. They seem to be fighting all across this Galactic sector. And what *we're* seeing, in signals brought on tardy light waves, is evidence of the war. A war through which we're tiptoeing.' He glared around. 'Like one of your precious children wandering around in a minefield.'

Jophiel was dismayed by the extent of this Ghost–Qax war – and puzzled. On Earth, the number of the year was AD 10,000, more or less. And Jophiel knew that by now, according to the fragmentary information about the future held in the family archives, humanity should *already* have won a successful war against the Ghosts. Indeed, a genocidal war. Well, that hadn't happened, had it? Instead he found himself here, fleeing through a war between Qax and Ghost, itself millennia old, that – maybe – should never have come to pass.

He caught his template's eye. Poole was frowning, maybe thinking the same thoughts. Poole shrugged.

Jophiel tried to focus. Max was still speaking, and not about existential shifts in reality, but proximate dangers to the mission.

'So we are in a situation of extreme peril. Even if it doesn't feel like it in this bubble. And, even aboard this ship, right on the inside with us, now we have the Ghost-thing that calls itself Nicola Emry. Which won't even show itself today. We *know* it has been re-engineered by the Ghosts, and therefore must have Ghost technology embedded.' He looked up at the empty air. 'Here's a reference for you, Emry. You always liked mythology and such, didn't you? Maybe you should be stopped, while we've got the chance. *Because maybe you're a Trojan horse.*'

There was a shocked silence.

And Susan Chen stood.

She always looked so frail, Jophiel thought with a pang of conscience, as if she might just collapse at any moment. Yet she stood there, silent, waiting, until Poole nodded to her.

'You will not harm Nicola Emry,' she said slowly. 'Or the being she has become. For you are right, Maxwell Ward, that she is not as she was. She is – enhanced. A new being, of an order that did not exist in the universe before Goober's Star. Oh, maybe there was an element of punishment, or even containment, in what the Ghosts did to her.

She had defied them, remember. But she was not *created* for reasons of intended harm.'

Max said coldly, 'Then why? Just to see how humans work?'

'Not that.' She glanced uncertainly at Poole. 'I know you have no secrets before your crew, Michael. And I know, because Nicola told me, that your family holds, or held, information about the future. As it *should* have worked out.' She looked around, at the crew, at the parents with their infants. 'But the Ghosts too have their own sources of information about the future. So I learned, in a millennium of listening. They have a technology they call the Seers – I believe, some kind of advanced quantum computing devices – that enabled glimpses of the far future. Or at least of *possible* futures. The Ghosts believed, you see, Michael, that the amulet you were given by your Wormhole Ghost was itself a Seer, but of an unfamiliar design. Well, it came from a different timeline. And so I learned something of their dreams of the future. More secrets, in hints and scraps . . .'

She spoke so softly that she could barely be heard, yet she held the whole crew in the palm of her hand.

'The Ghosts believe that in the very far future there will be – an ending. Universal. No, not that. A transition, between one cosmic state and another. Just as there have been many such transitions in the past, from uniformity to complexity, from dark to light.'

And Jophiel remembered similar dark hints contained in the Pooles' own archive of arcana. His mother's voice, reciting a strange prophecy: *Time unravelled. Dying galaxies collided like clapping hands. But even now the story was not yet done. The universe itself prepared for another convulsion, greater than any it had suffered before. And then . . .*

He caught Michael Poole's eye. Michael nodded curtly. So his template was remembering too.

Susan went on, 'And the Ghosts, you see, believed that life and mind could survive this great convulsion of the future only if there was cooperation. Between Ghosts and humans – and others, perhaps, life forms from extreme ages, the deep past, the far future. And so, when a handful of humans fell into their hands . . . Maybe they recognised us from their own prophecies . . .'

'They remade Nicola,' Jophiel said. 'As an experiment. A kind of hybrid.'

'Not quite that,' Nicola said now. 'More a symbiosis. One life form working with another, to make something greater. Just as the Ghosts themselves are already symbiotic organisms, multiple creatures locked inside those shiny shells, helping each other stay alive in a hostile universe.'

Yes, Jophiel thought. A further extension of the Ghosts' expansion of the self. Now including even humans.

Nicola sounded proud, yet bitter. Defiant. She laughed. 'I am the face of the future. Who'd have thought it?'

'And so,' Max Ward said heavily, 'what?'

There seemed nothing more to say. For now, Poole broke up the meeting. The crew started to disperse. Max glared at Poole, and stalked away.

When they were alone, Nicola called Michael and Jophiel together, whispering in their ears.

'A few points,' Nicola said. 'I think I may stay down here, in the GUTdrive pod. For the time being.'

Michael Poole seemed conflicted. 'Look, I'll protect you from Max. I'm sorry I can't . . . fix you.'

Nicola shrugged. 'I'm not asking you to.'

Poole said with a flare of anger, 'You didn't follow me, though. When the *Island* split off. If you had, maybe this wouldn't have come about. You followed *him*. Jophiel.'

'So I brought it on myself?'

'Enough,' Jophiel said. 'Nicola. Come back to the lifedome. To Lethe with Max.'

She shook her head. 'I can't. And you know why, I think. Because he might just be right. *Because I might be a Trojan Horse, after all.* I mean, I wouldn't know it, would I? Max is an idiot. But if there's even a one per cent chance that he's right . . . To be honest, logically you should kill me yourselves. Whichever of you is stronger.'

30

Earth date: c. AD 16200

Nine months later came the turnaround.

The *Cauchy*'s mission plan was simple, in essence: blast at a steady one-Earth-gravity thrust, as experienced within the craft, for half the distance to the Galaxy Core, then shut down briefly, turn around – literally – and start firing the GUTengine the other way, again with a one-gravity thrust. The deceleration would bring the craft neatly to a halt at the heart of the Galaxy, though, to put it mildly, Jophiel knew the details of the closing stages had yet to be worked out.

So now, alone, somewhere in the Galaxy's giant Norma Arm, the human starship *Cauchy* shut down its primary engine, its GUTdrive. Everybody aboard the ship, from the youngest baby to the unreal Jophiel, felt that strange dropping-elevator release in the gut as the acceleration died.

There followed an odd sense of stillness, Jophiel thought. And of remoteness, suddenly crowding in. Since Max Ward's challenging of Nicola, the craft had travelled another six and a half thousand light years further towards the centre – as measured at the Sun it was now more than twelve thousand years since their departure. Such numbers made no sense, in human terms. So it was best not to think about it, and to get on with the work.

And there was plenty of that. The planning of the turnaround, a key milestone in the voyage, had been the subject of much debate. It had been hard even to decide how long it should take. After nearly ten years of continuous flight, the engineers, including Jophiel himself, wanted plenty of time to run routine maintenance. On the other hand the medics, led by Harris Kemp, worried about the effect of extended periods of weightlessness on the crew – especially the latest cadre of infants, born within the last couple of years or so.

In the end, they had settled upon ten days of zero-thrust turnaround. And as soon as the shutdown came the crew got to work.

Jophiel helped Poole with much of the coordination. Crews of humans and bots crawled over the inert GUTdrive pod, worked the length of the ship's spine seeking cumulative stress problems, and picked their way over the lifedome's outer surface, patching flaws where, despite the shielding provided by the wormhole interface, the near-lightspeed sleet of the sparse interstellar material had managed to get through. From now on, of course, the burning engine pod would lead the way, thrusting against the direction of travel, and tweaks of the exhaust plumes would blast a tunnel through the ice, gas and dust that littered interstellar space.

There was some debate about ditching the wormhole interface altogether, now that even its secondary purpose, of shielding the ship, was gone. But Poole and Jophiel vetoed that. The exotic-matter frame itself represented a store of energy – and besides, though *Island* was lost for good, *Gea*, the flotilla's third vessel, was still out there somewhere, and the Pooles still had a notion, or a dream, of reconnecting with that lost crew some day.

Inside the lifedome too, there was work to do. Floor plates were taken up to expose a huge infrastructure of waste processors and food printers and pumps and vents and dehumidifiers and heaters, through which engineers worked their way. The children found this hugely exciting, and had to be kept from exploring the caves of steel revealed beneath their feet.

But in this strange interlude there also was an opportunity for some constructive work.

Asher Fennell and her small team ran through a programme of specialised observations. The crew of the *Cauchy* were already far into galactic realms unseen by human eyes before, not even telescopically from Earth thanks to intervening dust clouds. Beyond the plane of the Galaxy too there was the dark-matter halo and its mysterious structures to explore – and, further yet, what Asher Fennell called the 'crystalline clarity' of extragalactic space. Of course they had carried out such observations in flight, and now, such was their velocity even without thrust, the view was still folded up by the aberration of light. But, as Asher tried to explain tactfully, even Poole Industries' finest GUTengines did come with the slightest of murmurs, vibrations which could distract from the immensely delicate observations the astronomers were trying to make.

So, in this brief interval of stillness, Asher and her team worked feverishly.

Meanwhile Maxwell Ward took the chance to put every crew member he could get his hands on through zero-gravity military drill exercises. Max's training was always popular with the young, Jophiel had observed, if only because it gave them something to do, some structure in their lives.

There was time for fun too. Jophiel was astonished to see infants sent drifting in the air like balloons by their parents.

After five days, the turnover manoeuvre itself was another challenge for the engineers and crew. The whole ship had to be rotated, end over end, to get that big GUTengine pod pointed in the right direction.

The ship's frame was configured for greatest strength in the direction of thrust, with lifedome leading and engine pod at the rear. Of course it was designed to cope with off-axis manoeuvres too; the basic GUTship design had been intended primarily for short-haul missions within the Solar System, with a requirement for manoeuvring and docking at either end of a journey. But they were twelve thousand light years from home, and with only one ship left. So the engineers took the rotation manoeuvre slowly and carefully. The three-kilometres-long baton that was the ship tipped with painful slowness, a swarm of bots and engineers watching every step. Asher and her astronomy team complained bitterly about the loss of observing time, as the ship turned from a stable platform into a pinwheel, but Poole overrode her.

Then Asher called a meeting of the seniors, two days before the GUTdrive was scheduled to start up again.

31

Poole gave over his apex suite again. And Asher opened the debate with a grand sweep of her arm.

A Virtual of the Galaxy appeared in the air in the middle of the room.

A fat bright bulge of stars at the centre. The great surrounding disc with its spiral arms. The image was so beautiful, its appearance so dramatic, that it evoked gasps from the surrounding watchers, who were hanging in a rough sphere around the display, zero-gravity suspended in the air. The complex light cast highlights from Nicola's gleaming silver limbs. Asher Fennell, quiet and studious, was learning showmanship, Jophiel thought wistfully. Maybe it was in the nature of the subject matter. Astrophysics dealt with the grandest objects in the universe; how could you *not* be spectacular?

Asher looked around at them. 'Now I've got your attention,' she said drily, 'I need to tell you what we've been discovering. It's not just abstract knowledge. I think it changes our deepest understanding of – well, of the nature of the universe. And of the meaning of our own mission.'

Nicola grinned. 'Oh, good. I love it when that happens.'

Jophiel had to grin back. Physically Nicola, wary of Max, was still lodged safely in the engine compartment. But she had grown weary of her isolation, and she had started to project Virtuals like this one, despite her self-professed revulsion at throwing off short-lived partials. It was a price she was prepared to pay, for now, to keep out of Max's way, while not missing the good stuff like this.

'Get on with it,' growled Michael Poole.

Asher continued doggedly. 'What I'll show you is a synthesis of the observations we've been making since launch. Observations of phenomena no human eye, or probe, ever saw before us. And now backed up with some precision sightings taken during the turnaround.

'So,' Asher said, gesturing at her image. 'What you *see* is the baryonic-matter Galaxy. The light-matter stuff.' A beacon, bright blue, sparked into life in the disc, in a spiral arm halfway between edge and Core. 'Here *we* are. And what we've been looking for, primarily, has been infestations of intelligent life.'

Nicola laughed. 'Infestations. Good word. *Infestations*, like us, and the Ghosts, and the Qax.'

'Yes. Start with that. We've got two sources of information about intelligence in the spiral arms: the old data, from the Poole archives and the Wormhole Ghost's information, glimpses of a lost future, and our own new observations. So, at Goober's Star – leaving aside the Xeelee and the dark-matter creatures for now – we found that three species of intelligent, technological, starfaring species had made it there independently. Species of light matter, that is. As you say, Nicola, us, the Ghosts, the Qax. If you guess that that's a typical density, that you have three species interacting in a radius of a thousand light years—'

Nicola nodded. 'I like number puzzles. Three in a disc of a thousand light years radius. So in a spiral galaxy a hundred thousand light years across, you might expect – what, a few thousand civilisations?'

Asher shrugged. 'Well, that's a guess. Better than nothing. That might not seem so many in a Galaxy of hundreds of *billions* of stars. If you want my guess, life is common – maybe even universal – but technological starfarers are relatively rare.'

Michael Poole frowned. 'But you have been looking. And I'm guessing you found some even so, or you wouldn't be here talking about it. Right?'

Asher nodded. 'The Ghost–Qax war is far behind us now, despite the way hyperdrive transports allowed it to spread faster than light. But as we have crossed the Galaxy we have found – traces.'

Jophiel was fascinated. 'Traces?'

'Signatures,' Asher said gloomily. 'Of civilisation, of industry. Sparsely scattered. And not many are extensive, beyond a star system or two – not the way the Ghost–Qax war sprawled across thousands of light years. And a few times we've seen clear evidence of a kind of decadence, even destruction.'

She began to list classes of evidence of vanished cultures. She reminded them that the Goober's Star system had shown evidence of being mined out, regularised, perhaps by some culture that had vanished long before Ghosts, Qax, Xeelee or humans turned up. Even Anthropocene-era Earth could have destroyed itself in a way that would have been visible to cultures on Alpha Centauri or further out, Jophiel learned now. An all-out nuclear war would have produced a flash of gamma rays visible across interstellar distances, but only lasting a few hours, perhaps. Some of the longer-lasting effects – an atmosphere gone opaque through a nuclear winter, the depletion of ozone and other perturbations of the air – would have lingered, and would have been detectable from afar.

'We're probably not recognising all that we see,' Asher said. 'Maybe some of those who survive war and conquest go on to some advanced plane of existence we know nothing about. What we *don't* see is any sign of a thriving interstellar empire. No lanes of transports, no huge multi-species space liners crossing the stars . . .'

'Lots of diversity, though, it sounds like,' Nicola said.

'Yes – because *humans never got here,*' Jophiel said heavily. 'In this timeline. Not after the Xeelee intervention and the Scattering.'

'Right,' Asher said. 'By now there *should* have been a wave of human expansion out of the Solar System and the Orion Arm that was called, in some Poole-archive accounts, the Assimilation. A huge disruption, right across the Galactic disc. And an extinction event, if you like. To rival on a Galactic scale the Columbian exchange, when the Europeans of the Discovery Era started to ship slavery, diseases, and rats around the planet.'

Nicola grinned at Poole, not unsympathetically, Jophiel thought. She said, 'An extinction event, though. Which you seem to have – well, inspired in one timeline, Poole. At *least* one timeline. But then the Xeelee intervened. Here's something I've heard the crew muttering about, when they've seen some of this data. The younger ones, who don't have our cultural baggage. Who have grown up as refugees. Look – if the Xeelee that invaded the Solar System averted a Galaxy-wide extinction, a bonfire of life and culture, did it do a *good* thing? By some higher measure of morality. And if so, maybe we're wrong to try to kill it for its troubles.'

To describe the shocked silence that followed as awkward, Jophiel thought, didn't begin to cut it. What an astounding swivel of perspective.

'We are where we are,' Michael Poole said gruffly. 'We've made our choices. And we just have to continue, that's all. What else would you have me do? What?'

And even Jophiel, looking into his own simulated heart, had no answer.

With some relief, Asher said, 'Now for the bigger picture.'

Jophiel stared. 'Bigger than *this*?'

'Oh, yes. Like I said, at least we had some familiarity with what goes on in the spiral arms. Here's what we didn't understand so well.'

She waved her hands again.

Now the Galaxy image tipped up, shrank down to the size of a dinner plate – and a wider shell, transparent with a silvery glimmer, materialised around the Galaxy itself. Dwarfing it.

'Here's my representation of the Galaxy's dark-matter halo, on its grossest of scales. We relied a lot on the data compiled by the *Gea* in the early days, though we have built on that since.

'You can see most of the dark matter is out beyond the visible edge of the Galaxy – but not all of it. Look, see that silver plane embedded in the disc? There is actually a significant density of dark matter down there *within* the visible disc, which is, as I've said, very thin, comparatively, in itself. How does it get down there? We have records of some very ancient observations of these phenomena, and theories almost as ancient. Some of which we can confirm now, we think.

'You see, we do know some things about dark matter. We know it's made of "sparticles", in the jargon – supersymmetric copies of regular baryonic-matter particles. And we think now that dark matter has its own set of physical laws. Its own forces, like our nuclear, electromagnetic, gravitational forces. The complication is that the dark-matter suite of forces is *not* the same as ours. We only have one overlap, in fact: gravity. That's the only way dark matter influences our baryonic universe directly – but that is a pretty significant way. The lack of any further overlap makes dark matter hard even to observe. Hence "dark".

'But the existence of those other forces implies structure in the dark-matter realm.

'You see, it's just as a baryonic-matter star, say, has structure, coming from a balance between physical forces: gravity, which tends to compress its bulk, and electromagnetic energy from the core fusion, which tends to blow it apart. Similarly dark-matter structures can form from a balance of relevant forces. In particular if you have some equivalent of electromagnetism – a way to radiate energy – then you have a way to cool down. And objects that cool down can collapse down into a gravity well . . .'

And that, Jophiel realised now, was how come there was that fine dark-matter skim within the thin layer of the Galactic disc. Dark matter that had cooled, slowed down, got trapped in the gravity well of the Galaxy disc.

They debated this, questioning and speculating. There was an almost collegiate atmosphere at times like this, Jophiel thought. As if they were a field expedition from some far-distant university. Whereas Max Ward thought the ship should be more like a warship. Jophiel had always suspected that they weren't going to get anywhere near their objectives without learning, without acquiring a deep understanding of what they were facing and its context. So, collegiate made him happy.

'But – life?' Michael Poole broke in. 'You keep speaking of structure. Are you talking about life in the dark matter? Those big tendrils Flammarion said she saw, reaching down into the Galaxy disc. Life, even mind?'

Harris Kemp, the nearest to a biology specialist they had on board, rubbed his nose doubtfully. 'Well, maybe. That's still a heck of a stretch. But how could such things evolve? Or even breed?'

And Nicola's silver face was suddenly transformed, the mouth open, the eyes wide. Jophiel, startled, thought he had never seen such an authentic human expression on that reconstructed face of Ghost hide.

She disappeared.

Poole and Jophiel shared a glance. Jophiel said, 'She seems – over-excited. Do you think she's OK?'

Michael shrugged. 'She's suspicious of her own nature. Of herself. She will never be "OK" again. But she has a good brain, in her way . . . I think she's come up with something, that's all.'

And Nicola returned. With a box of construction material, or at least a Virtual replica: the big lens that she and Asher had saved from the Ghosts' station at Goober's Star.

32

The big lens-shaped box crowded out the suite.

Poole snapped, 'What in Lethe are you doing, Nicola?'

'Planning to return a child to its mother . . . I think. That's too anthropomorphic, but that's the basic idea.'

Jophiel frowned. 'What mother? What child? . . . Oh.' And he saw it, all at once, just as Nicola must have, before him. *The photino fish?*'

'Yes! Look, Jophiel, Michael, we should have put the pieces together before. You were there with me.'

'Where?'

'In the Sun, Jophiel! In the Sun. Where we discovered the photino fish for ourselves. And again, there they were inside Goober's Star, where this specimen was taken from. Probably in every star in the Galaxy, for all we know.'

'So?'

'So, look at the two places we think we've observed dark-matter life. In the halo of the Galaxy, and in the hearts of stars. Huge scale on one hand, tiny cramped confines on the other. Why would dark-matter creatures be found *there*, in those contrasting places? Unless—'

Asher nodded, excited herself now. 'I think I'm starting to see it. Unless they *needed* to be there.'

'That's it. Here's what I'm thinking now. The dark beasts, the big tentacled monsters out in the halo, represent only part of the – life cycle. I'm thinking salmon, and oceans, and rivers. Jophiel, salmon live in the ocean, but they have to go upriver to breed – right? Same here. These big dark-matter cloud-entities live out beyond the Galaxy, but they can't *breed* there. Why? I don't know. Maybe they need density, compression. Because of the information that must be exchanged between parent and offspring? Maybe two clouds couldn't mate; they would just – intermingle. Something like that.

'But there are places in the universe, little pits of gravity, where they *could* squeeze down and find the compression they need.'

'In the hearts of stars,' Asher said.

'Right! We know gravity works on dark-matter creatures; we know they are immune to heat and radiation. So the Galaxy is like a great reef, to them, full of these tight little pits, the gravity wells of stars, where they can deposit their . . .'

'Their eggs?'

'Which hatch out to become photino fish, as we called them, swimming around inside the stars, like the Sun. Like larvae. And when they are mature . . .'

Jophiel said, 'Ah. They hatch out. As if a star was an egg. They fly back up, out of the stars, out of the disc, up into the halo. And – open their wings.'

Asher laughed. 'Just like salmon swimming up rivers. Like turtles, coming to the beaches to spawn. I love it, Nicola. It's too beautiful to be wrong.'

'So now,' Nicola said, 'the right thing to do is obvious. We release the . . . larva from that hull-plate pod, that the Ghosts trapped it inside—'

Jophiel. No.

'*No.*' Jophiel snapped out the word.

He looked around, at surprised frowns. He looked at Michael, and got a blank stare back in response. He had surprised himself. But he knew he was right.

'No,' he said. 'I'm sorry. We need to hold on to that pod, for now. I can't explain . . . Call it intuition.'

Nicola grinned. 'Virtuals have intuition, do they?'

Jophiel glared at his template. 'Michael. You need to trust me. It's important.' And, he thought, how he wished he felt he could tell Michael of that other Poole, the reality-leak traveller, who seemed to hover over him like a guilty conscience.

Poole stared back at him. He looked oddly lost. Then he nodded curtly. 'Leave the pod in its store for now, Nicola. After all, we can always release the fish later.'

Asher looked baffled, irritated. 'Well, you did a good deed, Nicola. Or tried to.'

'Yes. Don't spread it around.'

'So you have it,' Asher said. Our journey, our ant-like crawl across the Galaxy. Even the fireworks between the Qax and the Ghosts. All against the context of a Galaxy-wide ecology that was so huge in scale we never even noticed it before.

'Moving on. Here's what else we saw.'

Jophiel gaped. 'There's more yet?'

'Further out.'

Another wave of her hand, and the Galaxy, dark-matter shell and all, shrank to the size of a toy, of a human hand.

And it was joined in the image by more toys.

More galaxies. Jophiel saw one big spiral that looked like it out-massed the Milky Way itself, and a clutter of others – perhaps two, three dozen, all of them much smaller than the two big dogs of the pack.

'So,' Asher said. 'Looking beyond our own Galaxy, here's what you get. The Local Group. The big beast is the Andromeda Galaxy, of course. Right now, around two million light years away. That's not much on the scale of these objects, maybe twenty Galaxy diameters. And in fact, as you probably know, Andromeda and our Galaxy may be heading for a collision, perhaps three, four billion years from now. I mention it as something we might have to deal with, if Michael keeps us plummeting into the future.' Polite laughter.

(Much later Jophiel would remember this exchange. Asher's gentle joke. The laughter.)

'And zooming out further—'

That compact little group shrank down to a detail in a much larger conglomeration of galaxies and galaxy clusters.

'The Virgo supercluster,' Asher said. 'A hundred million light years wide. Hundreds of galaxies. Which come in all sizes and ages, from dwarfs up to monsters about a hundred times our Galaxy's mass. Some galaxies are younger than ours. Some so old they are nothing but wrecks full of red dwarfs and stellar remnants. As for the scale: I'll expand again, and again.'

A zoom out. More clusters and superclusters, gathering in threads and planes, in three dimensions.

'You can see that the Virgo group is itself part of a greater mass, called the Pisces-Cetus supercluster, a *billion* light years across . . .'

The threads and sparks of light were assembling into an open structure. Now, to Jophiel, the image didn't look so much like a cosmological picture as something caught under a microscope: the cluster of atoms that made up a base molecule, say, which in turn were threaded on the fragile spiral of a DNA molecule . . .

'This is the universe on the largest of scales we can observe,' Asher said.

'Remarkable,' Susan Chen said. 'The cosmos is so empty.'

Nicola shook her head. 'It looks like a room full of cobwebs.'

'Well, that's not a bad analogy.' Asher pointed out details. 'Galaxies gather in clusters, which gather into superclusters, and features we call "walls" – these threads and sheets. We think all of this is a product of the way the early universe emerged from the Big Bang. A sea dominated by dark matter, more or less smooth, but with turbulence. And the baryonic matter, the light matter, gatherred in the dips and the cracks.'

Nicola grinned. 'A universe like the back of a giant turtle, like in some old myths. And the galaxies are like diamond dust scattered on the turtle's shell, gathering in the folds and pocks . . .'

'But it isn't static,' Asher said. 'All the galaxies, all of this structure, is in motion.'

Another wave of the hand, and the galaxy pinpoints were colour-coded in a manner obvious for a spacefarer: red for receding, blue for approaching, like Doppler shift.

Almost all of the picture was coloured red, Jophiel saw, startled.

Asher drew the obvious conclusion. 'You can see that aside from a little random motion, *all* the galaxies, including our own, and their clusters, are being pulled across space. And this organised flow is on a tremendous scale. All this has been measured before; we are only confirming models themselves thousands of years old.'

'That,' said Susan Chen, 'is a *lot* of moths. But what is the flame?'

Asher looked at her. 'This is what we *weren't* able to show you before the shutdown.' She clapped her hands, and the images disappeared, leaving the room feeling dark – and cold, and empty, Jophiel thought, though he was as unreal as those images himself.

And in the darkness, something appeared – Jophiel squinted to see – small, remote, blurred. Surrounded by mist.

Perhaps a torus, tilted up.

A ring.

Jophiel stared, and looked across at Michael Poole.

He, they, had seen this before. Another object enigmatically glimpsed in the amulet of the Silver Ghost.

'The generation who discovered this – I think it was the twenty-first century, or maybe the twentieth – called it the Great Attractor,'

Asher said softly. 'The great mass that is drawing in all the galaxies, across the observable universe. They couldn't see it, but they could infer its existence, its distance and mass, just by looking at your great cloud of moths, Susan. Now we can image it . . . almost.

'We think this thing is a hundred and fifty million light years away. We think it has as much mass as tens of thousands of galaxies. And we think *it*, itself, is perhaps ten million light years across.' She sketched out the ring shape with her finger. 'The whole of the Andromeda–Milky Way pair would fit *inside* that structure.'

'Structure.' Michael Poole turned his head sharply. 'Do you mean an artificial structure? A construct? Ten million light years wide?' He turned to Jophiel. 'And we thought our wormholes were big engineering.'

Jophiel asked, 'What in Lethe is it made of?'

'Well, we can't know,' Asher said a little testily. 'I've had one suggestion that it could be some variant of cosmic string.'

Which, Jophiel knew, was a defect in spacetime itself, a remnant of the initial singularity. Atom-thin, a rope-like flaw whipping through space at near lightspeed, and massive enough to bend spacetime around it . . . 'Somebody is using *that* as a building material? But what is this for, Asher?'

'We can only guess.' Now Asher, clearly cautious, began to describe measurements made right at the limit of her instruments' capabilities. 'For a start,' she said, 'there is some very exotic radiation coming from the ring's central region. We suspect the ring itself isn't just massive, it may be rotating. And is creating a singularity of some kind at the centre.'

'Ripping a hole in space,' Nicola murmured. 'I admit, I'm impressed.'

'Also,' Asher pushed on doggedly, 'we are seeing what looks like planetbuster-beam radiation backwash, around the central structure . . .'

'Xeelee,' Nicola said immediately. 'Fighting.'

'And further out *still*, a dense concentration of dark matter,' Asher concluded. 'Seriously dense. All around the ring. And complex, with powerful gravitational fields capable of manipulating masses on a very large scale. I mean, more than stellar masses. Clusters of stars, maybe even dwarf galaxies.'

'Lethe,' Nicola said. 'Huge energies being expended, across a tremendous volume. Masses hurled in at the ring, and planetbuster fire in return. Attack and defence. This is a war zone. Max Ward is going to love it.'

Asher said, 'We can't be sure of the interpretation—'

'Look, I'll jump to conclusions, if nobody else will. All the way out *there*, the Xeelee are building a tremendous artefact, in the middle of intergalactic space. So big it's distorting the entire structure of the cosmos around it. And creatures of dark matter are trying to stop them. That's how it looks to me.'

Jophiel shook his head. 'It's unbelievable . . . But if that's anywhere close to right, it shows that the war we're engaged in here – humanity's war with the Xeelee – is only a fraction of the bigger picture. A detail.'

'But a significant detail, maybe,' Asher said. She smiled. 'Questions?'

The meeting soon wound up after that. Jophiel knew he would spend a lot of time considering what he'd learned. Not least about himself. And Michael Poole.

They stood together, awkward mirror images.

Aside from the two of them, only Nicola remained.

Michael glared at her. 'Staying to gloat?'

'About what? Your personal angst? Look, Poole, from the minute that Xeelee poked its nose out of your wormhole it's obvious you've been mired in a tangled mess of overwhelming moral complexity. You're central to it, but it's not your *fault*. How could it be? Self-pity, in you, is a sign of arrogance.'

Jophiel had to laugh. 'Is that supposed to comfort us, Nicola? Maybe you should stick to the tough talk.'

She grinned. 'Fair enough. Well, here you are on a twenty-five-thousand-year punitive mission to the centre of the Galaxy, and that *is* your fault. You may be one of the few military despots in history who isn't actually a psychopath. No wonder you are screwed up.'

And she popped out of existence.

Two days later, with the turnover complete, the GUTdrive was smoothly restarted, and an agonisingly slow deceleration began.

FOUR

This is a key time in human history, Alia, a high-water mark of human ambition. We've been privileged to see it, I suppose. But now we must fall back.

Luru Parz, c. AD 500,000

33

Earth date: c. AD 28,700

It took six more years by crew time – as nearly thirteen *thousand* more years passed, beyond the ship's hull – before the *Cauchy* reached the Central Star Mass, the crowded space at the very heart of the ten-thousand-light-years-wide bulge of stars at the inner terminus of the great spiral star-lanes of the disc – a bulge that, Jophiel knew, the Exultant generation would have called 'the Core'.

And then ten more months' ship time, ten months in increasingly star-crowded skies, before the ship neared its next significant astrophysical landmark, known as the 'Cavity', a kind of spherical bubble of relatively low density, at the centre of which lay the black hole itself.

On the day the ship reached the edge of the Cavity, Asher summoned the seniors to the apex office. When Jophiel got there Asher was waiting, her old-young face blank, illuminated by the complex light of the Galaxy Core. She had been unusually vague about what was on her mind, Jophiel thought.

A Virtual Nicola was here too, as ever captivated by the view beyond the lifedome.

And that view . . .

Jophiel struggled to find words to describe it, A crowded sky that reflected from Nicola's Virtual silvered face. As ever, the view was an image unfolded from light aberration: even after years of deceleration the *Cauchy*, was still pressed hard against the light limit in its forward travel.

The others, too, were hushed.

'Take a starry night on Earth,' Nicola said at length. 'Somewhere clear. A high desert in South America, where the Anthropocene-era astronomers built their great telescopes. Or, better yet, a still, cold night on Mars. Between dust storms anyhow. Just you and the stars.

That's the kind of sky we evolved under, I guess. The kind of sky we're used to. Stars, a few thousand clearly visible to the average eye, in clear, familiar patterns that barely change in a human lifetime.

'Then double it.

'Overlay it. Again and again and again. Fill in all the gaps with stars, and vast, glowing dust clouds. And do it over again until the sky everywhere you look is deep with stars, the nearer ones sliding visibly over your field of view . . .'

Asher nodded. 'You know that we're close to the destination now. Only seven light years from Chandra, the black hole itself. Only three years of ship's time before we slow to zero. We are well inside the Central Star Mass. Ten million stars, in a volume of space that might hold ten thousand out in the vicinity of Sol. And from here on in it's going to get even more crowded.'

'Because we're falling into the gravity well of the central black hole,' Nicola said.

'That's it. But even before we get there, we're learning an enormous amount about stellar evolution.'

Jophiel grinned. 'And everything we thought we knew was wrong.'

Asher shrugged. 'How did you guess? You know that we are at the edge of the Cavity. That's the name the Exultants seem to have given this place, when this was a war zone. A kind of gap in the heart of the Galaxy, centred on Chandra – well, everything is centred on the black hole. A gap fifteen light years across.'

She expanded a patch of the complex sky, a patch scattered with stars and glowing clouds. In there was even what seemed to be a spiral structure, Jophiel thought, tangled lanes of stars and dust, quite distinct, like a fractal model of the Galaxy itself, here at its heart.

And at the very centre, a point of intense light.

'*That* is Chandra,' Asher said now. 'That central pinpoint. The black hole. You can't see the event horizon yet, because it's embedded in a cloud of stars, something like ten million of them within a light year. "Chandra" is another Exultant name, by the way. Like the "Baby Spiral", for that feature you see.'

Jophiel only half-listened. He, and he suspected Michael, was gazing at the black hole and its surrounds, looking for traces of the Wheel, as they had come to call the artefact in the amulet, the band around the black hole. Not yet visible. Not yet.

Asher said, 'Outside this Cavity there is a steady infalling of gas and dust – falling into the black hole's gravity well, that is. But there are a dozen or so superbright stars deep inside the Cavity, orbiting the black hole, which emit a ferocious stellar wind that pushes the infall back. Just a dozen stars, their energies sweeping this huge volume clear . . .

'So, behind us, there is a torus of molecular gases, relatively dense, where the infall is stalled by the starlight. The arrangement isn't particularly stable. Every hundred million years or so there's a loss of stability, a collapse of the torus, a burst of star formation.

'What we *don't* find here in the Cavity is any evidence of dark matter. And not as much modification of the stars as we've seen out in the spiral arms. None of the accelerated ageing. But—'

'Whoa,' Nicola said. 'You're running ahead of us. You've *seen* the stars ageing?'

Asher looked uncertain, Jophiel thought. Self-conscious. 'Sorry. It's just that we've learned so much, these last years, months – we lose track of what we've briefed. But, yes. We have been travelling for twenty-five thousand years, nearly, as measured in the external universe. And that's long enough to actually *see* some modification. In individual stars, I mean. Stars growing old too fast.'

'Ageing,' Poole said. 'Just as we suspected in the Sun. The photino fish clogging up the stars' fusion cores with helium ash. Pushing the stars towards the end of their lives too quickly—'

'How long?' Jophiel asked. 'How long until the stars die?'

'I can only tell you what we've observed,' Asher said cautiously. 'In twenty-five thousand years of travel, we think we've seen individual stars we've monitored age as much as they should in twenty-five *million*. The luminosity changes, the spectral profile—'

'A factor of a thousand,' Nicola said. 'So a star like the Sun, which is five billion years old, and should have billions more years ahead of it—'

'Only millions.' Asher laughed, hollowly. 'Sounds a lot. It's not. A million years is the age of the human genus, for instance. And we think we know why this is happening. I told you. It's not about physics. It's about life. No. Belay that. *War*. It's about war.'

A startled silence.

Poole asked, 'What war?'

'Just listen.'

In the beginning was the Big Bang.

Nothing but physics at first, Asher said, an unravelling of physical law, the crystallisation of matter from energy.

But life soon emerged. The Xeelee, from the tangled spacetime of the first splinters of time. Thus, one protagonist of the longest war.

The other soon followed.

'We don't know when dark-matter life first emerged,' Asher said. 'But we think it was very early – and we think we do know what the first structures of dark matter in the universe must have been. Immense stars, or starlike objects – from a hundred to a *thousand* times as massive as the Sun, generating heat purely from their gravitational collapse, and their own subtle internal forces – there are no fusion processes as in the cores of stars, not in dark matter. Different physical forces, remember. Still, clouds as bright as the Sun.

'Which in turn quickly collapsed to create black holes. Objects which slowly merged in turn to create the supermassive black holes like Chandra, here. Which in *their* turn gathered galactic masses, of light matter, around themselves.'

'Mm,' said Poole, wondering. 'And the black holes attracted the attention of the Xeelee.'

'We think so,' Asher said. 'The Xeelee are creatures of twisted spacetime themselves – relics of an even earlier cosmic era, probably. They would surely be attracted to the event horizons of the new, giant black holes.

'Perhaps that was the first interaction between Xeelee and dark-matter life. It wouldn't be the last.

'Because by then, you see, we believe dark-matter life was evolving quickly.

'The first true stars were born around six hundred million years after the Big Bang. Which would one day generate baryonic life on the planets they warmed.'

Nicola was nodding. 'But they were also useful for the dark-matter creatures.'

'Yes. As we know. With stars, for the first time in the history of the universe, you suddenly had small, deep and accessible gravity wells. And we think that dark-matter life quickly evolved to take advantage of that. Life on a tremendous, extragalactic scale, but with their breeding pools in individual stars.

'We think that once this form of life evolved it spread quickly. Probably faster than light, actually; we think it's most likely they used natural wormholes, another kind of defect left over from the Big Bang. Today, now we know what to look for, we see dark-matter fingerprints everywhere, in the stars of very distant galaxies.'

'And meanwhile,' Michael Poole said heavily, 'the stars evolved, and the planets stabilised, and in warm puddles on worlds like Earth—'

'Life evolved,' Asher said. 'Baryonic life, like our own. Busily breeding under the light of stable stars.'

Nicola prompted, 'Except—'

'Except the stars weren't all that stable after all.'

The great dark-matter Ancients had believed they ruled the universe. But their domain had flaws.

These pesky stars, with their so useful breeding-pond pinprick gravity wells, had an unfortunate propensity to blow up.

'Oh, they don't all explode,' Asher said. 'But even calm, sensible stars like the Sun will age. But here's the kicker. Only about a *tenth* of the hydrogen fuel available in the star is used up in the process.'

'Which wasn't good enough, for the lords of creation,' Jophiel said.

'Right. Inefficient. And they probably didn't much enjoy the explosions and expansions going on in their cosy little breeding pools. Novas and supernovas and such.

'And so we think – we *think* – the dark-matter Ancients began to tinker with the workings of the stars.

'At first they may have tried to make them more efficient, more stable. Lift away a little mass: smaller stars burn longer. Mix up the inner layers so more of that hydrogen fuel reaches the fusion engine: another way to stretch the lifetime of a star.'

Jophiel nodded grudgingly. 'And they do all this through the photino fish.'

'That's it,' Asher said, nodding. 'We think they must do it all through gravity – which *is* accessible to them. Flocks of photino fish wheeling in the cores of stars, spinning them up for mass loss, diverting mass flows in the interiors. Maybe the photino fish, basically a larval stage, evolved into a separate subspecies, a companion life form, to achieve all this.'

'Ah,' Jophiel said, grinning. Enjoying the play of ideas. 'But these tinkering Ancients had rivals as lords of creation, didn't they? Who might not have liked to see such widespread meddling with the light stuff, the baryonic matter – their own domain.'

'The baryonic lords,' Nicola said, rolling the words around her mouth. 'I like that. *The Xeelee*. There must have been a first confrontation. Xeelee against dark-matter creatures.'

Jophiel mused, 'If Max were here, he might be asking how you would fight a dark-matter enemy. If you had to, theoretically. Bullets, shells, energy beams would just pass through them. But, gravity—'

'Planetbusters,' Poole said flatly. 'That's it. Gravity is all that could touch them.' His eyes widened. 'Hey. No wonder the Xeelee have planetbuster beams. Like gravity-wave lasers. The planetbuster wasn't designed to smash up our planets. *It was designed to take on dark-matter creatures.* It was a weapon from a much older war than their conflict with us.'

Jophiel grunted. 'So, the Xeelee pushed back. Across the Galaxy, presumably. Across the cosmos? Lethe. It's unimaginable.'

Nicola mused, 'Makes you wonder if maybe we picked the wrong side to root for in this war in heaven.'

Poole's face was set. 'It was the Xeelee that attacked Earth. Not your dark-matter Ancients.'

'Good point,' Nicola said drily.

'Anyhow,' Asher said, 'at some point the Ancients changed their strategy. Now they targeted the big, bright stars, like the Sun. Infested their cores. And they started to *shorten* their life cycles, driving them to an early termination. You can see the logic. In one stroke they can eliminate baryonic life, *and* get rid of such stellar inconveniences as supernova explosions. The prize would be a universe full of cosy, safe, sterilised relics – a trillion years of stability, or more. Once they get the job done. They probably left most of the stars untouched, actually. The small ones, the red dwarfs – *they* were fine for the dark-matter life cycle.'

'One thing I don't understand,' Jophiel said. 'The stars are billions of years old. Once the Ancients finish their remodelling, the stars will have just millions of years of main-sequence life left. So this star-tampering strategy can only have begun recently—'

'"Recently" as an astrophysicist defines it,' Nicola said drily.

'Right. Meaning, millions of years ago, not billions. And it will be over in a few millions more years, not billions. So how come *we* are around to see it? Seems a coincidence that we evolved just as a war as old as the universe comes to its climax.'

'Not really,' Asher said gently. 'We think it's about efficiency. Look – the universe has an unknown future ahead of it. But already its age of star-making is coming to an end, in a sense, even without the Ancients' meddling. All the easily accessible star stuff, the hydrogen in the discs of the galaxies, is being used up. We think that nineteen out of twenty of all the stars that ever will be born, have been born already.

'And we think the Ancients have waited for this moment, waited for the maximum number of stars to be ready to be modified, in one grand sweep.'

Poole pressed, 'And as for us?'

Asher shrugged. 'It may have taken this long too for life like ours to have emerged, even after stars and planets were born. The long slow process of evolution from some chemical-rich scum in a warm, drying pond, to starships . . . So there's some coincidence about the timing, but not as much as you might think.'

'Lethe,' said Nicola. 'So they mount a *universe-wide* campaign of this star-ageing, all at once.'

Asher said cautiously, 'We're still – guessing. We now have data spanning twenty millennia or more. But even so, it's like a single snapshot in a war that reaches back to the birth of the universe. We *think* we've got this right . . .'

'But this doesn't change our basic objective,' Poole said now. 'Which is our encounter with the Xeelee from the Solar System, in whatever lair it inhabits *there*.' He pointed to Chandra, the black hole, and its attendant cloud of captive stars. 'We're still seven light years out. Three years left to travel. Three years we must use to prepare, for the end game.'

That killed the conversation. The others drifted out, one by one. Jophiel looked back at Poole, who stayed there, alone, staring at the complex Galaxy-hub sky.

34

The journey continued.

Time passed.

And on the two hundred and fifty-second day of the twentieth year of the flight, Michael Poole called Jophiel to his apex suite.

The GUTdrive had died away now; they were weightless once more, for the first time since the turnaround ten years earlier. And in the last months, as the *Cauchy* shed its velocity, the aberration of light had finally unravelled, and the sky began to look normal once more.

Normal. Depending on your perspective, Jophiel supposed. Beyond the lifedome's apex was a mush of stars and glowing gas. This was no projection now, Jophiel knew; this was a naked-eye view – if any unprotected human could have survived out there, in the sleeting radiation of the Galaxy Core.

'What a view,' Jophiel said to Poole. 'And what an achievement. We made it, Michael. Whatever comes next, we made it.'

Poole, glaring up at the crowded sky, looked fierce. And he opened his fist.

The Wormhole Ghost amulet, still attached to its lanyard, floated up from his palm into the air.

'Michael?'

Poole looked at his avatar. 'Remember the image my – our – mother extracted from this thing? I showed it to Nicola on the night before we left Cold Earth for good.'

'Of course I remember.'

'I've done a lot of thinking. Nicola's right. I'm no warlord. But I'm no criminal either. One human can't deflect the course of a Galaxy's history. On the other hand, that Lethe-spawned Xeelee came for *me*, and my planet. So I'm involved. Well, I hurt it in the Solar System, and I tracked it all the way here, and now I'm going to finish this. That's all. Are you with me, Jophiel?'

'I *am* you.'

Poole magnified the sky image with a wave of his hand.

And Jophiel saw it at last. Clearly distinguishable, against a backwash of hurtling stars.

The object at the very centre of the Galaxy. Just as in the amulet imagery.

Chandra.

A black hole with a ring around it.

The Wheel.

3 5

The Pooles, conferring, had decided to wait a week after the GUTdrive finally died before fixing on the next step.

There was a lot of muttering about that, Jophiel realised. It was too long a delay, according to the more hot-headed of the Pooles' advisors, notably Nicola and Max Ward. Or it was too *short*, according to others.

The Pooles reckoned they needed the time. Time to gather more detailed data than had been possible in flight. Time to run through a hasty programme of maintenance and refurbishment for the ship, after nearly ten more years of continuous thrust. Time to prepare equipment and strategies for the next phase of this lifelong mission – such as launching probes to explore the spaces around them. Time to hang, unpowered, at the edge of this extraordinary Galaxy-centre system, and just *look*.

A week? Too long or too short? It would do.

There was even more controversy when at the end of the week the Pooles announced that the next steps would be discussed at an open crew briefing.

'This is nuts,' Max Ward predictably groused as the meeting slowly assembled in the lifedome amphitheatre, the open space once more strung with zero-gravity webbing. 'We already spent too long on this mission bouncing babies and chasing chickens. And now, what, should we have a singalong before we start?'

Nicola had a grin on her silvered face. 'You hum it, I'll play it.'

Michael Poole took the opportunity to kick her foot. By now she was showing up to these events in person once more; Max seemed to have parked his decade-old threat to have Nicola dismantled. But it didn't pay to provoke him.

'Come on, Max,' Jophiel growled. 'This isn't just our war. It's *theirs*.' He waved a hand. 'The next generation. This is only the beginning, for them. I mean, we *know* this isn't the only Lethe-spawned Xeelee in the cosmos. Even if we win this battle the war has to be carried on. And that will be up to *them*.'

Susan Chen, sitting patiently cross-legged on the ground, looked up at him. 'A remarkably bleak perspective, Jophiel. So is this the future for mankind, or what's left of it? The child soldier?'

Max grinned. 'If it was good enough for the Exultants, it's good enough for me.'

As the due time approached the crew gathered, some bringing carry-bags and baby papooses that they tied to the zero-gravity guide ropes. Michael Poole opened the meeting by simply standing up, and waiting until the buzz of talk had died down.

'So,' he said. 'It was a long hard journey, but we got here.' A smattering of applause, a few whoops. 'We've had a week to celebrate. But now the hard work begins.'

He clapped his hands.

The lifedome went dark. There was a ripple of anticipation.

And a wash of red stars appeared in the air above all their heads. Within this cloud, Jophiel thought he saw a central knot, directly over his head, a point of light brighter than the rest. There were a few brighter stars close in around that mass, like planets around a sun.

He looked around. Saw the upturned faces of children, shining in Galaxy-centre light.

'We're close now,' Poole said. 'Just one and a half light years from the very centre,' and he pointed to that Sunlike knot.

'Chandra,' replied a very young voice.

'Right. The black hole. Which itself has a mass of four *million* stars. And within a few light years of the black hole there are around ten million stars. There's a paradox, though. Right here, about one and a half light years out, there's a drop off – a kind of hole within this inner star cluster. The stars are less densely packed than further out. Maybe, if an infant star gets too close, the black hole's tides disrupt its formation. Or maybe Chandra's gravity just slingshots stars away.

'Anyhow, that's precisely where we stopped,' Poole said now. 'On the edge of that inner cavity. We planned it that way, with the help of Ben Goober and his navigational tweaks. We figured this was a good vantage.' He pointed again. 'So there's the black hole, and its surrounds, the accretion disc, the close-in stars that orbit it. Asher and her people are taking a good hard look at *that*. But we're not going to the black hole, not yet—'

'I know where we're going.' A young voice.

A slim figure stood up. Jophiel recognised Chinelo Thomas, daughter of Alice, ten years old, one of the first of the new generation to be born on the *Cauchy*. Evidently a good kid, but, to Jophiel, a stranger, like all her generation. From the moment they'd been born, Jophiel had learned from bitter experience that, to children, Virtuals were creatures that looked like people but who you couldn't smell or touch, and were therefore to be feared. By the time the children were starting to walk and talk Jophiel had got used to keeping a polite distance from them, and in turn they from him.

Now Chinelo pointed upwards. 'We're going to the Wheel.'

Poole nodded gravely.

He clapped his hands again, and the image shifted, becoming a schematic. There was the central black hole, and its clutter of companion objects. Further out, the swarming red stars were reduced to pinpricks.

And there was a ring, a fine band, enhanced and now clearly visible. Subtly tilted, it swept across the foreground, and wrapped around the rear of that central glow, slim, perfect.

No matter how many times he considered it, Jophiel shivered with awe. It was obviously an artefact, a made thing two light years in diameter. *A ring around a supermassive black hole.* How could any finite living creature have the audacity to construct such a thing? But their best guess as to the origin of this thing was that, evidently, the Xeelee from the Solar System had done just that – for if the Wheel had existed before the Displacement of Earth, evidence of it would have shown up in deep-sky radio wavelength probes, probably millennia before Poole had been born. It was *that* big.

The crew were silent. Jophiel saw that every face was turned up to Poole's image – including Chinelo Thomas, who was still on her feet. And she was grinning, her perfect teeth white in the light. Again Jophiel shivered. Not because of the black-hole engineering this time. Because of this determined kid.

Poole said now, 'It's going to take us some time to explore all this. You know that. Years, even.

'Think about the sizes here. The black hole itself is built on the same scale as the Solar System. It is a big ball of darkness, of twisted spacetime, and it sits at the centre of all this, like the Sun in the Solar System – but it is much bigger than the Sun. Its event horizon would just about fill the orbit of Mercury. If you saw it from Earth's orbit its width would span *eighty* Suns, side by side.

'Outside that is the accretion disc. A mass of rubble, mostly broken-up stars, a great whirlpool that is slowly draining into the event horizon itself. In the Solar System, *that* would wash beyond the orbit of Mars, or even further out; the edge isn't well defined. And you see those close-by stars? Everything here is orbiting the black hole, and they come as close as they can get without being ripped apart by the tides. They orbit a few *hundred* astronomical units out – as far out as our Kuiper belt. Whole stars, orbiting like planets.'

'So all this is about the size of the Solar System,' Chinelo said now. 'Whereas the Wheel—' She spread out her arms.

Asher Fennell smiled now. 'The Wheel is a band a million kilometres wide, give or take. So wide that even at our distance of half a light year from the closest surface, there's some detail we can make out. For instance it seems to have a couple of decks raised up above an outer substructure . . . Sorry. I get caught up on the detail. Yes, a million kilometres wide.'

And it has a radius of a light year. It's easy just to say that. A Wheel with the radius of a light year. So what? So the whole thing is over *six* light years long, in circumference. Why, if you straightened it out it would stretch from the Solar System to beyond Alpha Centauri! A single structure. Not only that, it's also rotating. The whole Lethe-spawned thing. Rotating at near lightspeed. *Very* near lightspeed. And that has implications. Ask Einstein.'

'So it's big.' Chinelo was grinning, entirely unfazed. 'So we land on it, and take it. Right?'

Once again, Jophiel shivered.

36

Chinelo was right. That was the ultimate goal, to land on the artefact, to engage the Xeelee. Even if nobody knew how to do that right now. Even if all they could actually conceive of, for now, was a flyby in the *Cauchy*.

And even Poole didn't believe he could risk that before gathering data from a series of probes. Launched over the weeks following engine shut-down, these were automated, each a stubby cylinder just a metre or so long.

But the last of them, Poole decided, for this first human exploration of the environs of a black hole, was to be crewed, after a fashion: crewed by three Virtual humans, lodged within the probe's memory store.

It took a hundred days after the ship's arrival at its half-light year-out station to get the mission set up, a suitable probe modified.

And the designated crew was chosen after discussions in the apex suite. Afterwards, Jophiel was never sure if he, Nicola and Asher had volunteered or not. Nicola whispered to Jophiel, 'You know I hate these cast-off shadows of the living. No offence. But, you thought I'd miss this?'

So, on the hundredth day, the three of them found themselves drifting in the air, facing each other in an infirmary bay where they went through final medical checks, and Harris Kemp led them through a countdown to the spin-off. Jophiel knew the drill. The spun-off Virtuals would be stored, without activation, inside the probe's memory for more than a year until the first significant mission milestone. This was necessarily a pared-down, energy-conscious mission. So, in a few subjective seconds, either he was going to be here still, or—

'Three. Two. One.'

37

Not.

Jophiel and Nicola shared a glance.

Jophiel quickly checked his environment. Suddenly they were sitting in a flitter cabin. Or so it seemed. The big viewing window ahead of them showed a stripe across a complex sky. Artifice, like scaffolding, Jophiel thought.

Asher wasn't here, in the cabin.

'Lucked out,' Jophiel said.

'You mean, to find yourself the copy on a one-way mission to oblivion? Depends on your point of view. And what in Lethe are you doing in my seat?'

Jophiel found he was indeed sitting in the Virtual flitter's left-hand seat, Nicola on the right. Jophiel hadn't even noticed. He laughed.

'Just my little joke.' A disembodied voice.

'Asher? Is that you?'

'Mission control here.'

'And as Virtual as we are?'

'Indeed. I just thought I would keep from cluttering up the cabin. Not a lot of room with your two egos in there. In fact, as far as *I* can tell, I'm back aboard Larunda. Home from home. Orbiting Mercury, you remember? When Harris and I looked over the shoulder of Mitch Gibson as you two piloted your way down into the heart of the Sun.'

'As *I* piloted us down,' Nicola groused. 'So, Poole, are you going to give me my couch back, or do I have to reprogram you?'

Of course none of this was real, Jophiel knew. Just another couple of Virtual environments, inhabited by Virtual people, an illusion cast by a chip the size of a thumbnail within the carcass of a ship the size of a walking stick.

And yet – here he was.

Jophiel gave it up with good grace.

But he felt a faint nausea as he moved. *That* was an unusual side-effect of a spin-off, if that was what it was. He said nothing. He hoped it would pass before the others noticed.

'So,' said Asher, with a kind of glacial calm. 'We're committed, however we feel about it. You want to know where we are?'

'Or,' Jophiel said, 'more to the point, *when* we are.'

'Yes. Timing is going to be a little tricky. In terms of our direct experience, obviously it's only minutes, for us, since we were all sitting in the *Cauchy* infirmary being downloaded. We just skipped forward, in our dreamless sleep, about four hundred days. And then there are the complications of relativistic time dilation, for a probe which is travelling nearly at the speed of light while the *Cauchy* is effectively stationary—'

'Get to the point,' Nicola growled.

'I'm planning to log ship's time as measured at the *Cauchy*, as opposed to what we experience. So we are twenty-four days into year twenty-two since launch from Cold Earth.'

Jophiel did a quick mental conversion. 'A year, accelerating steadily. So we've already travelled about half a light year. Which means—'

'We're about to cross the perimeter of the Wheel. Take a look.'

And that structure that Jophiel had glimpsed before from a respectful distance, that complicated band across the sky, now swept over his field of view.

Huge, complex, detailed, hanging in space.

There and gone.

At Jophiel's insistence, they ran the visuals and other recordings of the flyby over and over.

Nicola grunted. 'This Wheel is about the biggest, dumbest object anybody ever built. Or dreamed of, anyhow. And I bet you *did* dream of stuff like this, Poole.'

'Big but not so dumb,' Asher murmured. '*How* you could ever build such a thing is another question – although I'm picking up a few clues. Look at this. I'm selecting images.'

In magnified images of the Wheel's elegant, curving sweep, Jophiel glimpsed structure. Layers, like strata, raised above the floor level on the inside curve, fixed by some kind of spokes.

'As we suspected there are more decks above a base level – the outermost shell, the closest to lightspeed. We're calling that the "c-floor".'

'Cute,' murmured Nicola.

'The lowest deck, a couple of hundred metres up, is itself only a whisker below lightspeed. Call it Deck One. The effects of time dilation down there – I'm estimating the numbers, and I frankly don't believe them. After that, Deck Two is twenty million kilometres above Deck One. The decks are connected, or supported, by what look like incomplete spokes. The highest of the decks, Deck Three, is more than a thousand astronomical units up from the c-floor.'

Jophiel tried to take that in. An astronomical unit was the distance of the Earth from the Sun. *A thousand AU*: you could have fit the entire Solar System, all the way out to the inner edge of the Oort cloud, *between* those decks. Yet, on the scale of the Wheel itself, it was all lost in the detail; the Wheel's light-year radius was more than *sixty* times larger again.

It was impossible to grasp.

But Asher was trying to grasp it even so. 'There are glimpses of detail on the decks themselves. Splashes of colour, discs and ellipses . . . Complex materials, evidently, contained in some kind of pits in the surface. I'm trying to compile maps. And I *think* I'm seeing signatures of chemistry in those pits. Some volatile compounds. Methane. Oxygen.'

Nicola looked startled. 'Life?'

'That's the obvious conclusion to jump to. But it is a jump . . . How could life *get* here?'

'Maybe it was brought here,' Jophiel said. 'Or drifted. This artefact could be over twenty-five thousand years old, if the Xeelee came straight here by hyperdrive from the Solar System. Not old enough for life to evolve here, but time enough for it to travel. As we did.'

Nicola, heroically, still refused to be impressed. 'It's just a big dumb machine. Even if it does have bugs growing in the clockwork. Anyway, how could life survive? I'm guessing the spin gravity down there is ferocious.'

'Actually, not,' Asher said. 'Surprising, maybe. The spin gravity even on the lowest deck is only about a gravity. I mean, an Earth gravity.'

'That makes *no* sense,' Nicola protested. 'That's no spinning toy, like Larunda at Mercury. You said the rim is moving at near lightspeed!'

'But,' Jophiel said gently, 'the turning radius is a whole light year, remember. It balances out. So if people do get to land there they will be able to walk about comfortably. You see, you can imagine wheels of varying sizes each with one-G spin gravity.'

Nicola grinned. '*Imagine*. Yeah. This is a wet dream for you, isn't it?

Did Jules Verne write about a ring around a black hole?'

'Not Verne, though he could have handled the maths. Later thinkers did, though. Storytellers. Visionaries, edge-of-the-possible engineers. The structures they imagined had names like Bishop rings and Banks orbitals and Niven ringworlds.'

Asher said, 'We ourselves built stations like Larunda – a wheel a couple of kilometres across, turning at a revolution a minute to give you that one-gravity spin weight. But you could imagine a much bigger artefact. A wheel a few kilometres wide would turn in an hour, say. And a one-gravity wheel a few *million* kilometres across would have to turn in a day. There are limits to the tensile strength of any material, though; enough spin would pull it apart. The tension in the structure scales as the square of the spin velocity. You can't build a one-gravity wheel out of steel much bigger than a few kilometres wide. With graphene you might reach a thousand kilometres.'

Nicola waved a hand. 'And to build a thing two light years across? With a velocity of lightspeed, nearly?'

Jophiel shrugged. 'This is Xeelee engineering. Remember we guessed that the Xeelee used cosmic string to hold their Great Attractor artefact together? Maybe . . .'

Asher nodded. 'Good thought. I'll look for that.'

Jophiel sighed. 'Maybe Michael will get the chance to figure it out. There are other technical issues. To put it mildly. Such as, isn't this thing dynamically unstable? If it is fixed on a central mass, like the black hole. Eventually it slips off centre, until one edge comes into contact with the middle. If it hasn't shaken itself to pieces by then.'

Asher said, 'Somehow I doubt very much that that is a problem for the Xeelee. There are probably layers of subtle engineering beyond our capabilities.'

'But it still makes no sense,' Nicola broke in. 'The whole design. Yes, this thing is clearly a Xeelee artefact. Maybe Asher is right that there are habitable zones, in those splashes of mud in the decks. But *why one Earth gravity?*'

'Not exactly,' Asher murmured. 'But near enough.'

'Why would the Xeelee build some monstrous habitat to suit *us*?'

That stumped Jophiel. 'Good point,' he said grudgingly.

But Asher said diffidently, 'Actually it does make a certain sense, Nicola. There is a peculiarity about the distribution of the gravity fields of planets . . .'

Planets came in all sizes, Asher said, from barely spherical balls of rock and ice smaller than Earth's Moon, all the way up to monstrous gas giants larger than Jupiter, blending into brown dwarfs and dwarf stars at the upper end of the mass scale.

'And you might think,' she said, 'that the bigger a world is, the higher its surface gravity. Because a bigger planet has more mass. But it doesn't work out that way. If you keep adding mass, there are complications. Rocky worlds get denser, with liquid cores. Giants of ice and gas heat up in their interiors, so they expand, and become *less* dense. So, it turns out, the gravity field graph has a kink in the curve . . .'

Jophiel, intrigued, pulled up some numbers on a softscreen. 'It shows up in the Solar System. This never struck me before, but she's right. Venus has – had, before the Xeelee destroyed it – eighty per cent Earth's mass, ninety per cent the gravity. Neptune had seventeen times Earth's mass, but only fourteen per cent higher gravity, in the high clouds anyhow. Saturn *ninety-five times* Earth's mass, but only six per cent higher gravity. Quite a plateau.'

'Not only that,' Asher said, 'the exobiologists came to believe that life was more likely to evolve on these transitional worlds – the plateau worlds. Neither too small so they lack a gravity field strong enough to retain an atmosphere, nor too large so the pressures are crushing . . . And therefore, if you had to build a single habitat to host a wide variety of planetary life forms, your best bet for the artificial gravity would be—'

'About Earth's,' Nicola said. 'OK. I'm impressed by the logic. But why build a habitat? And why on this scale?'

'I suspect that when we know that,' Jophiel said, 'we'll know most of it.'

Asher said, 'The flyby is over. We probably ought to shut down until the next mission milestone. This little missile we're living in has plenty of juice, but we don't want to burn out before we get to Chandra. There's one more thing you ought to see before we go to sleep, though. Another clue – not about what this thing is, but how the Xeelee built it. Maybe, anyhow . . .'

She assembled a series of images, to show them what she meant. Objects, swarms of them, crossing space in immense streams.

Both Nicola and Jophiel recognised them immediately.

Boxes of Xeelee hull plate, or so it appeared. Each the size of the object that had once been retrieved by the Xeelee from its five-billion-year storage deep in the crust of Mercury, then grown in the light of the Sun, and sent on a destructive course through the Solar System: a box a thousand kilometres on a side, a box big enough to contain a small moon. Humanity had called it the Cache.

Now they saw thousands of caches. Millions. Uncountable.

The individual caches were actually following orbits around the black hole, Asher said, elongated elliptical orbits that seemed to reach down to the black hole itself, and then came back out all this way, a light year out – orbits that must take millennia to complete.

Asher was able to pick out streams of the structures, running more or less parallel: one heading into the black-hole system, towards Chandra, the other coming back out the other way, and heading for the Wheel.

'I'm tweaking our course,' Asher said. 'To parallel the cache flow. You see, I figure this flow might have something to do with the Wheel's constructon. Well, the *Cauchy* crew can figure out what happens to these caches when they reach the Wheel. Our job is to see what happens at the black hole.

'We're following the stream in, towards Chandra.'

And Jophiel could only stare at a flow of material organised on a scale that matched the distances between the stars in the vicinity of Sol.

Another sleep. Another period of unconsciousness.

Another waking, to fresh wonders.

38

Jophiel found himself stretching, reflexively, as if waking. But he hadn't been asleep. Rather, non-existent.

He checked the screens. Over seven months this time, since the last revival. More than a year and a half, by the mother ship's clocks, since the probe had left the *Cauchy*. And, outside—

'Quite a view,' Nicola said.

The cache river was close now.

And it snaked through a sky full of stars. Crimson globes, many of them near enough to show as discs.

Jophiel ought to feel exhilarated by such a sight. He felt anything but. 'Another little death,' he said gloomily. 'Another unwelcome birth. And only, what, a half light year out from the black hole?'

Asher laughed. 'Just look, Poole. *Look* . . .'

Jophiel looked, and saw it.

An artefact. Not the wheel. Something else. Something closer.

That was obvious from his first glance. A plane sliding over the top of his field of view – sharp-edged, but the detail of its face elusive, even in the bright light of the swarming stars. And the colours were sombre, deep rust-reds and browns. The colours of a Martian autumn, he thought.

Still that great plane unfolded over them, and still more. Ever wider.

'Asher, can you give us an overall view?'

'We did swoop in from far out . . .'

The viewpoint zoomed out smartly. The window-filling plane dwindled, all its edges gathering – a triangular face, then – and then the complete object slid into view.

'Lethe,' Nicola said. 'Another tetrahedron. Maybe tetrahedra are some kind of universal. How big, Asher?'

'Over fifteen million kilometres to an edge.'

When Jophiel tried to make out the fine detail on that upper face, he lost his way again. It was like looking for patterns in frost congealing on a window. Indeed it looked fractal, a nesting, structure within structure. The artefact combined the finest of scales with the largest, it seemed.

It hung in the complex sky, motionless, elusive.

'What's it *for*?' Nicola snapped. 'Any signs of life?'

'No.'

'Motive power?'

'It seems to be following its own long, unpowered orbit around Chandra. Safely away from the accretion disc and other hazards. Just sitting there. The interior is very complex – well, you can see that. But it is . . . inert. Passive. My guess is it's some kind of observing instrument. That complex interior might reflect a rich memory store. The thing could be very ancient,' Asher murmured. 'I've no way of proving that, but—'

'It feels that way,' Jophiel said.

'Yeah. And this isn't the only, umm, *artefact* I've encountered here. I didn't wake you for them all.'

She gave them a quick show and tell. A blizzard of three-dimensional dioramas. Much of this had been glimpsed from afar, and much of it was bewildering.

A little family of cylinders, tumbling over each other like baby mice.

A crumpled sphere that looked no bigger than the *Cauchy*'s life-dome, orbiting a treelike structure of branches and sparkling leaves.

Bundles of spheroids and tetrahedrons, pencils and rods and wands.

Jophiel found it hard to retain the detail. There was no sign of life, no purposeful movement.

'Wrecks,' Nicola said. 'The sky is full of wrecks.'

'Well, it's a sparse scattering – but yes. Wrecks of what look like ships, what look like habitats – and stuff we can't classify, like this big fractal tetrahedron.'

Jophiel thought it over. 'We came into this space, around the black hole, from a more or less random direction. And if we're encountering this much clutter here—'

'It must be everywhere,' Asher said. 'Throughout the volume around the black hole.

'But it makes sense, if you think about it. These inner few light years are the most significant region in this entire hundred-thousand-light-year-wide Galaxy. The Xeelee came here; we followed it. The same idea must have occurred to other starfaring species. Everybody is going to send a probe here, looking for – what? Treasure? Scientific understanding? Their gods?'

Nicola grunted. 'Or vengeance, as we have.'

Jophiel nodded. 'And a fair proportion didn't make it out alive. Billions of years of detritus, trapped in this giant filter. Who knows what wonders we are hurrying past here? Archaeological, cultural, scientific.'

'And who knows,' Nicola said drily, 'what we might have found here in that other timeline, Jophiel? Human fortresses. Raging battles. Billions of corpses, maybe. Oh, and a statue.'

Asher said, 'I'm recording everything I see. Sending it all back to the *Cauchy*.'

Nicola said, 'These relics are depressing. Wake me when there's something life-threatening.' And she lay back in her couch, mummy style, eyes closed, hands crossed over her chest.

39

Nova dreams.

Dreams of burning forests, boiling seas. Of spacecraft fleeing a wall of light.

'. . . We are still following the cache stream, as it follows its own three-thousand-year orbit in from the Wheel, from a light year out . . .'

Jophiel woke with a start, sat up in his couch.

Nova dreams.

He tried to concentrate on where he was. He stared out of the window.

Dead ahead, a black sun, rising from a sea of fire. It wore a halo of white gold, smoothly drawn on one side.

The black hole.

Asher murmured, 'Jophiel? Are you OK?'

Jophiel felt as if he was having trouble waking, in this latest revival. Asher's words came into focus slowly, and his vision more slowly still. 'I'm fine.'

Nicola snapped, 'No, you're not. This gets worse every time you're revived.'

'I'm . . . sorry.'

'I mean, *look* at that.' She pointed at the view. 'We made it. There's Chandra. A supermassive black hole. Another first for human eyes, or quasi-human, and *you* made it here. Even big brother Michael never got this far, and never will. So why are you depressed?'

'Who says I'm depressed?'

'Come on, Poole. I know you. I met your mother.'

'Maybe the support software is faulty. Or my memory store got corrupted.'

'It's not that, Jophiel,' Asher said gently – more gently than Nicola anyhow, Jophiel thought wryly. 'I think she might be right. Virtuals are as human as their originals – or at least they start out that way.

208

With humans, depression is a complex thing, a negative feedback loop between body and mind. Similarly there could be a deleterious feedback between your projected consciousness and the systems supporting you. You feel bad, the software develops bugs, the memory corrupts, you feel even worse . . . And I think I know the cause. After one of the downloads from the *Cauchy*, your consciousness has been synced with a message that came in from Goober c. From the partial you left there, the witness.'

'I've been dreaming of novas,' Jophiel blurted.

Nicola laughed again. 'Are Virtuals supposed to dream?'

'Shut up, Nicola. Jophiel – nova dreams?'

Jophiel sighed. He closed his eyes. 'I'm fleeing in a ship which can't outrun the light.'

'This is clearly deriving from your upload from the Goober c witness. It will have sent its upload at lightspeed – a message that only just recently caught up with the *Cauchy*, and has been passed on to you.'

Jophiel smiled faintly. 'So I'm not going crazy.'

Nicola said, 'Maybe you should embrace the discomfort you're feeling, even the confusion, as a tribute to *it*. The witness. It was another you, and it died, after all. And it's all an entirely rational process.'

But Jophiel wasn't so sure about that. Because, floating in his mist of a memory, was an image of that *other* version of himself, older, in that battered coverall. His wry smile. How to figure out what *his* presence meant?

'I guess I earned this pain. But, Asher, if you think some problem I have is compromising the mission, you have my permission to close me down.'

Nicola just looked at him. 'You know, I always wondered why it was you who came on this trip. I mean, a Jophiel copy, as opposed to a new spin-off from Michael, the template. A fresh copy instead of a faded second-generation clone.' You're still *him*. You still bear his monstrous freight of guilt, don't you? Anyhow, you won't need to "survive" much longer, will you?'

'What do you . . . oh.'

And Jophiel started to take in where he was.

Chandra was close. And the mission was coming to an end.

The black hole itself was the heart of a complex system. It sat in a sea of fire, centred on that great hemispherical dome of darkness. And that dome itself was rimmed by brilliant white-gold light, a pure arc. Like a distorted dawn, Jophiel thought.

'That lake of fire. The accretion disc?'

Asher said, 'We'll make an astrophysicist of you yet, Jophiel. We are about five astronomical units from the event horizon. Meaning, about the orbit of Jupiter.'

'The orbit of Jupiter,' Nicola said. 'Sounds an awfully long way. But in this strange system we're falling awfully fast.'

'Right. How long before—'

'Forty-four minutes,' Asher said. 'Before the closest approach to the event horizon. Our velocity is over ninety per cent of lightspeed; our mission was to get here as fast as possible, so we didn't decelerate. I unfolded the light aberration . . . I thought we deserved to see the view. We aren't going to fall into the black hole itself. We won't get that far. But—'

'We know the plan,' Jophiel said. 'This probe was designed as a one-way mission. *I* designed it that way. At closest approach, or anyhow at closest safe approach, we'll send a message back to the *Cauchy*. They'll receive it in a year and a half – as they are one and a half light years out – and all the data we've retrieved, and the essences of us, will be returned. Reintegrated into the memories of our templates. We will be remembered. Everything we saw, felt – even this conversation, I guess. But *we*—'

'We all knew the deal,' Nicola said brutally. 'You said it yourself, Poole, when we woke up. Your first words.'

'I did?'

'"Lucked out."'

He forced a smile. 'Should be on my gravestone.'

'You're not going to get a gravestone. Still less a statue.'

'But what we have got,' Asher said, 'is work to do.'

They all shut up and focused.

And the fragile little missile, still tracking a stream of Xeelee caches like a cautious fish following a school of whales, fell steadily in towards the centre of everything.

The accretion disc itself was extraordinary. As the Virtual flitter, nestling in a ragged stream of caches, flew low over the swirling pool of debris, Jophiel stared out, stunned, baffled. Delighted.

Cautiously Asher identified features. Such as a long, streaky wound, evidently the relic of a recent explosion. 'Most of the accretion disc is star stuff. Every ten thousand years or so a star wanders in too close to the black hole. The tides get hold of it, and it is stretched out, turned into a tube of hydrogen – still fusing; the magnetic and gravitational fields close to the hole keep hold of it that tightly. But when it passes closest approach, those fields weaken, and the star explodes, with the savagery of a hundred supernovas. But even that is just a detail, this close to Chandra.'

As Jophiel looked further inwards, to the inner rim of the accretion disc, he saw that it glowed, hot and violent. There, infalling material was heated to billions of degrees. Most of it was hurled back into the wider disc – but a fraction fell into the hole, to be lost to the universe for ever.

And the black hole itself, a hemisphere rising up from the curdled light-sea of the accretion disc, had a kind of grand, sombre stillness, Jophiel thought.

The core of it was a shadow, in fact, deep and wide – three or four times the width of the event horizon, the ultimate inner surface from which not even light could escape – for the black hole deflected the light of the star fields behind it. A gravity shadow. Further out there was more evidence of the distortion of light. The spinning hole dragged at spacetime, a swirl that gathered and deflected the very starlight. So the black hole looked asymmetrical: its leading side was darker, as if shadowed, while the other was brightened by the collected light that the spinning hole hurled in Jophiel's direction. Gravitational lensing, of an extreme kind.

There was a purity about this display. A clarity to the light cloaking the singularity. A perfection in the delineation of the arcs. It was angelic, almost.

And all of it nothing, at heart, but an artefact of spacetime.

'I must remember this,' he muttered. 'All of it. For you, Michael. I saw *this*.' To Lethe with depression, he thought. He might never have got to see all this. How depressing was *that* thought?

Nicola was smiling at him. Black-hole light reflecting from her silver skin. 'Welcome back,' she said.

'Nearing closest approach,' Asher said calmly. 'I'm watching the innermost rim of the accretion disc.'

'The caches,' Nicola said now. 'Look at the caches!'

Jophiel looked out, peering along the stream of pale boxes. Their neat cubical forms were an extraordinary element of symmetry in this howling chaos, he thought.

And now he saw them *fission*. Individual boxes growing, splitting, folding up into two copies, four . . . As more and more were produced the boxes collided with each other; some went tumbling out of the stream altogether.

He immediately saw the principle.

'This is what it's all about,' he said. 'The caches, I mean. The purpose of all this, for the Xeelee. The caches are made of hull plate, right? And hull plate turns radiant energy to mass. The more area it has to catch the light, the more it grows. An exponential process.'

'Yes! That's it,' Nicola said, excited. 'Remember the Cache on the surface of the Sun? In *that* light, it could double in size in a couple of hours. And in the intensity of the infall glow here—'

'Seconds,' Asher said, wondering. 'A box a thousand kilometres across could double in size – or replicate – in seconds. Just by soaking up the mass-energy from the accretion disc.'

Jophiel thought it through. 'A cache's closest approach to the black hole will last only minutes. But that's enough for many doublings – dozens, maybe. One box could become a thousand, more. And then all those boxes – all that frozen mass-energy – start the long haul back out to the Wheel again. Then, in fifteen hundred years or so, when they get there—'

'And *that* is how the Xeelee made the Wheel,' Asher said. 'By turning black-hole energy into hull plate, and hurling that plate back out to the Wheel's orbit. It would take millennia, but the Xeelee got here by hyperdrive, and it has *had* millennia. While we limped along after it at mere lightspeed.'

Jophiel grinned. 'I *love* this—'

'Ah,' said Asher.

Nicola frowned. 'What do you mean, "Ah"?'

'Look ahead.'

Jophiel obeyed.

To see a cache, randomly deflected, wheeling out of the stream, spinning slowly.

Coming straight at them.

A thousand-kilometre wall.

'We knew this was a hazardous environment,' Nicola said softly. Her hands hovered over her control. 'Trying to evade—'

Asher snapped, 'Seconds to impact. Uploading last data dump back to the *Cauchy*.'

Nicola sighed. 'That's that, then.'

212

Jophiel Poole grabbed Nicola's silver glove of a hand. He called, 'Asher?'

'I'm here.'

'You know what?'

'What?'

'"Lucked out" my ass.'

Nicola laughed out loud.

And then—

40

Ship elapsed time since launch: 23 years 264 days

The last, compressed, heavily distorted neutrino-link message came through from the Chandra probe, just as the *Cauchy* prepared at last to leave its eyrie a half light year outside the perimeter of the Wheel, and begin its near-tangential journey towards the inner surface – a journey that would itself take over a year.

And as the last returned data were recorded and analysed, the principals, Jophiel, Nicola and Asher, finally integrated the memories of their partial copies into their own minds.

Or tried to. Jophiel found he struggled with conflicting memories, just as had his copy on the probe, it seemed. *Nova dreams.* Maybe casting off partials really was a dumb idea, in the long run.

He tried to lose himself in work. Medic Harris Kemp had no better remedy to recommend than that.

On the ninth day Nicola and Asher came to see him, in Poole's apex office.

Jophiel greeted them with a grunt. 'What's this, the probe crew reunited?'

Nicola studied him, silver face unreadable. 'Still feeling sorry for yourself? Get over it, Poole. We've got work to do.'

'She's right,' Asher said. 'It is pretty exciting. We've been able to figure it out from the data we returned.'

'Figure out what?'

'How the Xeelee built the Wheel.'

She conjured up a Virtual schematic of the Wheel. At the heart of the apex suite, it spun in mid-air.

'Slowed down for effect,' Asher said drily. 'Given the Wheel is spinning at lightspeed. We've detected three decks, as we've called them – three levels above the c-floor, the structural level. You can see the upper decks are supported by these struts, rising up from the c-floor.

The highest is over a thousand astronomical units above the base.

'We think the essential construction material of all this is Xeelee hull plate.

'Now, each deck is a ring a million kilometres wide and a light year in radius. That's an area equivalent to a hundred *billion* Earth surfaces, peeled off and spread out flat. Look, you're going to hear a lot of absurd numbers like this; just bear with me. But if it's all made of hull plate, which is very fine stuff – and if it was stationary – the mass isn't so big, actually. Less than one per cent that of Earth's Moon, say.'

Nicola grimaced. 'Only, she says.'

'It's going to get worse. Of course you have to multiply that up by a few factors to allow for the multiple decks and the support struts.

'But what's much more significant is the effects of motion. It's all spinning at near lightspeed, remember. And the consequence of that is paradoxical. But Einstein figured it all out, back in the nineteenth century.'

'The twentieth,' Jophiel said automatically. 'Actually, Einstein used spinning rings and discs as a thought experiment: a paradox to help him figure out relativity in the first place.'

Nicola was impassive. 'Just imagine I don't know what in Lethe you two are talking about.'

Asher grinned. 'Look – we know that the radius of the Wheel is a light year. So its circumference ought to be two times pi times a light year – a bit more than six light years – if it were static. But it's not. Imagine you had some giant pacing it out down there, with a measuring rod a light year long. She lays the rod down, over and over – six times and she's nearly back where she started.'

Jophiel knew where she was going with this. '*If* the Wheel were stationary.'

'Yes. But it isn't. We know what happens when objects approach lightspeed. Look at the *Cauchy*, at its peak velocity. As seen by observers on Earth, our clocks slowed to a crawl; they would have seen us take twenty-five thousand years to reach the Galaxy centre – whereas it seemed to us to take only twenty years. We were accelerated, they weren't; acceleration changes the nature of the spacetime you inhabit.

'And, if the Earth observers had been able to measure the apparent *length* of the *Cauchy* at its peak velocity, they'd have seen it squashed up lengthways. Space and time adjust to keep the speed of light constant for all observers . . .

'So. Go back to the giant pacing out the Wheel. She's moving at a speed close to that of light, compared to us. And so her clocks will slow down—'

'And her measuring rod will contract, from our point of view,' Nicola said.

'That's it. Her direction changes the whole time as she paces around the circle, but that makes no difference to the *speed* she's moving at, and the relativistic distortion. We watch her lay down that shrunken rod, over and over, as she paces around a circumference *that looks unchanged to us*. And so she must put it down a lot *more* than six or seven times before she gets back to her starting point.' She studied their faces. 'You see where I'm going with this? Our surveyor down on the Wheel is in a spacetime distorted by the Wheel's motion. She can *measure* that distortion, directly. Just by counting the number of times she lays down those sticks. She finds that the circumference of her circle is *bigger* than what Euclid said it should be . . . She would get the wrong answer for pi . . .'

'How much bigger?'

'Given our measure of how close the c-floor has approached the speed of light, the ultimate limit – we figure five *million* times.'

Nicola actually gasped. 'So let me get this right. This two-light-year-diameter Wheel has a circumference that isn't a mere six light years, a walk past Alpha Centauri, like you say. It's more like *thirty million* light years.'

Asher grinned. 'A walk that would take you out of the Galaxy. Out of the local group—'

'All jammed into this diddly hoop?'

'You got it.'

'That's outrageous.'

'No, it's not,' Asher said calmly. 'Einstein understood.'

But Jophiel was still puzzling at the numbers. 'Five million times. OK, the distance expansion is one thing. But that factor would only deliver enough rest mass to complete the structure. Then there's the kinetic energy to push it up to lightspeed in the first place.'

Asher smiled. 'You're right. Another factor of five million.'

Nicola said, 'That's got to mass a lot more than a slice of the Moon, then.'

'You're right. You're looking at the mass-equivalent of several *thousand* stars.' She glanced up at the spinning Wheel. 'And *most* of the mass-energy delivered to this thing has had to be converted into kinetic energy.'

Jophiel laughed.

Nicola glared at him. 'You can *laugh* at this. You are still a Poole, aren't you? A little boy with another big dumb toy to play with.'

'I'm just thinking how tricky such a thing would be to build. If you put together the Wheel, made it just long enough to close the six-light-year loop, and *then* spun it up – it would stretch, crack up, as space distorted. Conversely, once built, if somehow it slowed down, it could crumple, fold up. Not enough space to fit in its length. Einstein thought of that, in fact. He said that you'd have to build a spinning object of some kind of liquid – mercury, maybe – that would flow to fill the space as it distorts.'

Asher said, 'We think the Xeelee has done *something* like that. As to how they built it—'

'We saw the process, didn't we?' Nicola asked. 'A stream of caches, grown at the black hole and spun back out here – incorporated into the structure somehow . . . Maybe starting with a single Xeelee flower.'

Asher nodded. 'It all extrapolates from what Xeelee hull plate *does*. Put it in sunlight, in any strong radiation, it grows. Before long, it has doubled in size, and doubled again, growing faster and faster. You want to know how many doublings you'd need to get from a single Xeelee flower, with a few square centimetres of area, up to the Wheel – or its equivalent in hull plate, anyhow?'

Jophiel grinned. 'Don't guess, Nicola. I've fallen into these traps before. Always less than you think.'

'Around a hundred and forty,' Asher said with a kind of triumphant glee. 'That's all! As to how long a doubling would take – down at Chandra, you're talking about seconds, no more. The radiant energy out of Chandra, from the infall from the accretion disc, is about two and a half thousand times that of the Sun . . .

'So – you sit out here, a light year away from Chandra. You throw in *one* Xeelee flower. Just one. It takes over fifteen hundred years to sail in to the black hole, before whipping around in a few *minutes*, and beginning the long slow haul back out again. Still, we figure you could achieve twenty or thirty doublings, a quarter or a third of the total needed, in a single pass.

'Then you sail the whole lot out again, and go back in for another pass. Do it again and again—'

'We get the idea,' Nicola said, holding her hands up. 'The transfer across a light year each time is slow, though.'

'Only if you don't want to spend any energy on hauling the material out of the gravity well. To speed it up you could boost your climb out of the gravity well – for instance, sacrifice half the mass as reaction mass. There are other subtleties. The Wheel's mass-energy is huge, equivalent to thousands of times the mass-energy of the Sun. Compared to that, even the total output of the natural radiation from the accretion disc is minuscule. We think the Xeelee is manipulating the replication process to adjust the accretion-disc infall, and so to extract more mass-energy from the system – ultimately from the black hole itself, and the knot of spacetime around it. Using the accretion disc as a kind of siphon, you see. And since Chandra masses several *billion* solar masses—'

Jophiel nodded. 'The mass of a few thousand stars is small change. So it's plausible. Barely.'

'So that's our model.' Asher smiled. 'Proof of principle anyhow. We're sure the Xeelee has been smarter, more subtle.'

'But it is elegant, isn't it?' Jophiel said. 'I mean, the range of uses to which the Xeelee put the replicating hull plate, this single super-efficient technology. The Cache it used in the Solar System. We saw the forests of buildings down on Goober c. Now this.'

Asher nodded. 'Maybe that's the mark of a truly advanced technological culture.'

'You two just love all this, don't you?' Nicola said. 'So, Jophiel, you ready to come back to work yet?'

Jophiel grinned. 'Is that all the sympathy I'm to get?'

'You're a Poole. And your ship is heading for a close encounter with the Wheel, however it was constructed. You've got work to do.'

41

Twenty-five thousand light years from its home port, GUTdrive exhaust flaring, the crew of the lone ship *Cauchy* prepared to fly into the superstructure of the Xeelee Wheel.

The geometry was simple in principle, staggering in scale. The *Cauchy*, on arrival at the centre, had come to rest just above the plane of the Wheel, a half-radius outside its rim. The ship was, Nicola had remarked, like a fly cautiously inspecting the turning wheel of a tipped-over wagon. Now it was going further in – not towards the Wheel's hub, but at an angle, cutting an arc across the Wheel's open face. The plan was that it would pass through the plane of the Wheel, making a close approach to one deck, and then, heavily accelerating, rise up and make another pass back up through the plane, encountering another deck en routre.

It would use its main drive to achieve this; burning at a full gravity, it would still take more than a year to complete all this, to achieve a flyby.

It had felt like a long year.

Day by day the great structure swelled in the ship's forward vision, a million-kilometre-wide belt hurtling through space. The *Cauchy*'s instruments peered intently at the surface that slowly grew before them, measuring velocities and dimensions, seeking details. Slowly grew, from a line across space, to a band, to a wall that covered the forward sky. From a distance it must look defiant, Jophiel thought, a single spark challenging that monstrous structure.

And then, at nine-tenths of lightspeed, the *Cauchy* flew within the outer arc of the Wheel, and swept low over the Wheel's uppermost deck.

This deck – Deck Three – was thirteen hundred astronomical units above the lowest, Deck One, itself raised above the c-floor, the strange relativistic substrate. All Jophiel saw was a flat plane, soft grey Xeelee hull plate, infinite in all directions, fleeing below the lifedome. Jophiel had once walked on the surface of the Solar System Cache, when it had sailed past Mars. That had been a manufactured plain a mere thousand kilometres across. This great artefact was a *million* kilometres wide – as wide as eighty Earths, almost as wide as the Sun. He could repeat such statistics to himself as often as he liked, but it barely helped him grasp the reality.

Worse yet, the naked eye could make out no detail. After nearly five hundred days at a full gravity's acceleration, the *Cauchy* had reached nearly ninety per cent of lightspeed, enough for some significant light aberration. Even so the mighty structure they were exploring was turning that much faster still, nearly a tenth of lightspeed more. As relative velocities went, that was a lot. The proximity of the spacecraft to such a whirling mass, at such speeds, was, he knew, making instinctive pilots, like Nicola, deeply anxious. Most of the crew were in their skinsuits, strapped into their crash couches.

And for mere onlookers the velocity had the effect of blurring any detail virtually to invisibility – though Jophiel knew there were some *big* features down there. The trajectory had been designed to take them over several of Asher's hypothetical habitable patches, some measuring ten thousand kilometres across or more. More of these had been detected on Deck Two, far below, as well as on Deck Three.

They were features each as wide as a whole Earth, seen as a mere flash of discoloration for a fraction of a second before being whisked away. But once each encounter was over Asher retrieved images of those big patches, and slowed them down, suspended them in the air, magnified, enhanced, swivelled them for perspective.

The first she focused on was remarkably Earthlike.

'Or at least,' Nicola said, standing with Jophiel in the apex suite, 'what Earth might look like if you *peeled* it.'

Jophiel saw a smeared-out scattering of continents, grey or iron-rust red, their edges fractally irregular. Swathes of ocean, greyish-green, with complex ripples visible in the shallowing beds towards the continental coasts. No sign of ice save at the summits of the mountains of what looked like a spectacular chain: an unexpected Andes, snaking along one edge of the largest continent. It was more like an animated map than a world. The air seemed murky but clear, except over one of the lesser continents where what looked like a big storm system was gathering, a huge creamy swirl as seen from above.

Max Ward smiled at all this, as if surveying a world to conquer.

'Like Earth,' Michael Poole said. 'But not quite.'

'Not Earth as it is now, no,' Asher said. 'Or was before the Displacement. It looks a little like Earth as it was about a billion years ago. Hardly any oxygen in the air back then, though it was already building up as photosynthesising plants evolved and spread. There were no land plants or animals, but you'd have found trilobites and such in the sea . . . I've got Harris and his team looking for biology.'

Poole frowned. 'There is spin gravity, of course. But what's to keep that "world" of yours from smearing out across the deck?'

'It's in a kind of dimple,' Asher said. 'An indentation in the deck. We're calling them *cupworlds*. Might not look it – the scale of the Wheel overwhelms detail like this – but this one alone is a thousand kilometres deep. The edge is sculpted, like tremendous cliffs. And since the scale height of Earth's air is only a few kilometres—'

'All the air and water would be contained in the pit. OK. So what's keeping it warm? And safe? The radiation environment around here is pretty lethal.'

'For now I can only guess. We *think* there's some kind of shield over each cupworld. A force field. It reflects some of our sensor tracers. Maybe that serves as an artificial, umm, *sky*. And presumably all the radiant energy pouring down from the stars in this area is absorbed, filtered – the energy re-radiated.'

Poole nodded. 'A simulated sky, tuned to suit whatever is meant to live inside the bottle world. Makes sense.'

'Maybe.'

'Arcologies,' Jophiel said. 'These cupworlds are like arcologies. Enclosed environments on a grand scale, like we built on Mars.'

'Rather larger than our arcologies,' Asher said. 'These are planet-sized dimples, remember. But you could fit a hundred of these side by side across the width of the Wheel. There is room for them all. Some cupworlds are empty,' she said bluntly. She pulled up a couple of images to make the point, images of pits, broad and circular, sharp-walled, flat-floored, their interiors the same milk-white as the rest of this hull-plate construction. 'But most aren't.' She displayed more cupworld images – including one that looked a little like a flayed Mars. Another that might have been a Venus, a deep pond of super-hot carbon dioxide. And a much more exotic model world, a pool of hydrogen and helium and ammonia and ethane and propane and exotic organic molecules . . . Huge lightning bolts flared across the great bowl.

'We think *this* is a Saturn,' Asher said. 'Or at least a model of a gas giant's upper layers.'

'The one-gravity plateau,' Jophiel said. 'I suppose we guessed it would be this way, and here's the proof. This whole artefact, on one level anyway, seems to be a habitat for life. Or a range of habitats. That's what these structures were for, traditionally, by the way. Ring-worlds, in the legends. You'd take apart a planet or two, to create a *lot* of living space.'

Ward grunted, unimpressed. 'A zoo, then.'

Asher said, 'If so, it's a zoo with some exotic residents. Take a look.' She brought up another image.

This cupworld seemed quite unlike the others. It was around the same size as the Earth clone, but there the similarity ended. It was as if the land lay open to a dark, starlit sky. Under that sky there was form, texture, but not structure as Jophiel would have recognised on an Earthlike world. It looked like heaped-up quilts, carpets, overlying each other, silver on black, studded with silver specks.

Jophiel picked out a section for magnification, at random. He found he was looking down on a three-dimensional tangle of rope.

Through which swam silvered balls, like floating toys.

He stepped back, astonished. 'Ghosts.'

Asher was watching his reaction. 'As you said, this is a collection of habitats. A zoo if you like. Big enough, it seems, to sample a Galaxy. Why *shouldn't* there be Ghosts? Listen. Elsewhere we think we saw Spline warships. Or maybe their ancestors, beasts kilometres wide, gambolling in an oceanic cupworld. Maybe there are Qax here . . . we don't know what a Qax *looks* like. Maybe there are species here from all across the Galaxy. Drawn to this vast monument.

'But there's something else here, down on the Ghost cupworld. More relevant even than that. Keep watching.'

In the event Jophiel was one of the last to pick out what she meant, which was odd, given it was his own design, or his template's. In the heart of the silvery Ghost tangle – its signature easily discernible even in a cupworld the size of a planet – was human technology.

A GUTship lifedome.

An obvious wreck.

*

For the crew, that sudden, shocking, entirely unexpected glimpse of a human artefact was galvanising.

The questions flew. Could this be the relic of another plundered scattership, its human occupants held by this party of Ghosts, as their cousins had held Susan Chen's people for so long? And how long had it *been* here? Since both Ghosts and Xeelee had faster-than-light travel, this lifedome could have been brought there long ago – five, ten, twenty thousand years ago, perhaps captured quite close to Sol, as the *Gourd* had been. If so what might have become of its human crew, or their descendants?

Something must be done, about the Ghosts and their captive life-dome. Somehow. Some day. Some time.

But for now there was nothing they *could* do.

The *Cauchy* couldn't land. It couldn't so much as slow down. The ship had already passed the point of closest approach to this upper deck. Still moving at near lightspeed, GUTdrive flaring, now it was heading for its next target, the rendezvous with Deck One, the lowest deck above the c-floor itself – the latter being, according to Asher's best guess, the putative habitat of the Xeelee. Such was the scale of the Wheel that the distance between the two encounter points was itself a fifth of a light year. It would take over eighty days by such a path to get from Deck Three to Deck One.

And even when they got there, there would be no way to land, any more than on Deck Three. The relative velocities would be too high. The journey profile was designed that the ship would make another close flyby to the structure itself, and then sail on into space.

The eighty-two days to the encounter wore down, one by one. The crew spent what was left of the cruise, under Asher's supervision, continuing the remote reconnaissance of the rest of the Wheel. Asher continued to survey her cupworlds. She and her crew grew pretty excited over a couple of worlds they spotted now, one on Deck Three, one on Deck Two, both much closer to Earth-nominal conditions than any they had yet seen. While the Three world looked if anything more favourable, the Deck Two prospect was more accessible. Asher boldly labelled the Deck Two world 'Earth Two', the Deck Three world 'Earth Three', and she laboured to squeeze out more observations, more inferences from the data.

One last sleep for Jophiel.

He woke, on the day of the encounter, expecting fresh miracles.

Which was pretty much how it turned out. With a twist.

42

Jophiel sat with Nicola and others in Michael Poole's apex office. From here they had a grandstand view as the *Cauchy* yet again plummeted, at near lightspeed, towards a surface that itself moved faster still.

To maximise the viewing opportunity the trajectory would cut a shallow diagonal over Deck One, before passing on beyond its rim. So they had a fine close view of the Deck One floor.

But, disappointingly, to first glance it was a blank surface, with none of the detail of Deck Three – or indeed Deck Two, what they'd glimpsed of it.

'No cupworlds here,' Nicola said. 'No toy oceans, no bowls brimming with Saturn clouds.'

Asher said, 'I'm guessing this is the engineering deck – well, we have our own version of that, under the habitable levels of the lifedome. But there *is* some detail. Look at this . . .' She pulled up a magnified Virtual.

Jophiel saw a stream of caches, pouring down from the sky at a stretch of deck. It was like watching hail falling onto an ice sheet. But, he reminded himself, each of those 'hailstones' was the size of a small moon, like the Cache that had rampaged through the Solar System. And, when Asher magnified the image again, Jophiel saw that as the caches approached the deck, they broke up – dissolved into smaller forms, into drones like cut-down Xeelee sycamore seeds, and then further still.

'What hits the deck, by the time it gets there,' said Asher, 'is in the form of Xeelee flowers. After a journey of a light year and fifteen hundred years from Chandra. Quite remarkable.'

'But what then?' Jophiel asked. 'Does the stuff just dissolve into the surface?'

'Basically,' Asher said. 'We have seen great heaps of the stuff, gathered, subsiding, eventually disappearing. The usual seamless conversion of mass to energy, I guess. It's almost as if the Wheel is liquid, its substance expanding as the relativistic stresses gather. As Einstein foresaw.'

Poole said, 'But of course the infall, which is mostly concentrated at spots like this, needs to be distributed across the Wheel as a whole. And I think we're starting to see how that works.'

He pulled up a schematic of the Wheel's three decks, the radial struts that connected them. And branching blue lines, like veins, now spread across these pale, featureless surfaces.

'False colour,' Poole said briskly. 'But, if they look like veins to you, that's not a bad analogy. We've detected motion – streams of it. There seems to be a network of transport channels covering the structure – at every level, and up and down the supporting struts, as you can see. Material flowing back and forth. We don't know how material gets picked up by this network, or deposited at its destination. Those flows are pretty fast, though – a fraction of lightspeed themselves. They have to be that fast to be useful as a structure this size. We have wondered if we could somehow *use* this . . .'

Jophiel said, 'It almost looks alive, doesn't it?'

Nicola predictably scoffed. 'Not like you Pooles to be so poetic.'

Michael shrugged. 'The question is, could we get it to carry stuff? . . .'

That was when the alarms went off.

The whole ship shuddered.

The apex suite deflected sideways with a jolt that shook all the corporeal humans in the room, and Jophiel too, thanks to his consistency protocol routines.

This was the nerve centre of the ship. Every surface was covered with softscreens and other monitors. Now every screen flared red. The air was filled with a screeching howl.

Poole's fist slammed down on a master control. The audio alarm cut out, but the red glare didn't fade. And still that sideways shove was apparent.

They turned to monitors, looking for reports.

Jophiel called, 'Harris's medical system is reporting a mass of minor injuries. A broken wrist seems to be the worst so far. Most people were in their couches. The small children safe in their armoured cots.'

'We have systems crashing everywhere.' Asher seemed bewildered. She was a scientist at heart, Jophiel reflected, better at the slow assessment of evidence than a rapid response to a sudden crisis.

'That's not all that's crashing,' Nicola said angrily. *'We lost the GUT-drive.* And I think I know why. Poole, Jophiel, look at your displays. Don't you recognise the symptoms? Back when the Xeelee first came through your dumb wormhole, into Jupiter space . . .'

Poole punched down on his screen. 'You're right. Quagma phantoms. Suddenly the GUTdrive is full of them. The little critters that followed the Xeelee through the Jupiter wormhole – relics of the early universe, we thought, feasting on the high-density energy in the cores of our ships' drives. They crippled us then. Now they've crippled us again. Lethe. We should have been prepared for this.'

But Jophiel, watching his template, could see he was coming up with an idea, even as he spoke. Something outrageous. Probably suicidal. Something that might work.

Poole turned to him. 'Jophiel, listen. Sever the lifedome. The spine, the GUTdrive pod, is useless now.'

Jophiel felt a spark of unreasonable rebellion – but then, he remembered how the Ghosts had decapitated the *Island.* 'Are you sure? That will strand us here.'

'No choice. Do it! And fast. Slave a copy of my console. Jophiel, I need your help – there isn't the time—'

Jophiel got it.

With a subvocal command, he accelerated his personal processing rate a hundred times.

Sudden silence.

Everything congealed around him: the people, the slowly turning craft – even the flicker of the alarm lights was reduced to a pulse.

He hammered in the lifedome separation commands – a contingency routine he, or his template, had dreamed up long before the Xeelee had come to the Solar System, as a way to save the crew of a GUTship in extreme conditions. 'Doesn't get much more extreme than this,' he muttered. His own voice was loud in the accelerated silence.

The response of the system was swift, even in this high-speed domain. From the corner of one eye, through a clear patch of hull, he saw a flash, explosive bolts firing to cut the spine – to behead the *Cauchy.*

It was almost peaceful here, at high speed. The *Cauchy,* the drifting lifedome. He could stay in this state, and just watch the events of the crisis unfold in slow, exquisite detail.

He laughed. 'Where's the fun in that? *Resume—'*

*

Noise billowed around him. The lifedome lurched still more violently.

'Hold on!' Poole yelled. 'Whatever happens next it's going to be a rough ride.'

And he punched a control with a clenched fist.

Another savage lurch sideways.

Jophiel pawed at his displays, even as the thrust continued. 'The auxiliary thrusters – you're pushing us sideways. Michael, what in Lethe are you doing? We were freefalling, but at least the lifedome was going to miss the deck. Now we're on a *collision course*, thanks to that manoeuvre. Are you crazy? When we hit we'll shine hotter than the Sun—'

Nicola laughed, gripping the arms of her couch. 'I always thought you'd get me killed in the end, Poole, you crazy bastard!'

'We're not dead yet.' Poole just grinned, and rested his head back in his couch. Closed his eyes. 'Come on, Xeelee, don't make me look like an idiot.'

And the lifedome's shuddering stopped.

Just like that. The crew were jolted in their couches, one last time. The alarm lights flared, more angry than ever now that the ship had been truncated. But, otherwise, everything was still.

Jophiel, disbelieving, checked a display, and looked out of the hull.

At an infinite floor.

'We're *down*. Down on the deck. We landed. On the Wheel!'

Asher looked too. 'And, incidentally, we are now moving about a tenth of lightspeed *faster* than we were a heartbeat ago. But I felt no acceleration. It would take a month of a GUTdrive under thrust to do that . . .'

'Told you to hold on,' Poole said, eyes still closed.

'You gambled,' Jophiel said. 'When you deflected us towards the deck, to a projected impact—'

'I figured there had to be an impact defence. We're in a crowded sky; stuff must fall on the Wheel all the time. And we know the Xeelee has some kind of inertialess drive. Probably uses that technology in the internal transport system. Also I figured – well, I hoped – that once it saw we were on a collision course it would just pluck us out of the sky. And set us down, gentle as an egg.'

'You're a crazy bastard,' Asher said. 'It could just as easily have shot us out of the sky. *More* easily.'

'It didn't, though, did it?'

Nicola just grinned. 'Remember, this is the man who gave you the Cold Earth. A man given to wild, reckless gambles nobody else even thinks of.' She thought it over. 'The man, who, as his ship is crashing, *has a first instinct to turn to his enemy for help*. You expected it to have some kind of safety feature, didn't you? As opposed to, as Asher says, a bank of guns that could have blown us to atoms before we got near the deck. How is that oath of bloody revenge coming on, Poole?'

'Psychoanalyse all you like. Once again, Nicola, I'm the man who saved your life.'

'And I'll never forgive you. So what now?'

Poole smiled. 'We check on the crew. And then we work out what to do next.'

43

Poole, Jophiel and Nicola took an elevator down from the apex suite to the floor of the lifedome, where a bewildered crew had already scrambled to fix and secure what was left of their ship. For Jophiel this brought back bad memories of the destruction of the *Island* at Goober's star.

Beyond the dome, utter strangeness.

The lifedome rested on a plain of milky-white substrate, apparently infinite and featureless. There was certainly no sense of the Wheel's curvature.

Above, the Wheel's relativistic sky. No stars were visible, for their light was gathered up in a kind of wash: bluish in the direction the crew immediately started to call 'east', the Wheel's spinward direction, and reddish in the west. The Wheel whirled you around so rapidly that the very starlight was Doppler-shifted, red and blue. A permanent dawn and sunset.

And the sky was cut across by a wide band, sharp-edged, dead straight. That was the Wheel, the next deck up: Deck Two. A band, spanning horizon to horizon, several times wider than the Moon as seen from Earth – even though, Jophiel knew, the deck was fifty times further from this lower level than the Moon itself had been from the home world.

'So, we're down,' Nicola said. She looked at her silver feet. 'On a deck that's moving so fast that for every day that passes here—'

'Fourteen thousand years outside,' Jophiel said.

Nicola just looked at him.

Michael Poole grinned. 'Well, then. No time to waste. Let's get to work.'

With impressive briskness, Jophiel thought, Poole rattled off a set of emergency protocols and specific orders, addressed to the crew in earshot.

Nobody was allowed outside the lifedome, not for now. 'The

footprints and flags can wait until we've crawled over every square centimetre of this lifedome. We're stuck here, and we have to make sure we can survive here. I figure that will take seven days, minimum. I'll post draft schedules. Look, I know you worked hard to get here. Now we have to work just as hard to stay. Let's get organised. Let's do this.'

So, in this twenty-sixth year of their journey, the crew buckled down to this new phase of their lives.

Even Susan Chen was able to help. She did after all have a millennium's experience of survival dependent on ageing Poole Industries GUTship technology, and she was able to point out long-term failure modes nobody else had even thought of.

Meanwhile Poole asked Asher Fennell to begin a ground-level survey of the huge artefact on which they were now stranded. But there was security to think about too, not just the engineering. Who knew what threats waited for them on this artificial world? After all, they had come here precisely to confront such a threat, in the Xeelee. Max Ward was eager to start swivelling the whole crew into a military routine, but Poole resisted that. There was too much work to be done in simply staying alive.

Seven days, then, as they crawled over the lifedome securing their means of survival. Seven days that in the event turned into eight, nine . . .

It was on the tenth day after the crash that Michael Poole finally allowed the footprints and flags.

Ten days in which, thanks to the ferocious time dilation at this level of the Wheel, one hundred and thirty-seven thousand years passed in the outside universe.

44

'I'm stepping down from the lifedome now . . .'

The first human being to walk on the surface of the Wheel, in a heavy, upgraded skinsuit, was Chinelo Thomas. Jophiel, with the rest of the crew, watched through the lifedome hull, made transparent for the day, as sixteen-year-old Chinelo, carrying a small pack, took her first tentative steps away from the dome wall.

A brief meeting to decide on the first pioneer had quickly settled on her, once Max Ward had suggested her name. 'So what if it's Max's idea?' Nicola had murmured to Jophiel. 'She might be one of his acolytes right now but so are half the young people on the ship. She's young, she's smart, she's a leader, and she represents the future of mankind – whatever that turns out to be. Who else but her? Max is one of those incredibly dumb people who sometimes makes an incredibly smart decision, almost by accident.'

Jopohiel was impressed that Chinelo's first words were not some gushy reaction, but were calm, efficient, factual, precise.

'The gravity feels normal. Of course, just as inside the lifedome. Hull plate is almost perfectly smooth, and frictionless, but the Kahra pads on my boots seem to work well. Just think, I'm using stuff for moving around on Xeelee hull plate that was first developed when Michael Poole and Jack Grantt explored the Cache . . .'

'*That* should have been me,' Nicola muttered.

'Let it go,' Jophiel whispered.

'It feels a little sticky when I walk. I have to pick up my feet deliberately. Sooner that than I fall on my butt and everybody laughs.'

'And there's the sixteen-year-old,' Jophiel murmured.

Several paces away from the lifedome now, Chinelo looked around. Lifted her head.

'The view out here is . . . I won't try to describe it. You can feel how

231

big everything is. Those strange glows to east and west. That roadway in the sky, the upper deck, like it might fall down and crush me. It's all *too* big. Maybe we'll get used to it, with time. I'm only a short walk away, but the lifedome looks small already. Fragile. But it's all we've got; we should take care of it, like Mr Poole says . . .'

It occurred to Jophiel that Chinelo, and the other youngsters who hadn't even been to Goober's Star, must have a profoundly deprived sense of distance, of scale. In the lifedome, in interstellar space, everything in the universe had either been no more than a few hundred metres away, or at infinity. He wondered if that would help or hinder them as they tried to learn their way around the Wheel.

'I think I should get out the flags now.'

She opened her pack. She drew out a couple of fold-out poles with Kahra-pad bases that she stuck to the hull-plate floor. Then she shook out two flags, and fixed them to the poles. One was the ancient UN standard, a laurel wreath cradling the Earth against a blue background. The second was the flag of Mars, a bright red globe cut across by non-existent canals.

Michael murmured, 'She asked for the flags herself.'

'I know,' Nicola said. 'Sixteen years old and she looks back to the past. Smart kid.'

Chinelo had the flags set now. She put down her pack and stepped back, and looked around, at the sky, the Wheel floor, the lifedome. 'I know this is a big moment. The kind that only happened a few times before, in human history. Or prehistory. The first time people walked on new continents, on Earth. Like the First Australians. Or when the astronauts first walked on the Moon, the first human footsteps on another world. The first on Mars. And then the first footsteps on the Xeelee Cache, when humans came into contact with an alien artefact, a craft from beyond the stars, for the first time. Armstrong on the Moon said he came in peace for all mankind. Grantt on the Cache said the same thing. I think he meant it, even if it didn't work out that way. Because for sure, the Xeelee hadn't come in peace.

'Now we've come all the way out here. Everybody thinks we came to fight. That we came for revenge, against the Xeelee that wrecked the Earth. We are following Michael Poole, who inspired a whole galactic war against the Xeelee in a different timeline.

'But I was born on the *Cauchy*. I never saw Earth. And I know about relativity. Every time I take a breath here a whole *month* goes by in the universe outside.

'The past is gone. Earth is gone. Even *Cauchy* is gone. I'm not going to claim we came in peace. We did come here for all mankind, I think. I believe we came to understand above all. But if that means war, so be it.' She paused. 'That's all I want to say.' She turned, and Jophiel could see her grin, wide behind her faceplate. 'So, do you guys want to come out now? It's pretty amazing.'

45

It was on the following day, the eleventh since the crash, that Jophiel and Nicola finally got out of the lifedome themselves, and walked on the surface of the Wheel.

Asher was their guide. She seemed in a hurry from the beginning; she walked briskly, directly away from the lifedome, and Jophiel and Nicola hurried to keep up. Nicola wore a new armoured skinsuit of her own – a design had been guesswork by Nicola herself, Harris and others, as nobody quite knew how much her Ghost hide would protect her under the Galaxy-Core sky of the Wheel.

Nicola muttered as they walked, 'So why isn't Poole himself out here?'

Asher said, 'He *should* be. The engineering checks are taking up too much of his attention. Too much time.'

Jophiel nodded. 'It's an occupational hazard, if you're a Poole. But I take your point.'

'Do you?' Asher asked, sounding surprisingly bitter. 'Do you really? Do you *really* grasp what we're facing here?'

'We're out here now,' Nicola said seriously. 'We're listening.'

Asher drew to a halt, panting. 'Just so long as you do.' She spread her arms, and lifted her heavily protected face to the complicated sky. 'Look. Away from the human clutter, the lifedome . . . Take a few breaths to just *look*.'

Jophiel followed her advice. He turned, at random, to the 'east', as they called it, the direction of spin, where the sky glowed a rich blue. Nicola too was looking that way. Jophiel saw that the front of her silvered body reflected blue highlights from the complex sky ahead of her, and her back was painted red by the western sky.

Asher was agitated, one gloved hand pulling at the other. 'Nearly fourteen thousand years pass with every single day we spend here. *Time dilation*. That kid Chinelo got it, right from the beginning. Every breath takes a month, she said. Are none of you *thinking* about what that means? We are – my team and I. And we've been watching the sky – when we've been able to steal time away from Michael Poole's programme of chores. I've told him what we've seen, but he doesn't want to disturb the crew while—'

'Just tell us now,' Nicola said softly.

'Very well. Look, we're going through a new . . . phase now. When events come thick and fast, faster than we are programmed to deal with. One example.' She pointed at the sky, in a direction meaningless to Jophiel. 'Up there. Globular cluster M15. On our fifth day here. *Suddenly it turned green*. The stars, every one – all at once, in our accelerated frame . . .'

Nicola was baffled. 'M15? So what?'

But Jophiel understood, and his unreal heart hammered. 'Nicola. That cluster, seen from Earth, was in Pegasus. That was the way the *Gea* went. After the mutiny.'

Nicola's silver mouth dropped open, behind her faceplate. 'Oh. And if they went out there at lightspeed, nearly—'

'They'd have got there in our *second* day down here,' Asher said. 'And at lightspeed the evidence of whatever they're up to reached us on day five.'

Nicola looked up. 'So what are they doing?'

'Who can know? If they maintained Officer Country and its high-speed processing, They could have become an ancient and powerful culture even before they arrived. And now – well, now they have a whole globular cluster to play with. A hundred thousand stars. That's not all. *Cold Earth*, Jophiel. Remember what was to become of that? On the longest of timescales – timescales we are now jumping over—'

Immediately, he got it. 'Wolf 359.' He glanced at Nicola. 'After the Displacement, Cold Earth got flung out of the Solar System by its residual orbital velocity. Aimed more or less, by chance, at Wolf 359, a red dwarf star. It would have taken somewhere over eighty thousand years to get there.' He shook his head. 'A time that seemed impossibly far in the future—'

'Got there day five,' Asher said bluntly.

'Lethe—'

She held up a hand. 'And on day eight, we saw it.'

'Saw what?'

'We figure they initiated it around AD 100,000, Jophiel. Just

235

about the time we estimated the Xeelee, or its machines, would have finished its work in the Solar System. Reduced it all to dust. Well, that was when Wolf 359 lit up with a beacon. All wavelengths, from gravity waves on up. It reached us on day eight here.'

Jophiel frowned. 'They – whoever they are, whatever they have become on Cold Earth – are broadcasting their presence to the Galaxy, then.'

Asher grinned, uneasy – awed, even, Jophiel thought. 'Yes. A signal that can mean only one thing.'

'They're not hiding,' Nicola said. 'They aren't afraid, not any more. Maybe they are calling the Scattered home. Lethe.' She laughed, apparently from sheer wonder.

'But,' Asher said, 'look at it another way. That's *all* we found. Of humanity, I mean. M15, Wolf 359.'

Jophiel nodded slowly. 'Right. Whereas, if humans had established some Galaxy-spanning super-civilisation—'

'We'd know about it. They'd be *here* by now.'

'But all we found here,' Nicola said, 'is one shabby lifedome in that Ghost cupworld.'

'So there's just us,' Jophiel said. 'And we can't expect any help.'

'Correct. Which is why some of us,' Asher said carefully, 'think we need another solution. Another plan. For our long-term survival, I mean.'

Jophiel shook his head. 'Another solution based on what?'

Asher pointed to the sky. 'The cupworlds. We saw them on the way in. Earth-like habitats, more or less. The chances of survival, long term, in such a structure are much greater than in the wreck of the *Cauchy*. If we can pick the right one. Earth Two, on Deck Two, seems the favourite.'

Jophiel frowned. 'How would we get there? We can't fly any more . . .' Even as he spoke, though, a possible solution to that, at least, occurred to him. 'Anyway I suspect Michael will say this is all beside the point. We didn't come here for cupworlds. We came to confront the Xeelee.'

Asher said, 'But securing our survival needn't compromise that goal. Even if it takes a little more time. Jophiel, we need to put all this together, and to come up with a strategy. And we need to do it fast, because—'

'I know. Fourteen thousand years per day.'

'*The stars are dying*, Jophiel. We're running out of time. Literally.'

He nodded. 'You're right. We need to take this to Michael.'

46

The earthquake hit four days later.

That was what it felt like: a deep shuddering, in the bones of the ground.

Jophiel felt it, of course. His spacegoing instincts had him reach for a skinsuit. If a ship's drive faltered, or some object hit the hull, the first priority was protection from the vacuum. Then a deeper, planetbound reaction cut in. *Earthquake.* He felt a profound, irrational fear at this betrayal by the ground itself, the substrate of the world.

Then it occurred to him that he wasn't on a planet at all.

It took Asher twenty-four hours to come up with an explanation. 'Some kind of impact, we think,' she told the seniors. 'On the Wheel itself. We don't know enough about the Wheel's dynamic modes to figure out what struck, or where.'

'Something big, then,' Michael Poole said sternly. 'A rogue planet. Even a star. Well, there are plenty of those; this is a dangerous corner of the Galaxy.'

Nicola was sceptical. 'We've only been here a few days. How likely is it a rogue star is going to hit in that time?'

Asher shook her head. 'You're not seeing it right. Time dilation, remember. A day down here corresponds to about *fourteen thousand years* outside. One impactor in an interval like that doesn't seem so surprising, does it? As long as we're down on this deck we're going to have to get used to "rare" events happening all the time.'

Poole grunted. 'Good summary. Show's over.'

So Jophiel, and the rest, went back to work. Though Jophiel never felt quite as secure on this mighty construct as he had before.

The next day Michael Poole gathered his seniors at the centre of the lifedome amphitheatre.

Jophiel glanced at their attentive faces, all bathed in the Wheel's relativistic glow. Chinelo, first to walk on the Wheel, was here too, her face open, engaged.

'So,' Poole said without preamble. 'Let's sum up. Here we are, on the Wheel. We already endured an epic journey of unprecedented proportions to get here. We made it, mostly. A remarkable achievement.

'But now we have to do more.

'We have a number of problems.' He counted off on his fingers. 'One. We're stuck in this busted lifedome. And it's all we have. It's all we'll *ever* have, if we stay here. And the longer we sit here, the greater the chance of some catastrophic breakdown. The recycling loops are almost perfectly closed – but not quite; we'll run out of *something*. Or some random piece of debris will fall on us from out of the crowded sky up there.

'Meanwhile, we may be running out of another resource – *time itself*. As Asher pointed out, now that we're stuck in this pit of accelerated spacetime.

'Look, we know there's a kind of universal crisis going on. We know that, because of the infestation of dark-matter agents, all the Sunlike stars are being aged too rapidly. How rapidly? It would have taken the Sun about five billion years to blow up into its red giant stage. Now, it looks like that will happen in just a *million* years.' He forced a grin. 'It sounds a long time. It's not. On this relativistic Wheel of ours, on this deck anyhow, we'll go through five million years in twelve months. Just *one year*, as we experience it, on this deck.

'However . . .'

He nodded to Asher, who stood up now.

'However, we don't have to stay on this deck,' she said. 'We have somewhere else to go.'

'You're talking about the cupworlds,' Chinelo called up.

'You all saw them during the flyby of Deck Three. Environments the size of worlds, indeed – and we found at least two, we think, Earthlike enough for us to survive with a minimum of tech support. Though don't hold me to that before we get up there and figure it out.

'And, listen. The cupworlds may help us solve our other problem. If we climb back out of this relativity pit, *we'll gain more time*. Five million years out in the universe is just a year down here. But that Deck One year stretches out to ten thousand years on Deck Two, and a *million* years on Deck Three. You see? We can win living space, and living time, too. And better yet, we'll leave the Xeelee down here, in its time pit. Until we're ready to deal with it.'

Chinelo frowned. 'But when we get to a cupworld, what if there's somebody already there?'

Max Ward grinned, and bunched a fist. 'We negotiate.'

'I have a question, though,' Nicola said now. 'The cupworlds – *how* do we get there?'

Michael held up his hand. 'We have a solution. Trust me on that. We're working on the details. But we do have one more big problem. Which is—'

'I know *that* one,' Max Ward said. 'The Xeelee. Which is what we came all this way for. Where is it, and how do we get to it?'

Poole smiled. 'Good news – we spotted it. We think. One of Asher's surveys of Deck One. There were some signatures that don't appear to be replicated elsewhere on the Wheel, as far as we can see. Gravity waves, for instance.'

Nicola grunted. 'And the bad news?'

'It's light years away. On this deck, but off around the space-contracted curve of the Wheel. We came down at random, re-member. It could have been worse, but we lucked out.'

Nicola said, 'Tell me you have a way of getting to it . . . Oh. You're working on that too, right? Which is why we need to buy more time. And a place to live. And if that's going to be a cupworld— OK, Poole. What's your brilliant plan to get there?'

Poole kept smiling. 'We build trucks.'

In the end, it was estimated, it would take four months for – as Nicola put it – the crew of a crashed starship to convert themselves into a children's crusade. A hundred and twenty days after the landing on Deck One. A third of their star-life year.

So they got to work.

FIVE

Think of the story of the race. Our timelines emerged from the oceans, and for millions of years circled the Sun with Earth. Then, in a brief, spectacular explosion of causality, the timelines erupted in wild scribbles, across the universe. Humanity was everywhere. But now, our possibilities have reduced.

Lieserl, c. AD 5,000,000

FIVE

47

Earth date: c. AD 1,796,000

'Walk with me,' Michael Poole snapped.

Jophiel was happy to obey.

He rarely got any kind of attention from his template. Nicola and Asher tried to manage the two Pooles' fractious relationship: Asher with tact, Nicola with barbed jokes. As if they weren't to be trusted together.

Yet here they were, in their reinforced skinsuits – one authentic, one a consistency-protocol sham – just one day, three watches, away from departure time. A milestone that Max Ward, who Poole had appointed a particularly ferocious keeper of the schedule for this phase of the mission, insisted was *not* going to be missed by *anybody*. Walking out together, away from the *Cauchy* lifedome, and towards the trucks of the convoy, around which even now there was much frantic activity.

'Second pair of eyes,' Poole muttered, as they approached the first truck, the rearmost of the convoy. 'You know how it is. You *remember* how it is. On every big project, every big milestone, every irrevocable step—'

'I know. You make sure you haven't missed anything. Nicola has stories of the military flyers of the Anthropocene. They were pilots, not engineers. But they'd do the same for their planes. They'd walk around the birds – they'd kick the tyres, Nicola says. Just checking what they could see.'

Poole seemed uninterested in the anecdote. But then he might know it already. Jophiel couldn't remember if Nicola had recounted it before his split with Michael, or after. A shared past could make small talk tricky.

Poole was silent, his stony, AS-preserved face expressionless, softly underlit by the reflected glow from the hull-plate floor. Michael Poole was sixty-nine years old now, and yet he seemed ageless – unlike,

Jophiel thought, the grey avatar who occasionally visited him, who seemed to be ageing with acceptance and grace.

When they reached the trucks, they looked back at the lifedome. Already gutted of its essential systems, its smooth hull broken open by gaping gashes, its inner partitions and structures cannibalised, it sat, still almost elegant, almost wistful, on the pale floor of the Wheel deck. Jophiel reflected that he would never have guessed that the thing had crash-landed here. This fragile component had kept a lost crew alive. But now it had had to be sacrificed to support the next phase of the crew's strange journey.

The best estimate, given by Asher's scratch team of astronomers together with Poole and his engineers, was that they faced a journey of a hundred and fifty days – subjective – across the Wheel to reach Earth Two, the Earthlike cupworld up on Deck Two, that was their destination. Not an easy estimate to make, not an easy plan to construct. The Pooles had built wormholes amid the moons of Jupiter. Now they were planning to *drive* across interplanetary distances. And their cargo could not have been more precious, consisting of, for all they knew, the last humans anywhere, in this future age. The last, including infants and newborn – and, Jophiel thought, that other newborn, the dark-matter larva in its hull-plate pod, stolen from the Ghosts at Goober's Star, which had been carefully stowed in one of the trucks. If that *other* Michael Poole was correct, that particular orphan could turn out to be the most significant refugee of all.

Hence the convoy.

The core of it were the trucks themselves, hastily improvised. Their hulls had mostly been inner buildings, dismounted from the interior of the lifedome and hauled out here, set in a rough line, and equipped with GUTengines and wheelbases. These structures were already robust and had the rudiments of independent internal life support. Before its launch the *Cauchy*'s original design as an interstellar exploration craft had been heavily reworked to make it resilient in case of damage, even purposeful attack, so these inner buildings were like storm shelters. The wheels, meanwhile, were treated with so-called Kahra-pad hull-plate adhesive. Everybody hoped this feature wouldn't be necessary; after all, the simple spin gravity of this astounding artefact kept everything it carried stuck to its inner surface. But the Pooles couldn't be sure of that. After all, to reach Deck Two they were going to have to *climb* . . .

They had no space-capable flitters – all had been mounted in the

GUTship's spine or docked to the base of the lifedome, and had been lost when the dome had been severed from the rest of the ship. They did have one atmospheric-capable craft, a flyer, taken apart and to be carried as components within the convoy until needed. But Jophiel, like Poole, was anguished that they had lost all their spacegoing capability.

Anyhow the two of them walked around the convoy, checked what they could, softly spoke to people labouring to meet their deadlines – they even lent a hand with loading stuff. Everybody knew it was symbolic, nothing more. Just a day out from departure, all the decisions had been made, all the work that could reasonably be done had been finished.

They were committed.

One more sleep.

Then they began.

48

Ship elapsed time since launch: 25 years 257 days

Every step of the way was planned.

The trucks rumbled slowly forward, at no more than walking pace at first, with skinsuited observers outside watching softscreens with diagnostic data.

The convoy stopped after an hour with only a few kilometres covered, and the rest of the watch was spent checking over the vehicles, and fixing minor flaws: an unbalanced axle, one GUTengine running slightly out of true, an odd smell in one of the habitable compartments that turned out to be the result of a clogged algae filter.

The lifedome was still easily visible, a broken bubble on the flat infinite horizon.

At the restart there was a changeover of crew. Now Poole ordered that the vehicles be run up to their operating speed, of five hundred kilometres an hour. The engineers were confident of the capacity of the GUTengines, heavily screened against quagma phantoms, to handle the job. It was the much more primitive mechanics of the improvised wheels and axles and transmission linkages and gears, all hastily adapted from other uses or manufactured with matter printers, that concerned Poole and his team. So, after half a watch's running – a mere two thousand kilometres covered – Poole ordered another halt, another half watch of inspections, repairs, replacements.

On the third watch, at last, Poole allowed a running of a full eight hours at the nominal speed.

After that the expedition settled into a rhythm, of two watches on, one watch off each day. Soon they were making a respectable eight thousand kilometres a day – about a fifth of the Earth's circumference every day, Jophiel reminded himself, an epic journey in the context of most of humanity's history, but a baby's footstep on the Wheel.

After a couple of days there was grumbling about that two on, one off pattern, with a whole watch being 'wasted' every day. The vehicles ran with impressive efficiency, and there was rarely a repair or main-tenance task that could not be accomplished in motion.

But it wasn't just the machinery that needed a break from the end-less travelling. Soon, even Jophiel found himself counting down to the end of another sixteen-hour stretch in confinement, after which the trucks would be drawn up in a rough circle, and people would pour out of the airlocks in their skinsuits, to walk, run, exercise – even play some sport. The children, predictably, made the most of the breaks, with some of the older ones using their hours of freedom to dash away, as far as they could get towards an illusory horizon. Their parents groused that it was just as well that on this table-top of a surface it was impossible for them to get out of sight.

Conversely there were some people who seemed reluctant to leave their cosy interior environments, if they got too immersed in some project – a study, a hobby, work, a game, a relationship. Poole put Max Ward in charge of making sure that everybody got out of the vehicles at least once a day.

Even Susan Chen walked daily. Often she was accompanied by Nicola: two victims of Goober's Star, Jophiel thought, and they made an odd couple, the small, bent old woman, the awkward silver-plated statue. But Harris Kemp said they were good for each other, that Susan was slowly talking her way out of the profound shock of the final revelation of the Ghosts' manipulative kindness, their preservation of the illusion of her crewmates' descendants. 'Walking and talking,' Harris said. 'Best therapy we've got, for both of them.'

So the crew settled into a routine.

They travelled on, and on.

And, as Jophiel never forgot, for every day they travelled, nearly fourteen thousand more years shivered by in the universe beyond the Wheel.

The crew had declared the Wheel's spinward direction as 'east', which in turn determined north, west and south. In those terms the *Cauchy* had landed a hundred and sixty thousand kilometres south of the centre line of Deck One – about a sixth of the deck's width away from that axis.

And so the convoy now headed steadily north, seeking the centre.

They travelled over a featureless, edgeless plain, but with the mighty slash of Deck Two running across the sky above their heads, and the great relativistic washes of light, blue and red to east and west, at least it was impossible to lose their way, Jophiel thought drily. At this rate of travel, including the one-watch stops, it ought to take the convoy some twenty days to reach the centre axis.

On the nineteenth day, they reached the river.

They made an unscheduled stop. Poole left Max Ward in command of the convoy, and led a party forward to investigate: Jophiel, Nicola, Asher, Chinelo.

Asher and her colleagues had long known of the existence of the centre-line hull-plate 'river', in theory. It was part of the grand, networked flow of hull plate around the structure of the Wheel. Their whole strategy for the trip, the whole of their future lives, depended on them being able to understand this latest phenomenon. Understand, and safely exploit.

But they didn't even know how wide it was. It hadn't been clear exactly when they would come to what Jophiel supposed they had to call its 'bank'.

So now Poole and his companions confronted utter strangeness. Standing in a line, looking north, facing – nothing.

'I can't even *see* it,' Chinelo complained. She took a tentative step forward. Tapped the surface with her toe, flinched back. Set down her foot, firmly. Pulled it back. 'Can't *feel* anything strange.'

Asher said, 'But it's there. Look, Chinelo, here's a neutrino scan . . .'

Chinelo looked into the softscreen, and Jophiel looked over her shoulder. To his right, to the east, the 'river' glowed a subtle blue – a blue that intensified the further north he looked. And to the west, a redness, a pink fading to crimson.

Chinelo had grown up with this kind of symbolism. 'Blue shift and red shift.' She stared at the floor. 'It's flowing. From east to west. Even though you can't see a bank.'

'No discontinuity,' Poole said. 'Just a smooth transition. And it's actually a double stream. *Two* rivers, side by side, each ten thousand kilometres across. One flowing west, like this one, its partner flowing east. Each one is stationary at the bank, and at the interface between the streams. At their centre lines they flow the fastest. We actually know how fast. In their centre lines, you're looking at six per cent of lightspeed.'

Chinelo goggled. '*That* fast?'

'It is a big structure,' Jophiel said gently.

'It doesn't *look* like it's going at six per cent of lightspeed,' Chinelo said. Cautiously she probed again with her booted toe.

Asher said, 'There's room for a gradient. If the speed of this moving roadway builds up steadily towards the centre – which it probably doesn't – step in one metre and you'd be moving at about walking pace. Another metre, double that . . .'

'Lethe. So what now?'

Nicola laughed. 'Now we're going to ride this river.'

Chinelo just stared.

Michael Poole looked around, at the engineered sky, the ground, and pointed upwards. 'Chinelo, we don't have a lot of choice. I'm trying to get us to a cupworld up *there*, on Deck Two. And we're going the long way around.' Now he pointed west. '*That* way is the nearest strut – a connection between Deck One and Deck Two, a vertical shaft. It's about two and a half light-days away. That's not much on the scale of the Wheel, only about a thousandth of the circumference. If the wheel were stationary. But it's pretty far in our terms. Two and a half light-days out from Earth would have delivered you to the Oort Cloud. And that's the *nearest* strut. The next nearest, to the east – well, don't worry about that.'

'Two and a half light-days,' Chinelo said, frowning. 'But if we can ride the river at six per cent of lightspeed, that will take us, umm – about forty days?'

'Near enough. Well, that's the plan. The whole point of the flow system is to deliver new hull plate around the Wheel, as seamlessly and painlessly as possible. All we have to do is hitch a ride. But that's probably the easy part. When we get to the strut, we'll need to climb it. Luckily for us there's a river flowing *up* the strut, just as it flows along the deck, though the speed seems to be a lot slower. The distance up to Deck Two is only about a light-minute, but we think it might take us ten days to climb that high.'

Chinelo frowned. 'Going straight up? But we can't drive that way. It would be like driving up a wall.'

Jophiel grinned. 'Don't worry. If we get that far, we'll think of something.'

'OK,' Poole said now. He pointed up, at the line of Deck Two above their heads. 'So we hitch a ride up the strut, and *then* we'll have to ride the river that runs along *that* deck, all the way to the cupworld, which is a thousand astronomical units, more than five light-days, to the east of us.'

'And then?'

Nicola smiled. 'The cupworld. More footprints and flags.'

Chinelo seemed to think the whole thing through. Then she said: 'I'll believe it when I see it.'

At first, at least, the plan unfolded pretty much as intended.

It was on the nineteenth day of the expedition that they had found the river. They spent a day on cautious experimenting. Mapping and measuring. It turned out the river's speed gradient was smooth but not simple; there were stretches of relative stillness swept along by the wider flow, like huge invisible rafts. Driving a truck over the river itself was tricky, as that differential flow caused the wheels to slew. But you could park up in comfort on a 'raft', and just ride. The feature was so useful that Asher speculated it was designed this way, that the rivers had a secondary function, for the Xeelee itself, as a crude cargo transport system.

When they were satisfied, the convoy trundled forward. It took another day or so to reach a raft close to the river's centreline. That generous six per cent lightspeed was not enough to create any relativistic effects visible to the unaided senses. Indeed, even at this speed, the Wheel was so gross in its large scale, so featureless on the small scale, that there was no real sense of motion at all.

That was, until the strut became visible. A wall itself twenty thousand miles wide. Plummeting into view.

Forty-one days after reaching the river, they approached the strut base.

They drove off the river. The strut was a wall that reached from ground to sky, from horizon to horizon. More exploration proved there was indeed another hull-plate 'stream' flowing up the face of the strut surface.

And another day of cautious experimenting proved that getting a ride along the strut, straight up into the sky, would be easier than they had feared. Here, it turned out, the Xeelee had used its inertia-control technology. Somehow the tug of spin gravity was overcome, and a sense of gravity with 'down' pointing into the strut wall was established. Once the convoy was on the strut, the vehicles could simply ride the up-flowing central river as easily as they had followed the deck's own central flow.

Getting a vehicle onto the strut was a challenge, though. There seemed no obvious transitional equipment, no ramps or slings . . .

In the end cautious experiments, made by skinsuited people just walking in, showed that the inertial-control system seemed to incorporate a kind of invisible ramp. If you walked forward you were lifted up, through a smooth right-angle curve, until your feet hit the strut face. And there you were, standing at right angles to your crewmates.

So to get aboard the strut in a truck, you had to just drive forward and hope. It was an interesting experience, Jophiel discovered when he tried it.

It took two more days of trial and experiment before the convoy had been transferred to the strut.

Then ten more days to sit tight, and allow the convoy to be borne up the strut – or across it. To the senses the 'strut' now felt like a bridge between the upended decks, between two vertical walls. Walls that spanned the sky. The architecture of Heaven, Nicola said.

On the expedition's seventieth day, however – over halfway along the strut – they rode through an earthquake.

That was how it felt to Jophiel, who had been trying to get some sleep at the time. The truck he rode jolted, shuddered, rose a little, before settling back on its suspension.

Just like before.

With the trucks still travelling, Michael Poole called a conference, where they made observations, compared notes, and debated the matter. The best idea anybody had was that once again a rogue star, falling out of a Galaxy-centre sky full of rogue stars, had got through whatever defences the Xeelee had set up and slammed into the Wheel – into a strut or a deck.

Back in the Solar System, Michael Poole had once crashed a GUTship into a Xeelee artefact – and later, a whole minor moon had been hurled at the Xeelee sycamore-seed ship itself. Neither had shown the slightest deflection. It was as if, Highsmith Marsden had speculated, Xeelee technology was anchored to spacetime itself. Evidently that anchoring had limits. 'Hit it hard enough,' Poole concluded bleakly, 'and this thing would ring like a tuning fork.'

Asher logged the event carefully. This impact had happened seventy days into their odyssey by truck. As they rose up the strut they had very quickly climbed out of the deep time pit, but even so Asher ascribed the event an astounding external date of AD 2,710,000. Whereas the first impact they'd experienced had happened at around AD 220,000.

Jophiel was flummoxed; he hadn't tracked the cosmic dates so carefully.

They were approaching three million years since Cold Earth. And here was Galaxy Core weather. Raining stars.

He had trouble sleeping.

On the seventy-fourth day they reached the terminus of the strut. They passed through a peculiarly conventional-seeming tunnel, that led them over anther right-angle bent-gravity curve, to the upper surface of the new Deck, Deck Two.

Here they spent another interesting day in their transition to the new Deck, a fresh hull-plate river.

From there, another ninety days.

And they came to the rim of the cupworld.

Earth Two. A place glimpsed only in hasty flybys across astronomical distances. And now their best hope of salvation.

The convoy drove off the river, the trucks were circled, and a camp quickly established.

Then, after a couple of hours, a single truck dragging a trailer laden with the components of an aircraft cautiously approached the cupworld's edge.

49

Ship elapsed time since launch: 26 years 57 days

Earth date: c. AD 2,710,000

The crew emerged from the truck.

Jophiel deliberately took a step away from the others and looked around.

The sky was heavily distorted by their motion, but much less so than at the extreme of Deck One: stars, though blue-shifted and red-shifted, were clearly discernible, all around him, above and below this great platform in space. Time dilation was gentler here too. On Deck Two a subjective day corresponded to a mere seventeen months in the outside universe, compared to nearly fourteen thousand years on Deck One.

Above his head Deck Three, over a thousand astronomical units high, was invisible to the naked eye. Behind him the great flat expanse of Deck Two. Around him his companions, all in their heavy-duty skinsuits, their soles gripping the featureless hull-plate floor: Chinelo, Asher, Nicola, Poole. All looking around with evident curiosity, if not awe.

And before them a captive world, yet another vast feature on a vaster artefact. As if they stood on the other side of the sky.

Cautiously, they approached the rim of the pit. The texture of the ground itself changed at the edge, Jophiel saw. On this side, under his feet in the vacuum, hull plate. Beneath the lid, what looked convincingly like rock – a kind of granite, Asher had suggested.

There was no sense that this was an enclosed pit, no sense of curvature. It was, Jophiel thought, as though he stood at the straight-line edge of some tremendous canyon, as though he looked straight down fifty-kilometre cliffs to a rust-brown ground, where a few splashes of grey-green huddled. Asher had promised there was air down there, with a decent proportion of oxygen, and liquid water, and, evidently, life, though there hadn't been time yet to examine it up close.

Directly below him, near the clinging clumps, he could see a dark snake that might be a river. He lifted his head slowly, following the line of the river across an arid plain, as it made for a blue-grey expanse that might be a landlocked sea.

Then, beyond the sea, more mountains, rounded, eroded.

Beyond the mountains, a grey plain.

Beyond the plain, a distant horizon, perfectly flat as far as he could see, with no sense of curvature. This really was a bowl the size of a world.

All of this was faintly obscured; he was fifty kilometres high, and looking down through an entire atmosphere. He was struck by how few clouds he saw: a few wan layers, spread out below him. And he made out a kind of shading of the landscape, as if cast by banks of cloud – a striping, alternately bright and dark, though the pattern was complex; it swirled and knotted like flow lines. Not cloud shadows, surely . . .

Standing here, he could see there was something separating him, out here in the vacuum in his simulated skinsuit, from the apparently living world below. A layer over the sky. It was like a flat, almost transparent lid, stretching over the whole of the pit as far as he could tell. Or it was like the surface of a very still pond, Jophiel thought now, occasionally visible in elusive reflections.

They'd glimpsed this feature on cupworlds from afar, even during the flyby. The cupworlds were covered by some kind of force field, was the best guess so far. It was presumably meant to keep stuff *out*, such as the unending sleet of Galaxy-centre radiation, rather than keep stuff in; these rock walls were so high that even without this intangible lid the atmospheric loss, from the great puddle of air down there, would have been negligible.

To go further they would have to penetrate that shield.

Jophiel glanced around at his companions.

Chinelo stood and stared. Asher grinned widely, as if delighted by all she saw.

Poole frowned. There was a kind of impatience about Michael Poole, who, Jophiel suspected, saw all this not as an adventure but an obstacle, another hurdle to cross.

Nicola, in her custom skinsuit, seemed puzzled. 'Something odd about those oceans,' she said now. 'And the mountains, come to that.'

Jophiel glanced at her. 'Odd?'

'Odd that they exist at all. This isn't a world, it's a – toy. There's nothing underneath it all but hull plate – as far as we know. So, what about erosion? There has to be weather down there, and where there's weather there is erosion. What happens when those mountains wear away, and the oceans silt up? On Earth, tectonic cycling – the drifting of the continents, the recycling of material through the crust – would turn all the silt back into mountains.'

'There hasn't been the time,' Jophiel said. 'At this level, Deck Two, while the time dilation is a lot less than down in Deck One . . .'

It was a strange paradox of the Wheel's nature that the higher you climbed into its structure, rising up from Deck One, the younger it was – because the higher decks moved more slowly than the lower, and suffered less time dilation.

As seen from the external universe, the best part of three million years had elapsed since the Xeelee had come here to build this thing. On Deck One, the lowest level, less than a year had elapsed since then, as seen by a witness there. But this second deck was five *thousand* years old – and the upper deck, subjectively, was more than half a *million* years old. Such numbers had led to many wild hypotheses among the crew about the sequence in which the Wheel had been constructed.

Asher put in, 'She has a point, though. Even if this cupworld is only five thousand years old you'd build for the future, wouldn't you? A self-sustaining system?'

Jophiel shrugged. 'Maybe there are repair mechanisms, Asher. We just haven't found them yet.'

But Asher scowled, and Jophiel knew that expression. She didn't like it when the universe didn't make sense, and she would keep nagging at the detail until it did. Jophiel felt a spark of admiration. Here was a human dwarfed by her tremendous surroundings, three million years out of her time, staying calm, gathering data, interpreting, thinking.

'So,' Michael Poole said, 'we need to go forward. I'm thinking of a planned sequence of tests of that force-field barrier. Starting with a probe, attached to some kind of lanyard.'

Chinelo stared at him. 'A lanyard? How long is *that* going to take? Oh, look—'

She crumpled up a softscreen and just hurled it at the shield.

They were in vacuum, and in close to a full gravity; the screen sailed over like a brick, even as it unfolded. It fell, and passed through the shield, that elusive meniscus, without any apparent hindrance, and landed flat on the rocky surface beyond.

'Ha!' Chinelo walked forward, and peered down. 'There, I can see the screen is working.' She tapped at a wrist unit. 'Picking up and returning data, just fine.'

Nicola laughed. 'Well done, kid. I have a feeling that if this barrier was meant to hurt us, we wouldn't be able to get even this close. But don't you go marching through it yet, Chinelo. Let's see if it lets through something as complex as a Virtual first.'

Which meant Jophiel. 'Thanks a lot, Nicola.'

Chinelo scowled. 'Not fair.'

Poole said, with the weary tone of an exasperated father, 'Let's just get it done. Jophiel—'

Asher held up her own screen. 'Ready.'

So Jophiel, Virtual heart hammering, stepped forward.

The hull plate dipped down, slightly, so that it passed under the shield surface. Jophiel took one step, two, until his boots were covered by the shining meniscus.

'I feel nothing.'

'It looks like you're standing in a shallow lake,' Asher said.

'Stepping off the hull plate and onto the rock . . . I can feel the unevenness; my boot soles are thin enough for that. It's pretty steep but I think I can walk down it . . .'

The shield, all but invisible, rose up across his body. He could feel nothing.

When he was immersed, he looked back up at the others, standing on the hull plate, looking down. 'Here I am, as intact as I ever was. I can see you, the stars. So.' He struck a pose. 'On behalf of all mankind, I name this world—'

'Oh, no, you don't.' Chinelo came stumbling down the slope after him.

They still had some hours of work to get through before moving on.

The next step was to carry their flyer down through the lid – not an easy chore given the quickening steepness of the rocky rim inside the cupworld. Once through they test-fired the craft's fusion engine and other systems. They checked too, at Poole's insistence, that the flyer could be hauled back out of the pit and would still function.

All this procedure was built on earlier, cautious planning, Jophiel knew. Although the GUTengines in the trucks seemed to have been protected from quagma-phantom attack by improvised shelters of hull plate, Poole had never been happy with similar attempts to rig a GUTengine inside the tight hull of the flyer; there wasn't the room for shielding. Hence, fusion power only, with various kinds of battery backup.

Poole ran the fusion engine through one final startup-shutdown cycle. Then, at last, he nodded. 'Let's get aboard.'

50

With Nicola, inevitably, at the controls, the flyer lifted smoothly off the tilted rock surface of the rim.

At first, with the air density negligible, the flyer was powered as if for vacuum flight, by high-performance fusion-heat rockets with internal propellant tanks. Nicola tested out the controls, careful not to let the flyer ride up and touch the force-field 'sky'.

Then, with an extravagant gesture, she sent the craft on a long sweeping dive, down, down past the rocky face of the peripheral cliffs, down and seeking the thicker air, where the ramjets would cut in: atmospheric air sucked in and superheated to be used as propellant. Deeper yet, when the atmosphere was thick enough, the flyer would become a true aircraft, relying for lift on the thickness of the air flowing over its wings.

Poole, sitting up front with Nicola, glared out. Asher was intent on her screens and other monitors.

Chinelo pointed back over her shoulder. 'The Rim Mountains.' She pointed up. 'The Lid. We ought to start naming stuff, if we're going to live here.'

Nicola said, 'There may be people here already, of course. Who already gave stuff names of their own. Kind of disrespectful not to ask, don't you think?'

Chinelo scoffed. 'Look down there. What people? Where?'

'I can't answer that,' Asher said. 'Not yet. But I can tell you that this world not only looks like Earth, it is turning out to *be* like Earth, in the detail. Oxygen-nitrogen atmosphere, thick enough down there to be breathable for us, and without any nasties – not an excessive carbon dioxide percentage, for instance. A lack of ozone, but maybe that's insignificant given the shielding effect of the Lid. Earth*like*, if not Earth. But the humidity is down, compared to the Earth average.'

'You mean it's dry,' Chinelo said. 'Like a desert.'

'Not quite—'

'I can tell that much. And *I* never saw a planet before.'

'At forty kilometres now,' Nicola said. 'Aero surfaces starting to bite . . .'

A glance out of the window showed Jophiel how she was still tracking down the face of the Rim Mountains, leading the craft through smooth S-shaped curves as the flyer's aerosurfaces explored the unfamiliar air.

Asher said thoughtfully, 'Well, you're right, Chinelo. My first estimates say there is about one-third ocean cover here, to two-thirds land. The reverse of the proportions on Earth. And the air is a little thin, and lacking water vapour – there must be a ferocious dip in temperature at night, even if it's hot during the day. Like a high desert on Earth.'

Nicola grunted. 'You're missing the fundamentals. What night? This *isn't a planet*. It doesn't spin on its axis, it doesn't orbit a sun – it can't have a day-night cycle. I know there are worlds that keep one face to their stars the whole time. But life like ours evolved on worlds that spin.'

'True enough,' Asher murmured. 'So, if you were going to build a refuge maybe you'd mimic some kind of day-night cycle. Life from Earth, at least, depends on it.'

Jophiel nodded, and he leaned forward so he could see the sky, the Lid. 'Hence, maybe, those stripes of shadow.'

From underneath, that flow-like effect in the sky was much more marked, a clear diminution of the light in huge, swirling, interlocking bands. And where the bands were at their most opaque, Jophiel saw, significant shadows were cast on the ground below.

'Like zebra stripes,' Chinelo said. 'Not that I ever saw a zebra.'

Asher stared. 'You're right, though. That *is* how it looks, a sort of organic, self-organising pattern. And this must be it – the key to day and night. Over a given spot on the ground, those bands coalesce or scatter, blocking or admitting the light through the Lid. It's going to take some analysing, starting with a timing of the cycle. I wonder if it's smart enough to mimic seasonality? Or the effect of latitude – long polar nights?'

Nicola grinned, not unkindly, as far as Jophiel could read the expression on her silvered face. 'You've got a lot of fun studying to do, that's for sure.'

Abruptly, reflected light flared through the pilot's window.

Even Jophiel winced, before the windows cut down the incident light. Looking out, he saw they were descending past a brilliant white surface.

'Sorry,' Nicola said. 'Got too interested in your fascinating conversation. Flying down smooth and easy. We just ducked down under eight kilometres from the mean surface. We're no higher than the tallest mountains on Earth, now. And we're flying parallel to that reflective layer in the rock face.'

Jophiel looked out at what looked like a snowfield, clinging to the upper flanks of the Rim Mountains. 'So I guess we're at an altitude where ice is going to form?'

'Maybe,' Asher said, staring at her softscreen rather than the view. 'But that's not ice – or not all of it. That's hull plate – I think. Or some variant. Not much of it, just a skim.'

Poole frowned. 'It doesn't *look* like hull plate. Not the usual texture. And look at its lower edge. It looks like it's turning brown. Crumbling, even . . .'

'Aha,' Asher said.

That irritated Nicola. 'You can be smug, Fennell. Some new puzzle you figured out?'

'I think I know how the mountains stay up, instead of eroding away. I'll tell you when I'm sure.'

Flying low now, and evidently handling easily, the flyer fled directly away from the Rim Mountains into the interior of the cupworld.

51

They flew low over rusty plains. Briny-looking lakes. It resembled Mars, Jophiel thought – or at any rate a partially terraformed Mars, one dream that had never been fulfilled before the Xeelee came.

Yet there was life here. Jophiel made out clumps of tough-looking grasses now, and even stubby trees, their leaves small, the species unrecognisable – to Jophiel, anyhow. But then the Pooles had never been naturalists.

'High Australia,' Chinelo said now.

They looked at her.

'The name for this place. I was thinking. I saw Virtuals of Australia on the *Cauchy*.'

Probably, Jophiel knew, last-chance-to-see records of Earth, before it was lost to the Displacement, and the cold.

'You wouldn't let me be first out through the Lid; at least you can let me *name* it.'

'I keep reminding you,' Nicola said, 'there might be people here already, human or not. And they might already have their own name . . . What is *that*?'

Jophiel glimpsed motion on the ground below. It was gone in a glimpse, such was the flyer's speed.

But Jophiel thought he had seen a gaggle of what looked like big, long-legged chickens.

Being chased by what looked like a big, long-legged rat.

'Earthlike,' was Nicola's only comment. 'Slightly evolved, maybe. But clearly Earth stock.'

'From the scatterships?' Jophiel said. 'Captured, like the Ghosts took Chen's ship, brought here, released into the wild?'

'Not much time for evolution,' Asher murmured. 'Like we said, this cupworld can't be more than a few thousand years old, locally. I suppose some quick adaptation is possible. Plenty of ecological niches to fill in such an empty landscape.'

Poole just shrugged. 'We don't know enough yet.'

'So,' Nicola said, 'should I divert and chase those . . . chickens?'

Asher asked, 'Are we still heading for the ocean?'

'Right now, yes.'

'Then keep on in that direction.'

Poole frowned. 'Why the ocean?'

'I'll tell you when I know.'

So they flew on, over more flat terrain, across which wandered rivers, wide and shallow, their water sluggish, red-tinged – Jophiel wondered if the stream he had seen coming out of the Rim Mountains had become a tributary of one of these weary flows. He glimpsed more life, trees and scrub grass and other less identifiable vegetation, mainly growing close to the water courses.

And here and there – where the water was more accessible, at shallow banks, and around oases that reflected the sky with pink glimmers – he saw animals. Cautiously gathering to drink, he supposed.

More variants, he thought at first glance, on the theme of rat and bird. If this was a biosphere it was an impoverished one. Although, from what he recalled of the original Australia, watching from the air you would have seen little of life but kangaroos and wallabies and humans, with much of the detail of a still-rich fauna to be discovered down at ground level.

The 'daylight' seemed to be getting brighter, Jophiel thought. Evidently they had arrived, by chance, in a simulated 'morning'.

As they approached the ocean, the landscape subtly changed, with a sandy soil mounting up into fields of long, shallow dunes, and the grass becoming scrubbier, paler, longer.

Then they flew out over the ocean itself. Asher was intent on her screens.

Nicola murmured, 'Do you think there are tides here? I wonder how you would simulate *that* . . . How far out do you want me to go? This pond could be pretty wide.'

'And,' said Poole, ever cautious, 'by flying over water we lose several failsafe modes.'

'Just keep on,' Asher snapped, still intent.

Jophiel stared down at the grey ocean, low waves rushing beneath the craft's prow. He wondered what life might be found down there. Some of the scatterships, carrying scraps of Earth's doomed ecosphere to the stars, had been more or less aquatic, he recalled; some had even carried fish, dolphins, dwarf whales – and the plankton and the rest of the food chain they depended on. He pictured all of them spilling out of some cargo hold, spreading out into another huge, empty biome. And, maybe, land grasses mutating to some kind of seaweed, perhaps, or rats evolving into the equivalents of otters or seals—

'I knew it!' Asher shouted now.

Nicola grunted. 'Thanks for yelling in the pilot's ear. *What* did you know?'

'The answer.'

'To what?'

'That puzzle about the erosion. How can a world without any geology not get worn flat, all of the mountains eroded away into sea-bottom ooze? I think I have it . . .'

Nicola said, 'Terrific. Now, do you mind if we turn around and head back before we run out of fusion fuel?'

As the flyer banked, Asher spoke eagerly. 'You were right, of course, Nicola. Erosion *must* occur, even here. Now, there's no geological process of uplift to compensate for that erosion. This is just a big machine. And so I knew there must be some mechanical solution.'

'Huge pumps,' Poole guessed. 'Taking the sea-bottom ooze, consolidating it, and pumping it up to be dumped on top of the mountains again.'

'No,' Asher said bluntly. 'I thought of that. Firstly we saw no sign of pumps and pipes. Second – it's not the Xeelee way. It's not *elegant*. I think they would do it using the hull-plate approach.'

Jophiel thought that over. 'Umm. Converting energy to mass. Suppose they repaired the erosion on the mountain tops with mass nucleated out of energy flows from the sky. The result might be that odd-looking hull plate we saw at five kilometres.'

Asher nodded eagerly. 'That's what I'm thinking. Just where the erosion would start kicking in, where the air is thick enough, yes. I looked it up. On Earth, before the Displacement, weathering around the world would deliver dust to the abyssal plains – the ocean deeps – at a slow but steady rate. Two or three centimetres' thickness, per *thousand* years. But that is a lot of stuff, a few centimetres over deeps that covered half the planet's surface.'

'OK. So you're suggesting the Xeelee fix the loss from the mountains with an energy-mass transformation. Even at such a rate that must be an expensive power drain.'

'I figure it's pretty high, yes. Something like a *hundred thousand* times the energy Earth once received from the Sun. But this isn't the Earth.

But you'd need to deal with the deposition in the ocean basins, as well as the erosion from the peaks. I was looking for mass *loss* down there, to match the deposition rate. And I found it.' She tapped her softscreen. 'A tiny effect, but we have sensitive instruments. Probably the mass loss and creation are connected to the wider hull-plate river network, a tremendous flow of massed energy; compared to *that*, all of this is a detail.'

Poole scowled. 'Good work,' he said, sounding indifferent.

Asher scowled and shut up.

They turned and flew back over the coast at a lower altitude. And Jophiel started to make out a new set of features, now. At first they looked like shallow craters, like the Moon's, each a neat circle of rim wall a couple of kilometres across, with a stubby hill, or mound, in the centre. Yet the features seemed somehow too orderly, too similar in size, to be the product of impacts – and besides, he'd have expected the Xeelee defence to keep out minor impactors. These features were sparsely scattered, but there were a lot of them, he saw now, panning over the landscape. Some vaguely clustered close to visible water sources, others were more haphazard.

They flew on for a while. Then Nicola banked the flyer sharply, heading to the right. 'Hey, Chinelo. You want to know what this place is called?'

She pointed out of her window.

Jophiel leaned over to look.

There was a woman on the ground.

'Ask her,' Nicola said.

Nicola brought the flyer down, slow, smooth and quiet, a good distance from the woman – the native, Jophiel thought they would have to call her. 'Don't want to rustle a hair on her head,' Nicola murmured.

She stood alone, near a rock bluff. Her skin dark, her hair wild, her clothing looking like rags. Her feet bare. She had some kind of pack on her back.

On Poole's command they climbed out one at a time, slowly, hands away from the body, empty and open. As unthreatening as possible. Nicola, the scary silver statue, was ordered to follow behind the rest.

If Nicola was last out, Chinelo had been first. 'Lethe,' she murmured. 'Another first footstep for me, and nobody even noticed.'

'Can it,' Poole said. 'No sudden moves, nobody call out. We've got no idea what we've walked into here. She needs to know we've come in peace. Let's go forward, together.'

The light was quite bright, Jophiel noticed as he walked into this new world – indeed, a new kind of world. Like a hazy sunlight, flat and shadowless, from a glowing sky.

The woman stood alone, a scrap of verticality in a flat landscape, beside her rock bluff. Quite unmoving. Hands loose at her sides, as empty as the visitors'. Jophiel made out a few more details. A black scar on the ground behind her might be the remains of a fire. She seemed to have backed this rudimentary camp site up against the bluff, as if for cover. Which in turn implied, of course, there was something she needed cover from.

When they had got to within twenty or thirty paces, they stopped, and Jophiel held his hands up. 'Let me go first.'

Nicola snorted. 'You aren't even real!'

'I look real enough,' Jophiel said. 'And I can't come to any harm. I can't *do* any harm.'

'Just go,' Poole said tensely.

Jophiel spread his hands wider, fixed a grin, and walked forward alone, towards the woman.

And he didn't even see the woman's motions. Not until later, when he relived the experience as a slow-motion flashback.

She had reached behind her back with two hands. One had emerged with a small but sturdy bow, the other with an arrow.

She nocked the arrow. Fired. Turned and ran.

Later Jophiel would muse on how many hours, years, of practice those simple, artful motions represented. The arrow was well made too, a finely sharpened stick, apparently fire-hardened, a flight of what looked like chicken feathers.

In real time, he had little chance to observe any of this as the arrow passed through the space between his eyes.

There was a wrenching, unreal sensation as his consistency protocols were violated as never before. He staggered, but didn't fall.

Chinelo grunted, 'Leave her to me.' And she ran after the fleeing woman.

That was when Jophiel heard Nicola cry out. He whirled around.

The arrow had dipped a little in its path, as it had flown on to its second target. It was buried in Nicola's chest – buried up to its flight. And she was already falling.

Ignoring his own consistency-violation agony, Jophiel started to run back. Poole and Asher moved too, trying to grab Nicola before she hit the ground.

'Got her,' Chinelo called over their comms link. 'The local. With my blaster. Shot her in the back. Just stunned her. Bet you're glad now that Max Ward put us through weapons drill, Michael.

'Oh, one thing I noticed.

'She's from the *Gourd*.'

52

Up close the woman was surprisingly small in stature. Jophiel might have mistaken her for a ten-year-old among the crew. But she was clearly much older than that, lithe, strong-looking, and her hair was a scraped-short frizz of grey curls.

They had to get both Nicola and the cupworld woman back to the flyer. Chinelo was able to carry the unconscious woman over one shoulder, her blaster in the other hand.

Asher and Poole, meanwhile, cradled Nicola, one to either side, their arms interlocked around her waist. That arrow protruded horribly from the centre of her silvered chest, but there was no blood – or blood equivalent – and Jophiel realised uneasily how little he knew in detail of Nicola's adapted anatomy. He hoped Harris Kemp and his team would know more.

Such was Nicola's weight that both Poole and Asher were struggling, sweating, stumbling as they made for the flyer.

Jophiel, feeling useless, hurried alongside. 'I'm sorry I can't help you.'

Poole grunted. 'I wonder if Columbus had this kind of trouble.'

'The Hawaiians killed Captain Cook,' Nicola mumbled now. She raised a blank face; her voice too was eerily expressionless. Jophiel was surprised she was conscious at all, and he wondered if some kind of backup system was cutting in. 'Just for once will you shut up, Poole? Every time you flap your mouth this Lethe-spawned arrow feels like it twists around.'

'You keep quiet too, then,' Poole said with grim determination. 'Nearly there.'

Back at the flyer, they found that Harris Kemp had already thrown down a skinsuited Virtual copy from the convoy at the top of the Rim Mountains. He supervised briskly as Asher and Poole manhandled their limp, heavy, awkward, precious load through a hatch that suddenly seemed much too small for the purpose.

Chinelo, meanwhile, carried her prisoner around the back of the flyer, where there was a small cargo hold with no access to the cabin. She dumped the native inside, leaving the woman's pack on the ground outside, climbed in herself, and pulled the hatch closed after her.

Jophiel said uncertainly, 'I *guess* that's the right thing to do. What else could she do, stake the woman to the ground? But—'

'But we just imprisoned the first local we saw. Some first contact. And Chinelo is only sixteen years old,' Asher said.

She and Poole were, under Kemp's instructions, scrubbing down a couch with antiseptic gel in preparation for laying Nicola on top of it. Nicola herself for now was slumped over in her favoured pilot's couch – not that she was going to be doing any piloting any time soon. And, in a chilling bit of ship's procedure, Asher had already slapped a bracelet on her wrist, stamped with the name of the *Cauchy*, and Nicola's name, ship's date, time of injury.

Still that arrow protruded from her chest. It was only wood and feathers and some kind of glue, Jophiel saw. Yet it was a thing of artistry in itself.

Harris said to Jophiel, 'We have to stabilise her. But the good news is that I'm confident Nicola is going to survive. That's because her inner layout is a jumble compared to ours. In fact Nicola's heart is down in her stomach cavity, and the arrow hit one of the complementary components the Ghosts loaded in there – it's like a sac of seaweed. But look, this will be a complex procedure. That's precisely *because* her inner layout is a mess.

'You two.' He pointed to Asher and Poole. 'Scrub with gel. I can instruct, but you're going to have to do the heavy lifting. In the meantime, Jophiel—'

'You're in the way,' Poole growled.

Jophiel glanced over at Nicola once more. 'Tell me when you have news.'

And with a subvocal command he threw himself into the hold.

Where, among smooth-walled boxes of supplies and spare parts, the captive woman was awake, and wide-eyed, and facing an armed Chinelo.

When Jophiel materialised out of nowhere, the local did an admirable job, Jophiel thought, of staying calm. In fact, when she had got over a reflex startle, she jabbered a string of words at him. Her tone was challenging, her words incomprehensible – though Jophiel thought some of the vocabulary was elusively on the edge of familiar.

Chinelo, a little glassy-eyed, kept her blaster pointing at the woman. Maybe she was working through the shock, Jophiel thought.

'Keep her talking,' Jophiel said.

'She won't *stop* talking.'

'Good. So we already have a few minutes' worth of records to work with.' With a subvocal command, he set a translation routine working in the ship's processing suite, ordering it to download any results straight to his own awareness.

Meanwhile he smiled at the woman, as calmly and reassuringly as he could. Trying not to think of the arrow this woman had shot into his friend – an arrow meant for him, in fact. After all, he was the alien invader here.

'My name is Jophiel. I imagine you're wondering why I'm an identical copy of the other man you saw. He's called Michael . . .'

The woman just stared back, and gabbled some more.

'That's it, good, just keep talking, give the translator processor a chance to work . . .'

Chinelo said, 'She tried to bust out twice.'

'What did you do?'

Chinelo waggled her blaster. 'Stun setting. Milder than when I took her down outside.'

Jophiel stared. 'How old are you again? . . . You don't fool around, do you?'

For the first time Chinelo sounded uncertain. 'Did I do wrong? This is how Max trained us. A weapon isn't some magic wand that controls people when you wave it around; you have to *use* it. I was on my own in here. If she had got away, broken out—'

'It's OK. As far as I can see you did exactly the right thing. In fact if not for your quick decision-making, the rest of us couldn't have concentrated on Nicola as we did . . . I'll report back to Max, when he gets here. Good job, Chinelo.'

She stayed expressionless, but seemed calmer. 'OK. But what now?'

'Now we need to make contact with this woman. Just be patient.'

Still she spoke; still they waited for the translator software to cut in, though again he thought he detected repeated words, phrases – some of them sounded like much-evolved versions of Standard, his own language. Her name, maybe. Demands to be let free. Threats of retribution. Not, he thought, pleas for her life; she looked too defiant for that.

At least he had the opportunity to study the woman up close. She wore a smock of some kind of hide, scraped and stitched together, quite finely, with threads of what looked like tree bark, leaving her arms and legs bare. Boots of a tougher leather. The bare skin of her arms, legs, even her face, was covered, he saw now, by a fine pattern, a tracery of lines, thin and black, nowhere interlocking. Tattoos, like an image of the sky.

'This is how people live, in an environment like this,' he said to Chinelo. 'A bare landscape, resource-depleted. They turn in on themselves, in a way. Their own bodies become a canvas. We called this place High Australia because of the landscape; maybe it has some cultural similarities too.'

'She's kind of short,' Chinelo said. 'Shorter than me. Shorter even than you.'

'Thanks,' Jophiel said drily. 'But it's a common adaptation, among animals anyhow. Any place where there isn't much to eat. A person half your height would need only an eighth the food you eat. The square-cube law.'

'Do you think she's still human? I mean, these people have been here all on their own, for a long time.'

He shook his head. 'Not that long. On this Deck it's only a few thousand subjective years since the Wheel was created, remember. These people can't have been here longer than that. That's enough time for cultural institutions to collapse, changes in language – and for this woman's people to adapt to a lousy food supply by growing a little shorter than her ancestors. But she's human, all right.' He looked at Chinelo. 'Out there, you said she was from the *Gourd*. The ship that was captured and taken to Goober c by the Ghosts.'

The woman looked startled at that evidently familiar word. *Gourd.*

'How could you know that?'

Chinelo grinned. 'My young eyes are sharper than yours, I guess, Jophiel.' She pointed. 'Look for yourself.'

On one wrist, Jophiel saw now, the woman wore a medical bracelet – just like the one Nicola was wearing right now, in the cabin. Virtually indestructible, it could well last for millennia if cared for, Jophiel realised. And, on its worn surface, one word was clearly visible. The name of the ship it had come from, from whose crew this woman's ancestors must derive: *Gourd.*

Suddenly her speech became clear, rendered into accent-free Standard by the flyer's software.

'. . . My name is Wina. I am of the People of the Vanquished First Slaver. You need not thank me for saving you from the First Slaver woman.'

'I – what people? Who? . . . Never mind. Very well. I won't thank you. She was, is, a friend. The, umm, First Slaver woman. My name is Jophiel.'

She listened carefully. 'Jophiel.'

'That's right. This is Chinelo.'

Chinelo grinned, and raised the weapon. 'And *this* is called a blaster.'

The woman looked at the blaster dismissively, then studied Jophiel, evidently suspicious.

He nodded. 'You may have observed I am different from the others. Different from you.' Jophiel passed his hand into the wall, and out again, with a tingle of consistency-protocol violation. 'You must not be alarmed by this.'

The woman thought it over. 'Can you use a bow?'

'No, I—'

'You will soon go hungry, then.'

Chinelo suppressed a snort of laughter.

'And you may have wondered why I am identical to the other man you saw.'

She thought that over. 'He who carried the wounded First Slaver woman.'

'Why do you call her Slaver? . . . Never mind. Yes, that man.'

She shrugged. 'You are nothing like him. Will you let me go now? I must hunt, or my family we will soon go hungry.'

Then came a message from Max. Aerial surveys had revealed what looked like the woman's home base.

Tepees, built in the corpse of a downed Spline ship.

53

Seven days later, a party from the convoy took the local woman home.

It had been easy enough to locate the woman's community, out in this table-top of a landscape. Max Ward had flown down from the rim and put himself in charge, however. And he decreed the *Cauchy* crew should walk in from the site where the flyer had first grounded, rather than fly. The less obtrusive an entrance they made the better; a flying machine would presumably terrify, or enrage, a people dependent on bows and arrows. And, Max argued, the less they showed of their strength, the better.

They did leave Nicola behind, over her protests, as she was still recuperating – and in the interests of diplomacy, given the way she had alarmed Wina enough on first contact that the woman had immediately tried to kill her.

So, led by Wina, the party set off. It turned out to be a tough ten-kilometre march over bare, unyielding ground.

En route they were chased by chickens.

At least, Jophiel thought they were chickens, or some kind of descendants. Muscular-looking birds the size of turkeys, with colourful plumages of gold and green, stocky legs, and crests of virulent red. All males, according to Harris Kemp. And, according to his softscreens, they looked a little like the guinea fowl from which domesticated chickens had descended. The birds took great offence to the passage of these unfamiliar humans, and their determination to give chase wasn't deflected by the felling of a couple of them by Max Ward's blasters. Wina showed them that standing still, shouting, and waving your arms worked a lot better.

Still, they got through the journey in a reasonable time. Max Ward had planned it out: they had started early, not long after this cupworld's eerie 'dawn', and arrived mid-afternoon of the local twenty-three-hour 'day'.

And even from the ground the village of the People of the Vanquished First Slaver was not hard to find. For, as the aerial surveys had already discovered, it nestled in the shadow of the great carcass of a Spline starship.

A few hundred metres from the village, the *Cauchy* party hung back, to recover, re-equip, and spy out the land before going in. From this distance the relic of the Spline looked like the stripped skeleton of a whale, Jophiel thought. Giant ribs towered over the scrappy human settlement, like the ruin of some tremendous cathedral. It was a relic of some incomprehensible, forgotten war, Jophiel supposed. Yes, and this was how interstellar war would leave a Galaxy. Monumental wrecks looming over diminished populations of survivors scrubbing for survival in the dirt. He wondered how it had been in that other timeline, in that other Galaxy which had been overrun, not by Ghosts and Qax and Spline ships, but by humanity: what ruins might have been left behind.

They were soon spotted. Jophiel could see people climbing high in that enormous ribcage, looking back at him. Descendants of the crew of a scattership – descendants of Jophiel's own contemporaries in fact. Clambering over the ribs of a dead alien.

Max Ward was studying a rough map sketched on a softscreen. 'Just so we know where we are.' He pointed. 'Here are the Rim Mountains. Here *we* are. The village of the People of the Vanquished First Slaver. Here's the river it sits by.' He traced with a finger. 'You can see how the river is a tributary of a greater artery that feeds into the ocean *here*. We think we see one of those crater-like structures there.' He pointed to pyramidal icons. 'And here, here, here, more of them.'

'Not surprising.' Asher consulted her own screen. 'From the air, we spotted these structures all over the landscape. All about the same size, crater-like ring walls centred on mounds. We asked Wina about them. She called them Libraries. That's the best translation of her word, anyhow.'

Max scowled. 'Why would an illiterate culture need a library?'

'Illiterate maybe, but highly intelligent, and highly sophisticated,' Asher said. 'That's been evident since the start of our contact with them a week back. They are the descendants of a scattership crew, remember. We shouldn't make any assumptions.'

'OK,' Max said grudgingly. 'But – look, we landed at random, and hit on these village folks at random. My view is we should go straight for the ocean. The flybys picked up more settlements there, even boats

273

of some kind. The more sophisticated the culture the more we'd have to gain. We'd even learn a lot more by cracking open one of those Libraries.'

Poole looked stern. 'We aren't "cracking open" anything, Max. We have two goals, remember. The ultimate aim is to find a way to get to the Xeelee. But the second is to find the crew a place to live, now and in the future. And if that's to be here, we need to find a way to get along with the neighbours. These people know their world. We know nothing, yet. We need to learn.'

Max laughed. 'What's to learn from a bunch of degenerate savages?'

The answer, as Jophiel was not surprised to discover, turned out to be a great deal.

They walked on.

The village was a gaggle of tepees and other, more functional structures – racks for hanging meat and furs, small workshops evidently for the manufacture of bows, arrows, clothing, various tools. Jophiel saw low fences. Stockades, which contained what looked like big, strong-looking rabbits.

The tepees were of all sizes – but oddly, the apparently ceremonial structure to which the guests were led was only the second largest. Two young people, one female, one male, sat watchfully on the ground outside the largest of all, which was sealed up. Chinelo asked bluntly what was in there; the response was silence.

Inside the designated tepee, under a conical roof, the elders of the village sat in a circle. Among them was Wina, who seemed more impressed to be allowed into the elders' tent than by the presence of the folk from the *Cauchy*.

The visitors were handed clay cups containing what tasted like strong beer.

Jophiel discreetly conjured up his own Virtual beer cup, in order to join the party. None of the elders showed any alarm, any more than when he had pulled similar stunts before Wina back in the flyer. These seemed a phlegmatic people. Maybe that came from growing up under the wreck of a living starship.

Jophiel, or his template, had always been more interested in engineering than people. Technology rather than anthropology. Yet he had the feeling that this scene must have been played out in one form or another across the Earth over many millennia. The strangers greeted in the tent, the sharing of gifts. The essence of what it was to be human, surviving at the centre of the Galaxy. Jophiel found it somehow pleasing.

Michael Poole, meanwhile, had quickly entered grave, if not very pointed, discussions with the elders, both sides translated by *Cauchy* software. The villagers' talk was dominated by descriptions of relationships, marriages, legacies, hunting trophies – and some complex discussions of the mixture of farming, stock-rearing and hunting that kept the people alive here. Primitive they were, but not ignorant.

Not only that, they knew exactly where they had come from. And when.

The most wizened of the elders said now, 'The people were brought to this world many days ago. How many days?' She worked her fingers in a complex sequence, which Jophiel guessed was some kind of finger-counting mnemonic.

As she worked, Jophiel studied the fine tattoos on her face. He had already learned, by asking Wina about something she took for granted, that every person here was marked with an impression of the light-and-shade patterns in the sky on the day of their birth. If more than one was born on a particular day, especial care was taken to distinguish the zebra stripes. Thus, every person was made as unique as an individual day, maybe even a particular hour. Wina had been curious about why so many of the crew didn't wear tattoos at all – and what was the meaning of the green tetrahedra some wore on their foreheads . . .

At length the elder pronounced, 'Two million, sixty-four thousand, seven hundred and fifty-two days on this world . . .' The translation back to Standard, from which these people's language had evidently descended, was clearer when numbers were pronounced. Perhaps such core words defied linguistic shifting a little more than others. Now she flashed her withered fingers once more. 'Twenty-three hours in the world's day. Twenty-four in the ship's day. This is the true age of the land. Every hundred days we send a runner to the Library with the number we count, as do others like ourselves. The Library remembers . . .'

Asher leaned over to Jophiel and whispered, 'They've remembered the key facts, after all this time. And they must have counted *every* day since they came here . . . The First Australians were good astronomers, in the same way, with a deep shared memory of the sky. Not that the colonialists ever cared to learn about that.'

Jophiel was working it out. 'That number, though. It translates back to five thousand, four hundred years, give or take – which maps to more than two and a half million years, outside. These people really are descended from *Gourd* crew, aren't they? Just as Wina's bracelet was a clue. Crew who left Earth about when we did, twenty-six years ago by our ship's time, by *our* time, and were abducted not long into their journey. Five thousand years for them. Two hundred generations . . . I know we have been through lots of relativistic distortions on this journey. Every so often it hits you in the face, the human reality of it.'

Asher nodded. 'The flora and fauna here. After Susan Chen and the rest were dumped at Goober's Star, soon after the ship was captured, I imagine the rest of the *Gourd* crew being dropped here, along with samples of the lifedome's contents. The basic frame of the cupworld must already have been in place: the land and oceans, the matter and energy cycles, the weather systems. Maybe even some kind of basic ecosystem, or a support for one. Maybe the Xeelee had some way of subtly helping out with that. I mean, if you can build mountains and oceans, making a little of the right type of soil, maybe, with some kind of engineered bacteria sympathetic to our kind of life, isn't such a stretch.

'So the crew was dumped here, and they unpacked, and started to adapt, to build a home. Once Earth life got a foothold, it would have dug in and expanded. The *Gourd* was a greenship, like the *Island*. Parkland. Trees and bushes and grass, and a little museum-piece farming: corn, root vegetables, potatoes. And the animals, not much besides chickens and rabbits—'

'And rats,' Jophiel said. 'Don't forget the rats. I saw a gaggle of village kids playing with what I thought was a small dog. It wasn't.'

'So they survived, and spread out to the ocean shore and the mountains. The animals would have grown wild, and evolved into new forms – or maybe, rather, recovered some of the characteristics that had been domesticated out of them. Human-driven adaptations that were only a few thousand years deep themselves, of course.'

Jophiel glanced up. 'That's the wreck of a Spline ship up there. At Goober's Star, the Ghosts were using their own tangleships. Their opponents, the Qax, used the Spline.'

Asher shrugged. 'So maybe the Qax came here too. Or the Ghosts captured their ships. It was a long war they fought—'

This aspect of the Wheel was troubling Jophiel, whenever he thought about it. The Xeelee had crossed the Galaxy to wipe out mankind. Why, then, create refuges for it here? But then, he realised, everything about the true agenda of the Xeelee in this place was still a mystery . . .

A distant scream.

Inside the tepee, everybody fell silent. A mutual wariness now turned to suspicious glares.

The scream cut off abruptly.

Max stood up. 'That sounded like Chinelo.'

Now Jophiel heard a new voice, steadily repeating some kind of incantation, or prayer – or maybe a simple request. A voice that was familiar. But not human.

A voice that was flat, mechanical, a wheezing, groaning tone.

A voice that sounded to Jophiel *like a Ghost*.

Everybody was on their feet now.

Poole said, 'Let's keep calm. Max, you make sure that squad of yours keeps their weapons out of sight. I mean it. I don't think our fragile relationship with these folks will stand another attempted murder.'

'Maybe not,' Max said, glowering. 'Even if it is our turn.'

'Elder Toma,' Poole said, bowing, 'I suggest we see what the trouble is before we start blaming anybody. Our crew member Chinelo is a child—'

'A child soldier,' Max muttered.

The elder woman glared at him.

Poole insisted, 'There may be some simple explanation for this.'

As it turned out, he was quite wrong.

Outside that largest tepee, Chinelo was being held by two burly locals, with sharp stone blades at her throat. She looked alarmed, but not panicked.

She was at the centre of quite a tableau, it seemed to Jophiel. Everybody in the village seemed to have come to see what the excitement was. Skin tattoos swirled across psychedelic faces.

And a big rat, with a collar like a pet dog, ran excited through a forest of legs.

Max Ward had to be physically held back from retrieving Chinelo, by Asher and Harris.

'I didn't do anything,' Chinelo said, as the party of seniors came bustling up. 'Well, not much. I didn't *mean* to.'

Poole walked forward, grave, calm, and spoke to the elders. 'This is a misunderstanding. This one is a child – shut up, Max. Could she be released? I vouch for her behaviour.'

The elders shared glances; one nodded.

Chinelo was released, and was left rubbing her shoulders and wrists. But her guards did not back off very far.

'Tell us what happened,' Poole commanded.

'It was that tepee. The big one. They wouldn't let us see. So I went to look inside. Wouldn't you?'

'No,' Poole said bluntly.

Chinelo wasn't too frightened for a cocky grin, Jophiel saw. 'Well, I just ducked under the door. It was dark inside. No windows, and door flaps like the tepee you went to. Before I could see what I was in there with—'

'Yes?'

'It spoke! Loud as the ship's general alarm. I jumped out of my skin. Then I *saw* it. I had to get out of there; that was all I thought. So I got my knife—'

'*Please kill me now.*'

The voice was clipped, somewhat artificial, stilted, but resonant, clear. It carried on the cool air.

And it spoke Standard.

Everybody shut up.

Asher was by the tepee, sneaking a peek, Jophiel saw. 'Lethe. I can *see* it. Where Chinelo ripped the cover . . . You'd better come look, Michael.'

Jophiel stepped forward, with the others from the *Cauchy*.

As these strangers approached their violated holy of holies, at a gesture from the elder, the locals held back. But Jophiel had the impression that if this incident unfolded badly over the next few minutes, there would be a lot of arrows flying. Max was fingering a blaster at his waist.

That big tepee had ripped open from top to bottom, far beyond Chinelo's reach. Jophiel wondered if the covering was so old it had been ready to fall apart anyhow. Through the rent, the tepee's interior, enclosed by a frame of sapling trunks, was easily visible. And inside—

At first Jophiel saw only a glint of silver. A smooth curve.

A silver sphere, fat and full, two metres wide.

It was a Ghost.

And it was pinned in place. A pyramid of wooden stakes had been driven *through* it, from above – into its skin and out again – and then thrust into the ground. Also there was a wider cubical frame around the Ghost, sturdily tied together and rooted in the ground. From this more stakes pierced the Ghost, from side to side, from top to bottom.

It was a peculiarly precise arrangement. Like a geometrical demonstration, a frame around a sphere. But the perfection of it was marred by what looked like dried blood on the hide, near the wounds.

The elder gestured, as if in disgust and contempt. 'Behold. The First Slaver. Vanquished, as you can see.'

And the Ghost said, 'Save me, Michael Poole.'

54

Poole reached out a hand, as if to touch the silver hide within the wooden cage, but pulled back. 'It's as if it has been crucified.'

Jophiel murmured to Max, '*Slaver*. They call themselves the People of the First Slavers. But that implies there were other slavers.'

'Yeah,' Max growled. 'Folk from the ocean. I talked to some of their youngsters. They have bloodthirsty stories of raiders coming on ships. Every few generations, it seems to happen. Maybe originating in other colonies along the coast, or islands. We haven't properly surveyed this place. They invade, murder and rape, and take your children. The settled folk recover, band together to drive them out, even exterminate them. But then a new generation rises, and it starts all over again.'

'So they know about slavers. And their folk memory of the Ghosts—'

'Is of slavers who brought their distant ancestors to this world in the first place. The First Slavers. Seems apt.' Max grinned cruelly. 'Except, it seems, that one of them got caught. Hey, no wonder that savage Wina took a dislike to Nicola. She must have recognised the Ghost hide. To her, Nicola was a human-shaped Ghost, walking free. She took no chances. Nor would I have. Good reaction.'

The Ghost had fallen silent, as if waiting.

Poole faced it. 'I am Michael Poole. You spoke my name.'

'You are feared. You are worshipped.'

'Not for anything *I* did. Some of your kind know of me, of my actions in another timeline . . . Are you in pain?'

'Yes.'

'How long have you been held like this?'

'Since the first coming of the Ghosts to this structure.'

'We call it the Wheel.'

'Yes.'

'When was this?'

'Over five thousand years ago. As the crew of the *Gourd* count time. We used faster-than-light technology which—'

'You brought them here.'

280

'We came to colonise. That is evidently the purpose of the structure – the spin gravity, the confined worlds – there are environments suitable for Ghosts and humans and many other kinds. Even Spline, or their aquatic forebears. We came here to accept the implicit invitation of the structure. It was an experiment, to study the artefact and its purpose. To see how well we could live here, on the terraces—'

'The *decks*. This is a *cupworld*. The structure is the *Wheel*. These are the words we have used.'

'Yes. Decks. Cupworlds. I will use your words, as I learn them.'

'So you brought humans too.'

'Yes. We brought some of the crew of the ship called the *Gourd*. We preserved the rest of the crew in other places.'

'We know. We found them. At Goober's Star . . . I'll show you a star map.'

The Ghost said nothing to that. 'We brought samples of the ecohab with which the vessel had been equipped. We wished to study humans. If we witnessed the evolution of a human culture without prior resources, we could learn a great deal. Later, more of us came here, in our own ships and captured Qax vessels.'

'We call your craft trangleships. What happened here? What happened to you?'

'We planted colonies across the artefact, the Wheel. We kept in touch using the trangleships. Sometimes we transferred personnel – humans and Ghosts – from one habitat to another. Once, humans, being transported between cupworlds on a Spline vessel, rebelled. Escaped from their cages. They managed to disable the Spline. It crashed, here, on this cupworld. Crashed and died.'

Jophiel was aware of a fist-pumping gesture by Max Ward.

Poole said, 'There were survivors? Humans and Ghosts?'

'There was a rescue, by trangleship. Most of the Ghosts were taken off.'

'Not all.'

'Not all. All but one of those left behind were killed by the rebellious humans.'

'All but one. All but you.'

'Yes.'

Poole walked around the frame, the pinned Ghost. 'They did this to ensure you could not escape.'

'Yes. If I tried I would rip—'

'I understand.'

'But to prevent my escape was not the only purpose of the framing. They thought I would die, slowly. In pain.'

'You did not die.'

'Ghosts are not designed to die. My damaged organs, internally, recovered. My skin heals continually over the wood of the stakes. I am not fed, but my body ingests organic matter from the stakes themselves. Which are periodically replaced. And, periodically, my skin is exposed to daylight, for energy. Thus, I have lived for five thousand years. Michael Poole, will you help me?'

Poole seemed to consider. Then he turned and walked away.

Jophiel stormed over. 'What are you doing? You can't leave this creature in such torment. Shame Nicola isn't here. She'd compare this to a circle in Hell – and we, human beings from *your* fleet of scatter-ships, Michael, put this Ghost in it.'

'But the Ghosts brought that crew here in the first place.' Poole seemed distracted.

Max Ward joined them, with Asher, others. 'Are you talking about the Ghost? Who cares about that Lethe-spawned monster? None of that matters, Michael. None of it. All that matters is that we get out of here while we can. Leave this world.'

Poole frowned. 'Why the rush?'

Max said, 'Because this world is poor, Michael. Because there's nothing for us in this environment.' He grimaced. 'Look at this place. The whole world is a lie, in a way. It has wood and sandstone, but dig down a little way and you find nothing but hull plate. There are going to be no fossil fuels or metals. Nothing but soft rock you can't even make decent arrowheads from. You noticed that? They just sharpen wooden shafts. These people were descended from scattership crew, remember. Our own colleagues, from just a few years back. Who set out equipped as we are, with fourth-millennium technology, with flyers and flitters and food printers. All of it lost, forgotten, after five thousand years.

'If we stay here we'll be the same, in a few generations. Living through the same cycle, over and over: slavers, and war, and a bit of peace, and then more slavers. That's all there is here. That and counting the days, and tattooing your face.'

Asher said, 'These people have survived. They have built a culture. There are worse fates.'

Max shrugged. 'So what? This isn't what we came for.'

Poole was silent. He might or might not have become a good leader,

Jophiel reflected, but he had become a good listener.

'We should take our time,' Poole said at length. 'In the tepee, the elders told me a bit about the Libraries – the crater features – especially the one at the mouth of the big river, the Great River as they call it, where they deposit their own information, their counts of the days. Let's go there. Like you said, Max, whatever there is to learn we'll find it there. Then we'll decide on our next steps.' He started to walk away, out of the village, in the direction of the flyer.

Jophiel took a step after him. 'But we can't leave the Ghost behind. Not like this. Michael. Michael!'

'He hears you,' Max said softly. 'He just doesn't want to decide yet. Listen, I think I changed my mind. About the Ghost, I mean. You want my advice? We should bring it.'

Jophiel scowled. 'Why?'

'It would be interesting to explore ways to kill it.' He grinned. 'Hypothetically.'

55

Jophiel thought that the smartest decision Michael Poole made in the aftermath of the discovery of the Ghost was to decree two full days of rest before they took another step forward. All of them, travellers, locals – and one representative of an entirely alien species – had been through huge conceptual shocks. If Jophiel had learned one thing, in the tangled history he shared with Michael going back to the first irruption of the Xeelee into the Solar System, it was that the effects of such upheavals took time to work through the soul.

And a couple of days' delay also happened to fit with the villagers' plans for their next regular expedition to the Library at the mouth of the Great River.

In the interim, Max Ward got to work setting out a perimeter around the flyer, and establishing guard routines. Local children trailed around wide-eyed after Chinelo and other young skinsuited warriors from the *Cauchy* as they made their patrols. Jophiel wondered if that would work out as a subtle way of building bridges.

Harris Kemp, meanwhile, had two patients to attend to: Nicola in the flyer, and the crucified Ghost, which he was treating in a hastily improvised lean-to outside the aircraft. 'Because there is no way,' Max Ward had insisted, 'that I am going to allow a potentially hostile alien inside our one and only means of escape from this cupworld.'

Even Jophiel, who instinctively opposed everything that came out of Max's mouth, couldn't argue with that.

Harris, for one, was glad to have the Ghost on hand. 'It's helping me treat Nicola,' he admitted on the first day. 'Nicola is a kind of cartoon version of a Ghost; having an original to study is helping me figure out some of her internal scrambles. Now I can figure out what Wina's arrow actually broke, and what just *looks* like it's broken . . .'

The Ghost itself was quiet, passive. It would respond to questions put to it by Jophiel and others, but stayed silent otherwise.

It did seem to appreciate the effort it had taken by Poole and the rest to get the locals to release it. 'You have saved me from torment,' it said on the second day. 'I am in your debt, for ever.'

'That might be true,' Jophiel said drily. 'But you haven't actually told us much about your people, your ships, your mission here.'

Which was true. To the detailed questions put to it by Jophiel, Max Ward and others, its default answer was 'I do not have that information.' Or, 'I was a very junior component of a very large mission.'

'There must be more of you,' Jophiel said. 'The chances of us stumbling so quickly upon the *only* Ghost in this cupworld are pretty slim. Don't you have any curiosity about others of your kind? What if they're having as bad a time as you were? Wouldn't you wish to help them?'

'I do not have that information. Even if I did I could not help them. I can scarcely travel in camouflage, in a human world. Even if I were free.'

'You've said nothing meaningful about your ship.'

'I had specific duties concerning food provision units.' Which, when described, sounded to Jophiel like nothing so much as artificial mock-ups of deep-sea mineral vents on Earth, black smokers around which bacteria, crabs and pale fish would gather to feed off seeping minerals – perhaps a clue to the Ghosts' ultimate origin, Asher had suggested.

'What was your ship's mission?'

'I do not have that information.' But the Ghost rolled as it said this, its motions visible from the orbits of scuffs and scars on its once-seamless silver hide, and Jophiel had the vague, unquantifiable impression that it was glancing up at the sky.

'Do you fight wars? I mean, among yourselves.'

He expected another deflection, but to his surprise the Ghost replied, 'Only historically.'

'Historically?'

'That may not be the right term. We evolved out of war-making against each other.'

Jophiel barked a laugh. 'As we aspire to, I suppose. So maybe we have something in common.'

'All sentient beings in this universe have something in common,' the Ghost said.

Jophiel asked on impulse, 'What is your name?'

'Name?'

'Do you have a name?'

'Our identities are evident to other Ghosts. At a level below symbolic communication.'

That sounded to Jophiel like a pompous circumlocution describing a kind of telepathy.

The Ghost said now, 'Besides, I am alone here. Perhaps alone on all this Wheel, despite your statistical arguments. To you I am unique. What need have I of a name?'

Jophiel had no answer.

56

On the third day, a rough expedition assembled. It was going to take about a day, they were told, to reach the Library by the Great River.

Cauchy crew members gathered diffidently around a group of villagers, who carried offerings of food: roots, fruit, dried lizards, even fish from the lesser rivers, in baskets woven of tree bark. For the Library, Jophiel supposed. And there were a few warrior types, bearing spears and bows, though the mood seemed light enough.

As for the crew, Michael Poole and Jophiel were leading, with Harris Kemp taking a day off from the care of his two unique patients. Asher came too, in case the Library did turn out to contain useful information for her to decipher. Max Ward sent along Chinelo and a couple more of his cadets as guards, but stayed back himself to watch the flyer, and Jophiel couldn't argue with that priority.

And Wina proudly presented herself to Michael Poole. 'I, Wina, will guide your folk,' she announced. 'For I wounded your warrior.'

'You don't need to be paying us back,' Asher said. 'You were only doing your duty, as you saw it.'

'That is true. But now I have a duty to you. As long as you live among us.'

'Then we accept,' Jophiel said gently.

So the expedition, led by Wina, set off. Not that the *Cauchy* crew needed a guide, geographically anyhow. They would simply walk along a well-trodden trail to the nearby stream, then follow that downstream to its confluence with the Great River, and then track *that* to the ocean shore. From there, it seemed, the Library would be obvious.

But if the geographic landscape was simple, the human landscape was deeply complex. It turned out that they would have to skirt the territories of two other groups en route.

At the first such encounter, the *Cauchy* folk quickly learned the rules. There were special places, indistinguishable to Jophiel, where you had to stand and wait until noticed by a scout from the local community. There would be some shouting, a few ritual challenges, a spear-waving. Then you said where you were going and how long you would be, and permission to pass was grudgingly given – or not, but Jophiel suspected that was rare. Then, with the formalities over, you sat down in the shade for the more important business of the day: gossip, nostalgia, and speculations about who was likely to be marrying whom soon.

The *Cauchy* crew were the subject of polite curiosity, but as they seemed to be the property of Wina's folk, nobody questioned them directly. Jophiel wondered, in fact, if maybe the First Slaver villagers had been so keen to make this trip just so they could show off the crew to their neighbours.

All this with warriors, like Wina, carrying lethal weapons always close to hand. But Jophiel suspected that most clashes between groups of people here were going to be more symbolic than deadly. Displays of identity; territory-marking rituals, yes – maybe some blowing off of steam when there were disputes. A couple of champions swinging their fists. Surely the folk here were too spread out for intense conflicts to be common, with too little property to be worth fighting over. And besides, these long-established groups evidently had deep shared links of territory marking and marriage bonds, reliant on a deep and intricate knowledge of past history.

'Which is,' Jophiel muttered as he discussed this with Asher, 'what we're likely to find locked up in this Library of theirs. Generations of gossip.'

'Yes, but how rich all this is,' Asher said, with a kind of fond enthusiasm in her voice. 'I mean, look around. Here we are in a world like a bowl of dust, the people with nothing but animal skins and bits of wood. Their origins almost forgotten. Yet their cultural life is so complex, so colourful. Like a cloud of light over all their heads. That's humanity for you. It was just the same on the ships, of course. Environments that were even more deprived, in many ways, and Chinelo's generation were evolving their own intricate culture in response, right under the noses of the adults.'

Jophiel smiled. 'I remember. Graffiti in the corners. The bracelets and necklets they made out of bits of waste—'

'Well, I don't recall that stuff,' Michael Poole broke in grumpily. 'And all the gossip in the world about whose aunt is marrying whose uncle isn't going to get us any closer to the Xeelee.'

Despite this impatience, however, Poole kept a polite smile on his face through all this complicated manoeuvring, and Jophiel felt obscurely proud of him for that.

The meeting ended with a still more elaborate round of farewells, with all the visitors touching heads one at a time with all their hosts, and a slow, almost regretful departure.

A little further along the river bank, they crossed yet another band's territory, and had to go through the same ritual all over again. But Wina and their guides seemed relaxed; evidently they had factored all this delay into their estimate of a day's march to the Library.

It was well past the middle of the day by the time they reached the Great River itself. It was wide, sluggish, tinged red with dust.

Jophiel knew from the hasty aerial surveys they had made that this was an impressive enough waterway, kilometres wide here – draining a continent, a veritable Mississippi twenty-five thousand light years from the frozen relic of the original. And there was some traffic on the slow-moving water, Jophiel saw: canoes, and larger vessels made up of many canoes bolted together, like multiple-hull catamarans. Their occupants seemed to be dredging up a kind of water-adapted grass, as well as setting out nets for fish. The river-borne folk waved to the walkers as they passed, without any territorial challenges. Evidently the river was seen as a common good, shared by all. During times of peace anyhow.

And there was wildlife here, as Jophiel might have expected, close to the water.

Asher pointed out some detail. 'Those swimming mammals by the bank.'

'They look like otters. They're rats, aren't they?'

'And *those* are big, long-legged rabbits on the far bank, taking a drink. Those wading birds with the bright crests—'

'Chickens.'

'And those trees by the water, a little like banyans, look like a variant of willow. The *Gourd* carried a parkland ecohab. Turn all that out onto a dusty plain, leave it to adapt for a few thousand years—'

'And this is the result.'

After tracking the river a while, Jophiel sensed they were approaching the sea; he thought he heard the deeper rumble of a more massive body of water, smelled salt in the air. He never got to see the ocean, however. There was no horizon on this table-top of a landscape, but the mist in the air limited visibility. And before the ocean came into view the path, well trodden, veered away from the river bank and cut directly across the landscape.

Soon they came to a rise in the land, like a ridge or an earthwork, heaped-up rusty dirt two or three times Jophiel's own height. Jophiel could see it followed a broad circle, like the wall of a crater; he guessed the diameter was a couple of kilometres, maybe more. Evidently one of the features that had looked so common, and prominent, viewed from the air.

The trail they now followed converged on a circular track, heavily worn, that looped around the exterior of the earthwork. They trudged along this. More tracks trailed in from the wider landscape to join this perimeter; this was evidently a common destination point.

The villagers bunched up closer together as they walked on. They had all fallen silent now, villagers and crew alike, as if through some shared perception. Jophiel knew that his template, Michael Poole, had never been swayed much by intuition, by *feelings* about places and situations. But Jophiel did sense a general unease.

At last they came to a break in the wall, a wide gap. There was nothing like a gate. Within the enclosure, Jophiel could see a kind of pyramid: a roughly finished, four-sided heap, standing on heavily trodden ground at the centre of the big circular earthwork.

The group started to move through the gap in the wall.

And Asher brushed Jophiel's hand, creating consistency-protocol warning tingles. 'Look around,' she muttered. 'At the wall itself.'

The sides of the cutting through which they passed were quite steep slopes, earth bound together by coarse grass; the earth was so dry it was almost like a sand dune, Jophiel thought.

A sand dune from which bones protruded. He recoiled. Then he forced himself to look more closely.

Skulls, ribs, joints. Some of them smashed, perhaps by animals seeking marrow. Jophiel had an absurd image of one of those big, tough-looking chicken descendants pecking angrily at this ossuary.

His companions reacted too. Chinelo gaped in horror. Asher glared, as if affronted. The villagers kept their heads down, as if in respect, as they passed through the bank.

By now Jophiel was pretty sure he knew what they were encountering. And so did Michael Poole, he saw, glancing over at his template.

'Uncle George Poole,' Jophiel said. 'More murky secrets from the family archive.'

Poole nodded curtly. 'This is a ring cemetery.'

'I know what that means,' Harris said to the two of them. 'This isn't just some Poole family secret, you know. The biologists and ecologists have studied the phenomenon ever since the days of your "Uncle George".'

Chinelo frowned. 'Studied what? What is this place?'

Harris glared at the Pooles, and turned to Chinelo. 'This is a hive, Chinelo. A hive of people. Don't let it . . . upset you. *This* is all quite characteristic. Unfortunately. As you said, Michael, this earthwork is a ring cemetery. They just haul out the bodies of the dead and dump them when they get far enough out, more or less equidistantly from the central structures. So you get this ring of corpses around the centre. Just as the insects do. The ants. And some animals, the mole rats. Evidently the human versions do the same, if you give them room.'

Chinelo stared at him. 'But all those bodies, heaped up. How many people can be in there? The pyramid's not that big. I mean . . . Even in five thousand years—'

'There may be more people in there than you think,' Harris said gently.

'We can't be sure what we'll find in there,' Poole muttered. 'The account George Poole left of the incident in Rome, back in the twenty-first century – of the very first of these hives, the first to be discovered anyhow – is still the most complete. But that was a very young system. There were a couple of near-misses on Mars before the Recovery-Era colonisation waves opened that world up properly. We don't know how the social structures and the rest will have evolved across five thousand years, if undisturbed—'

'Stop!'

'Halt!'

'Stop walking! Go back! Go back!'

The cries they heard now were hastily translated by their systems from a language not unlike the villagers'.

The group halted, bunching up. Jophiel saw they had nearly come through the barrier of bones and earth.

But the way was blocked now by a thin line of maybe twenty individuals. All had shaven scalps, and the sexes were hard to differentiate, though Jophiel had the impression there were more females than males. They were dressed in shapeless, colourless smocks of some vegetable weave. They seemed *old* to Jophiel, their skin wrinkled and spotted, their postures stooped. But they all held weapons of some sort, spears, clubs, even a few bows and arrows. They could put up a fight if necessary, Jophiel saw.

He made out more of these elderly guards coming out to join those at the barrier. Rushing, as best they could.

Chinelo's hand went to her blaster.

Wina touched her arm. 'No. They will not harm us. They only mean to protect the Library. See, already our elders go forward to name us, our people, our reason for coming. They expect us, you see. We sent runners from the village while we waited for you to be ready.'

Chinelo took her hand off her weapon. 'They have good discipline,' she said. 'I didn't hear an alarm being raised. Yet here they all are, this big number.'

'Not discipline,' Harris said. 'Not in the manner you mean. They just react, and follow each other's lead. They *swarm*. They are less like a trained military formation than – than antibodies, clustering around a wound.'

'Regina's three rules,' Poole said. 'Remember, Jophiel?'

Jophiel nodded reluctantly. '*Listen to your sisters*. Do that, and you swarm. I read about this stuff. I never thought we'd get to see it. I think we're being allowed through . . .'

The guards had backed off to form a kind of corridor, through which the visiting party would have to walk to reach the pyramid. But the guards kept hold of their weapons, and were silently watchful.

The group moved forward.

'Ugh,' Chinelo whispered. 'They smell of milk. And they're all so *old*.'

'Sacrificing the elderly,' Harris murmured. 'Another trick adapted from the animals and insects. If an attack comes, block it with the bodies of the old, the worn down, the useless.' He shook his head. 'Lethe. I'm supposed to be a doctor now—'

Poole murmured, 'It's tough for all of us. There's nothing you can do for them. We just have to get through this.'

Asher said, 'Certainly we're learning a lot about High Australia, that such places as this exist – and in quantity. We saw many of these ring features from the air, remember.'

Chinelo stared at them all. 'I still don't know what you're talking about. Hives?'

'All in good time,' Jophiel said. 'I think we all just want to be sure.'

After perhaps twenty minutes of very slow walking they approached the central structure.

Jophiel saw that the pyramid wasn't built of anything like concrete or brick, still less the more advanced technologies of Earth before the Xeelee. It seemed to consist of little but heaped-up stone, big red sandstone boulders that must have been quarried from what passed for bedrock on this cupworld. Stone that was smoothed over by what looked like heat-hardened mud, as Mars red as the rest of the landscape. And, here and there, Jophiel made out the marks of the fingers that must have done the smoothing, and maintained it, over millennia.

Now more people came out to greet them. Mostly female again, Jophiel saw, most dressed in garments that were just as plain as the guards' – one-piece tunics tied at the waist – but cleaner and of a better quality. They were all silent, but they all smiled, a little nervously, Jophiel thought.

And they bunched together like frightened sheep before these strangers, the *Cauchy* crew.

The First Slaver elders advanced with their baskets of food, meat and fruit and roots, and the girls and women took these with nods of gratitude.

'So,' Poole said. 'With these gifts the plains folk are paying. But for what?'

'Stories,' Wina said, when she had puzzled out what seemed to be a clumsy translation of the question. '*Our* stories, that we'd forget if we didn't tell. Stories of the days gone by, and the people who went before. When I die, my children will come here and sing of my life, my loves, the battles I fought. And the Library will remember it for ever, and sing of me to my children's children when they come in their turn.' She grinned. 'Already my aunt, that lady over there, is telling of how I brought down the Ghost-woman. Though I regret that sincerely. Here.' She handed out baskets of fruit, like heavy apples, to Poole, Harris. 'The Librarians like fruit.'

Asher nodded. 'And in return—'

'They will let you in.' She pointed at an entrance, dark. 'Through there. You are special visitors. Newcomers. The Librarians will want to learn of your battles, so they may sing them to your children in future. Sometimes people choose to stay. A few boys, mostly girls. Well, there is plenty of food. You see, people stay for the food. Just don't touch anything. Or anybody. Don't *steal* anything.'

Poole grinned. 'Thank you, Wina. Come on, Harris, Jophiel. Asher, you stay outside. And try to figure out if there is anything useful here.' He looked at the doorway and tensed. 'Let's get this done.'

'Keep turning right,' Wina murmured. 'That's the way to the birthing pools. Well, that's what my grandmother told me. On the other hand, the last time she went in there she never came out again.'

57

The pyramid was a place of narrow shafts, cut low through the stone, wide enough for two or three of them to pass side by side, if they ducked beneath the low ceilings.

There was light inside. The deeper they went the dimmer the light, Jophiel soon discovered, but it was there. It came from shafts, artfully cut through the walls.

Artfully cut. Maybe, but Jophiel was prepared to bet that everything he saw was the product of trial and error, repeated over and over across centuries, millennia even, until the best solution was found.

That applied to the air ducts he spotted too, he suspected. Shafts in the walls and ceilings, through which, when he passed, he could feel breezes, laden with a cloying smell of milk. As an air-conditioning system it was primitive, it was crude, but it worked – and all without any external power source, save the Galaxy-centre heat that poured down on this world through its filter of a sky, and human body heat, and convections.

He was reminded of a family monument, Lilian Poole's Recovery-Era Goonhilly Mound, in southern England, a conscious expansion of the design principles of a termite mound.

Anyhow it had evidently worked for centuries.

As was proved by the people that pressed close, as soon as they got more than a dozen paces in from the daylight. A crowd, all around them, filling the passageways: apparently mostly female, short, bald, blank-faced, eyes wide in the perpetual shade. They pushed along the corridors and practically flowed around the strangers. They were always in contact with each other, Jophiel noticed immediately, always rubbing shoulders, holding hands, whispering – even kissing softly. And at first they reacted to the newcomers too, with gentle touches – not in a hostile way, and still less sexual – just a brush of the arm, a stroke of the back.

That all changed when one of them tried to touch Jophiel. He kept silent, as his flesh crumbled into a cloud of brilliant pixels.

Immediately, their behaviour changed. They stopped coming so close, and instead a group of more or less permanent escorts closed up, in a tight wall so that no others could bump up against Jophiel. And as they moved on, Jophiel observed how others backed off and squirmed out of the way as they passed.

'Soon they'll all know about us,' Chinelo said. 'Jophiel and his consistency protocols.'

'*Listen to your sisters,*' Poole said. 'That rule is mostly what governs their behaviour. If one gets alarmed, they all get alarmed. Mostly it works – and is very efficient . . . Another right turn. Let's keep following Wina's advice.'

They passed a couple of chambers, big rooms cut into the rock mound, pierced by air and light shafts of their own. Here Jophiel saw huge vats of what looked like some kind of broth, itself glowing pale green – bioluminescence, perhaps, a useful trait down here. People lined up in their dozens, hundreds, bowls in their hands, to scoop up portions of the soup, while others stirred the vats with vast wooden ladles. If this was a cookhouse, or a refectory, it was just as crowded as the corridors. The room was filled with a susurrus of soft whispers; the people here spoke constantly, but no words could be made out.

Chinelo said, 'So *many* of them. All of them underground too! You'd never have known they were all here, thousands under this pyramid.'

Asher said, 'And all those other pyramids too, remember, all across the cupworld. Thousands and thousands.'

'That is the big advantage,' Harris said. 'For the genes, anyhow. The sheer numbers. This is a way of living that delivers a *lot* of people, all living comfortably together.'

Chinelo thought that over. 'Comfortable, yeah. That's the right word. They all look comfortable. But *I* wouldn't be comfortable here.'

Poole asked, 'Why not?'

'Because they're all the same. Doing the same thing.'

Poole considered. 'Good answer.'

They passed another chamber, another big room, which seemed to be a dormitory. There were no beds, no bunks, not even blankets. Instead people were just piled up on top of each other, snuggled in, adults, children. A single big heap, a mound of humanity. Like puppies, Jophiel thought.

Wordless, they moved on.

Then Chinelo coughed, seemed to stagger slightly, and shook her head. 'I'm fine . . .'

'Oxygen levels are very low in here,' Harris said, consulting a soft-screen that glowed in the semi-dark. 'Low in terms of normal human requirements. Another common characteristic. The inhabitants here will have a tolerance. Maybe they're even able to withstand extended periods, such as minutes or hours, with no oxygen at all, if there's a cave-in for example. Like the naked mole rats on Earth . . .'

But he fell silent, as they had come to the entrance to another chamber.

This was even vaster than the refectory. This time Jophiel had the sense of a large pool – like an indoor swimming pool – but a pool brimming with a pale white liquid, that looked, and smelled, like milk.

In the pool, women swam. Some of them were heavily pregnant, their milk-coated bellies shining in the dim light. One or two had infants with them, very young, who shared the pool with the expectant mothers. Babies, swimming as confident as otters, Jophiel thought. And there were others here too, all female, all naked, slipping through the liquid to supervise the infants, or to bring the mothers bits of food or cups of drink.

Chinelo looked shocked at the sight, as Jophiel might have expected. There's so many of them. And they all look alike. Like one big family.'

'That's exactly it. That's what they are. Almost all sisters,' Harris said gently. 'I know it seems strange . . . This is a hive, Chinelo. A hive of humans. Like a colony of ants or bees – and it works the same way. At any one time there are only a few mothers, giving birth to the rest. If you aren't a mother you give up your right to have children of your own in order to help your mother produce more babies – more sisters. It seems strange to us, but in nature it's a very common way of living. It's called eusociality – which actually means a *perfect society*. On Earth it turned up among the insects, the birds, the mammals, like rats and dogs—'

'And humans,' Michael Poole said. 'As my distant ancestor George found in Rome – which was a very old city on Earth – when he went looking for his lost sister.'

Jophiel grunted. 'And he figured out how it worked. Regina's three rules. *Sisters matter more than daughters.*'

Harris said, 'This is what you get in situations where there is nowhere to spread out, to get away from your mother. Probably there was something like a spring here, a bit of well-watered ground. Nothing else for kilometres around – nothing between here and the river, say. When you can't get away from home, you have to cooperate with the family – and that becomes more important than thinking for yourself. You just copy your sisters, and they copy you. And the hive organises itself, out of all those little interactions.'

'*Ignorance is strength*,' Poole quoted. '*Listen to your sisters*. You just follow what everybody else is doing, and it generally works out . . .'

Now one of the swimming women came close to a gravid mother-to-be. She leaned over, as if meaning to kiss the mother. But she seemed to vomit, and regurgitated food flowed easily into the mother's mouth.

'I have to get out,' Chinelo said suddenly. 'I feel like I'm choking.'

'Maybe you are,' Harris said sternly. 'The hive is rejecting you, just as you are rejecting it. Come on, let's get you out of here.' He consulted a softscreen map, and led the way out. Chinelo followed, with Poole.

Jophiel brought up the rear, feeling unreasonably glad to be escaping himself.

When they got out of the pyramid, Chinelo stumbled away into the light, and took deep, shuddering breaths. Harris discreetly checked her over.

But Chinelo looked less scared than angry, Jophiel thought.

She said, 'Why would anybody want to live like this?'

'Nobody would *want* to,' Harris said. 'The genes want us to. And what the genes want they generally get.'

'I've always thought it's a kind of trap for humanity,' Jophiel said. 'People survive, lots of them. And the genes win out. But it's the end of history. The people here descended from *Gourd* crew, remember. They were just like us. But they have no meaningful future. A hive is an end.'

'I don't think there's anything here for us,' Asher called softly. 'In the Library's collection of data, I mean. The attendants out here were prepared to a answer questions. Much of it was surprisingly comprehensible for us. Max was right, actually. There is a lot of family history stuff. Who married who, who murdered who, dynastic squabbles. Some useful lore, on unusual weather systems for instance. Records of once-in-a-generation events. Useful for the locals, I mean.'

Poole prompted, 'But for us—'

'Nothing. They've forgotten where they came from, save for a few trace origin legends. They've forgotten they live on a big Wheel. I think it's going to be like this all over this cupworld, Michael. This is an arid world, and it's going to be studded by Coalescences like this. To quote the name George Poole gave to the hives.'

'This whole cupworld is a trap,' Poole muttered. 'Max is right. The people here aren't going anywhere. And if we don't leave now, while we still have the technology to do it, we never will.' He glanced around. 'Everybody agreed? Then let's get out of here.'

58

The departure of the *Cauchy* crew from High Australia turned out to be a surprisingly moving sundering.

After five weeks here, as measured by the local time of Deck Two, it took several flights of the *Cauchy*'s solitary flyer to lift the crew and their materiel back from the First Slaver village and up to the Rim Mountains, and then through the Lid to the vacuum of the upper Deck itself.

As this process neared its end, with Jophiel intently watching from the village as the flyer disappeared into the sky yet again, Susan Chen approached him. 'You are missing all the fun,' she said.

He turned; he hadn't heard her approach. He noticed Wina standing behind her, a few paces back, looking awkward – avoiding eye contact, yet clearly wanting something.

'Sorry, Susan. I'm kind of distracted today.'

'In case something goes wrong?'

'We're short of fall-back options. I mean, we only have one functioning flyer. I suppose we could walk out of here, if we had to.' He glanced towards the horizon, where mist hid the Rim Mountains. 'Heck of a climb, up into the vacuum – you'd need skinsuits in the end . . .'

She smiled, her ageless face barely moving. 'I do worry when you Pooles begin to dream of such stunts. It is as if you might do it just for the fun of it.'

He had to grin. 'You got that right. But I suppose if we Pooles hadn't had that restless streak we wouldn't be out here in the first place. Which is a pretty damning thing to say, given the ruin that has been brought down on the human race.'

She shook her head. 'You have a sense of perspective your template lacks, I think. But it would be true arrogance if you Pooles imagined that the whole of human destiny, indeed the whole of Galactic history, had been shaped by your own character flaws.'

'Hasn't it?'

She shrugged. 'If you hadn't built your wormholes in the thirty-seventh century, isn't it possible one of your competitors might have done the same thing in the thirty-eighth?'

He rubbed his nose ruefully. 'There would have been a different statue at the Galaxy centre, though. To Bill Dzik, maybe.'

'Quite. And, simply because you strive for some goal, it may not be true that any alternative is failure, so much as – well, as a choice of a different path. Suppose your flyer did fail; suppose we did find ourselves stranded here, on High Australia. Would that really be so bad? As you know there have been some who have taken that very option.'

He nodded. Somewhat to his surprise a half-dozen of the *Cauchy* complement had chosen to stay here, with Wina's people. Four were older, veterans of Cold Earth, who had had enough displacement in their lives, and Jophiel, in retrospect, supposed they would likely have jumped ship at the first reasonably acceptable port of call. Another was Ben Goober, who had fallen in love, it seemed, with a boy from the village. Given the varying relativistic time shifts to be endured as humans crawled over this tremendous artefact, Jophiel could think of no way in which Ben and the other stay-behinds, once sundered from the crew, could be kept in touch. And yet Ben, like the others, was determined.

'How does Michael feel?'

Jophiel shrugged. 'Conflicted, I guess. Well, there's no change there. I do share some of it. I am him . . . I think he can see why people aren't following. He understands the logic. But he's clinging to a kind of inner core. "People have died to get us this far. I have to finish it."'

'Is that healthy?'

'I have literally no idea. He goes on, anyhow.'

Susan said now, 'And we do in fact have one volunteer coming the other way.'

'Volunteer? . . .' Slowly, understanding ground through his mind. 'Ah. And that's why you wanted to see me.' He looked again at Wina. He saw that she carried her hunting pack, with its bow and arrows, as well as another bag filled with what looked like clothes, mementoes such as a chicken-doll made of wood and feathers, other junk.

Wina seemed intensely nervous, but intensely determined. 'It is true. I, Wina, wish to travel with you from the *Cauchy*.'

He studied her, trying to think this through – trying to work out what was best for her. 'You're the only one of the village who's asked to travel on with us.'

'Our people were once like you. *We* travelled, before we were brought to this place by the First Slavers. Now I would travel on, in my turn.'

He looked around, at the village of wood and leather on this rusty plain. The girl before him in skins, with a bow and arrow in her pack. 'Do you understand what it means to travel with us?'

She shrugged. 'I know now that this world is a bowl set in a great table. We will climb out of this bowl, and travel to other bowls.'

'Yes, but the relativistic time displacements – there would be no way back. That's the important thing. You will be as if dead to your family. They will be as if dead to you.'

'I understand,' she said, quietly but firmly. 'But I have my duty, you see.'

'Duty?'

'I might have killed Nicola Emry.'

'You were only doing what you thought was best.'

She shook her head. 'It was bad judgement. You had weapons that could have destroyed us all in a heartbeat. We were lucky that you were merciful. I should have been more patient. Watchful. Spared Nicola. Or, when I did strike, strike without fail. Murdered you in your sleep, for instance.'

Jophiel nodded, suppressing a grin. 'Fair point.'

'In the event I wounded Nicola unnecessarily. Our code is that in that circumstance I must support the victim, for as long as is deemed necessary.'

'Well, if you're sure—'

'I have another duty too.'

'And what's that?'

She eyed them frankly. 'I am told you intend to carry the First Slaver with you, away from this world.'

Jophiel nodded. 'The Ghost, yes. We didn't believe we should leave it here. Not when we have the capacity to—'

'Rescue it?' Susan Chen smiled. 'Michael Poole always comes to the rescue.'

'I will guard you,' Wina said. 'From the First Slaver. Just as my elders guarded me from it, while I grew up.'

He thought it over. 'Very well. Valid arguments. Welcome aboard.'

'One other thing.'

'What's that?'

'Will you tell my mother for me?'

Jophiel himself rode the flyer on its last journey out of the village.

In all they had spent nearly forty days in High Australia, in the cupworld. They had been so high out of the Wheel's relativistic pit that a mere fifty years had elapsed in the external universe.

And just five minutes on Deck One, where the Xeelee lurked.

59

Like the journey from Deck One to High Australia, the journey of the *Cauchy* convoy to their new destination was simple in principle.

Simple if you drew it on a softscreen sketch diagram. As always, Jophiel reflected, it was the sheer, immense, mind-crushing scale of the great artefact over which they crawled that was the real challenge.

Their nominal target now was 'Earth Three', the second Earthlike cupworld they had spotted in the hasty survey carried out during the *Cauchy*'s first flyby across the Wheel, up on Deck Three. The seniors all felt nervous, Jophiel thought, about their reliance on this target. After all, they hadn't been able to update their records since the flyby. Once stuck on Deck One they had been looking up at the underside of Deck Two, with none of the upper decks' surfaces visible. And given they faced a journey of significant fractions of a light year by tracked vehicle, they couldn't afford to make a wrong choice of destination.

The best guess was still that Earth Three was the nearest easily habitable world within their reach. And besides, as Michael Poole pointed out, Deck Three would give them an even greater time-dilation advantage over Deck One and the Xeelee itself, their ultimate target.

So that was where they determined to make for.

To get there, they would need to climb a strut, up to the third deck.

And *that* meant going back the way they had come, to the nearest strut, ninety days at a brisk six per cent of lightspeed, returning via the counter-current of the hull-plate river that had carried them to High Australia.

Ninety more days. It sounded fine in theory, but now, after the open spaces of High Australia, to be shut up again inside the convoy trucks was frustrating. Harris spoke darkly of mental health issues among the crew.

Still, they got through it.

Climbing the strut was the next challenge. As before it took them a day to transfer the trucks cautiously to the strut's vertical face.

Then the climb began. The trucks were like a line of ants, Jophiel thought, climbing through the structure of a giant Ferris wheel. For the first hours Jophiel huddled with Poole, Asher and Nicola in the lead truck's cabin, watching the Deck Two surface slowly recede behind them, now looking like an apparently vertical wall.

The greatest uncertainty this time was how long it would take to traverse the strut from Deck Two up to Deck Three.

Poole set out the numbers. 'We know we took ten days, in the hull-plate stream, to climb the strut from Deck One to Two. Which was only about an eighth of an astronomical unit. Just a third of the distance of Mercury from the Sun, say. The climb to Deck Three is ten thousand times further. More like a jaunt to the Oort cloud.'

They laid bets on the journey time. Michael Poole aggressively predicted a mere ten days, a super-fast transition. Jophiel thought it would take a lot longer – a thousand days, perhaps, still by far exceeding the speeds of the first leg of the climb.

Nicola frowned as they discussed this, her flawless silver face reproducing the expression with precision, Jophiel thought. But she had a habit now of rubbing her chest, where Wina's arrow had penetrated her Ghost-hide flesh. 'Look – we're crossing an interplanetary distance here. One a Poole GUTship could once have covered in a hundred days, burning at one gravity. Not so slow it takes for ever, not so fast it's risky. I figure the Xeelee will make the same kind of calculation. I say a hundred days, give or take.'

In the event it took one hundred and three days before they reached the under-surface of Deck Three. Jophiel avoided a gloating Nicola for hours.

Then it was a day of transfer to Deck Three, and to find the river of hull plate that would sweep them to their next destination.

Earth Three was estimated as two hundred and forty-one more days away. Again the crew settled down, more or less reluctantly, to their truck-bound regime, for another eight months.

On the eightieth day, one-third of the way there, Asher called a meeting.

The seniors gathered in the lead truck. Jophiel turned up with a sense of inchoate dread. He thought they all seemed restless, nervous, afflicted by cabin fever. What now?

The fun part, relatively, turned out to be a review of Asher's team's latest observations of the Wheel, and its cupworlds.

'We've refined our observations of the worlds we spotted before, on the flyby before we came down on Deck One. And we spotted plenty more on Deck Two, as we rose up along the spoke and had a chance to take a look back. Even on this deck we've managed to spy out new worlds, using high-flying remote probes. Glimpses anyhow.

'You do realise we have no sensible estimate of how many cupworlds this structure might support. The cupworlds are pretty sparsely set out, and we don't have a good model for their spacing, let alone their distribution—'

Poole waved a hand. 'Show us some pretty pictures.'

Images lit up on softscreens spread over the walls of this small cabin. Dimples in the hull plate.

Most cupworlds seemed never to have been occupied at all. They stood empty, like healed scars.

Of the rest, only a few were remotely Earthlike.

Asher commented as the images flickered by. 'You'll understand we're selecting for suitability here. We left out the Venus-like ovens, the gas-giant cloud worlds . . .' She showed them quick highlights, images of increasingly exotic worlds. Worlds so cold that rivers of liquid helium flowed *up* mountains of water ice that was harder than basalt. Worlds hotter than Mercury, with surfaces of molten rock and rivers of iron, Asher said.

Airless, Moonlike worlds, on some of which, Asher said, traces of Ghost technologies may have been detected. Ambiguous evidence. But no Ghost activity had been spotted on this Deck . . .

'Let's ask the First Slaver,' Jophiel suggested.

'Let's not,' growled Max Ward. 'Enough with the scenery. Show us the Earths.'

Most of the supposedly Earthlike cupworlds showed nothing but the blue-grey of ocean, Jophiel had already learned. Water worlds. Maybe that reflected the distribution of real worlds out in the Galaxy. Some bore scatterings of ice, and one or two were roofed over entirely by ice sheets. Others featured scraps of land breasting the ocean, island chains or summits that looked like volcanic calderas.

At the other extreme was another subset of worlds superficially like High Australia, Jophiel thought: mostly arid landscapes, with any seas and oceans standing like puddles.

Only a handful of worlds had expansive land masses dividing large oceans, like Earth.

Earth Three was one such.

Asher looked around at them. 'The world we've called Earth Three is still the most Earthlike we've spotted – and that includes High Australia.'

Something in her tone indicated to Jophiel that this was where the bad news would be coming. Bad news, about their best hope of refuge. That sense of dread deepened.

'*But*,' he prompted.

'But,' she said ruefully. 'You need to be prepared for what I'm going to show you. For one thing, time dilation is a lot less up on Deck Three. Half a million years have passed, for worlds up on Deck Three, since we launched the *Cauchy*. Over two and a half million years outside the Wheel, of course. And so the glimpse of Earth Three we saw on the way in, when we first arrived at the Wheel – well. It's out of date.'

Poole looked alarmed. 'What are you hinting at, Asher? Is there some problem?'

'See for yourselves.'

Jophiel knew very well what Earth Three had looked like, before. The crew's scientists had examined those few, sketchy flyby images closely, even obsessively, trying to tease the meaning out of every pixel. Jophiel remembered a world that had looked like a scrambled Earth – a mix of oceans, ice and land in about the right proportions – like Earth itself, perhaps, in some past age, with photosynthetic life of some kind busily using sunlight to generate an oxygen-nitrogen atmosphere. If Earth life couldn't prosper there, it couldn't prosper anywhere.

'Half a million years later,' Asher said. 'The good news is that atmospheric chemistry has advanced quickly. A lot more oxygen. It's breathable, we think. However—'

She showed her images.

As seen from above, Earth Three looked broken.

That was Jophiel's first impression. That much-studied scramble of continents and oceans was broken up into segments, plates separated by what looked like wide, white rivers. And those segments themselves were a crazy patchwork, some flooded with grey water, some caked in ice, some just bare rock or sand – though some were islands of green and grey that, it seemed, bore life, just as they had promised before.

And at the centre of the crater-like dimple within which the cupworld rested, a mountain reared up, a smooth cone, monstrously tall.

'Cracked,' he muttered. 'The cupworld is cracked.'

Nicola grunted. 'Not like you to find the right word, Jophiel. But that's it. Like it was some fine piece of crockery, dropped and smashed to bits, and put crudely back together. These white bands between the segments—'

'Hull plate,' Asher said. 'If it looks like some kind of repair job, it probably is. We think. And those hull-plate joins are pretty crude welds.'

'The impacts we experienced,' Poole said. 'When stuff hit the Wheel. Too big for even the Xeelee's defence mechanisms to deal with. This is the result. Smashed worlds.'

Asher nodded. 'That's what I think. We discussed this before. We've already been here for two million years ourselves – we're fast-forwarding through time, especially when we were down on Deck One – and on such timescales we were *likely* to see most kinds of exceptional incident. Including catastrophic accidents. We think, in fact, this is a relic of the first impact we experienced, or thought we did, when we were back on Deck One. Half a million years ago for this cupworld, give or take.

'You can see the cupworld is damaged. You can also see life of some kind is surviving down there.' She hesitated. 'We do think we see the signature of Earth-type life. Our kind of photosynthesis, for example. We're still too far away to be sure.'

Nicola frowned. 'So? Look, we know the Ghosts came to this place, the Wheel. We know they brought humans, if only from the *Gourd*. If they dropped people into High Australia, couldn't they have dropped them into this world too? And if so—'

'If so,' Asher said patiently, 'they will have had to endure half a million years, subjectively, in this place already. That's an evolutionary timescale. Time enough for a *lot* to change. Especially after a cataclysmic upheaval. So this cupworld may be more . . . exotic than we might have expected.'

'So what?' Poole asked. 'We have no place else to go. And ultimately it's only a waystation. Our purpose is to get to the Xeelee. Which would have meant using Earth Three as a base, and going on. An expeditionary force. On to the next strut, descending back to Deck One from where we could travel to meet the Xeelee at the site where we observed it . . .'

'That may be problematic too. And it's the second thing we need to discuss.' Asher pulled up more images, some direct, some extrapolated, this time of the wider structure of the Wheel. 'I can only show you what we found.'

And Jophiel saw the problem immediately.

The next strut, which might have delivered Michael Poole to his foe, was damaged too. Buckled, its surface twisted and broken.

'Lethe,' said Michael Poole. 'An impact, somewhere close by. Has to be.'

'We're still trying to resolve the finer detail. We can't know what effect this might have on the Wheel's structural resilience—'

'He doesn't care about that, Asher,' Nicola murmured. 'Not Michael Poole. He came to this place to confront the Xeelee. We all came so far, just for that. Now, in this last leg, through sheer bad luck, he's lost his means of moving on.'

Poole snapped, 'It's just another obstacle.' He was clearly thinking hard. 'Our plan of action from here is clear enough. We proceed to Earth Three. We find a way to live there. And then we find another way to move on.'

Nicola murmured to Jophiel, 'You know, you Pooles are always more scary when you are calm than when you are angry.'

60

On the one hundred and fifty-seventh day since the strut, Jophiel was summoned again to Asher's truck.

Poole was here, with Asher, Max, Nicola. Wina stared, wide-eyed.

And the Ghost, First Slaver, was here too. Wina had her bow and arrow in her hands, an arrow nocked, ready to fire.

'Jophiel Poole,' the Ghost said politely.

Jophiel nodded. He walked deeper into the truck. On the soft-screens were images of what looked like a Ghost tangleship, after a spectacular crash. He looked around. 'What's going on here?'

Max Ward was glaring. 'What do you see, Jophiel?'

'A crashed Ghost ship.'

'Right. Which one of our crew just detected in a cupworld, up here on Deck Three. But we know that this fatball,' he pointed his thumb at the Ghost hovering impassively beside him, 'didn't arrive in *this* crashed Ghost ship. He came from a crash down on Deck Two. High Australia. And now, this,'

Poole sighed heavily. 'You see the problem, Jophiel. Consider the odds. We've crawled a fraction across this huge structure. And if we've found two crashed Ghost ships, so close together, there must have been whole armadas of them, descending on this structure, across the ages, perhaps across a couple of million years. So why did they come here? What did they want?'

Max glared at the Ghost. '*And where did they go?* Are we going to turn a corner and find they took over this whole Wheel?'

'No,' the Ghost said.

'Then where?'

'I have no objection to telling you.'

Asher frowned. 'Why didn't you tell us before?'

'You didn't ask.'

Max would have interjected again, but Poole held him back.

'We followed the Xeelee,' said the Ghost. 'That became a policy. Across millennia, a species policy. And, before I became isolated, I was aware that some of our parties had followed the Xeelee to the Great Attractor.'

Asher stared. 'The extragalactic centre? You mean the artefact there? The cosmic-string ring?'

'I know you have been observing it,' the Ghost said. 'This object so distorts spacetime that whole galactic clusters are drawn to it. Species across much of the observable universe *must* see it. Many must travel there. We follow the Xeelee, we Ghosts. We followed a Xeelee here, to the Galaxy centre. And we followed them to the Attractor too.'

Asher looked baffled. 'Very well. The ring. It is obvious that the Xeelee are undertaking a massive manipulation of spacetime. Even we have been observing it long enough that we've been able to track its construction. We now think it will be finished around five million years AD – that is, five million years after the date we of the *Cauchy* encountered you Ghosts at Goober's Star. Five million years: just when we expect the stars to have died. But we still don't know what it's for . . .'

Ask it.

Jophiel felt . . . giddy, perhaps. Disoriented. Too much information, pouring in. He tried to think, to speak clearly.

'You know, I lost track of Asher's observations of the Great Attractor. That dating is news. Five million years more until the death of the stars . . .' And he remembered that the *Cauchy* crew was already some three million years through that tremendous interval. 'But we still didn't know the ring's purpose. The Xeelee's objective.'

Ask the Ghost, then.

Michael Poole, murmuring in Jophiel's ear.

Jophiel didn't look round. 'Ask it what?'

Ask the Ghost about the ultimate purpose of the ring. Or at any rate what it believes that purpose is. What have you got to lose? You're all in this together now.

Jophiel turned his head.

It was Poole. But it was not Poole. He smiled at Jophiel. He was thin, tired-looking. He wore his drab one-piece coverall. He looked older than before.

Jophiel turned to the Ghost, and then back to the other Poole.

Who was no longer there.

*

'I'll take the hint,' he said.

The others looked at him curiously. Michael, template Michael, looked suspicious.

'Look,' Jophiel said. 'Here we all are glaring at the Ghost. Maybe we should try talking to the thing. Ghost – you say your kind have been travelling to the Xeelee ring. If you know its purpose, tell us.'

'I have been isolated for a long time. I can only guess.'

'Guess, then.'

'The war rages,' the Ghost said simply. 'Across this universe. The Xeelee and their light-matter kin battle against the dark-matter swarms. You have witnessed the infestation of *all* the bright stars by the larval forms you call photino fish – and I know that you have one such larva locked up in a box of construction material, in your vehicles, stolen from the Ghosts at Goober's Star. And you have witnessed for yourselves that the dark-matter creatures are winning.'

'Across this universe,' Asher said. 'You said, the war rages across *this* universe.'

'Quite. And so the Xeelee are seeking to escape from *this* universe, and flee to another.'

A simple statement. A long silence. The Pooles, Michael and Jophiel, stared at each other.

Asher laughed, in wonder. 'A naked singularity. Is that what the Xeelee are cooking up? At the centre of the ring. All that mass-energy whirling around at relativistic speeds—'

'Yes. They're creating a rip in this universe,' Poole said, nodding. 'Acting as a doorway to another.'

The First Slaver said, 'The Ghosts have no ambition to become extinct. You may know that the universe betrayed us once already—'

'When a pulsar ate your star,' Jophiel said. 'Your Destroyer God.'

'Indeed. Now the Destroyer God is loose once more, and is wreaking havoc on a cosmic scale. The Xeelee, however, are seeking a way out.'

Poole laughed. 'And you Ghosts are going to follow them. Right? What audacity!'

Ward growled, 'So what's that got to do with the Ghost wreck below? Why come here, to the Wheel?'

'We follow the Xeelee,' the Ghost said laconically. 'As I said. We watch them. When the Xeelee which you wounded, Michael Poole, began building a significant artefact at the centre of our Galaxy, we came to study it. We believe that *this* Xeelee, unable perhaps to reach the Great Attractor in this epoch – and certainly unable to contribute to the dark-matter war – is seeking to survive by accelerating through time. Thus it inhabits the extreme dilation zone, down on the lowest levels of the Wheel.'

'Ah,' Poole said. 'Only a few months subjective, five million years objective.'

'We believe the Xeelee will then attempt to join its conspecifics, in their flight through the ring – after the dark-matter war is done, while the ring is still functional, before the ring is abandoned, collapsed, destroyed. This is what I and my colleagues concluded as we explored the Wheel.'

Poole said, 'So this Wheel, this whole vast artefact, is a crude, one-way time machine! . . . I suppose it makes sense. But why the cupworlds? Why make it a harbour for other forms of life?'

The Ghost said, 'We cannot be sure. We believe that the Xeelee, though apparently powerful and indifferent, do in fact have an instinct to protect other life forms. To preserve them, even through cosmic transformations.'

Asher nodded. 'We thought we saw that. The client species that came through the wormhole with the Solar System Xeelee. The quagma phantoms, the Paragons . . . They may have been relics of the past – preservations. I wonder if our Xeelee has built this big fly-trap as a way of *collecting* species to take with it through the Attractor.'

'So you Ghosts were going to follow the Xeelee through their escape hatch,' Poole said. 'But some of you never got further than this Wheel.'

'That is my tragedy, yes.'

'And ours,' Nicola said softly.

Poole looked around at them all, one by one. 'Does all of this make any difference to our own next steps? No? Then we continue.'

So they travelled on.

And after a journey across the deck of two hundred and forty-one days, and having driven in their trucks a distance equivalent to eighty times the gulf between Earth and Neptune, the convoy reached Earth Three.

61

Earth date: c. AD 2,710,000

A world like a smashed plate, clumsily stuck back together. Just as Jophiel and the rest had seen from afar. But now, a week after the arrival of the *Cauchy* crew at the edge of this new cupworld, after surveys from their Rim Mountain station and flights of their single flyer, the maps Asher Fennell showed her colleagues were far more detailed than anything they'd had when they had chosen this world as their next destination.

Asher and her team of amateur geographers had divided this world into sectors – roughly like pie slices – around the great monument that was Central Mountain. Pie slices that contained significantly distinct climatic zones, separated by thick ridges of hull plate, folds themselves the size of mountain ranges.

And now Jophiel stood with Asher and their colleagues on the edge of the Rim Mountains himself, looking down through the Lid over the sky on this new world.

Down on one of these zones. A bare, arid plain.

'Like we travelled all this way and ended back at High Australia,' Chinelo said.

Jophiel too felt only a kind of incuriosity, even dismay. He raised his head and looked to a dusty horizon. Just as at High Australia, all of the cupworld's atmosphere was below him, and it was like looking down into a very shallow, very clear sea, with a sandy sunlit floor. He could see nothing of the neighbouring continent-sized pie slices. It would be hard work to live here, in this pie-slice desert at least, for the crew and their putative descendants.

And he couldn't make out Central Mountain, all of five thousand kilometres away. The telescopes revealed a hull-plate summit sticking out above the dusty air, like a tethered moon. Nobody imagined that

314

the mountain, or the rest of this world's detail, was as it had been designed by the Xeelee.

Asher was holding up her map. 'So we came in from the west, and we're looking east, spinward. If I show you an altitude chart . . .'

Coded with false colours, this was a disc of shades, varying from yellow in the west to deep brown in the east. And a dazzling pinprick of yellow-white at the centre.

'The lighter the shade, the higher the altitude. You can see Central Mountain, towering above the mean. But if you look at the cupworld as a whole—'

Chinelo saw it immediately. 'It's tipped up. Higher in the west, where we are, lower in the east.'

'That's it. The collision that disrupted the Wheel left this particular world on a tilt.' On her screens, she sketched detail on the maps. 'You can see that the altitude slope has affected the climate zones – presumably because of the distortion of weather systems, the water distribution. And those big hull-plate ridges between the zones act like tall mountain ranges also – *very* tall, and presumably immune to erosion. There do seem to be passes through them; life can cross between the zones. But they cast mighty rain shadows.

'We haven't stayed still long enough to study cupworlds properly, not even at High Australia. We certainly don't know how they are *supposed* to work. And if this cupworld has suffered sufficient damage – maybe even the basic day-night cycle has been disrupted, let alone the seasonality and average temperatures . . . Well, we're just going to have to keep on measuring, and studying, and figuring it out.

'In the meantime, this is what we found.' She gestured at her pie-slice map, sweeping her gloved hand. 'Working anticlockwise from here, there is an oceanic sector – a few scattered islands and one major continent – and then a frozen zone. Glaciers descending from the foothills of the local Rim Mountains, and what looks like tundra below. The ice piles up at the cupworld's easternmost point, so its lowest in terms of mean altitude. Beyond the frozen zone you have what looks like temperate grassland. Wide sweeps of open land. What may be big herds. And after that the final sector, to the "north" of us. Dense forest, apparently tropical. Which gives way to the desert before us.'

Poole frowned. 'On the grasslands. Herds of what?'

'Well, we don't know. Not yet. Presumably herbivorous . . . something. We haven't had the resources to check. We do know the ecology is essentially Earthlike. The grass is grass, for instance; the photosynthesis uses the same chlorophyll chemistry as Earth life evolved.'

'So you think this is another place where the Ghosts emptied out some of the *Gourd* crew, and their ecohab? Or some other scattership.'

'Maybe. But even if so, we have to expect everything will be . . . changed. That's what I've been trying to explain in the briefings.'

Chinelo frowned. 'What kind of changes?'

'Evolution. In ecological niches,' Jophiel murmured. 'She's talking about what happens when a landscape fragments. Breaks up. This cupworld is like the African rift valley maybe, where the hominins evolved. Us, I mean. The Mediterranean drying and flooding, pulses of aridity. Once there had been continent-spanning forests. Then it all broke up, and we started to adapt, some to the remnant forests, some to the broadening plains . . .'

'Africa,' Poole murmured. 'Maybe that's what we should call Earth Three. We left High Australia behind. Now – High Africa.'

'Niches, yes,' Asher said. 'And half a million years is plenty of time for adaptation. Even for people,' she added grimly. 'And we think we've seen signs.'

Jophiel was startled. 'Of people. From up here?'

She looked around. 'You need to understand what I'm going to show you. Remember the Coalescents on High Australia?'

Chinelo said, 'The hive people.'

'Right. We know from the historical accounts that Coalescences take only millennia, if not centuries, to evolve. But once established they keep *on* evolving. Presumably. Given the right conditions.'

Jophiel turned, turned to face the sweep of desert below the Rim Mountains. 'Conditions such as here,' he said, guessing.

'Such as here. But we have never observed just how, before. We've surveyed this dry sector. You can see it's pretty open country. A few oases, a few heavily adapted trees, looking more like cacti. There's probably animal life, but if so it's on too small a scale, too dispersed, for us to see from here. But, what we have seen . . .'

Jophiel had a deep foreboding in his Virtual gut about the images she pulled up now on the softscreens.

He was expecting something like the pyramids of stone and dirt that they'd observed in High Australia. Here, he saw much more complex forms, vaguely conical, but with vents and shafts and ducts. The basic forms *glistened*, their surfaces smooth and hard, and the complex light of the sky cast highlights from the tan carapaces.

And around each and every structure, a circular earthwork.

Asher said, 'These structures are all over the desert zone. They seem to have been drawn to water sources. Aquifers, deep springs – on this engineered world you'd probably call them leaks, from the wetter zones to either side. We've counted hundreds; there are no doubt more. We've no idea of their age. Water courses do shift, on natural landscapes anyhow; it may be that the colonies move, with time – or are even abandoned. We don't really know. What we do know is that nobody has encountered human Coalescences this old before. Not before we left Cold Earth anyhow.'

Chinelo seemed awestruck. 'If they're like the Libraries on High Australia, there might be millions of people down there. Billions.'

Poole grunted. 'But, after half a million years, are Coalescents still people in any meaningful sense? I doubt that there's anything here for us. In this arid zone, I mean. And we stay away from the Coalescences. Agreed? We're most likely to find people like us in places suited for people like us to inhabit. '

Jophiel had to smile. 'A brusque summary of the theory of evolution, but I take your point.'

Poole ignored him. 'And that means going to the north and east, in the forest zone, and the grasslands. So we send a scouting party, down off these Rim Mountains into that big wedge of forest, then track roughly north-east, if we can, until we reach the grasslands . . . Are we done here? Let's go back to the convoy and plan it out.'

Jophiel thought their spirits had been raised a little by Poole's crisp decision-making. Maybe it was all illusory. Michael Poole was an earthworm crawling through the track of some immense excavating machine, making a plan to conquer the next centimetre of broken soil. But it helped for now, and maybe you could ask no more of a leader than that.

Even Nicola had no sarcastic comments to make.

62

They allowed seven more days to prepare for the expedition into the rainforest. Temporary habitats were set up, the trucks and other gear were checked over. Their passengers received some attention. Nicola and Asher even ran non-intrusive probes through the hull-plate shell containing their pet dark-matter larva, as Max called it. Trying to detect if it was still alive. And Jophiel briefed their captive Ghost, alone in the truck that was its prison.

Wina, in a lightweight skinsuit, ran as far and as fast as she could, to an unattainable horizon.

Poole used the time constructively. At his orders the flyer, broken down for haulage in the convoy, was taken out of store, assembled, tested. But the only place to check out an aircraft was in the air. So Poole mandated test flights, down over the desert zone. Asher leapt on these, so as not to miss a quick opportunity for close-up observations.

And Jophiel grabbed the chance to go on the first flight of all, over the new world.

The descent from the Rim Mountains was every bit as exhilarating, as terrifying, as he remembered from High Australia. And soon they were swooping low over a new landscape.

He had anticipated that this dry landscape would be every bit as dull as High Australia had seemed, up close. But it wasn't so. Barren it was. In places they crossed dune-fields that stretched as far as the eye could see. Asher pointed out a salt flat: cracked ground that glimmered in the light of the rippling sky: the relic of a vanished sea.

But a little further from the Rim Mountains they came to a region where oases seemed more common. Jophiel spotted the scrubby brown-green of vegetation, presumably deep-rooted and drought-tolerant.

Vegetation, and animals.

The flyer swept down on one oasis, all but silent, but nonetheless its rushing passage and complex shadow disturbed the busy, wary fauna. Jophiel saw what looked like small, erect rodents, with big back legs capable of springing high in the air. Insectivores, maybe. They scattered and scurried for shade, while other rodents, pale, with stubby tails, burrowed out of sight into the ground.

And now a bird came stalking past, big, evidently flightless, its red crest the only sign of colour on a body covered with dun feathers. It snapped at the rodents with a powerful-looking beak, and glared up at the flyer, as if challenging a rival.

Then they flew over a herd of what were presumably herbivores. Animals the size of big dogs, maybe, or small horses. They had long fur, and humps on their backs, like camels. When the flyer passed over, they huddled together, fleeing, and it was hard for Jophiel to make out details. But he saw how the 'camels' had big ears, folded back against their heads, and powerful-looking back legs, and white lumps of fur for tails. And when they did scatter he saw that they moved with great leaps, propelled by those big back legs.

When the flyer had moved on, Asher eyed him. 'What do you make of that?'

'I hope we got decent images to convince Harris and the other biologists back at the Rim . . .'

'Convince them of what?'

'Those camel-like creatures looked like big rabbits. The burrowers and insect-catchers back at the water hole were rats. And the big flightless birds—'

'Chickens. I know.'

Jophiel felt himself shiver at the strangeness of it. 'This is what you get when you dump out a bit of parkland and leave it to evolve for a few hundred thousand years.'

'An ecology with everything but the people,' Asher said. 'But then, aside from Coalescents, who would want to live *here*, when there's a continent-sized forest next door? Although the climate might have kept shifting. Driven them on. It's evident the Wheel was pretty badly damaged in this area, and maybe when the Xeelee came to make its repairs there was a limit even to its capability. The job was crude – look at all the exposed hull-plate welding. Maybe the cupworld's systems were permanently destabilised – the erosion cycle, for instance.'

Jophiel frowned. *'When the Xeelee came* . . . I hadn't thought of that. You think that's what happened? I've tended to imagine the Xeelee stayed camped down on Deck One, down in the deepest time pit, with some kind of remote repair system to take care of any flaws. But maybe that's anthropomorphising. Look at its pattern of operation in the Solar System. When it came to the destruction of the worlds, the planetbuster Cages, the Xeelee itself was part of the attack. Its sycamore-seed primary ship was stationed at one vertex of the tetrahedron that caged each planet, with the other corners occupied by drones.'

'Correct. The distinction between a Xeelee and its technology may be blurred. So it does seem quite possible that the Xeelee came here, somehow, to this part of the Wheel, to supervise the repair work itself.'

Jophiel looked east, in the direction of Central Mountain. 'And if so it would have needed some kind of repair shack, you'd think . . . Equipped with some way of getting back to its base on Deck One. Something quicker than our crawl across the Decks.'

'Something like a Poole wormhole would do it,' Asher said, grinning. 'And stuck on top of that mountain, probably. Centrally placed, with access to all the zones of the cupworld.'

Jophiel said, 'We must discuss this with Michael. I mean, if we could find some kind of rapid-transit route back to the Xeelee base on Deck One – that could change everything. *If* we could find it . . .'

The flyer rose high in the sky, and the detail of the sparsely scattered inhabitants of the plain below became indistinct, the fleeing herds reduced to smudges against the broad, austere landscape.

63

Poole was predictably electrified by the notion of a work shack, and a transit route for the Xeelee. He immediately dispatched small drone craft across the landscape of the cupworld – and to the summit of Central Mountain, which, he agreed, was the most likely place to find a Xeelee portal.

Then, after seven days of aerial surveys, Poole – clearly suppressing impatience as he waited for the drones' results – decreed that the ground exploration of High Africa could begin in earnest. Predictably, he insisted on leading the first expedition himself. And, using aerial imaging, he quickly plotted out a course. 'That forest looks pretty thick. But there must be river courses we could follow. Where there's an Africa, there must be a Congo . . .'

So the flyer was loaded up, in search of a river through the forest sector. As ever, Nicola was at the controls. Harris and Asher were both aboard.

Max Ward wanted to come along, with a view, Jophiel thought, to scouting out a potentially hostile landscape. He had a squad of his trained-up cadets on board too, including Chinelo. 'After all,' he growled, 'if we do find any descendants of the *Gourd* crew half a million years late, let's hope they don't bear a grudge.'

Susan Chen was here too – in her own way, Jophiel realised, hoping for just such an encounter.

And Wina of High Australia, hunting pack, bow and arrows and all.

'My idea,' Poole said. 'Although she volunteered anyhow. Maybe a native of one cupworld will help us make some kind of contact with the natives of another.'

Nicola snorted. 'That is so deeply patronising. Natives they might be, but separated by half a million years. As if you brought along Isambard Kingdom Brunel to make contact with a Neanderthal.'

'You want I should kick her off the plane?' Poole said.

Jophiel considered. 'No. She will surely have better instincts in this kind of environment than you or me, Michael. Come to think of it, so would Brunel, probably. Or the Neanderthal. Let's get on with it.'

So they flew.

Once over the forest, as Poole had predicted, it took just an hour to find a river. A veritable Congo.

At this point in its course it was a broad, placid stream cutting through a blanket of green, eventually feeding a delta that led into a shallow inland sea – that in turn, a thousand kilometres away, broke against the hull-plate walls that separated this forest sector from the grassland beyond.

Nicola took the flyer on a course down the river's middle line.

Harris said his best first guess was that the evergreen trees that crowded the forest, and even the banyan-like colonists of the shallow waters near the river bank, were hastily evolved relatives of oaks – which, Jophiel learned now, had once had evergreen subspecies as well as deciduous. And in the shallower water the river itself was choked with mats of algae, and what looked like tremendous lilies.

Green, everywhere. Jophiel the engineer found himself trying to estimate the sheer mass of life he saw in one glance: a biosphere that had presumably developed from the scraps that had tumbled out of the captured wreck of the *Gourd*, and flourished, adapted, spread, and turned trillions of tonnes of the raw material of this Xeelee artefact into copies of itself.

Soon the river widened dramatically, and even from a decent altitude, Jophiel had to turn his head deliberately from side to side to see the river's banks. A Congo indeed, here in High Africa. But such thoughts, of purpose and planning, seemed to dissolve as they flew on and on across green immensity. This forest, Jophiel reminded himself, was a detail in a cupworld that was itself a mere blemish on the face of the Wheel. And all of this, he marvelled, ultimately derived from the mass-energy of a supermassive black hole a light year away.

Poole had estimated that the crossing of the forest zone, measured out as ten thousand kilometres, would take three watches' flying at a conservative four hundred kilometres an hour. These would be spaced by two more watches on the ground, to allow for exploration, rest, maintenance.

So, after the first eight hours, Nicola and Poole started looking for a place to land.

That turned out to be not so easy. With the river itself a mystery

– there were surely no crocodiles or alligators, but maybe something else had taken the initiative to occupy the relevant ecological niches – they did not want to land too close to the water. But the forest was a jungle, and the trees, competing for light, packed about as densely as they could get, Jophiel thought.

Eventually they spotted a clearing. It was a rough circle blasted into the forest cover, with burned and fallen trees littering the ground, the green shoots of a new generation already showing.

'A lightning strike,' Nicola called back to her passengers. 'So now we know there are electrical storms here.

'We're going down.'

64

As soon as they touched down, even as they threw open the doors of the flyer, Max Ward began issuing orders about guard rotas and perimeters.

Chinelo went off to join Michael Poole and the scouting party he was putting together.

And Jophiel, walking with Nicola, emerged into a world of green gloom. Tree trunks like pillars rose up to a sky obscured by a distant canopy. Where a little light penetrated to the ground, saplings, scrub, sparse grass struggled to grow, but otherwise the ground was bare, save for a thin carpet of leaves, dry and curled.

'It's like the cathedral at Achinet,' Jophiel murmured. 'The light here. Do you remember? On Tenerife. After the Xeelee probe strike in the Atlantic—'

'I remember,' Nicola said.

'I knew it, once,' Susan Chen said. Jophiel saw that she had set up a kind of camp in the open, just a few fold-out chairs, and a small galley unit that would deliver hot drinks and military-style rations. Susan waved a hand. 'Come, sit with me. One thing that I don't regret about age is not needing to be busy, busy all the time. We land in a place like this and immediately we are fiddling with equipment and making plans. To achieve what? We are here. The forest is all around us. If we pursue it, it will elude us. If we wait, it will come to us.'

Nicola was grinning. 'Good idea. As for me, whatever Poole does, do the opposite. I've always found that a good default strategy.'

Jophiel shrugged, sat on a Virtual equivalent of Susan's canvas chairs, and snapped his fingers to give himself a Virtual cup of hot mint tea.

Once the guards were set, the flyer closed up, and the scouting parties had finally marched off into the green shadows, a kind of peace did indeed settle over the landing site.

And with the human sounds receding, for a few minutes they sat in silence. Jophiel seemed to hear further, clearer. Distant cries, echoing, that might have been birds, small animals – monkeys maybe.

Susan lifted her face, her eyes closed, a faint smile on her lips. Jophiel thought she must once have been very beautiful. 'Perhaps it is no coincidence that a forest reminds us of a cathedral. Perhaps that is why we built churches like forest glades in the first place: the towering columns, the gloom, the contained hush. Gaudí's Sagrada Familia in Barcelona, you know. Lost now, of course. We re-created the spaces where our ancestors once walked. And,' she said, pointing, 'the forest has never forgotten us either.'

Jophiel followed her gesture.

And there, in the shade of nearby trees, he saw hulking forms. Low, heavy, moving almost silently – no, not quite silently. He heard a rustle of leaves as big hands explored the ground. Cracks, sharp and brisk, as massive jaws closed around nut shells.

Bright blue eyes, startlingly clear, looking out of the shadows at him.

'Stay calm,' Susan Chen said softly, whether to the two of them or the forest inhabitants Jophiel wasn't sure. She was still smiling.

Nicola murmured, 'You were right, Susan. Michael Poole will kick himself when he discovers he's missed this.'

'I'm recording it all.' Asher walked out to join them, treading softly. 'They seem curious about us. And the flyer. I tracked back through the records; they moved in, cautiously, as soon as the trek parties moved out. I think there's one adult, and several children.'

'Oh, no,' Susan said. 'Take a closer look.' She pointed. '*That's* an adult female. Those lesser ones are males. There are children with them, but a lot smaller – see, the infant clinging to the female's back?'

It was difficult to make out details. The visitors were all squatting, and it was hard to judge their height. They didn't look tall, but massive, heavy, like bloated weightlifters. They were nude, but wore their hair long and unkempt. Their skin, scuffed with dirt and the stains of leaves and other vegetation, was dark too, both male and female, apparently. And the skin was not covered in hair, Jophiel thought, not like an ape, though hairier than a human. Their hands worked at the ground continually, scratching for nuts, roots, lifting the goodies to those robust mouths, even as they stared at the *Cauchy* crew.

Their squatting bodies looked almost conical, Jophiel thought. And their heads looked oddly small, behind very human faces.

'That big female,' Nicola said. 'She's staring straight at us.'

'I wouldn't make eye contact,' Susan said. 'She's curious. Wondering if we are another pack, probably. She won't fear us, but she might misinterpret a stare as a challenge. A fight over her pack of males, maybe – it looks to me as if females are dominant.'

Jophiel accepted this wisdom, thinking of the bleak millennium of study and observation Susan must have endured while she cared for the diminished descendants of the *Gourd* crew on Goober c.

'They eat all the time,' Nicola observed. 'Nuts and roots they grub up. They're so big it's hard to imagine anything much smaller than a lion taking them down. But they look so heavy – surely they would have trouble hunting down meat.'

Asher nodded. 'Vegetarians, probably. And—'

A crack, from high above.

'Look out!' Asher shoved at Jophiel, instinctively, her hands passing into his Virtual flesh. The protocol-violation sting of that was bad enough.

Then a tree branch came crashing down from above, and passed *through* his sitting body. He jumped up, stumbled back. The protocol-generated pain was astounding.

Max Ward's perimeter guards came running, vaguely waving their blasters at shadows in the trees above.

But Susan Chen, still sitting, was holding out her hands, palms forward. 'Jophiel! Stay quiet. You people, put away those guns. It was an accident – look at that branch, it's rotten, it just broke away – believe me, they intended no harm. Anyhow the root-eaters have gone. And the other sort, they'd rather we didn't notice them at all.'

Asher seemed confused. 'What other sort?'

Susan, cautiously, pointed upwards.

Jophiel looked up. It was difficult to see anything, so shadowy was the lower canopy above him. He subvocalised system commands to enhance his vision; generally he didn't like to cheat . . .

A touch of night vision showed them clearly.

Human forms, up in the branches, clambering, squatting, even swinging from one arm at a time. All but silent. More bright eyes looking back at him.

'A different kind,' Asher murmured. 'They look a little more – human. The body plan. Hairier, though.'

'Not quite,' Nicola said. 'The proportions of the arms and legs are subtly off. Big hands – and big feet too, which look like they could grip.'

'And small brains,' Asher said with a tinge of sadness.

Jophiel said, 'Thus the crew of the *Gourd*, I guess. Or some other captured scatterships. Or rather their remote descendants.'

Susan nodded. 'Certainly it is must be generations since they re-membered their origins. Generations more since they knew anything more than an endless present in the green. A present of no significant events save those of their own small lives. Births and deaths, hungry days, days of feast. No change, no challenge. And so—'

Another irruption of noise.

This time it came from the edge of the clearing. An animal, howling, burst out of cover, dashed into the open space, and stumbled to a halt.

Everybody scrambled out of the way.

Jophiel glimpsed a low body, big and muscular, but with the body plan of a hunting cat: long, supple legs, paws tipped with claws, a meaty tail, black eyes, folded-back ears – and incisor teeth like kitchen knives.

The perimeter guards, surprised, yelled and waved their blasters around, threatening more harm to the humans than the animal, Jo-phiel thought. Nicola, evidently with the same instinct, hauled Susan Chen back out of the way. But the animal was already wounded, Jophiel saw, with a cruel-looking arrow sticking out of one bloodied haunch.

It stood still for a heartbeat, panting hard.

Then it dashed across the open space and was gone.

It was followed by a silent, intent Wina, running almost as fast, another arrow ready to fire from her bow.

Hunter and prey passed out of sight. A kind of stunned peace returned.

Jophiel looked around. Nobody, it seemed, had come to any harm.

But, he saw, the humanoids, the big forest-floor browsers and the agile climbers both, had all gone.

When Poole and his party returned, the explorers compared notes.

'We walked to the river from the clearing where we landed,' Mi-chael Poole said. 'Keeping to cover, moving quietly. Plenty of animal life, if you give it a chance to show itself. I thought we saw something like wild boar. Did the *Gourd* carry pigs? And a flightless bird, on the prowl – a *big* one.'

Ward grunted. 'Wina saw a nest on the ground, and was all for raiding it for eggs. I put a stop to that.'

'I mean, *really* big,' Poole said, apparently shaken. 'It saw us, but it ran off after what looked like rabbits, with long heads, pointed snouts—'

'Maybe they were ant eaters, I thought. Or specialists on termite mounds.' Harris seemed bewildered too. 'But with the bodies of rabbits.'

'And at the river itself, when we got close to the bank, more big beasts. Fat browsers, like hippos. A thing not unlike a crocodile, but mammalian . . . Whereas here—'

'We had visitors,' Jophiel summed it up. 'Things like gorillas. Things like chimpanzees.' He briefly described the experience.

Susan Chen said, 'I know that in the forests of Earth, gorilla packs were dominated by single males, with smaller females. Sexual dimorphism. Here, the same, but with the dominant figure a female.'

Harris was interested, but shrugged. 'If we get the chance we should study this. How the sexual role-reversal affects pack politics. Evidently the genes found a way to make it work . . .

'Still, chimps and gorillas. I guess there are only so many ways for big primates to make a living in a dense forest. Floor dwellers living off fruit, nuts, roots, with big heavy jaws to take food nobody else could – jaws that could break through tough shells, chew up stringy roots. Or else you live like chimps, competing for fruit in the canopy – maybe indulging in a little opportunistic meat-eating.'

Poole nodded gravely. 'But aren't you missing the main point? There were no apes or monkeys in the *Gourd* parkland inventory. Just chickens and rats and rabbits—'

'And people,' Max Ward growled.

Asher nodded. 'The old forms were still there, in our genes. They just needed the time, the opportunity to bring them back.'

Max grunted. 'You're saying they lost their minds, and went climbing trees, or sat on their butts cracking nuts?'

'And for a long time too,' Harris said, looking now at softscreen images of the 'gorillas'. 'You can see by the adaptation of the jaw, the big muscles hinged on the upper skull . . .'

'How come they didn't stay smart?' Chinelo asked. 'Wouldn't that be an advantage when you're facing a rat that's evolving into a, a leopard?'

Asher sighed. 'Only if you're in an environment that favours smartness. Max said it, back in High Australia. The forest looks spectacular, but that's pretty much all there is here. The soil is shallow; almost all of the organic matter here is above ground, in the trees. And under the shallow soil, a layer of soft rock, like sandstone, and, not much deeper than *that*, hull plate. Just imagine how it must have been. Half a million years. Generation upon generation, the tools they must have brought with them from the *Gourd* breaking down with no way of repair. There was no way they could escape from the cupworld, of course. You'd make spears and bows from wood – like the High Australia folk. But with time you would see your grandchildren growing ever clumsier, ever less interested. Because the ability to run and fight counted for a lot more than the ability to *make* stuff. Minds like burning-out candles.'

As Asher spoke, Jophiel glanced at Susan Chen. These hominins, tree-climbing, nut-cracking, could well have descended from the crew of the *Gourd*. And yet she did not seem distressed. Not bitter, or angry, still less horrified. Oddly content with what she was finding.

'That's enough.' Michael Poole stood decisively. 'It's clear to me there's nothing for us here. Take whatever samples and readings you need, Asher, Harris. We'll stay here one watch. Try to get some sleep. Rotate the guard.' He looked up, as if seeking the sky. 'Then we go on. To the grasslands.

'And beyond.'

65

Jophiel felt a great sense of relief to be back aboard the flyer, in the air and over an expansive grassland: a sea of rippling grass broken by scattered rivers and lakes, and small clumps of trees, a few rocky outcrops. A sense of release, he thought, to have been lifted out of the shadows of the trees.

'Of course you feel like that,' Harris Kemp said, when they talked about this. '*You* are evolved for the plain. Open and full of light. Long eye lines, where you can see what's coming over the horizon, and it can see *you*. So both predators and prey are adapted for speed, for long-distance running. On a grassland everything is in flight, all the time . . .'

He was right.

The flyer passed over fleeing herds.

Big heavy rabbits with thick, hairless hides. They were like elephants, or rhinos perhaps, equipped with horny skulls and sharp claws for defence. Or slimmer, more agile rabbits, with those big muscular rear legs adapted to running, or in some cases jumping. Rabbits distorted like gazelles, or kangaroos. Some of these herds were enormous. And as the flyer crossed over, the streams of herbivores would be disrupted, the animals scattering.

Then there were the carnivores that preyed upon the herbivores. Big flightless birds that seemed, as Poole observed, to be reaching for genetic memories of the dinosaurs.

And people.

Max, sharp-eyed, was the first to spot them. He sat up in his couch and pointed. '*There*. Look. No doubt about it. A band, must be about fifty . . .'

Jophiel peered down.

They didn't look like chimps or gorillas this time. Slim, tall-looking, they were naked, out on the plain. Adults, some children, a few infants on their parents' backs. He saw that some of them surrounded a fallen animal, apparently one of the elephantine rabbits, and were hastily butchering it.

They didn't look up as the flyer crossed over. Evidently they didn't expect any visitors from the sky.

'So, hunters,' Max said. 'And carnivores.'

Wina spoke, surprising Jophiel.

'No. Not hunters. Look.'

She rarely contributed to the discussions of the group. It wasn't that she was shy, Jophiel thought; it was just that she stuck to her own area of expertise, and spoke only when she had something to say. A habit, Nicola had once observed drily, that a few others among this crew could do with copying.

Now she showed Jophiel a magnified image on a softscreen. 'This animal was not brought down by weapons, by spears or arrows. See? Its throat has been torn out. By big teeth.'

'Ah,' Asher said, blowing up the image further. 'Killed by one of the big predators, then. So the real killers abandoned their catch, for some reason.'

Wina nodded. 'And these . . . people moved in, to take the meat.'

'They are scavengers,' Max said. 'Humans, scavenging over prey brought down by rats.' He laughed. 'How pathetic.'

Wina looked angry, offended. 'There is no shame. If you are hungry you take your meat where you find it.'

'You're right,' Harris said grimly. 'And you, Max, shouldn't believe the stories about the heroic advance of humanity they told you when you were a kid. *We* always scavenged – or our ancestors did.'

'Let's take her down and see,' Poole said firmly.

That turned out not to be so easy. As soon as the flyer started to descend, the human types noticed it, at last. They broke up into smaller groups, adults grabbing children, and scattered.

Wina laughed now. 'They are so fast! A race between them and the best runners of the People of the Vanquished First Slaver would be interesting.'

Jophiel saw that one small group, away from the flyer, had paused. They had taken chunks of meat from the kill; now they dumped this on the ground and began to eat, hastily, almost furtively – expecting it to be stolen, Jophiel saw. The lure of the food overcame their fear, for now, though they stared fixedly at the flyer.

'Send me down,' Jophiel said on impulse. 'Split off a copy. Let's just take one close look, before we move on.'

Nicola raised a silver sketch of an eyebrow. 'Dressed like that?'

He glanced down at his bright blue coverall. 'So give me a neutral colour.' He thought of that other Poole. 'Give me grey. *He* suits it.'

Michael Poole looked at him oddly. 'Who?'

'Never mind. Just do it . . .'

And he was on the plain. In an infinity of grass, an abstraction – it was like a Virtual environment on the *Gea*, perhaps.

He stood, facing the group.

One child, looking over its mother's shoulder, spotted him. It gurgled, and pointed.

Jophiel smiled.

One by one the runners turned, saw him, eyes widening. Parents instinctively reached for their young. But they did not flee.

Harris murmured in his ear, 'They don't know if you are a threat, or prey. They've never seen anything like you. Just stand still.'

One tall male stood up, stared at Jophiel, and jabbered what sounded like a paragraph of speech but probably wasn't. He walked forward.

And he loomed over Jophiel.

They were all so *tall*, Jophiel saw immediately, women and men alike, and their bodies well balanced, with muscular limbs, broad shoulders, flat torsos. Like decathletes, perhaps, trained for a variety of sports, for speed and strength and agility.

'Sit down,' Harris murmured now. 'Sit on the ground. The less you look like a threat, the better.'

Good idea, but too late, Jophiel thought. Even as he sat, the big male hurried off, apparently alarmed. The group gathered back at the spot where they had been eating, and stood in a circle, the younger adults facing out, the older adults and the infants inside. Jophiel saw now that a couple of the adults held weapons, just roughly sharpened wooden spears, though the tips were blackened.

Asher had noticed the same thing. 'Fire-hardened,' she murmured to Jophiel.

'So maybe they still have fire?'

She shrugged. 'Or they just exploit lightning strikes.'

When no immediate threat came from Jophiel, the next step seemed to be exploration.

One young woman walked out of the group, hesitantly – and yet defiantly, for she walked straight up to Jophiel.

'Remarkable,' Jophiel breathed. Cautiously he got to his feet, and approached her.

The woman flinched back.

Then, when he offered no threat, she walked around him. Jophiel could see the fine hairs on her bare skin, smell a scent of dust and sweat. She was quite naked, her hands empty.

'She's – beautiful. They all are. Perfect bodies, almost an idealised human form. Like the stars of some Virtual soap opera.' He laughed, making the woman flinch, but she stood her ground. 'Sorry,' he said. 'Flat stomach. Strong shoulders, well-muscled limbs. She's meant for running. Very well adapted to this plain of grass, evidently.' He had to look up to meet her eyes. 'Taller than me. Eyes quite normal, as far as I can see. Human eyes, with whites, not like an ape's. But the head, the shape of the face . . .'

Her jaw was too heavy, too strong. Her nose was broad and flat. Her eyes were sheltered from the light of the sky by a heavy, bony ridge. And the brow behind that eye ridge was flat, receding, and her skull small at the back. For all her athlete's body, Jophiel felt he could have cupped that skull in one hand, as if cradling a baby's head.

'Her eyes look human,' Jophiel said. 'As human as mine. *Bright*. But – calculating. It's like looking into the eyes of an animal. A lion, maybe—'

Abruptly she raised a hand and thrust it, as if to grab Jophiel's throat. Jophiel recoiled instinctively, though she could not harm him. There was a stinging flare of pixels where her flesh touched his, and she flinched back. Her face twisted in anger, in threat, and she jabbered a string of syllables at him.

Harris murmured, 'Just stay calm. They're acting on instinct. They can't work out if you're a predator out to eat them, or a rival runner meaning to attack them, or steal their kids. So you have a mix of instinctive responses.'

Jophiel frowned. 'Instinctive?'

'I agree,' Asher said. 'Instinctive, not decision-making as we understand it. I've been analysing their speech. That threat she just uttered, Jophiel. Barely any semantic content. Just a screech of challenge, or warning. As we said, just like in the jungle, this isn't an environment where a big heavy brain is an asset. If you put all that energy into running, instead . . .'

'And give it half a million years,' Jophiel said a little bitterly, 'then the result is this. Beautiful emptiness.'

'Now you're being parochial, Jophiel. These are animals, perfectly fit to their environment. In fact I think they're a close analogue of *Homo erectus*. More of those, umm, *living solutions*, evidently still there in our genomes for when they are needed again. And probably easy for evolution to reach for – if I can put it that way. Just changes in the relative growth rates of organs, for instance.'

'Bigger hearts. Smaller heads.'

'Something like that.'

Max Ward growled, 'Maybe so. But they lost their humanity. And they're not even the dominant animal on this savannah. Are they? As Wina said, they're just scavengers.'

Susan scowled. 'What of it? *Homo erectus* lasted millions of years. Maybe they will last just as long here. When we are long gone, pursuing our foolish dreams, *their* children will still be here, running in the light—'

Without warning, with a snap, Jophiel was brought back to the flyer.

He staggered, feeling a little drunk. '*Ow*. A little warning would have been nice. And I bet you scared the runners again.'

Michael Poole stood before him, grinning. 'Never mind the runners. We've got much bigger news than that.'

Jophiel guessed wildly, 'Your drones have reported in.'

Nicola stood back, arms folded. 'Some of them. In particular the one we sent to the summit of Central Mountain—'

'Just tell me.'

'It found a wormhole.'

SIX

In case of emergency, break laws of physics.

Harry Poole, AD 3829

66

Ship elapsed time since launch: 27 years 182 days

Earth date: c. AD 2,710,000

Nicola stayed at the top of the mountain, and sent the uncrewed flyer back for the rest. They loaded up quickly.

Then, under Michael Poole's piloting, the flyer swept smoothly up the western flank of Central Mountain.

The higher they climbed, the more fake the mountain looked to Jophiel. The lower slopes, where the mountain emerged from a sea of grassland, seemed authentic enough, with grass, scrub, and scattered clumps of trees clinging to an increasingly steep rocky face. There were animals there too, post-rabbits with skinny frames and long legs that made them look like goats – and, in one place, as Chinelo excitedly pointed out, people: or post-people anyhow, a small band of enterprising hunters who scattered at the approach of this unfamiliar monster, the flyer.

From here, when Jophiel turned and glanced back, he got a wide view of the landscapes of the cupworld. A swathe of grassland, a patch of forest, a river decanting into a lake that flooded a strangely angular basin. From up here the land *looked* as if it had been cracked and broken, the fragments crudely glued back together.

Past a certain height the efforts of life to colonise gave way to bare rock.

Then, higher still as the flyer continued its relentless climb towards a sky of rippling light, the rock itself started to show gaps, like a canvas stretched so far its paint had cracked and flaked away, and Jophiel saw the pale uniform gleam of hull plate, the true substrate of this mask world. But the hull plate itself looked jumbled, tipped up, distorted. Nicola pointed out ridges of thicker material where, apparently, new hull plate had been grown over to seal wounds.

And a mountain that was evidently no mountain at all.

Jophiel wondered if it had been something like the creation of a

337

central mountain in a lunar crater, caused by a strike by an asteroid or comet nucleus. Such a mountain was a kind of frozen, reflected ripple at the centre of a circular scar, in bedrock that had been smashed and broken and melted and *splashed*. Hull plate wasn't bedrock, but maybe this mountain was a similar phenomenon, a wave of destruction that had focused here at the geometric centre of the roughly circular cup-world – a focused distortion that had thrust up this kilometres-high peak – and then, as the hull plate somehow recovered, been left frozen in place.

There was a kick as the flyer's small fusion-powered rockets cut in and an aircraft morphed into a spacecraft. They flew above the air now. Above Jophiel's head, the artificial sky was deepening to a blue-black, across which the strange day-night bands of brighter illumination were strikingly obvious, and through which the red stars of the Galaxy centre could clearly be seen, a dismal veil.

The flyer at last soared up and over a rim.

Here, Xeelee hull plate had been stretched beyond endurance and, at last, had torn and cracked. The result was a fence of jagged, lethal-looking peaks, spikes of stretched hull plate, through which the flyer swam smoothly.

And beyond the fence, the summit itself spread out before them. It was a plain of what looked like pure hull plate, more smashed fragments crudely stitched together, with here and there clumps of broken rock. Poole brought the flyer low down as it crossed an expanse fully fifty kilometres wide, enclosed by those hull-plate spikes. Jophiel was reminded of flights over Olympus Mons, greatest mountain on Mars, a volcano whose summit was a plain pocked by multiple calderas.

And there, at what looked to Jophiel like the geometric centre, a bright spot of Earth green: a dome, the shelter that had supported Nicola through her stay up here, while she had sent back the flyer for Poole and the rest.

Beside the dome, a scrap of sky blue.

A cube.

Floating above the ground.

The flyer landed a respectful distance away. The crew clambered down to the surface.

And *surface*, not *ground*, Jophiel thought, was the right word for this section of the artificial world. Here at the climax of this tremendous wound, the hull plate was bare, exposed in places, fractured into overlapping plates that were stitched together by clumsy, thick welds.

The *Cauchy* crew, in their skinsuits, clambered cautiously over this as they made for Nicola's dome.

'Take it slow,' Nicola said, greeting them. She wore her custom-adapted skinsuit. 'Easy to crack an ankle up here; we're still under a full gravity, remember.'

And she led them to her discovery. The sky-blue artefact.

They clustered around it. Close to, the object seemed as simple as it had from a distance, Jophiel thought. Just a cube, maybe ten metres on a side. Jophiel thought he saw faint lines in the surface, nested squares engraved within the otherwise smooth faces.

And the cube was floating, a metre off the ground. No apparent support.

Asher checked this out. She got down on her hands and knees, waved a gloved hand under the floating box. Repeated the exercise with a grappling rod she took from the flyer. 'Nothing holding it up.' She shrugged. 'Antigravity? Electrostatics? Some kind of repulsion effect from the hull plate?'

Poole growled, 'In the circumstances that seems a minor miracle. But this doesn't look like any kind of wormhole to me, Nicola.'

She shrugged. 'Maybe it isn't a wormhole. You're the specialist, Michael. You haven't seen it all, yet. "Wormhole" was the best label I had for it.'

'Show me, then.'

She walked up to the cube and traced the engravings in the nearest face. 'See these marks? That look like the edges of hatches? That's exactly what they are. Hatches. And remarkably simple.' With one gloved hand she pushed at the innermost panel, which swung up and back as if from a hinge set in the top edge, revealing a way into the cube, a hole in the wall maybe a metre across.

A blue glow within, Jophiel saw.

'It just seems to fold back. I didn't investigate the mechanics of *that* too closely. The lack of a hinge seemed another minor miracle, as you put it, Poole. But before I went in I did establish that the bigger groove marks are indeed the edges of another hatch. For passing wider loads, I guess. Very practical.'

'Hold up,' Max Ward said. 'You were up here alone. You *went in*? Without reporting back, without backup?'

'Spare me the military protocol, Max. Tell me you wouldn't have done the same thing.'

'Never mind,' Poole said. 'Show us.'

She fetched a short ladder from her life-support dome, set it against the floating cube, stepped back, and grinned. 'Cube off the ground, ladder leaning against its side. Looks like some surrealist art installation, don't you think? And an unassuming bit of kit for such an epochal discovery, you'll agree.'

'Get on with it,' Poole growled.

'Barbarian.' With a fluid grace that belied her bulk, she climbed the ladder, then gripped the frame, swung her legs into the hatchway, and dropped through and out of sight. 'Still hear me? Have to admit I kept that hatch propped open when I was in here on my own.'

Chinelo immediately said, 'I'll go in with her—'

'No,' Poole said. 'Not until we know what we're dealing with.' He glanced at Jophiel. 'You, Jophiel. You next.'

Asher frowned. 'His survival or otherwise will prove nothing about the safety of the containment for regular humans.'

Jophiel smiled. 'True. But, once again, it is a test of our systems. And I am disposable, relatively. Only one way to find out,' he muttered. He snapped his fingers.

And here he was, inside the cube. Standing beside Nicola on a smooth floor. Within blank walls that seemed to glow with their own soft blue light. The floor and ceiling too.

In this wash of light the two of them cast no shadows.

Nicola was grinning at him. 'Once again, the two of us into the unknown. The heart of the Sun, the centre of the Galaxy. Now this. It's getting to be a habit, Jophiel.'

Jophiel grinned back.

Poole called, 'Still with us, Jophiel?'

'Still here,' he reported. 'The systems embedded in Nicola's suit are evidently maintaining my projection. Like they're supposed to.' All human tech was designed to support augmented reality, unobtrusively. And it worked, even in an environment as extreme as this.

He looked around. This was an almost featureless box. There were more of those hatchway grooves, their function obvious, in walls, roof and floor. Otherwise, nothing. He pulled a softscreen from a pouch on his skinsuit leg, shook it out; it was a Virtual construct but slaved to the flyer's systems. He began to upload instrument analyses, hoping Asher would be able to squeeze out more meaning than he had so far.

340

He felt a little lost.

Nicola was watching him with a mocking grin. 'Come on, Jophiel, even I made faster progress than this. What do you see?'

'Lots more hatches,' he said lamely.

'Well spotted. All functional as well.'

'Big hatches and little hatches?'

'They all work. Try them . . . Oh, you can't. Poor ghostly Jophiel. Well, I discovered you can just push them open from either side. I felt like a rat in a lab cage, exploring all this. All leading nowhere, just out of the cube. Save for . . .' She glanced at the floor.

He looked down at the usual set of nested edges. 'Save for what? A trapdoor to the ground? I mean, it's only a metre's clearance between the ground and this floating box; those big hatches wouldn't even open all the way before fouling.'

She shrugged. 'If you say so.'

'Show me.'

She knelt, a little stiffly in her confining skinsuit, leaned forward, and pressed on the floor's innermost hatch. It hinged down easily, not impeded at all by the ground that was, Jophiel thought, supposed to be in the way.

Hinged down, to reveal a blue glow. Shining up from the hole.

Jophiel came forward cautiously. He should have been looking through a hole in the floor to a ground of scarred hull plate and scattered dirt. Instead—

Another room.

He knelt and ducked down to see more.

The lower chamber was identical to the room he was in, complete with hatch marks on the walls and floor – and, presumably, in the ceiling he was looking down through. It was like looking into a mirror, or a still pond, a reflection of the room behind him – but without his own face peering back at him.

He leaned back. 'A room ten metres deep, where there should be a metre of vacuum above a solid floor.'

'You got it.'

'A paradox? Some kind of illusion? Like a Virtual trick?'

She shook her head. 'More physical than that. I went further. I climbed down . . .'

Jophiel suppressed a groan, not wishing to sound like Max Ward. 'Of course you did. Thousands of kilometres from the nearest backup.'

'If it's some illusion, it's a remarkable one. I was able to stand up straight, down there. I even improvised a measuring rod from the flyer's repair kit. I opened it out to twenty metres, from the floor of that lower chamber to the ceiling of this upper. This space is as real as that measuring rod, as me – and a lot more real than *you*.'

He stood up. 'Fine. But, Nicola, you called this a wormhole. Some kind of – of higher-dimensional trickery doesn't make it that.'

'I know that. A wormhole is a road, a route. But, you see, I went further. I opened the lower hatch, down in the cellar there. Nothing but darkness. Even I didn't take the chance of going further. But I did drop in a drone probe. It passed through the hatch space easily enough. I think it's still down there. Well, I know it is. I programmed it to observe, report back. But there was a mismatch. It took seventeen minutes, here, to capture a single microsecond's worth of data, gathered down there.'

Jophiel ran those numbers in his head. 'Ah. A million to one.'

'Yes, you see it. Time down there, in the sub-cellar, is running at the same rate as down on Deck One, where the Xeelee lives. And so the obvious conclusion—'

'Is that it *is* down on Deck One. That this nest of cubes is a passage-way. Good thinking.'

'And *that* is why I called it a wormhole. It's not, but it's obviously a – transit system. Across more than a thousand astronomical units, from up here to down there. It somehow manages the speed-up transition, the time dilation. But because of that—'

'It's effectively one-way.'

She looked at him. 'Michael Poole *is* going to go through.'

Jophiel nodded. 'And we must follow,' he said.

67

'I knew it,' said Michael Poole. 'As soon as Nicola and Asher suggested it, I knew they were right. This mountaintop had to be a construction shack.'

Poole was pacing in the confined space of Nicola's survival shelter, his skinsuit hood lying back on his neck to reveal thick hair that was greying despite decades of AS treatment. A blunt face, Jophiel thought, once again watching himself from the outside, the skin space-pale, somehow coarsened by habitual expressions of determination. And a very different Poole from Jophiel's occasional visitor – who was maybe no older, physically, but wiser. Gentler. *This* was a Michael Poole whose life, whose universe, had taken a wrong turning, Jophiel thought now. Yet still this damaged, flawed Michael Poole led all the humans on this Wheel – and Jophiel himself.

They sat and listened: Jophiel, Nicola, Max, Susan, Chinelo. The rest of the crew was scattered: back up at the Rim Mountains with the trucks, some still down on the plain. But some had projected Virtuals over – including, to Jophiel's mild surprise, Michaela Nadathur, first of the next generation. Maybe the wider crew sensed this was a key moment.

They probably weren't wrong, Jophiel thought.

'I knew it,' Poole said again. 'There had to be an access point, a base, for the work required to fix up this cupworld, if not the whole of this part of the Wheel. And the mountain, not really part of the cupworld at all, was an obvious place to put the wormhole.'

Which was the name they had settled on for a transport technology that was, Jophiel thought, as far advanced over the old Poole Industries spacetime wormholes as those wormholes themselves were advanced over George Stephenson's first passenger railways. But Nicola's label had stuck.

'Maybe it even came through itself, if its physical size allowed it.' Poole glared around. 'Maybe the Xeelee was *right here*, on this cupworld. And maybe it left the wormhole in place in case it needed to come back here and fix more stuff.

'And if the Xeelee can travel this way, then we can follow it. Just as Nicola already proved with her drone . . . We thought we were cut off from Deck One by the damage done to the Wheel. Well, we aren't – thanks to the Xeelee itself. Now we can go and finish the job we came to do.'

By Michael Poole's standards, that was meant to be an uplifting speech, Jophiel realised.

He was met by flat silence.

At length Chinelo Thomas, eighteen years old, got to her feet. 'We've followed you this far, Michael, and I guess we'll go the rest of the way too.' She sat again.

Wina of High Australia stood too. 'You have my arrows, Michael Poole.'

But now Michaela Nadathur stood up. Thirty-one years old, quiet, grave, slim, and apparently more interested in sports challenges than the affairs of the ship. Jophiel didn't think he'd ever heard her speak at a crew briefing before. Yet she had a certain quiet authority. And, it seemed, this time she had something to say.

She glanced around at Poole, Max. 'Some others asked me to speak today, because you oldsters might listen to me. What with me being like a symbol. I was the firstborn of the second generation of the flotilla. Why, my parents named me after you, Michael. And, with all respect, Chinelo, you do what you like. I admire you. You're always out there in front. But you don't speak for all of us.'

Chinelo stayed seated, but frowned.

Max Ward was watching all this warily, as if they were close to a mutiny.

Jophiel saw Nicola grinning.

Poole was gracious enough. 'Fair enough. If you speak for the others—'

'No,' she said. 'We're not that organised. We just want to ask questions. You said you wanted to finish the job you started. Which is to find the Xeelee, and . . . well, then what? I mean, so much has changed. What is the Xeelee *doing* here, on this Wheel?'

Poole was evidently reining in his impatience. 'You heard the briefings. You know what it's doing. As best we can guess. Look – we know the Wheel is basically a time machine. One-way. The Xeelee was wounded during the battle for the Solar System. So it came here, to the Galaxy Core black hole, and is hiding out. Perhaps even healing, until—'

'But that can't be all of it,' Michaela said. *'Why build the Wheel?* I mean, the decks, the cupworlds. Why build all these refuges, for all these alien races? See, I think – many of *us* think – that this Wheel is exactly what it looks like. It's not some kind of fortress. It's an ark. It's a haven for our kind of life – life like ours, like the Xeelee, life made of light matter, as opposed to the spooky dark-matter stuff that the Xeelee are fighting in their big war. The Wheel has already lasted a long time, as a haven. Why, the runners and tree-climbers on this cupworld have been here so long they've had time to evolve. And not only that, when this cupworld was damaged, the Xeelee came out here to fix it. You proved that yourself, Michael.

'The Xeelee . . . *cares* for its creation. And, presumably, the creatures that live on it. Maybe the Xeelee means to save us all, somehow. Not just itself.'

Poole studied her, as if baffled. 'Make your point, Michaela. What are you saying?'

She seemed to take some time to summon up the courage to reply – but then, Jophiel was slowly realising, she was challenging the orthodoxy that had governed this mission since before she had been born. Which, he supposed, was just what a new generation was supposed to do.

He found himself silently urging her on. *Speak well, Michaela.*

'I'm saying that we do understand what you mean when you say you'll finish the job. You don't want to just find the Xeelee. You don't want to understand it. You want to hunt it down, and destroy it.'

Poole frowned. 'We crossed the Galaxy to do just that. After it came to the Solar System, and tried to eliminate humanity altogether—'

Michaela said in a rush, 'But it came from a timeline where humans inflicted a huge extinction event on the whole Galaxy. From its point of view it isn't just destroying stuff for the sake of it. It's putting something right.'

'I came here to destroy it. That was the purpose of the expedition.'

'Yes. Because of what happened before any of us were born. *We* never knew Earth. We never even knew Cold Earth . . .'

Michael Poole paced, looking furious, frustrated.

Jophiel found himself intrigued, disturbed.

Of course she was right. An oath of vengeance taken by a forty-four-year-old Poole back on the frozen ruin of the home world had seemed noble, even inevitable at the time. And it had propelled this quixotic mission across the face of the Galaxy. But nobody back then had ever imagined *this*. Nobody had planned for how the next generation might feel about it. They must have managed things better in that other, lost timeline, he thought now. Where, according to the Poole family archive, a twenty-thousand-year war had been fought and won with child soldiers. Endless generations shaped under a ghastly Galaxy-wide authority, apparently called the Coalition of Interim Governance. We look like amateurs compared to that lot, he reflected. Yet here we are.

He asked now, gently, 'What would you have us do, Michaela?'

'We did come here for a purpose. To defeat the Xeelee. But that doesn't look so simple now. Across this vast distance, through so much time . . . We should deal with what we've actually found.'

'And so—'

'*The Xeelee.* Spare it. Let it finish the job it started here. Let it save itself, and whatever else it has collected here. Because killing it won't bring back Earth.'

Susan nodded earnestly. 'And then – what for you, child?'

'We've thought about that,' Michaela said quickly. 'It's not that we've been conspiring . . .'

Max Ward glared.

'*We want to stay here.* Here, in High Africa. Look, it's another Earth. It's been stable a long time, and evidently even survived the star impacts on the Wheel. We can live here, safely. That was the point, wasn't it? We thought this cupworld, High Africa, would be a refuge for the long term.'

Max growled, 'And a base from which to strike at the Xeelee.'

Michaela insisted, 'But we don't have to follow that through. Instead—'

Max Ward sneered. 'Instead, what? Climb trees, and run away from giant rats? And wait for your mind to dissolve?'

'It doesn't have to be that way,' Michaela said defiantly. 'And it's not as if there's anywhere else to go. This is all there is. This world is the only home we will ever have, except for the inside of a truck.

'And now it's our turn to choose.

'We don't want to go through that wormhole, Michael. Whatever lies beyond. Some of us, anyhow. We can't stop you going through and facing the Xeelee. But we don't want to wage war. We want to live, and we want to live *here*.' She grinned. 'We have a whole world. Who knows what we'll achieve?'

She seemed to stumble to a halt, looked around uncertainly, and sat down.

Jophiel had to smile. 'It's just like when the *Island* broke away. Here we go again.'

And Nicola started to clap, a heavy, unreal sound with human hands encased in glove-like Ghost hide. 'Well said, Michaela. We may be a bunch of brutalised relics, but somehow we managed to raise a bunch of smart kids.'

For a few more seconds she clapped alone. Then Susan Chen joined in. And Harris Kemp. And Chinelo, Michaela's tentative rival for the leadership of the new generation.

Then Jophiel.

Though that earned him an angry glare from Max Ward. And a baffled glance from Poole, who stood unsmiling.

When the applause died down, Poole stepped forward. 'I hear you, Michaela.' He looked around. 'I hear you all. But I'm – look, I'm not a soldier. This isn't a troop ship. Or a prison. I can't, won't, force anyone who chooses not to follow.'

'But,' Asher said, standing up, 'if we're talking about splitting again, before we go on with this, there's something I need to make crystal clear, to all of you – all of us. Suppose you do stay, while Michael and others go on. The choice to separate, once made, *can't be unmade*. Because of the time dilation. If Michael goes down into the time pit, down to Deck One . . . in an hour, for Michael, a century will pass up here. And if he comes back after a day, this moment, which we experience now, will be more than two millennia gone. If your descendants survive at all, he will be history at best, or legend – or forgotten, at worst. And after a week, a month . . . Look, if we split now, it's for good. Well. That's all I have to say.' She sat down.

Poole stepped forward. 'Fine. Are we done? Given all that's been said – and we're going to have to consult the whole crew properly, I know – how many of you want to stay?'

It really was just like the *Island* split all over again. Max glowered, the vote was a hesitant one, and Jophiel wondered if some of the rebels feared some kind of reprisal.

But the result was clear enough.

Chinelo came to stand by Poole's side.

But about half the crew, including most of Michaela's generation, did not want to follow Michael Poole any further.

68

It was another complicated and painful separation. Sharing out the trucks and other equipment was the easy part. Splitting the people was trickier.

Most of the seniors opted to stay with Poole. Jophiel himself. Max Ward, Nicola, Asher, Harris, Chinelo. Susan Chen too. 'To the end, Michael Poole! To the end!'

But as far as the crew was concerned, that preliminary vote proved not to be quite definitive. Some crew changed sides through fear, or perhaps hope, Jophiel thought, regarding the strange alternative destinies on offer: a life either on a damaged artificial world or in the bowels of a Xeelee artefact.

Then there was some rejigging of the lists when Harris, with the backup of Poole and others, gave stern warnings about the need to maximise genetic diversity within each of the two halves of the crew. Twenty-five or so was a low number for a colony's founding population, but not impossibly so – not if the founders were genetically diverse enough to begin with. But Harris, having the data to hand, was able to show that the split as initially proposed was far from optimal, genetically speaking. He insisted on a few tweaks. Poole asked for volunteers to switch sides, and was deeply relieved, Jophiel thought, to get them, and not to have to transfer crew by order, or even compulsion.

It did mean that a few sets of siblings were broken up. Bob Thomas would go through with Chinelo, but there were cases of children leaving their parents.

Even after that, Jophiel found himself hesitantly approaching Poole with more issues.

'We have some oddities,' Jophiel said.

'Oddities?'

'Wina from High Australia wants to go through.'

'Let her.'

'Our captured Ghost?'

'Bring it.' Poole grinned, wolfish. 'Might be entertaining to bring the two great enemies of mankind together. What else?'

Jophiel hesitated. He had a vision of that other Poole. The one who should have existed. And the one urgent request he had made of Jophiel.

'The dark-matter pod. With the photino fish inside.'

Poole frowned. 'That we retrieved at Goober's Star.'

'Yes.'

'So?'

'So,' Jophiel said, his voice an urgent whisper, 'we need to make sure we take it with us. Down to Deck One.'

Poole rubbed his nose. 'Why? Those fish are in a lifeboat of their own already. They'll be safe here, on Deck Three. Why should we clutter up our trucks with that?'

Jophiel wrestled with a decision. 'I can't tell you that. Not yet. It's complicated. Look, I'll see to it myself. But I'm a Virtual, I'm only ever one system crash away from extinction. I want to be sure this happens. And I want you to promise me you'll do it.'

Poole rarely looked his Virtual copy in the face; he did so now. 'Why do you care so much?'

Jophiel sighed. 'Suppose I said, because *you* told me so.'

Poole thought that over, and grinned. 'We're Pooles. For us that doesn't even register as odd. Sure, I'll make sure it is saved. OK? Now leave me alone, you fruitcake, and get back to work.'

Because of the time dilation, the final passage through the wormhole was complicated, and extended.

They soon worked out that you couldn't shove people and materiel down at random through the wormhole. A second down there mapped to eleven *days* on Deck Three. Just shove stuff through and there would soon be a disorderly heap. So the transition was planned, rehearsed, and the crew took their time. The party's trucks and other equipment were disassembled and passed through, component by component, with bots on either side of the wormhole, and people followed too, each in their skinsuit, lugging personal gear, two or three at a time.

It took a whole year by Deck Three time. A year more, after a quarter-century mission.

But on Deck One, the whole pile came through in seconds, and the bots worked frantically to retrieve the gear and hustle the people out of the way.

And when it was done, Poole and Jophiel were the last to enter the Xeelee wormhole. And pass through—

To the other side.

In the gloom of what felt like a basement, for a moment the two of them stood side by side, in an anonymous blue box. Jophiel thought he could *feel* the heaviness of time down here, gummed up as it was with the glue of relativity. And they were surrounded by a slowly dispersing crowd of people and their gear, that year of flow compressed into a minute. Jophiel glimpsed the Ghost, caged and heavily guarded.

'Take a deep breath,' he said now. 'Another. Say five seconds a breath. Down here, five seconds maps onto sixty days up there. Take five more breaths – a year. Michaela and her crew are already forgetting us. Ten or twelve breaths, two years gone already—'

'Enough,' Poole growled. 'We have work to do. And, listen, now we're down here I figure we have just a hundred and sixty-seven ship days left before the Xeelee hits its Great Attractor completion milestone. Five million years. Whatever we do, it has to be before then. Let's get started.' And he stomped out of the chamber.

Jophiel stayed for a while, just counting his breaths. Remembering faces he would never see again, no matter what the future held.

Then he followed his template.

69

Back on Deck One.

It all felt familiar to Jophiel: the bare hull-plate surface, the relativistic sky, red and blue. A sky where rays of light followed curved lines, he realised. The people standing around, with their stuff. It almost seemed mundane.

Once the wormhole hatch was closed, Max Ward immediately took charge.

He called together most of the crew into one of the trucks. Only a few were left outside on what he called guard duty. They crowded in.

And Max faced down Michael Poole.

'Look,' Max said bluntly. 'We're now back in enemy territory, and we're going to get a lot closer to the foe. Right? Because we're here to take on the Xeelee. This situation is why you brought me here, Michael. Precisely why. If you aren't going to listen to me now, then when?'

Jophiel watched uncertainly as Poole faced him, neither aggressively nor passively, Jophiel thought.

Jophiel was uneasy about Max's general demeanour. Tense. Impatient. Nicola caught Jophiel's eye. Her silvered face was all but expressionless, but he could see what she was thinking – how she was harbouring the same doubts. Maybe the man had just been through too much strangeness, too much change – the latest being this strange time-shift isolation from so many of the crew he had been training for years.

If Poole felt the same, he didn't show it. 'Your priorities, Max? I guess to get a habitat of some kind established . . .'

Max shook his head. 'There you go. That's not the priority at all. Our priority now, our only priority, is engagement with the Xeelee. And everything we do has to be shaped by that. And why? Because we're so close, and we have so little time. Just a hundred and sixty-seven days, remember, before that weird five-million-year deadline. So how far away is the Xeelee?'

Asher said, 'We think around a million kilometres.' A rueful smile. 'In most circumstances that would seem a long way. Now we've got here we can confirm that, anyhow. That's based on observation of gravity-wave anomalies. A known signature of Xeelee tech.'

Chinelo, default leader of the younger crew, frowned at that. 'And does the Xeelee know we're here?'

Max pointed at her. 'Good question. We have to assume it does, unless proven otherwise. I mean, here we are crawling around the artefact like we escaped from a cupworld – monkeys out of a cage. It must *know*, it must sense us and our crawling caravans.'

Somehow Jophiel hadn't thought that through. Why was it the Xeelee *hadn't* dealt with the rogue humans long before? It must have sensed the crash of the *Cauchy* in the first place. Was it watching them even now? Was it waiting for them to fall into some kind of trap? Or . . .

Keep going, Jophiel. Finish the thought. That odd, gravelly voice in his unreal ear.

Or, he thought, the Xeelee meant them no harm.

Heretical. I'd keep that to myself if I were you . . .

'So,' Max said. 'A million klicks. How do we get there?'

'A million kilometres.' Poole gazed into a softscreen. 'We have the trucks, and the flyer. We need the trucks to live in. The flyer's a lot faster. But it has a small capacity, and is really meant for high-altitude flight. And that's a risk; the *Cauchy* was downed by the Wheel's impact defences, remember? Also we already know that the hull-plate river solution won't work; it's not flowing in this part of the Wheel – maybe because of the stellar-impact damage.'

'Then we need speed close to the ground,' Max said.

Poole nodded. 'So we rig something up with the flyer. A low-level capability, maybe based on some kind of ground effect – downward thrusters to keep us above the hull-plate floor, effectively frictionless. Essentially we adapt the flyer as a hovercraft. You could reach some pretty high speeds that way, even at low level.'

'How fast?'

Poole shrugged. 'A thousand kilometres an hour? So it would take forty, fifty days of flight to get to the Xeelee.'

Max rubbed his chin. 'That will have to do. But we only have a hundred and sixty-seven days. Realistically, at that rate, we won't have time for more than one return mission. Right? We need to get it right first time.'

Nicola grinned. 'A ride at super-speed a few metres above the floor of an alien artefact? I volunteer to pilot.'

'Fine,' Max snarled. 'So pick a backup, and a backup for the backup, and *train yourselves up*. This isn't some stunt, Emry. We're taking on an enemy here, and we have to assume the environment itself is hostile. Seven days,' he said now.

Poole looked confused. 'Seven days?'

'To finalise a plan. To sort out our gear and prepare our assault. Look, I know we just went through a trauma. There is such a thing as pushing too hard. But seven days is enough. We haven't time for much more anyhow.' He glanced around, at sombre faces. 'You can all contribute. Keep your eyes open. Observe, think, make a note, report. When we come up with a plan, question it, probe it, figure out your own part in it, and rehearse it over and over. And prepare your survival options. Wherever you are, work out where you would go, what you would do, who you would need to help, if the worst came to the worst. Practise it, over and over.

'Seven days, until we go get that Xeelee. Are we done? Are we all clear? Then let's make a start.'

As the meeting broke up Jophiel stood with Nicola.

He whispered, 'You think I should have said something? Michael should have responded to that challenge. Make it clear this is his mission as much as Max's.'

She snorted softly – and quite artificially, a special effect, Jophiel realised; her nostrils were smooth, inflexible air ducts. 'What, intervene in the stand-off of the two alpha males? This is the moment Max has been waiting for since we left Cold Earth. As for Michael, maybe the only thing worse than not achieving a lifelong goal is achieving it. Michaela's mutiny affected him, I think. Maybe he feels he's lost his way . . .'

'Yeah. Max, though. For all the tough talk, don't you think he seems – brittle?'

'Terrific perception,' Nicola said sourly. 'Remind me again why I followed you losers from Jupiter? Well, at least we know what the plan is. As Max says, let's make a start.'

So they made their seven-day plan, and followed it through.

While, in the universe beyond the Wheel, ninety-six thousand years shivered past.

*

On the seventh day Max assembled selected seniors: Poole, Jophiel, Nicola, Harris, Asher, Chinelo. He pre-empted the use of one whole truck so they could have some privacy.

And he projected a Virtual map along one long wall. It had a green cross close to the left-hand end, Jophiel saw, a red cross to the right. Otherwise it was blank.

Max glared around at them. 'Behold your neighbourhood. A stretch of the deck a bit more than a million kilometres long. And it's not to scale, by the way; the section on the chart should be as wide as it is long. Spinward, which we call east, is to the right.

'Here we are, the green mark to the left. Still close to the Xeelee wormhole assembly.

'And over *there*,' – and he walked the length of the cabin to make the point – 'is the Xeelee. As far as we can tell. Right, Asher?'

She nodded. 'Confirmed, by the drones we dared send up. It has a distinctive signature – gravity waves, for instance. Physically it is a knot of spacetime anomalies.

'But we have also detected some kind of structure out there. Hull plate: with its opacity to neutrinos, that's easy to identify. We sent up some drones, and have some long-range visuals. And we see some similarities with the wormhole close by here: a cube, it looks like, and the same colour, visually, that soft blue. The same kind of signature in other spectra. Nicola really wasn't so far off when she called that transit system from Deck Three a "wormhole". It *is* an artefact of folded spacetime, in part, just like a wormhole, and it emits some of the signatures of a wormhole: negative-energy particle cascades, for instance.'

Poole grunted. 'So the Xeelee has another wormhole over there?'

She shook her head. 'We don't think so. Similar engineering maybe, but this is bigger, apparently more complex. We think the structure has some other purpose.' She grinned. 'We're calling it the Nest. Not very scientific, I know.'

Max snapped his fingers, and more detail coalesced on the map, between the two locations: pale circles, mostly, Jophiel saw, with no interior detail.

'There is some structure between us and the Xeelee,' Max said. 'Which we're probably going to have to see close up, to figure out.' He pointed to the circular notations on the map. 'These are like craters, or so they look from afar, each maybe a thousand kilometres across. Like small cupworlds, maybe? A thousand kilometres might not sound much – lost against this background – but that's as wide as the Mare Imbrium on the Moon. Anyhow we don't think these circular features are any threat. So we bypass them. Most of them, anyhow.'

'Bypass?' Harris Kemp said. 'Something you admit we haven't even seen before? And we just ignore them?'

Max shrugged. 'This isn't science we're doing here. This isn't *exploration*.' He pronounced that word as if it was an obscenity. 'We're trying to achieve a goal. And whatever is irrelevant en route to that goal we can leave aside. But we have to secure our base first.' He snapped his fingers again, and a new green mark appeared in the map, some distance to the left of the symbol that marked the human camp. 'We know the Xeelee has used our wormhole to get through to Deck Three, and supervise repairs. That's how we got here, correct? So we *know* it has travelled anti-spinward along this swathe of Deck One, from its nest as far as this hatch. So now I propose we make our permanent camp in the *other* direction. Further anti-spinward. Just in case the Xeelee comes out to its wormhole again.'

Jophiel nodded now. 'That makes sense. Make your base outside its known range.'

'Right. So we load the trucks, and send them *thataway*. Away from the Xeelee. While the rest of us go visit the Xeelee ourselves.'

'One chance only,' Nicola said. 'No time to scout, even. It's all or nothing.' She grinned, feral. 'I love it.'

Jophiel, having thought it over, didn't. 'Michael, what about backup options? I mean, we only have one flyer. How would we retrieve the crew if . . .?'

Poole looked uncomfortable too. But he shrugged. 'This is all we have.'

Max snapped, 'Look, it's the hand we've been dealt. And at least we have a play.'

Chinelo looked alert, engaged, excited. 'We really are going out there, aren't we, Max? Going to face the Xeelee.'

He grinned at her. 'Well, that is why we came all this way.'

But Jophiel found the strange blankness of Poole's expression, as he took one step nearer to his goal, deeply troubling.

70

It took them two more days to prepare. To finish the stripping-down and checking out of the flyer itself. To select and load their gear. Two days in which the remainder of the crew started the process of moving the trucks and other gear which sustained their lives westward, away from the Deck hatch installation, and the sullen Xeelee.

There were to be just six in the flyer, all that the craft would take comfortably, with their gear and supplies for the ninety-day round trip Max had planned for.

The six:

Max, of course. Expedition leader.

Michael Poole.

Asher Fennell, never a warrior but the nearest thing Max had to a source of intelligence on the Xeelee.

Nicola, the pilot. Anticipation for the extraordinary flight shone from her silvered face.

Chinelo Thomas. Max called her the best fighter of the new generation. And Jophiel agreed it was right that at least one of the ship-born should be present to witness the climax of a saga with roots reaching back all the way to the Solar System and Cold Earth. A witness for the future, however it turned out.

And Jophiel himself. Who at least didn't take up any room, he reflected wryly.

Michael Poole was the last to scramble aboard, carrying one last item: a box of what looked like bamboo.

Jophiel saw this.

Nicola missed it. She and Chinelo were too caught up in preparing the flyer's systems to pay attention. Nicola said she intended to use the mission to teach Chinelo to fly, and she had started that process already. Asher was immersed in her softscreens, as usual, as if saying goodbye to her own projects.

But Max noticed the bamboo box, and raised a quizzical eyebrow.

Jophiel recognised the style of the box, though he didn't know what was inside. 'Bamboo. From Gallia Three, right?'

Poole nodded curtly. 'A gift from Miriam Berg. Keep it to yourself.'

Gallia Three, a heavily stealthed station in Jovian orbit, had been a key source of intelligence and weaponry for Poole's effort to resist the Xeelee during its assault on the Solar System. And Miriam Berg had been one of Poole's closest allies and colleagues. Never quite a lover. So this was significant.

And Jophiel thought hard. Looked inwards, looked for memories, or rather gaps in his memory.

'I don't know what's in that box. Yet when Miriam handed it over, it was long before I was spun off. I was there, so to speak. *Why* don't I know what you do?'

Poole looked embarrassed. 'Security. In this case, it applies even to you. I apologise. I can imagine how it must feel to know that you've been – edited.'

Jophiel was bemused. Furious. 'You don't trust *me*? You didn't trust yourself?'

Poole's expression hardened. 'It was done when you were spun off. You were being sent over to the *Gea*, remember, where, it turned out, there was a mutiny going on.'

'Have you tinkered with my head any other way?'

'No. I swear. Just this.'

'But I'll never know if that's the truth, will I?'

'You'd have done the same,' Poole said bluntly.

And Jophiel knew he was probably right. He turned away, conflicted, confused. 'Well, I hope whatever Lethe-spawned thing you have in that box is worth it.'

'So do I.'

One last round of goodbyes. Another break-up, just as when they had all climbed down through the wormhole from Deck Three, Jophiel thought. He thought there was a sense of relief once the flyer hatch was finally closed.

Nicola touched the controls, lifted the flyer to a height of fifty metres above the smooth hull-plate floor, and steadily, cautiously, began the ramp-up to full speed.

Jophiel, strapped into a passenger couch, locked into his consistency protocols, barely felt a touch of acceleration. Once they were out of the clutter of trucks and temporary shelters the extraordinary sky of the Wheel opened up around them, light curved into a false dawn, an unending sunset.

A thousand kilometres an hour.

'Sweet as a nut,' Nicola said.

'Well, let's keep it that way,' Poole said. 'No stunts, Nicola. No matter how bored you get.'

She grinned. 'Oh, I'm all grown up now, don't worry about that. Let's just hope it stays as smooth and calm all the way to the Xeelee, in six weeks' time.'

'Well said.' Max pulled his skinsuit hood up around his face – following Max's crew rules, they were all to wear their skinsuits all the time – and settled down in his couch, his legs stretched out before him. 'Wake me up when there's something to see.' He opened one eye and looked over at Chinelo. 'Part of the drill, kid. You sleep when you can, eat when you can. You never know when you'll get the next chance.'

But Chinelo, wide-eyed, looked as if she would never sleep again.

Jophiel leaned over to her. 'Why don't you go out back and get some exercise? There's room in the hold. You can rig up a rower, a treadmill.'

Chinelo seemed reluctant to leave the control cabin, but it was apparent that nothing was going to happen any time soon. 'You'll call me if—'

'I suspect you'll know all about it. If.'

She grinned. 'OK. Thanks, Jophiel.'

And Jophiel had the uneasy feeling that Max wasn't asleep at all, despite his performance.

As it turned out, there was no 'if' for four days.

Then, early on the fifth day, more than a hundred thousand kilometres from the *Cauchy* camp, they found something.

It was as if the flyer flew over a cliff edge.

Jophiel watched from a side window. The aircraft kept to its course, and he saw a neat hull-plate floor far below.

He glanced around. Nicola and the rest were staring out at the scenery, intent – all save Asher, who was frowning into a softscreen.

'OK,' Nicola said. 'I used pilot's prerogative on how to deal with this. We're flying over one of the teeny circle marks on Max's map. You remember? Craters a mere thousand kilometres across. So we should take an hour to cross it. And a few kilometres deep, as you can see. Just like Max said back at camp, it's a feature as big as the largest seas on the Moon, but lost in the detail of this deck.

'We came onto this one roughly along its centre line. Which is why I decided to fly over it instead of around. There's no sign of danger. If we'd skirted the feature it would have added half an hour to the journey. And I kept our altitude constant. I could fly down if you feel it's worth inspecting the surface.'

Max shook his head. 'Nothing down there, you can see it. Good choice about the route, Nicola. No evident threat. You have to prioritise. We're not here to explore.'

Asher sniffed. 'Maybe, but we ought to make time for finding out *what* this is. Otherwise we're flying blind.'

'It's like a cupworld,' Chinelo said. 'Don't you think? A lot smaller; they were more like ten or twenty thousand kilometres across, I think. With all that detail . . .' She trailed off, uncertain. 'Maybe not so much like it, then.'

'No, I think you're right, Chinelo,' Asher said. 'There are similarities. An order of magnitude smaller, yes, no detailed sculpting. But – here's one of the things you can't see in a glance, Max – it does have a Lid over it. Like the force-field "skies" we saw over the true cupworlds. So maybe it is meant as a habitat of some kind, even if it's empty for now.

'Other differences, though . . .' She pointed at a softscreen. 'That perimeter, the edge we flew over, looks remarkably fragile to me. Loosely coupled to the wider Wheel structure, by remarkably thin strips of hull plate. As if the whole thing, this great bowl, is meant to be *detached*.'

Poole looked baffled. 'Detached?'

'And more odd energy signatures,' she said. 'This time of the kind we associated with the Xeelee when it was in flight. Planar spacetime flaws, like the Xeelee discontinuity drive.'

'Propulsion systems?' Poole stared at her. 'Are you saying this – dish – has a propulsion system? Independent of the Wheel?'

'Looks that way. As if the whole thing could just detach and fly off.'

'A disc-ship,' Jophiel said. 'We need to name this, right? Always the first step in managing the unknown. It's a disc and it's a ship, too. Probably. A disc-ship.' He frowned. 'But I don't recall us observing these features before, when we first hit this deck. Before we went off up to the higher decks, I mean.'

Asher shook her head. 'No indeed. So maybe this is new. Maybe the Wheel is moving to some new configuration, as the end of its five-million-year mission approaches – always assuming we're right about *that*.'

'Maybe it's a lifeboat,' Chinelo said now. 'The disc-ship, I mean. A lifeboat for a whole world – I mean, a cupworld. If you really had to take off the whole population, if something went badly enough wrong on the Wheel.'

Nicola laughed.

'You think it's crazy,' Chinelo said defensively.

'No! No, not at all. I think it's a beautiful idea. And just crazy enough to be true.'

Max Ward grunted. 'Maybe so. But if this is a lifeboat, what kind of iceberg is the Xeelee anticipating up ahead?'

As Nicola predicted, it took them an hour to cross the disc-ship.

They flew on.

The days settled into a rhythm of sameness.

Max slept an astounding amount of the time.

On the nineteenth day – not yet halfway through the journey – they came upon another disc-ship. It was the same size and configuration as the first.

But this one was occupied.

It brimmed with roiling gas, a sombre red tainted with purple and black – a bowl of clouds, illuminated from within by immense lightning bolts. The disc-ship seemed to contain a single huge storm, a thousand kilometres wide.

Nicola gave this disc-ship a cautious wide berth, but Asher gathered data eagerly.

'Jupiter cloud-tops,' Poole murmured. 'When I was at Io I spent many hours staring up at views like that.'

'Like a sample,' Jophiel said. 'Cupworlds are as big as planets. This disc-ship is like a piece of a world. Like an ecohab in one of our greenships, like the *Island*. You were right, Chinelo. A disc-ship is a lifeboat.'

They flew on. In the next hours, days, they observed more disc-ships: mostly empty, but some were bowls of rock and metal, liquid and gas. Asher gathered data assiduously, muttering to herself, sometimes speaking to Harris Kemp and others back at the trucks.

When she fell silent at last, some days beyond the Jupiter disc-ship, Jophiel prompted her. 'Come on, Asher, we know you by now. You have some new unsettling idea fermenting, don't you?'

She looked at him sourly. 'If you want to put it like that. I'm ex-changing data with the trucks all the time. The observations are still chancy.' She said hesitantly, 'It's hard to be sure. I think we're seeing evidence of a wider reconfiguration.'

'Of what?'

'Of the Wheel. The *whole* Wheel, Michael. We're surveying the wider structure of the Wheel as we move through it. With triangulation we can see some dramatic changes up there on the decks, even the struts . . . The cupworlds seem to be *moving*.'

Jophiel was astonished.

It did make made sense that the Wheel would reconfigure, as the end of its five-million-year mission approached, and a new phase began. But it was profoundly unsettling to have this tremendous habitat rebuild itself around them all.

Asher said, 'And when we put it together with what we've learned of the disc-ships . . .' She ducked her head, and looked out of the flyer, peering up at the Galaxy-centre sky, as if seeking to see the rest of the Wheel up there. 'It's so remote, and on such a large scale, and so slow, it's like tracking the motion of planets. But we *think* that the cupworlds are sliding along their Decks. Even descending, down the struts. This is all very partial.'

'Wow!' Chinelo sat up. 'And I bet the cupworlds are being brought down here, to be – emptied out.'

'Or sampled, at least,' Asher said. 'Maybe using wormhole links, given the time dilation. It does look that way, doesn't it?'

'But you couldn't empty a whole world into a lifeboat. How would you *choose* what to put in?'

Asher spread her hands. 'We don't know. We may never know. We're like ants crawling around this mechanism ourselves, Chinelo.'

Jophiel, stunned, tried to picture it. The Wheel like some vast piece of clockwork, with whole worlds, or world-sized artefacts, being moved around like beads on an abacus. The disc-ship lifeboats filling up with samples of life. And then—

And then what? Would the lifeboats be released, to go flying off into the dark?

'It's wonderful, though,' Chinelo said. 'Isn't it?'

Max Ward just glowered. 'That's one word for it.'

They crossed over one particularly notable occupied disc-ship dimple, thirty-four days out from the *Cauchy* camp. In this one, tangles of silver rope lay inert across an ice-strewn landscape. In the larger concentration, a tower lifted above the tangle, the jewel-like sculpture at its tip inert.

Ghosts, again. Asher made her records. There was little discussion.

On the forty-second day of the flyer's journey, they arrived at the Xeelee Nest.

Just as Asher's remote sensor results had suggested, it was like an enlarged twin of the wormhole facility on Deck Three.

A blue box, floating above the hull plate.

71

Earth date: c. AD 3,409,000

Nicola set down the flyer perhaps five hundred metres from the Xeelee structure.

Ward and Michael Poole prepared to set off for a preliminary scout. Ward checked out his own skinsuit briskly, hefted a weapon, a laser rifle, and glared around. 'You've all got plenty to do. Secure the flyer. Prepare for a full raid. Let's keep this simple.'

Nicola frowned. 'Simple? There's nothing simple about this, Ward. Save for your weapon, which won't be a scrap of use against the Xeelee.'

But Jophiel saw how Ward glanced at the orange pack on Poole's back. In there, Jophiel knew, was the bamboo box, the gift from Gallia Three. So Ward knew something about that.

Ward grinned back at Nicola. 'We'll see. On the other hand, we may achieve something here that probably no other species has managed in ten million years. Ten billion, for all I know. Strike back at the Xeelee.' He winked at Chinelo, who stared at him wide-eyed. 'Come on, Poole.'

Jophiel and Nicola watched them go.

'You're not happy,' Jophiel said.

Nicola's expression, always hard to read, was pinched. 'I give Max credit. He was a hero of Cold Earth. He was a big figure, then. But now we've dragged him across the Galaxy, and he's – small.'

Jophiel shrugged. 'But he's all we have.'

'True enough. You know, I've never believed in fretting about problems before they turn up. Now look at me. Must be the Ghost in me. Or I've spent too much time with you morbid Pooles. Come on. Let's go and oil our six-shooters like the Marshal said.'

After an hour, the scouts returned.

Back in the enclosure of the flyer, pulling open their skinsuits, a grim-faced Poole gave a quick summary. 'We learned nothing new we didn't get from the drones, and the remote survey. We didn't actually touch it, or ping it with anything more threatening than a gravity-wave probe. The Nest looks to be the same kind of mechanism as the wormhole between the Decks. A big blue box, floating maybe a metre off the floor. There are nested ports in each of the faces we could see, just like the Deck hatches. It didn't react to our presence. Seems to be the same kind of hull-plate material as Nicola's wormhole. But bigger.'

'A lot bigger,' Ward said. 'Two hundred metres on a side, roughly.'

Nicola shrugged. 'The next step is obvious. We go inside.'

'Not until we're fresh.' Ward glared around. 'We'll rest for one watch. Get some sleep if you can.' He glanced at Jophiel. 'Those of you without an off switch, anyhow.'

Poole nodded curtly.

For Jophiel, sleepless, the watch lasted a geological age.

At last they started moving.

Inside the flyer, under Ward's guidance, they checked out their gear. Each wore a skinsuit, and carried a first-aid kit. Weapons, from knives up to laser rifles. Softscreens in pockets and mounted on their sleeves. For communications, once they were inside a structure that was likely to be opaque even to neutrinos, they would trail cables in from the exterior. And as a backup, in case the cables failed or were cut, Asher had rigged up a backpack containing a minute lump of condensed matter. The lump was not heavy, but extremely dense, and when manipulated by electromagnetic fields it gave off gravity waves, weak but detectable even through Xeelee hull plate.

They even had a short stepladder and lengths of rope for climbing around inside the putative interior of the structure.

And Poole hefted his orange backpack, containing the bamboo box.

As they checked their stuff, Ward gathered them together to talk through his plan of action one last time. 'If the Deck wormhole is a precedent, we're expecting to find multiple chambers within that box.' He shook his head. 'Or *beyond*. Whatever. So, we leave a trail as we go. And the comms cable.

'Also we have to think about securing a retreat. One person stays outside. And we leave one person in each chamber we encounter, until we get to . . . whatever we find. I know that spreads us out, but it gives us cover, front and back. Ideally I'd leave somebody back in the flyer, but there may be too few of us as it is.'

'We need to keep talking,' Poole put in. 'Describe what you're seeing. Make sketches, maps. We must expect the geometry to be strange. We may be able to piece it together later, from our differing perceptions.'

'Last chance to send a message home,' Ward said. 'Back to the convoy, I mean. We might even get a reply or two before we deploy. Even at this distance a lightspeed signal will only take a few seconds.'

Chinelo stared; she evidently hadn't thought that far. 'What kind of message, Max?'

'Anything you want to say. Put your affairs in order. If you've got anybody you need to apologise to, do it now.'

Chinelo considered that. 'What will you be saying?'

He grinned. '"Don't touch my stuff."'

Obeying one last insistent order from Max, in pairs they checked over each other's skinsuits.

Then Max took a deep breath. 'Let's do this.' And he pushed open the flyer's airlock door.

Once outside, Jophiel looked back at the flyer. Stranded on the clean hull-plate floor of the Deck, against the smooth red wash of the Wheel's western sky, it looked crude, ungainly, primitive.

It seemed to take another age to walk the final five hundred metres to the Xeelee structure.

Nicola was watchful. Even quiet, for her. After a few paces, Jophiel leaned over to her. 'Something on your mind?'

Her expression was enigmatic, even given the stiffness of her artificial face. 'Just looking around. Looking at *us*. Max Ward, the gung-ho soldier, as brittle as an over-sharpened blade. A wide-eyed kid, an even more wide-eyed astrophysicist, *me*, a miracle of alien technological tinkering – and you, a Virtual copy. Quite a comet-tail of losers and freaks, trailing Michael Poole across a Galaxy and three million years.'

Jophiel smiled. 'That's life. Michael's life anyhow. And it's all we have.'

So they reached the artefact. Just as advertised, a floating blue box, a big one.

The Xeelee Nest.

The group instinctively gathered closer together.

Max glared. 'Scatter. Move away. You, Chinelo, over there, you, Nicola . . . Come on, guys. Basic field craft, that I've been drumming into you for a quarter of a century. Or trying to. Don't let yourself get put in a position where you could be taken out by one shot.'

Nicola looked around, theatrically. 'One shot from what?'

'Don't get smart. You. Fennell. You only attended one of my drill classes that I recall, and you were the worst cadet I ever had.'

Asher smiled. 'That makes me obscurely proud.'

'Good. That's why I'm leaving you out here. Hold this.' It was one end of a spool of multiple cables. 'Stay in touch with us, and with the convoy, as long as you can. And if we fail, do your best to report back. So that next time they don't make the same mistakes.'

Asher seemed lost for words.

Poole stepped up to her. 'Just observe like you always have, Asher,' he said, solemn-faced. 'All the way back to Larunda, and our dive into the Sun. What you always did best.'

After that, it was down to business.

Max walked up to the wall of the Xeelee structure, and studied the hatch lines. This wasn't a simple nesting as with the much smaller structure of the mountaintop wormhole, Jophiel saw, rather a mosaic of varying hatch sizes, some looking large enough to admit a craft the size of the flyer, others more human-scale, many lined up along the lower edge. All very practical – even mundane, he thought. But then, a hatch was a hatch no matter how advanced you were.

Max reached up with his gloved hand – and pressed his palm against the pale blue wall, in the middle of one of those lower inscribed hatches.

There was no reaction from the structure. No harm done to Max. He turned around and grinned. 'So much for first contact. Now to open this thing up.'

He pushed again, more firmly.

The hatch swung back, on an invisible hinge over his head. More blue light spilled from the interior, reflecting from Max's helmet, the folds of his armoured skinsuit.

'Good. I'm still in one piece. And it looks just like before, like the wormhole between the decks. But bigger. OK, Chinelo, you have that stepladder?'

The little ladder, extended to about a metre and a half so it rested on the lower lip of the open hatch, itself could not have been a more mundane sight in the circumstances, Jophiel thought. Just like Nicola's ladder at the wormhole in Deck Three. Something about it lifted his spirits. Basic human practicality in the face of mystery. And so far, the mystery was cooperating.

'Now,' Max said. 'We do it like I said, like we rehearsed. We move in two at a time, with the rest hanging back, providing cover if you can, being ready to help us draw back if necessary. The first pair is me and Poole. If we get separated, if anything goes wrong, we rendezvous back here, with Asher. Remember, whenever you make a move, always name a fall-back rendezvous point first. Got that?' He turned to Poole. 'So, you want to take the first step?'

'You lead,' Poole said. 'You said it. This is a military expedition, not exploration.'

Max nodded, unsmiling. 'Here we go, then. After me . . .'

He scrambled up the ladder, gripped the door frame, swung in his legs, and, trailing the comms cable, dropped out of sight.

Hastily, a little clumsily, Poole scrambled up the ladder and followed him in.

'That looked awkward,' Nicola murmured to Jophiel. 'We should have practised with the Lethe-spawned ladder.'

So they should. A detail missed for all Max's apparent thoroughness. Jophiel's sense of dread deepened.

Max and Poole looked back out through the hatch, waved at their crewmates, gave thumbs-up gestures. Then they turned and walked deeper into the structure, soon vanishing into the shadows, lost from sight.

'Nothing to report,' Max called back. His voice sounded tight, strained. 'An empty chamber. Big, though. Just pinging it with my laser . . . Two hundred metres on a side. Big enough to fill the whole structure.'

'Except that I'm confident it doesn't,' Poole said now. 'There are more ports in the walls, and the roof, and floor. Funny geometries in here, I'll bet, just like the wormhole between the decks. Asher, how's the comms working?'

'The cable is functioning fine. For now your radio and neutrino links are also working through the open hatchway. And the gravity-wave transmitter . . . It's gone. Dropped out. Looking at the analysis . . . oh.'

'"Oh"?' Jophiel couldn't see Max's face, but could imagine the glare. 'What is "oh"? Why don't I like "oh"?'

'You have quagma phantoms in there. Just like the bugs that came through the wormhole with the Xeelee, in Jovian orbit—'

'And brought down the *Cauchy*,' Poole said. 'Lethe. I guess they chomped down on the fragment of condensed matter in Max's backpack. We should have anticipated this. Where the Xeelee goes, the quagma phantoms seem to follow. Predictably, we're under attack immediately. So we have to abort. We only came a hundred metres and we've already lost one of our comms channels—'

Max snapped, 'And what? We fly all the way back to the convoy, and rig up some other fall-back, and fly all the way back and try again, until something else fails?' He sounded almost panicky to Jophiel, but he pressed on. 'Look, the bugs won't hurt *us*. Aside from the condensed matter, we brought nothing for them to eat. They'll pass through our bodies like we were Virtuals. Right?'

'Right,' Poole said. 'I guess.'

Max seemed to pull himself together. '*So we go on*. We came a long way for this, and we may not have the resources to mount another try. We do this today, or never,' he finished flatly.

Nicola touched Jophiel, evoking protocol-violation pixel sparks, and spoke on a private line. 'I think he means, *he* may not have the resources to try again. He's more scared than we are.'

Jophiel frowned. 'Yeah. Fragile. Yet he is going on.'

She nodded. 'Give him that.'

Max growled, 'Asher, you hold the rendezvous point, as before. The other three of you, follow us in.'

72

Once he was inside the structure himself – inside a huge blue box, like an abstract cathedral, flooded with sourceless light – Jophiel found his unreal heart beating fast.

All these years after his own Virtual creation, it did him no good to tell himself that, in theory, he was subject to the least personal danger of any individual here. The walls of Xeelee technology blocked most human signals, but the equipment carried by each of the team, like all human tech, was embedded with the hardware that projected his existence. Even a few metres of the comms cables they were trailing would do the job. And if all went wrong he could fall back to stored copies, held by Asher outside the Nest, or back in the flyer, even in the convoy a million kilometres away.

All that logic made no difference. He was here, now, and he *felt* he was in just as much mortal danger as the rest.

Nicola, to her credit, seemed to recognise this. As the rest were staring around at featureless walls, she was gazing at him. 'Hey. Take it easy.'

He looked into her enigmatic face, a mixture of human and Ghost he could barely read, even now. 'Take it easy? I'm *scared*, Nicola.'

'I know you are. I know some people think that Virtuals are immune to such feelings. Of course you're scared. You have a right to be. *You are alive*, whatever your physical form. You have lived as long as your oldest memory. You see, I've had time to think this over. You're scared because you are alive, not because you're crazy.' She glanced over her shoulder. 'Though I'm not so sure about our crewmates. Chinelo is grinning . . . Come on.'

Max, for better or worse, was making quick decisions. Now, without further talk, he pushed open another hatch – in the wall opposite the one the five of them had entered through. Jophiel, approaching, could see nothing of what lay beyond. Nothing but an elusive darkness, as if his gaze slid from one side of the open hatchway to the other, without taking in the intervening space.

Max said now, 'We go through. To the next room . . .'

'We're in the Third Room,' Poole murmured. 'Counting the exterior as the First Room. Here we are in the second Room . . . Which might not occupy the same space as the First Room, you see . . .'

And, of course, that next hatch was the first impossible doorway, Jophiel realised. If this structure was as simple as it looked outside, that door ought to have opened up to the exterior, to the Wheel, its relativistic sky. Instead, another room, Room Three where no room ought to be. The others didn't seem to have noticed. Or, he thought, glancing at Nicola and Poole, if they had, they weren't remarking on it. Good policy, he decided.

'Let's go on,' he said.

'Fine,' Max snapped now, edgy again. 'All five go on to the Third Room. We can see back through the Second to Asher, out there, and she can see us, so a sentry would be wasted here. We don't know how extensive this structure is going to be . . . Same arrangement as before. Michael and I will lead. You three cover us, and prepare to retrieve if necessary. Let's go.'

Poole first this time, Max following, they disappeared through that enigmatic hatch, into darkness.

Chinelo, Nicola, Jophiel hung back. Jophiel was aware of Asher, outside, watching anxiously.

After a few heartbeats Nicola called, 'Michael? Max? Are you OK in there?'

'I . . .' Poole's voice. 'Come through.'

They glanced at each other. Then Nicola climbed through, followed by Chinelo.

Jophiel was the last. And he climbed, through a mundane hole in the wall, into—

Twisted horror.

At first he could make no sense of the shapes he saw. The patches of colour that slid through his field of view. The lack of clear edges. No absence of any sense of relative positions, distances. When he turned his head, the scene seemed to swim around him – as if projected from his own eyes – and yet not quite, as if the very act of his turning caused the space around him to distort.

There was no roof above, just what looked like the interior of a pyramid, of four, five, six sides – the number was meaningless; the order of it changed as he tried to count his way around. The floor underneath his feet, though it *felt* as flat as that of the Second Room had been, rippled in his field of view, slowly, like viscous oil.

And on that shifting surface stood Max. Standing straight, but at an odd, oblique angle.

He determinedly closed his eyes. He dropped his head. When he looked again, it was at his own body. Trying to ignore the background under his feet, he concentrated on finding the Virtual comms cable that trailed from his own waist. *There*, there it was, a silver line of human artifice snaking back through the chaos.

And he followed other cables, and found Chinelo, and then Nicola, her bulk unmistakable. They stood as still as he was, upright, apparently calm. And yet at angles, as if in a tipped gravity field. Stiff toys roughly scattered.

'It's like Gallia Three,' Michael Poole said.

Nicola's voice sounded faint. 'What? What did you say?'

'Or Larunda. A spinning habitat. Think about it. Where gravity doesn't just point *down*, but at odd angles. Where the sky is a grassy field above your head. Think, Nicola. Imagine if you dropped a few of the grassland runners from High Africa into a place like Gallia. Wouldn't they be baffled? Scared? *We* could understand the logic, figure it out. But—'

'But not this,' Jophiel said. 'An artefact beyond our comprehension.'

A kind of snow seemed to be coalescing around him now: not falling from any sky, not condensing like a mist, but big, soggy flakes just appearing, as if blowing around some invisible corner.

'That's all this is,' Michael Poole said, determined, dogged. 'An artefact. We know the Xeelee is a relic of a different age – when the universe was very young, when spacetime itself was chaotic. Maybe this is some reflection of how it sees the world – a mixture of our perceptions, and its own . . . I don't know. *But it doesn't matter*. Listen. We knew it would be like this. Didn't we? Even the wormhole between the Decks was – folded. But our instruments still work. Things still make sense. In the end it's just another big room. And we can walk to the far side. Max? Max, you agree?'

There was no reply from Max. It was hard even to see him in the chaos. A glance at Jophiel's wrist screen showed that the man was still breathing, if raggedly, heart still pumping but too fast.

Poole said, 'Lethe, I didn't pay him enough attention. Look – Max

– close your eyes if you have to. Stay still, and I'll come to get you . . .'

'No,' Chinelo said, sounding calm. Unimpressed even, Jophiel thought. 'I'm closer, Michael, and I'm behind him. I can see him. I'll fetch him, and bring him to you . . .'

After she had brought him back they gathered around a silent, stiff Max Ward. Huddled, for human companionship, comfort. After a quick conference they decided to go on, at least one more chamber. And by common consent, despite Max's feeble protests, they decided not to leave a sentry in the twisted-up space of the Third Room.

So they advanced together, holding gloved hands – save Jophiel – human beings helping each other creep through twisting distorted strangeness. One step at a time.

Until they reached the hatch on the far wall.

All five clambered through. Max moved without a murmur, obeying simple orders, responding when gently pushed or pulled.

And, in the next room, Jophiel found himself staring at the Great Attractor.

This Fourth Room at least seemed conventional, as far as its floor, ceiling, and three of its walls were concerned. Just that ubiquitous sky-blue surface, engraved with the usual marks of hatches, nested in their different sizes.

But the fourth wall:

Open space. A curtain of stars. A magnificent diorama two hundred metres across. Almost overwhelming.

And there, hanging in space, a loop, a thing of lines and curves.

The viewpoint was positioned somewhere above the plane of the loop. The near side of the construct formed a tangled, impenetrable fence, twisted exuberantly, with shards of light glittering through the morass – light distorted by spacetime defects, perhaps, Jophiel thought. The far side of the object was visible as a pale, braided band, remote across the sky. The rough disc of space enclosed by the artefact seemed virtually clear – save, Jophiel saw as he looked more carefully, for a single, glowing point of light, right at the geometric centre of the loop.

They all must have known immediately what this was, Jophiel reflected. They had all studied Asher's blurred, edge-of-resolution images, of – this. The Great Attractor. The Xeelee Ring. And that central pinpoint was a doorway to another universe, if Asher, and the Ghost, were right.

Nicola murmured, 'A sense of perspective.'

'What?'

'What we need above all in this universe. Especially you Pooles. And just to give you a sense of perceptive—' She pointed, off to the right of the image. 'My Ghost eyes are better than yours. See that blur?'

Jophiel frowned, staring. He gave in to the rare temptation to enhance his vision, to use his Virtual eyes' zoom feature. His eyes itched as he stared.

Nicola's 'blur', a mere detail on the image wall, was a handsome spiral.

'That's a galaxy,' he murmured. 'A whole galaxy. As big as ours, maybe, that we just took twenty-five thousand years to cross. And it's dwarfed by this ring, this single object.'

A damaged galaxy too. Its structure seemed broken, one spiral arm twisting out like a tail – perhaps it had been distorted by the gravity field of the immense object nearby.

'And, look further.' Poole pointed at more distant stars. Jophiel imagined they must be brilliant, supergiants, to be individually visible across such distances. 'The stars on the far side of the ring, the galaxies . . . I think their light is tinged blue. Blue-shifted. But it would be, wouldn't it? This is the Great Attractor. The place all the stars are falling into. Where all the *light* is falling. And at the heart of it all, the Xeelee artefact.'

'It is . . . wonderful,' Chinelo said. 'And horrible.'

Nicola said, 'Whatever it is, it's a hundred and fifty million light years away from our Galaxy. Yet we see it. How? This whole Xeelee structure is about folded spacetime, isn't it? And I guess we are looking across one Lethe-spawned monster of a fold.' She held up a silver hand, reached out. 'I wonder what would happen if you tried to walk through this wall.'

'I wouldn't advise it,' Michael Poole said.

'Why not?' Chinelo asked. 'It looks so real.'

'I know . . . I suspect it is real, in some sense,' Poole said. 'A true image of the artefact, not some simulation. Given that to ask what is "true", what is "real", what is there "now", is only going to produce unsatisfactory answers across intervals of millions of light years. But I don't think this is another Xeelee transit system – another super-wormhole. I think this is some kind of viewer. Like a light pipe maybe. The Xeelee can see where its fellows are, has been able to watch the construction of this ring. Obviously useful. But it can only get there using its faster-than-light drive, when the construction is done.'

'Right,' Jophiel said. 'Otherwise it would have gone through by now. I guess their wormhole technology has its limits.'

'If this is just a pretty picture,' Chinelo said, 'we should copy it back to Asher and move on. We haven't found what we came for. Not yet.'

'Agreed,' Poole said. He glanced around at his team; Jophiel and Nicola nodded their acceptance.

Jophiel was impressed by Chinelo's briskness.

Max, though, just stared at the light show.

When Poole touched his shoulder, he seemed to come back to himself with a start. He looked at Poole, glanced at the others, and walked off, curtly, to the far wall of the chamber, the next hatch.

Jophiel and Nicola shared a concerned glance.

Another hatch, easily pushed open. The stepladder unfolded once more.

They stepped into another room of twisted space, just as baffling and incomprehensible as the Third Room had been.

But Chinelo stared at the floor, the walls. 'I think there's something in here with us.'

They all froze.

Poole glared around. 'Not quagma phantoms.'

'No. Something bigger. More – ordinary-looking. There!' She pointed, sharply.

Jophiel saw it. A couple of creatures – if creatures they were – fist-sized, scurrying across the floor and out of sight in the chaos. A blur of legs.

And Chinelo said softly, '*Look*. Look at me.'

When Jophiel glanced over he saw that one of the 'beetles' was climbing up her arm, as if inquisitive. It was insect-like, about the size of Chinelo's hand, with a smooth black carapace. It looked like an Anthropocene-era artillery shell, Jophiel thought, a museum piece, cut in half.

'I can't tell how it's moving,' Chinelo said. 'I don't think it has legs, like a regular insect. I can't *feel* any legs, through my suit. I can feel – like rippling.' Cautiously she turned her arm over. The beetle clung on, apparently unperturbed.

'I think you're safe enough,' Poole said cautiously. 'If they were going to do us or our stuff any harm – like the quagma phantoms – they'd have done it as soon as we walked through the hatch. Take care, though.'

Now a beetle approached Max, scurrying over the floor. Max seemed to recoil; he actually staggered backwards, calling out, until Chinelo, following close behind, caught him.

'Private line,' Nicola muttered now. 'To you two Pooles. I knew it. I knew this guy would crack up. A quarter-century of marching and drilling and posturing, and now this.'

Jophiel murmured, 'We were expecting conflict. Max knows conflict. He fought a human war, and won. He's been able to cope, as we've progressed to this point. One long straight line across the Galaxy. But, crawling around this Wheel like ants around an empty swimming pool, he can't expand his mind to accommodate this strangeness.'

Poole grunted. 'Which doesn't necessarily mean he's less sane than us, if you think about it. All right. I'll give him an out. But we go on. Agreed? Nicola?'

'We go on,' she said quietly.

Poole's solution was simple. They went back one step, to the Fourth Room, the Great Attractor diorama. He told Ward he needed him to stay here as sentry. He would be doing his duty, serving as a key link back to Asher and the rest of the crew. Ward seemed barely able to nod, but he accepted the arrangement.

'He's trapped,' Nicola said brutally. 'Can't go forward because of existential fear. Can't go back because of his pride. Hate to admit it, Poole, but you found a smart solution there. Ha! And this is the man who was going to dismantle *me*.'

'He came up against his limits, that's all. Let's see what happens when you reach your limit, Nicola.'

'Yes,' she said coldly. 'Let's see.'

So the four of them, Nicola, Poole, Jophiel, Chinelo, leaving Max behind, scrambled back through the doorway into the Fifth Room.

Chinelo led the way this time, boldly striding through chaos. She even carried the spool of comms cable that had previously been fixed to Max's waist. At least they had figured out how to cross such spaces now. You pretty much shut your eyes, stuck out your hands, stepped forward one pace at a time, and hoped, Jophiel thought.

Another wall, another hatch. They all looked through, into another empty room – roof, floor, and four walls this time. Except that a hatch was already open in one side wall.

And through that hatch Asher Fennell was staring back at them. The comms cable trailed away from that hatch, off into the interior of the Nest through another open hatch in the opposite wall.

'No,' Chinelo said. 'That can't be right. That's the Second Room, with the quagma phantoms. We walked in a straight line through all those rooms and we ended up back where we started. A straight line!'

Jophiel found himself staring at the comms cable they had dragged through room after room, which now, somehow, was meeting its other end, an impossible loop.

Asher grinned. 'I've been expecting you,' she called.

'A straight line, though!' Chinelo said.

Jophiel and Poole shared a glance. They, like Asher and presumably Nicola, had been aware of the Nest's peculiar hypergeometry from the time they had walked across the first chamber and into the next, where no chamber had been. And perhaps it was that dichotomy, impossible to resolve in a human perspective, that had pushed Max over the edge.

'Indeed,' Jophiel said. 'Odd, isn't it?'

Poole suddenly seemed to remember he was de facto leader of the little unit. Brusquely, he ordered everybody to clamber through the hatch back to the Second Room – and out, out of the Nest, back to the hull-plate floor, under relativistic Wheel light, with Asher. There were ration packs and water bottles here; Poole and Chinelo grabbed some of these and replenished their suits' stores.

Jophiel just waited, ignoring simulated hunger. Just relieved to be out, for a while. Nicola stood apart, her silver face bathed in hull-plate glow.

'A straight line!' Chinelo kept protesting. 'We walked in a straight line and still came in a circle. We could tie the ends of the comms cables together in a loop! How can that be? Some kind of trick?'

'Not that,' Asher said. 'It's all about distorted spacetime, Chinelo. I think this structure, and maybe the Deck Three wormhole too, is like a tesseract. A four-dimensional cube. You know the idea? On a softscreen you can draw a square, in two dimensions. Print out six squares and you can fold them up and over to make a cube, the two-dimensional surfaces surrounding a three-dimensional space. And similarly, if you print out eight of those cubes, you can, *in theory*, fold them up into a fourth dimension. You get a hypercube, with eight faces – each of them an ordinary three-dimensional cube – enclosing a four-dimensional volume. When you were walking through the Rooms, you were walking over the three-dimensional surface of a four-dimensional hypercube. You were like ants crawling over the surface of a box – but never noticing the ninety-degree tilts where one square face joins the other, and never seeing the interior.'

Chinelo was, almost visibly, picturing this – imagining the ants with which the green areas of the *Island's* life-dome had been infested – her face screwed into a frown. 'And if the ant on the cube just kept walking in a straight line, after four faces—'

'It would come back to where it started. You got it.'

Chinelo was nothing if not practical; she seemed to move on from that conceptual nightmare without skipping a beat. 'So,' she said. 'What do we do now? If we went all around this – tesseract – and we didn't find the Xeelee – oh, but we didn't see it all.'

Poole nodded. 'That's it. We saw five Rooms – including this outer box, the one that's stuck in our three-dimensional space – out of eight.'

'Three more to find, then. Where?'

Asher stepped forward and pointed back into the Second Room. 'Doorways in all four walls – and in the floor and ceiling too.'

'Ah.' Chinelo nodded. 'I get it. From here we can go up or down.'

Nicola smiled. 'You choose.'

'Down.'

'Why?'

'We've got rope to climb down. We haven't got a long enough ladder to go up.'

Poole laughed out loud, and Jophiel wondered how long it had been since he'd heard that sound. 'Good answer.'

Poole briskly started a new comms-cable trail from Asher's position.

Then he hefted his orange Gallia Three backpack, checked his laser weapon, and tugged at the comms line attached to his suit. 'Everybody ready? Let's try again. Follow me . . .'

So they went back into the Second Room, through the still open hatch. Once again Asher stood and watched them go.

This time Poole made straight for the nest of hatches in the floor, and pushed at one of the larger squares. A major section of the floor swung down, unimpeded. Jophiel remembered a similar setup at the High Africa construction shack. There was no *room*, beneath a structure floating in the air a metre off the ground, for that hatch to swing down. But it swung down even so.

Jophiel, standing back, glimpsed a textured darkness through the hatch. *Textured*, that was it: a gloom, but he seemed to see structure in there. Parallel planes, like shelving, but at an odd angle, like radiator louvres, maybe.

And – movement. Drifting lights.

Scuttling things, like beetles. He shuddered, an instinctive reaction.

Poole seemed fearless.

They let down a fine rope through the hatch, fixed to the upper floor by a Kahra pad. The rope, oddly, seemed to dangle at a slant inside the lower room.

Once the rope was in place, Poole knelt down and stuck his helmeted head through the hole, and looked around at the room below. Then he straightened up, and swivelled so his legs were dangling over the hatch rim, and wrapped the rope around his waist, making sure his comms line wouldn't snag or tangle. 'Getting into this one is a little tricky.'

Jophiel grinned. 'More funny geometry?'

'You got it. But different again. Just do what I do, and you should be OK.'

Chinelo frowned. 'You haven't done it yet.'

'Here goes . . .'

Poole twisted around again, so he was on his belly, with his legs dangling in the hole. Then he slithered backwards. Once his legs were in free space Jophiel thought he would fall through quickly. But instead he tipped back, clinging with his arms to the Room floor, as if his legs were being drawn *up* towards the underside of the floor – to the ceiling of the chamber beneath. He slid further, so he was clutching the edge with his hands.

Then he let go, and, holding onto the rope with both gloved hands, slid out of sight.

And, a heart-stopping few seconds later, Jophiel heard his feet thump down on a solid surface.

Nicola called, 'Poole? Did you live through that?'

'I . . . More or less. The drop was harder work than I expected. Maybe you should help each other down.'

Chinelo was staring at the hole in the floor. 'I don't understand any of this. What just happened?'

'I think I know,' Jophiel said. 'Come see.'

He, Nicola and Chinelo cautiously approached the hole. Together, they knelt down and stuck their heads through the hatch.

And saw Michael Poole, *standing on one wall*. His body horizontal, from their point of view. He was surrounded by what looked like fireflies.

Poole smiled. 'Come on in.'

Once inside, the three of them looked around, apprehensive.

'The images you're sending me are a jumble,' Asher called from outside. 'Tell me what you see, Michael. All of you.'

'Shelves,' Jophiel said. 'Surfaces sticking out of the walls. And dropping from the ceiling, poking up from the floor. That is, the ceiling and floor as we see it from our current angles. Like a big cave with stalagmites and stalactites. Not quite natural, not quite artificial.'

'I don't know what any of that means,' Chinelo said. 'But there's no funny stuff. I mean, everything stays where you look at it, at least. The room furniture, anyhow.'

'No funny stuff,' said Nicola drily, 'except that we're all sticking out of one wall like coat pegs.'

Chinelo laughed. 'We're crawling around a tesseract. Get used to it.'

'Cocky, isn't she?' Asher murmured.

Nicola smiled. 'So she should be. She's shown she's got twice the intellectual capacity of Max Ward, and twice the imagination. And I think you're right, Michael. We're safe enough here. And if the beetles liked Chinelo, the fireflies *love* you.'

It seemed to be true, Jophiel saw. Like tiny, free-flying lanterns, emitting a bluish light, the 'fireflies' were everywhere, but a good number of them had formed a kind of cloud around Poole's helmet. Jophiel felt an odd stab of jealousy. The life forms seemed to like the other three – the fireflies were clustering around Nicola too now, casting highlights from her smooth, silvered belly, and they hovered over a smiling Chinelo's open, gloved hands – but they left *him* alone entirely.

He fell back on analysis. 'So, Asher. Have you figured it out yet? What do we have here?'

'Life,' Asher said. 'That's obvious, isn't it? More life – the structure is evidently full of it. Maybe "Nest" was a good name for it after all. Life that looks to me like at least three divergent types: the quagma phantoms, the beetles, those fireflies. But not *our* kind of life. Not at all. And not from our time, if they are naturally evolved. Any more than the quagma phantoms were. Not even from the *same* time . . .'

Jophiel and Nicola shared a glance.

Poole said, 'Come on, Fennell, spill it. This isn't a college seminar.'

'Life of exotic physics. I think Chinelo's beetles are creatures of condensed matter. And the fireflies – they appear to be minute flaws in spacetime. Highly structured, highly compressed.'

Jophiel looked over at Michael Poole, who stared back at him, and Nicola, and at the swarming fireflies.

Poole asked, 'Flaws? Like monopoles? *Alive?*'

'Flaws, yes, but . . . One of those fireflies is to a monopole as a bacterium is to a grain of sand. These life forms must have spawned deep in a fractured spacetime. Life from condensed matter, life from spacetime flaws. Relics of different times, different cosmic epochs – evidently all early. Just as the quagma phantoms came from a still *earlier* time. We think the Xeelee itself is a kind of symbiosis of life forms like this, don't we? In fact a symbiosis between survivors from different eras.'

Michael Poole said brutally, 'Then if you're right, if these are more of its client species, the Xeelee itself must be close. Any ideas, Asher?'

'I have no sensor data. But there is a logic to the tesseract, the Nest. Surely the Xeelee will be at the safest point – the Room furthest from the First Room, the one tethered in our spacetime – the furthest in a four-dimensional sense, I mean.'

Poole glared around. 'Which way?'

'To your left. The wall to your left.'

'Fine. Chinelo, you stay here as sentry. Nicola, Jophiel, with me.' Then he impatiently brushed away the fireflies that still hovered around his helmet. Stalked over to the left-hand wall.

Punched the surface.

A blue hatch swung open.

And Jophiel prepared to die.

For, in the room beyond, the Xeelee hovered above the floor.

73

They stepped through, one after another.

The Xeelee dominated this space, this Seventh Room – this two-hundred-metre cube, just like the other faces of the tesseract. The humans stood before it, diminished.

Jophiel could not have said how he knew that this was the Xeelee itself, the enemy, naked. But the form was so familiar. The Xeelee was, he thought, like a scale model of its own ship, the sycamore-seed craft Poole had first seen when it came bursting out of the Jupiter wormhole. There was the core body, squat, compact, like an elongated artillery shell – but Jophiel could recognise, now, that this central core had much in common in its form with the beetle-like condensate creatures they had seen in the Fifth Room. Maybe it was made of the same stuff, a condensate, an exotic state of matter. It had no head, as such. Yet the forward rim of the main body seemed to be equipped with tentacles, narrow, slimy, surrounding what might be a circular mouth. Tentacles capable of manipulation more finely than human fingers, perhaps.

And there were the wings, delicate, lobed, sweeping back. So fine he could see the pale glow of the walls through them. Jophiel thought he made out structure in those wings: lines, a kind of webbing, almost too fine for him to see, and if there was a pattern that was elusive too.

But those delicate wings were rent by holes, he saw now, that looked only partially healed. And in that broken webbing he saw electric-blue sparkles. What looked like the spacetime-flaw fireflies of the Sixth Room, crawling through these warped wings . . .

His analytical thinking gave way to raw fear. Surely this monster, in its lair, could wipe them out of existence effortlessly. Out of the corner of his eye he saw Chinelo, so young, so close to death. His own mind rattled with doubts, fears, regrets. What in Lethe were they doing here? They should have taken it slower, surveyed, worked out a strategy . . . Anything rather than just walk in like this.

Yet, for now, he still breathed. Virtually, anyhow.

And so far the Xeelee hadn't done anything.

Michael Poole stepped up and stood directly before it, glaring.

It was just as when, Jophiel remembered, the Xeelee had sought Poole out on the edge of the fusing core of the Sun, and had faced him, cocooned within his ship. Now Michael Poole had found the Xeelee, here at the pivot of the Galaxy. And now he faced it again, Jophiel to his right, Nicola to his left, Chinelo behind the three of them. The three archangels of an angry god, Jophiel thought.

But Jophiel did not feel angelic. What did he feel, then? He couldn't tell. He imagined what Miriam Berg would say. *Just observe. Feel, when you have the time.*

'There are quagma phantoms,' Asher murmured in their ears. 'In this room. They won't harm you. The condensed matter was all you brought that they could eat. They seem to be hovering around that carapace – which is condensed matter too. Landing, ascending. Why would the Xeelee *need* a hard shell like that? Maybe it had to survive some kind of age of predation . . .'

'Symbiosis?' Nicola murmured. 'Of the quagma phantoms and the Xeelee?'

'Maybe, yes. As birds would land on the backs of elephants, seeking grubs and ticks.

'The wings are different. They each embed a kind of spacetime flaw, a sheet discontinuity. Just as do their extensions in the sycamore-seed ship, which is what powers the Xeelee at sublight speeds, we believe. Those discontinuities propagating through spacetime itself. Those wings aren't simple structures, though; they look as if they are . . . woven. And those spacetime-flaw fireflies are working over those spacetime-flaw wings . . .'

'They look as if they are fixing it. More symbiosis?' Jophiel asked.

'Maybe,' Asher said. 'You know, the sycamore-seed ship design now looks like just an extension of its body form, doesn't it? What the Anthropocene-Era weapons designers would have called a mecha . . . I think it *hears* you, Michael. Certainly it knows you're there.'

'How can you tell?'

'The wings. The discontinuities. They are never still. They ripple, Michael. Ripple with meaning – the radiation is gravity waves, and there's a kind of focus – oh, Jophiel, at least I can show *you*.'

And now Jophiel's eyes, subtly upgraded, showed him a shimmering, rippling pattern, a full spectrum of false colours, washing across the wings. 'Lethe, it's beautiful. And, she's right, Michael. There is a kind of – halo – around you. It knows who you are, I guess.'

Michael Poole took another step closer to the Xeelee, his motions stiff, angry. That halo of reflected gravity waves moved with him now, Jophiel saw.

'So it knows I'm here. So what? Why doesn't it react? It must have seen us coming, we crashed in its impactor-deflection net, we've been crawling all over this structure, and now *here we are*, in its own holy of holies. Why hasn't it killed us before now? Why doesn't it kill me now? Never mind the lost history, the million-year war. *We* hurt it, after all.' Michael Poole pointed at the wounds in the wings. '*We* did that, back in the Solar System. With a monopole cannon.'

'Yes, we did,' Jophiel said. 'But look what followed, Michael. It fled, and it came here, and built . . . this. We know the Wheel is a kind of fast-forward time machine. And our best bet is that it is trying to get home. Just a few more months subjective and then it can get back to its fellows at the Great Attractor. So close.'

'Yes,' Asher said urgently. 'And it must have intended to take a lot of secondary life forms with it. Look at what it surrounded itself with here. Even wounded, even here in its own innermost sanctum. All these immature species, the bugs and fireflies and beetles . . .'

Nicola looked up. '*Immature*. What are you saying, Asher?'

Asher said, 'Think about it. The Xeelee was utterly alone. Injured. Hundreds of millions of light years away from its own kind. And it surrounded itself with symbiotes, and immature forms of itself, its components.

'It built a nursery.'

Michael Poole seemed to consider that for one heartbeat – and Jophiel had the deep sense that all of human history might pivot on what Poole did next. Not for the first time.

Then, with a practised move, Poole he slipped off his orange pack, opened the bamboo box, and pulled out a cylinder, stubby, with a handle and simple controls.

Jophiel immediately knew what this was. 'Ah. Your gift from Gallia Three. Where Highsmith Marsden developed the monopole cannon that did all this damage. They upgraded it to a handgun, right? I should have guessed.'

'Yes. And here we are. The Xeelee thought it had stomped on us in the Solar System. But we managed to survive all it could do, and we limped after it in our dugout-canoe spaceships, and here we are. Here *I* am. Look at it,' Poole said with contempt. 'Cobbled together. A shambling thing. A relic of vanished ages. Begging to be put down.'

The Xeelee lifted off the floor. Just a fraction. As if provoking a response.

Jophiel said, 'Michael, you can't—'

Michael Poole raised the weapon.

Fired.

Jophiel saw only a wash of light.

Then, suddenly the room seemed full of huge, thrashing shapes.

Jophiel stepped back, and stumbled against, or through, Chinelo; protocol-violation pain sparked. Nicola was a mass of highlights, cringing back.

There was no sound.

When there was relative stillness and he could see again, Jophiel looked down at the Xeelee.

There was a crude cut along the junction of the Xeelee's right wing with the central body, a ragged sawing, as if by the bullets of an automatic weapon. The Xeelee slipped down on that side now, ruining the clean geometry of its position in the room.

But the amputated wing itself was not motionless. A great severed sheet, it twitched and flapped and pulsed. Thrashing, the wing seemed as huge as the Xeelee from which it had been sliced.

'Independently alive,' Asher breathed in Jophiel's ear. 'That wing. Just as if you cut off a tentacle from an octopus. Which has a body plan where the neurons aren't as concentrated in the spine and brain as in our bodies; an octopus's tentacles are in some way independently conscious. The Xeelee is built something like that, perhaps . . .'

Jophiel felt a stab of admiration. Even now, in this moment of utmost peril, she was still observing, recording, deducing.

She said, 'Oh, now the quagma phantoms are back. They are clustering around the, the *wound*. Trying to close a severance that can never be healed.'

Even the ruined wing was awash with harsh colours in Jophiel's vision, still attuned to gravity waves. 'It's in huge pain,' he said. 'You can see that.'

'So am I,' Poole yelled. He raised the gun again.

'Don't kill it,' Nicola said quickly. 'You already hurt it enough. And surely it can't reach the Great Attractor now. You've already stranded it, you've taken away all it has worked for across millions of years.'

Jophiel said, 'Think about it, Michael. You said it yourself. This isn't a fortress. The Xeelee must have known we were here since the day the *Cauchy* crashlanded. But it hasn't tried to harm us in any way. It hasn't tried to kill us, even threaten us. It's not at war now. So why kill it?'

Michael faced his Virtual copy, his face hard, old, empty. 'Because it's all I've got left. Because it made me kill the Earth to save it. Because this is my only redemption.'

Nicola pushed forward. 'Michael—'

'A brief life burns brightly,' said Michael Poole.

'No!' Nicola leapt.

Poole fired.

Nicola was hit in the stomach.

It happened in a flash. Jophiel, Chinelo could do nothing about it.

Nicola, in mid-air, folded over, and was – *stretched*. She was hurled back, the core of her body pulling back as if her body was made of some extensible plastic, Jophiel thought, watching in horror. Then the Ghost hide at last gave way, and her torso *broke*: it burst, split in two, blood spurting and freezing instantly in the vacuum. Behind her, her legs, splayed and spasming, thrashed against the amputated Xeelee wing, which still twitched and writhed in its own agony.

Her upper half dropped at Poole's feet. Poole, astonished, fell back.

Yet she was alive, Jophiel saw with overwhelming shock, with sympathy mixed with horror: still alive, her eyes open, one arm still mobile and scrabbling for purchase on the floor. Blood poured from severed vessels, boiling in the vacuum.

And organs spilled, heavy, almost languid, pink and white, from the broken silver skin as if from a split sack.

Poole dropped the handgun, fell to his knees. The blood was forming a slick ice on the floor, and he stumbled and slipped before he had hold of her, the severed torso. He cradled her head in his arms. His face was hidden behind a blood-smeared visor. 'Nicola. Nicola!'

Jophiel pushed forward, reached for Nicola, but his gloved hands broke up uselessly, painfully, into clouds of pixels.

Nicola's eyes were open. She saw this, the consistency-protocol failure. She even forced a smile. 'Just like your mother.'

Poole said, 'I – Nicola, I never—'

'Shut up.' She was whispering now. Her voice was losing its human tone, Jophiel thought, becoming metallic, distant. Ghost-like. 'It doesn't hurt. Odd, that. I've been saving you from yourself since the day we met, Poole. Well, the Xeelee saved the Galaxy from humanity. Then you saved humanity from the Xeelee. And now I saved the Xeelee from *you*. Stopped a monopole, huh? Make sure you tell Highsmith Marsden, if you ever . . .' She coughed, gurgled, and a black liquid, viscous, bubbling, seeped from her silver lips. 'And the Ghosts even saved me. Nearly. That's the clue, Poole. You think I'm the cynic, but in the end we have to work together to . . .' Another cough, choking this time.

Michael Poole broke down at last. Jophiel saw tears splash against the inside of a grimy faceplate.

Jophiel stared. He couldn't remember the last time he, or Michael, had wept.

Nicola stirred. 'I wonder . . .' Just a whisper.

Jophiel bent closer. 'What, Nicola? What do you wonder?'

'This is the Seventh Room, right? I lost count.'

Poole clung to her. 'I lost it all. I lost Miriam. I can't lose you too.'

'I just . . . What's in the Eighth Room?'

'Nicola? Nicola! . . .'

74

Once they were outside the Nest, while the others cared for Nicola, Jophiel was dispatched to bring Max back.

The man stood rigid at his post as a sentinel. Without being able to touch him, it took Jophiel a lot of murmured reassurances, distractions and commands before Max allowed himself to be led out of the Nest.

Meanwhile, Asher and Chinelo salvaged what they could of Nicola's skeletal structure, reconstructed it, patched up her hide, stuffed it with bandaging. And they set her before the Xeelee artefact, which floated serenely above the hull-plate floor.

So Nicola stood, naked in her silvered Ghost hide – no need for a skinsuit now – stood tall and straight, legs together, her arms crossed at her chest. Eyes wide open, staring at the Xeelee Nest.

When Jophiel returned with Max, Chinelo and Asher, having set Nicola up in this place, were standing back, considering. Jophiel knew that Michael Poole, trying to immerse himself in work, was huddled in the flyer. Max looked on silently, blankly bewildered.

Tentatively Chinelo ran her gloved hand over Nicola's belly. 'We did a good job putting her back together, didn't we? You would never know.'

Asher nodded. 'She would have liked that. She was never one to complain about weakness, or pain. Or even to show it. She'd appreciate dignity, though. Although I do wonder now if she'd have wanted to stand there making an obscene gesture at the Xeelee, for all eternity. Or at Michael Poole.'

Jophiel grinned. 'I don't think she'd have cared much, one way or another. I never met anybody with less sense of – an afterlife. Of continuity beyond death. I think that's why, of all the religious creeds she studied, she was so attracted to the old Norse stories. For the Norse there was no creator god, no reward for virtue or courage, no salvation. The world came from nothing, is filled with brutal and destructive gods, and will go back to nothing.

'But I think she'd like the irony that in the end she gave her life to *save* Poole's mortal enemy, the Xeelee.' He grinned again. 'Also that she was the one who ended up with a statue at the centre of the Galaxy, instead of *him*. Even if it isn't two kilometres tall.'

Asher said gently, 'It's been a long watch. Back to the flyer?'

Jophiel hesitated. 'In a moment. There's something Nicola would have wanted. Remember? One room we never explored. I need to go back in and finish the job.' He looked up at the blank silver face. 'For you, Nicola.'

When the others had returned to the flyer, Jophiel walked, alone, back towards the floating blue box.

Entered it.

From memory, and following discarded comms cables, he pieced together his route back through the higher-dimensional maze of the first seven Rooms.

Found the Eighth Room.

And then—

75

He was the last human.

He was beyond time and space. The great quantum functions which encompassed the universe slid past him like a vast, turbulent river, and his eyes were filled with the grey light against which all phenomena are shadows.

Time wore away, unmarked.

And then, millions of years after the Qax invasion, millions of years after his own descent into the wormholes, and deep time—

There was a box, drifting in space, cubical, clear-walled.

From around an impossible corner a human walked into the box. He wore a battered skinsuit, of an old-fashioned design.

He stared out, astonished, at stars, bright, teeming, young. Detonating.

Michael Poole's extended awareness stirred.

Something had changed. History had resumed.

76

Earth date: c. AD 3,998,000

After the return of the party to the main *Cauchy* convoy, events began to move quickly.

Once back in the womb-like interior of the flyer, Max had withdrawn even further into himself, and had scarcely spoken during the weeks of the journey. Now, as soon as the exploratory party got out of the flyer, Harris Kemp came rushing out to greet them, shot up Max with tranquillisers, and took him into the truck he used as his clinic. Harris ordered Max to relinquish all his duties for the foreseeable future, and Michael Poole himself took over Max's role, as head of security and discipline.

Just now, Jophiel thought, that seemed to suit Poole's mood.

After that brief, devastating burst of emotion following his assault on the Xeelee and the loss of Nicola, it was as if Poole had retreated to a kind of rigid core, a robotic inner self. Harris, the nearest thing the crew had to a psychologist, speculated that Poole's attack on the Xeelee had been cathartic, even if it hadn't resulted in the destruction of the Xeelee itself. He had, in a way, Harris speculated, resolved issues that had plagued him all his life, the eerie predestination that had always haunted him – certainly since the irruption of the Xeelee into the Solar System in Poole's twenty-fifth year.

Maybe, Jophiel thought. If so, it had been at a terrible cost. But that was the Pooles for you.

Meanwhile, with some curiosity Harris studied Jophiel himself. 'I don't see why this shouldn't have hit you as hard as it did your template.'

Jophiel didn't see that either. He grieved badly for Nicola – worse than he would have imagined; maybe he had cared for her a lot more than he had realised. And, perhaps, she for him. Now he would never know.

As for himself, Jophiel had a private, unscientific theory that once he, Jophiel, had been cast into existence, he and Poole had grown apart – or had become opposites though still bound together. The opposing ends of that dipole. Poole had kept his sternness; Jophiel had developed softer qualities, doubt, compassion – and, maybe, a little more psychological depth, even self-knowledge. Two halves of one person, neither complete without the other. Well, maybe.

So Jophiel seemed able to observe Poole's suffering. While Jophiel didn't seem able to feel anything at all.

All this trauma among the leadership, meanwhile, couldn't have come at a worse time.

The completion of the Xeelee ring at the Great Attractor was still forecast to occur at around five million years after the departure of the *Cauchy* from the Solar System – one million years more by Earth time, only *seventy more days* by the relativistically accelerated calendar of Deck One of the Wheel.

The crew still had no clear idea what the Xeelee had intended to do when the five-million-year mark was reached. But even if the Xeelee itself appeared to have been disabled, the great mechanisms of the Wheel were still reconfiguring. Still the cupworlds and disc-ships slid along the Decks and down the struts, like beads over that light-year-scale abacus. Still, drone surveys reported, more of those Deck One disc-ships were filling up, becoming puddles of dirt and rock and water and air and life.

And meanwhile, at the extragalactic Great Attractor, the climax of a contest as old as the universe itself was approaching.

Remarkably, the *Cauchy* crew were able actually to see the final stages of the construction of the Xeelee ring, the Great Attractor artefact. The exploration party had left drone observers inside the Xeelee Nest, able to communicate with the convoy thanks to cables that still trailed to the exterior. And the images returned were astonishing.

Images of departure.

By now a massive tide of materiel was flowing from across space into the ring, apparently heading for the knot of broken spacetime at its heart. Though the detail was impossible to make out, it was evidently a massive evacuation through a naked singularity, Jophiel saw: a flight from the universe itself.

But by just seven crew days later – another hundred thousand years – war was flaring.

So Asher interpreted. She pointed out huge disorderly masses, flung at the ring's tangle of cosmic string from all directions: masses themselves the size of galaxies, Asher reported, unbelieving. The ring itself was orders of magnitude larger yet than these immense projectiles, but gradually its structure was damaged, cosmic-string threads cut, broken and decaying.

And the brilliant other-universe light at its heart quietly dimmed.

After another eight weeks – eight hundred *thousand* more years in the outside universe – the singularity light finally died. The Xeelee evacuation was done at last, for good or ill, the ring a massive, drifting ruin.

It had been the last war, Jophiel thought. Played out around the most tremendous construction project this universe had ever seen. And now, apparently, ending in destruction, defeat, and evacuation by the Xeelee.

All this against the background of a sky growing dark, as the dark-matter infestation reached its own end game, five million years after Cold Earth, and all the stars turned red.

Yet still the Wheel itself remained inert. Still the disc-ships did not fly.

The last humans, bemused, even as they began to absorb this vast spectacle, made tentative plans for their own future. Even while the gigantic artefact on which they lived rebuilt itself, all around them.

Then, three months after the destruction of the Great Attractor, they found High Africa.

77

Ship elapsed time since launch: 29 years 86 days

Earth date: c. AD 6,233,000

'Or anyhow,' Michael Poole said, 'the disc-ship that High Africa was dumped into.'

Poole, unusually for him, immediately gave Jophiel the news; he'd called Jophiel to the truck cabin that Poole had pre-empted as an office. Now Poole snapped his fingers, and the air filled up with images of grasslands.

'Remember what we saw before? On Earth Three, High Africa? On a cupworld that, when we encountered it, had hosted humans for about half a million years, local time. Those runners on the plains, like small-brained humans? Well, by now, up on Deck Three, it's been well over half a million years more . . . *There*. Look: a troupe of them.' Poole manipulated the recordings to magnify, inspect, swoop around.

Jophiel stared, wordless, at shadows on the grassland.

Their habitual motion seemed to be a crawl, though occasionally they would stand straight, showing their big low-slung bellies. They were still bipedal, just. They had big jaws, with which they grazed steadily on the long grass through which they moved. An infant, fast asleep, clung to the hairy back of its mother.

'Grazers,' Poole said. 'Big bellies to help digest the cellulose. They're all over these grassy plains. The rat-lions take some of them, but they fight back. They can still make simple tools – they wield bones as clubs. And they can move surprisingly quickly, given their bulk. Well, horses were grass-eaters, and they were pretty fast.'

Jophiel followed this analysis, but he felt as if his own thinking, and his emotional reactions, were slow, sclerotic. Maybe he had seen too much, he thought. 'People,' he said now. 'Those are people, right?'

'Descended from people, yes,' Poole said. 'There's another species, in a colder area, which have bulked up to the size of small elephants. But the most successful variants, measured by size of population, seem to

395

have specialised on ants and termites. They have these long, clawed fingers they use to dig into the nests, the mounds.' He flexed his own hand. 'You know what breaks my heart when I see all this? It's not the adaptation for the climate, or the food sources. It's the group sizes. I mean, just count them. You see them in bands of ten, twenty – rarely more. Harris will tell you that group size is a key indicator of cognitive ability. Even those *Homo erectus* runners we saw before had bands of up to a hundred or so. Modern humans have networks of a hundred and fifty direct acquaintances . . .'

'Brains gone, then.'

'A lot of the higher functions, yes. Just as Harris observed. Smarts are no use in these toy worlds. Better to spend your blood and energy on a big belly to digest all that grass, and on running faster than the tyrannosaur chickens.'

'Tyrannosaur chickens?'

'Don't ask. Take a look at this.'

He clapped his hands. A startling shift of scene, like a piece of stage scenery falling away. Now Jophiel saw what looked like tundra, a bleak treeless landscape with shallow lakes, scrubby grass. In the distance, hills with gleaming snow caps, and a coast where sleek animals swam, dipping in and out of the grey water.

And on the land, distant herds.

Jophiel leaned forward to see. 'They look like musk oxen.'

'Bigger than that. Post-rabbits, the size of small mammoths. It pays to be big on the tundra – the bigger you are the better you keep your body warmth. They're preyed on by sabre-tooth rats.'

'So where are the people this time? What about the crew we left behind?'

Michael pointed to the water, as if it was obvious. 'In these cold climes, mostly in the ocean. Living like seals, walruses. You want to see the forests? There, the reversion to ape forms continues, the chimp and gorilla types and others. The chimps still walk upright. Still use tools of wood and bone, some of them, but it's hard to tell if that's a cultural memory or a rediscovery.' He eyed Jophiel. 'We also found Coalescences.'

He brought up images of huge clay structures, on flat plains. To Jophiel they looked like medieval castles, if the stone were melted after a nearby nuclear strike. And around each one, a cemetery ring towered high.

Jophiel, appalled, had no comment.

'There are some spectacular sights. The disc-ship's equivalent of the Rim Mountains have been colonised, by panther-like rats that chase antelope-like rabbits—'

'I've seen enough.'

'Suit yourself.' The screens blanked out.

Jophiel studied his template. Poole looked so much older now, Jophiel thought, older, blunter. Coarser. A shell he had grown over the trauma, or catharsis, of his final encounter with the Xeelee.

Yet he still functioned.

Yet he went on, day to day, task to task.

'Why are you showing me this, Michael? You don't do anything without a good reason.'

'I'll take that as a compliment,' Poole said gruffly. He eyed his counterpart. 'We have a job for you, Jophiel.'

'That sounds ominous.'

'So it should. Look, there's a lot of detail; I'll give you the summary.

'We think the Xeelee has a new plan. A new way to save itself, and presumably the other life forms on the Wheel. And we intend to go along for the ride.'

Jophiel nodded cautiously. 'Tell me more.'

'We believe that the whole purpose of this Wheel was as a shelter, a means for the Xeelee to survive until the year AD five million, when the Great Attractor ring would be completed, and the Xeelee could fly off faster than light to join its fleeing cousins. Along with, apparently, the disc-ships, samples of life from the Wheel – which in turn had acted as a honeytrap for life from across the Galaxy for millions of years. A strategy it evidently improvised after we damaged it at the Solar System. A flight of survivors, led by the Xeelee.'

'Right. The Wheel as galactic ark. But that didn't work. Because of us. In the Nest, you wounded it grievously enough that—'

'I like to think so,' Poole said grimly. 'So the Xeelee is stranded in the future, with the rest of us. The point is, since we got past that five-million-year mark – about three months ago for us – the Xeelee's mode of operation has changed. We've still got to survey a lot of the disc-ships, but we think that the transfer operation, from cupworld to disc-ship samplers, is complete. Well, that makes sense if the original grand plan was to have evacuated before now.

'And on the other hand, the Xeelee seems to be . . . rebuilding the Wheel itself. The hull-plate rivers have started flowing again. New material, flowing along the veins of the Wheel – reinforcing the basic structure, maybe. And building up what looks like additional shield-ing on the disc-ships.'

He snapped his fingers, and pulled up a graph, showing a steep climb to a peak, then a very gentle decline.

'This is an overview, based on the material flows we observed. It did a lot, very quickly, and then settled into this long phase of consolidation.'

'That looks like a very long tail.'

'Right.' Michael eyed him. 'It's all an extreme extrapolation, and Asher doesn't like me pushing her on this . . .'

Jophiel grinned. 'That's Asher.'

'She is predicting that this activity will continue, at this rate, for centuries. Maybe even a millennium, until the Xeelee has finished – doing whatever it's doing.'

Jophiel nodded. 'OK. So the Xeelee is embarking on some kind of upgrade job on the Wheel that might take a thousand years, Deck One time. And then—'

'And then, we don't know. Maybe the thousand years correlates to some process in the external universe we haven't figured out yet.'

Jophiel thought that over. 'A thousand years down here is five *billion* outside.'

'Maybe by then there will be some new refuge for all these particles of life. And maybe the Xeelee will send the disc-ships off somewhere after all. If not through a ring, then to some destination in this universe.'

'Where? There's nowhere to go. Thanks to the dark-matter crea-tures all the stars are dead, or red.'

'There may be habitable worlds, even around red dwarf stars. Re-member Proxima, for instance . . . Look, we don't know.' A rueful grin. 'We have to trust the Xeelee to come up with something.'

'I can see that would be a little awkward, for you,' Jophiel said. 'Anyhow you're thinking about finding a destination for us. The crew.'

'Right. But the *Cauchy* is wrecked, of course.'

'*That's* an understatement.'

'We can't get off this roundabout under our own steam.'

'Ah. I see. Ultimately, to escape, we'll need to get into one of those disc-ships ourselves.'

'Correct. That's how I'm thinking. The High Africa one, presum-ably, though there may be other choices. And then, after a thousand years, when – we expect, we guess – the Xeelee is ready to send the disc-ships out to some new destination, we'll be aboard too. Or our descendants. So in principle all we have to do is wait.

'*But*—' Poole looked at the tundra images. 'The chances of us, or our descendants, lasting that long are bleak. Look – our trucks won't last for ever. And even if they did, could our culture survive a thousand years? If not, if our archiving failed, our descendants might finish up with no memory of how they got here, and no experience to handle whatever might lie ahead when the disc-ships reach their destination. By then, our great-grandchildren won't quite be reduced to eating grass and running from the rats, but—'

'Some of *us* could survive. The present crew, I mean, AS-preserved. Like Susan Chen on Goober c.'

Poole said grimly, 'We'd have the same trouble as Susan. We don't have the infrastructure to keep up the supply of AS treatments. Not over a thousand years.'

'Good point. I take it you have a solution.'

He nodded. 'I've gone over this with the crew. Asher, Harris. Look – we do have the trucks. We think we *could* keep them functioning, on some level, for the thousand years. The technology itself is smart, we have matter printers to make replacement parts.'

'Keep the trucks functioning as what? Not vehicles.'

'No. Simpler than that. As sleeper bays. Hibernation pods. A human being is a much simpler beast to keep alive asleep, rather than awake. I've done some fault-tree analyses . . .'

More graphs, which Jophiel glanced over with an eye as expert as his template's. 'Looks like good work,' he said. 'I can see one omission. The cache of photino fish needs to be put into suitable storage too.'

'Fair enough.'

'And what do you plan to do with our captive Ghost? The First Slaver. If it broke out with everybody asleep—'

Poole shrugged. 'We have containment systems.'

Jophiel looked at him. 'Which I don't want to know about.'

'No, you don't.'

'So we get to the point. You're going to put the crew to sleep for a thousand years – including yourself. Right? I have a feeling you're getting to the part where you tell me what this has to do with me.'

'Actually,' Poole said, faintly apologetic, 'I already showed you, if you'd looked closely enough. I put you in the fault analysis. The odds of survival improve by an order of magnitude if—'

'You put *me* in your fault tree?' Jophiel looked again.

'Jophiel, a thousand years is a long time to last, for the smartest self-repairing machine. But the software and hardware that generates a Virtual, like you, has no moving parts, is descended from systems that have already been proved to work on millennia-long interstellar flights—'

'The Outriggers.'

'Right. You're getting the point. Look, our options are shutting down. It's extinction – or hibernation for a thousand years. And for *that*, Jophiel, we need a caretaker.'

'So you're asking me to spend a thousand years alone. Or, five *billion*, depending on how you look at it.'

'That's about the size of it.'

'Is this some kind of obscure revenge, Poole? Some kind of displaced sibling rivalry?'

'Well, I have no siblings, so I wouldn't know. It won't be so bad. The time will fly. Pack a book.' He grinned. 'A long book. So, will you take the job?'

SEVEN

At last, life will cover the universe, still observing, still building the regressing chains of quantum functions . . . Consciousness must exist as long as the cosmos itself . . . in order that *all* events may be Observed . . . And at Timelike Infinity resides the Ultimate Observer. And the last Observation will be made . . . Which [will make] the cosmos through all of time into a shining place, a garden free of waste, pain and death.

Shira, AD 3829

78

Ship elapsed time since launch: 30 years 108 days

Earth date: c. AD *11,535,000*

It took over a year by ship's time to get the sleep pods established to the satisfaction of Poole, Harris and others. Established, tested, loaded with their population of *Cauchy* crew. There were High Africa natives too, there at Harris Kemp's suggestion to widen their genetic diversity, as well as ensuring some of those strange descendants of a scattered mankind survived. All sealed up, in trucks drawn into a loose circle on a desolate plain at the heart of the High Africa disc-ship.

Jophiel took it on himself to make sure that the hull-plate pod with its cargo of dark-matter life was safely loaded – more participants in whatever adventure was to come, perhaps. And that the Ghost, in a custom-built cage, facing another long imprisonment at human hands, was at least not uncomfortable.

A year. While five *million* more years shivered past in the external universe.

After that, Jophiel was alone.

While the rest lay in their caskets, they had left Jophiel a truck all of his own. Just as if he was a regular human, with regular human needs, such as the comfort of four walls around him. He didn't *need* the physical shelter, but the truck did contain extensive backups of the hardware and software that sustained him.

Still, for the first few days after the last of the crew had gone into their sleeper pods, Jophiel let himself settle into a pretty ordinary human routine. He slept, ate his Virtual food, even showered. He looked over the latest reports from the drones patiently exploring the disc-ships and other aspects of the Wheel.

And he looked at the sky, through software that filtered out the relativistic distortion of the Wheel's endless cycling. It was a sky of steadily dimming stars, now, every one of them infested by dark matter, and settling down to crimson longevity.

It was a new age in the grand history of the universe, he supposed. A new epoch. He wondered what the scholars might have called it, if any had still been around. What myth Nicola might have mined for a parallel. Perhaps she would have called this after Erebos, the goddess of darkness in Greek myth. Human eras like the Anthropocene were long over: this was the Erobocene, the age of endless dark. And it was five million years deep already.

He felt profoundly aware of time, now. Poole and the rest of the crew had been concerned only about how to survive a thousand subjective years, a millennium of what they still called ship's time, without harm. But the crew would actually sleep away five *billion* years. Jophiel would have to live through all that, travelling the long way. What new convulsions would he have witnessed by the time the universe was more than a third as much older than it had been when humanity evolved?

Jophiel was no cosmologist. He had no clear idea what was to come.

He grinned. 'But I expect to find out,' he said to himself.

For the first few days, in order to check on the functioning of the sleep systems as they settled into their thousand-year cycles – and, also, whenever he felt lonely – he regularly passed among the crew trucks. Checking softscreen readouts. Looking at the names on the panels.

Studying faces.

Here was Max Ward. A man who had weaponised his whole life, only to find, when it came to the crisis, he was crippled by the limitations of his imagination. He had seemed grateful to be laid down in his sleep pod. Perhaps something of his spirit would be wakened on the new world, Jophiel hoped.

Alice Thomas. The first rebellious parent of the crew. Her daughter, Chinelo, sleeping peacefully, a competent young human ready for the challenge of the frontier of a new world.

Susan Chen. Survivor of a millennial vigil of her own, and now facing an unexpected new destiny. Hers was perhaps the strangest story of all, Jophiel thought. Yet here she was.

Asher Fennell and Harris Kemp. Old friends of Poole and Nicola since their days at Mercury. Never lovers, but steadfast companions, intelligent and inquiring. As they would be still, Jophiel was confident, on the other side of their long sleep.

Wina, not far away from the Ghost who had become her strange companion. Both already sole survivors of lost worlds.

And along with the rest of his crew, Michael Poole. At peace. For now, anyhow.

The first time he visited his template, Jophiel laughed. 'At last you have a statue at the centre of the Galaxy, Michael. Even if you had to become it yourself. Like poor Jocelyn Lang Poole on Venus . . . Like Nicola at the Xeelee Nest.

'It was never about you, you know. Never about us. I've been thinking it over, you see.

'We're locked inside a universe that is itself evolving, from hot to cold, dense to sparse. And life arises, and spreads as fast and as far as it can. We humans, and the Ghosts, and the Xeelee, and even the dark-matter entities, we just got . . . tangled up in the machinery.' He touched the transparent panel over his template's face; protocol-violation pixels sparked. 'It was never about me, or even you. Sleep tight, brother. I hope you wake up forgiving yourself. As we forgive you. And hey, have children, grandchildren. What would you sooner have, after all, a kilometres-high statue or a grandkid to catch the ball you throw?'

He turned away. Then back again.

'And remember me to your family.'

For Jophiel had the odd intuition that however his thousand years turned out, *he* was never going to join the *Cauchy* crew again.

Thus, the first few days.

Then Jophiel began to relax.

He was still an engineer. He, or his template, had had a hand in designing these long-term sleeper systems, for use on the scatterships that had fled Cold Earth. He knew that if no faults showed up in the first few days, they weren't likely to show up in centuries. And even then the layers of redundancy, backup and maintenance that swathed every component reduced the risk of catastrophic fault almost to nil.

No need for a daily walk around, it occurred to him.

And no need even for him to live through each day at a snail's pace.

Time to take a lesson from the *Gea* crew.

He set up the software, tested it, and various alarm protocols. Then he walked away from the trucks, just a short distance.

Softly uttered enabling codes.

The software routines he now invoked, permeating the systems that sustained his own Virtual existence, had been developed without authorisation on *Gea*, and copied down to the archives of *Cauchy* and *Island* before *Gea* had itself been lost. Jophiel had checked it all through himself. It worked as specified.

Now, for Jophiel, time compressed. It felt odd, briefly, as if he was walking through some thickening liquid.

He was slowing down. His own system's pace, compared to the systems cannibalised for the trucks from the *Cauchy*, was slowed by a factor of ten, a hundred . . .

Just like the Virtual officers of the *Gea*, he stabilised at a factor of one to fifteen hundred – but he was running slower than nominal, not faster. He resembled one of *Gea*'s statue-like reserve crew, trapped in slow time. Now, a minute for him corresponded to a whole day on this deck. But he was doubly slowed, of course, by the software and by relativistic time dilation. So that his minute, Deck One's day, would span fourteen thousand years in the outside universe.

Time enough for the rise and fall of a civilisation.

Every minute. He laughed.

He walked around, testing himself, steadily, comfortably. He experienced no difference, yet he knew that to a normal-paced witness his motions would be barely perceptible. He was yet another Galaxy-centre statue, he realised. 'Place is getting cluttered,' he said to himself. 'But I did just reduce my load on the power grid by a factor of a thousand. No, don't thank me.'

So he settled down to a new routine.

He set timers to remind him to check over the sleeper pods once every six hours. Four times a day for him; once a year for the sleepers. And he had alarms to draw his attention if anything failed in the interim.

Other than that, he ate when he liked, slept when he felt like it. 'At this rate, only eight months before they all wake up,' he said to himself. 'I better not start that long book, Michael.'

It was after a couple of days of this that he got around to resetting a few softscreens to give him a steady, time-averaged view of the sky beyond the Wheel – a view otherwise distorted by the Wheel's ferocious relativistic blue shift, and by its own spin around the black hole Chandra.

And that was when he got his first big surprise.

*

He could see it coming, from out of the northern Galactic sky. A blur of light maybe half the size of a full Moon, seen from Earth.

After a few weeks, it was twice that size. And getting rapidly larger.

A few weeks. He had to keep reminding himself that that mapped onto a billion years, outside. Whole species could rise and fall without seeing any perceptible motion up in that sky at all, he realised.

'Whereas I am stuck on fast-forward. What a spectacle.'

Now he could see structure in the approaching entity. It was a tipped-up puddle of light, with a glaring pinpoint at the very centre, surrounded by a wide swirl of spiral arms. The colours, at least as rendered by his visioning system, were spectacular, though tinged with red.

It got bigger, and brighter, every time he looked at it. And it seemed to be tilting further, as if coming in edge-on, right at him.

It was a galaxy: the Andromeda Galaxy, of course. The closest large galaxy to the Milky Way – *the* Galaxy.

He checked all this over quickly. The two big spirals were bound gravitationally into a group with a number of scattered dwarf galaxies. Andromeda, bigger than the Galaxy, was just as tarnished, it seemed, by the infestation of dark-matter life. Andromeda looked like some huge cruise liner in the night, festooned with crimson lights.

And the two huge systems, each hosting hundreds of billions of stars, were heading, it looked like, for a collision.

He remembered now a joshing exchange with Asher Fennell, long ago, about such a collision. *I mention it as something we might have to deal with, if Michael keeps us plummeting into the future.* There had been polite laughter. 'Well, the joke's on me now, Asher,' Jophiel murmured. '*What* collision, though?'

He looked it up.

He found that the ship's records contained predictions of such an event, but they relied on observations and models made even before the Xeelee invasion of the Solar System – and therefore, by now, a billion years out of date. They told him nothing about the details of the collision, or its likely consequences. Nothing save that the inexorable law of gravity had made the smash-up inevitable, even as seen from that long-gone epoch.

And now here he was, sitting right under it.

He half-thought of waking up Asher Fennell to advise him about it, and to share the experience. He did do his best to set up systems to obtain comprehensive records of the event. 'If we survive to look it over,' he muttered, 'Asher *will* thank me for that . . .'

He kept watching, as his smart systems monitored the sky.

And, ninety days in, he spotted something else unexpected. At first glance it was just a blur, deeply reddened, swimming out of the plane of the Galaxy, disappearing fast. A cluster of stars, made red by Doppler shift, he quickly realised, as well as by the photino fishes' tinkering. It had been a globular cluster, a bundle of hundreds of thousands of stars, one of many quietly orbiting the central mass of the Galaxy. Most of these star masses still followed their orbits – and would do so, presumably, until their final scattering and disruption during the galaxies' collision.

All save the one that had flown away, before the galaxies closed.

His systems gave no clue as to what kind of propulsion mechanism could have shifted an entire star cluster, at what appeared to be immense accelerations. But he was able to identify the cluster in catalogues that dated back to the astronomers' observations on pre-Displacement Earth. And then he understood.

It had been M15.

The place the *Gea* crew had gone, after the rebellion of the officers.

'So you used a globular cluster as a lifeboat from a galaxy smash.' He saluted the sky. 'Nicely played, Flammarion. Remember me.'

At last – at about a hundred days in for Jophiel, a couple of billion years outside – the galaxies passed each other.

Andromeda, coming in edge-on like a monstrous shield, with the glaring boss of its central bulge easily visible, slid *under* Jophiel's view. Under the plane of the home Galaxy.

For the next few weeks Jophiel watched, astonished, as Andromeda receded. The galaxies' two dense cores seemed undisturbed. But ragged lanes of stars that had been spiral arms were wrenched from both galaxies, and trailed like intermingling spider webs. Webs that were chains of stars and planets, and scatterings of gas and dust.

Then Andromeda seemed to slow. Jophiel tried to estimate this, watching the apparent shrinking of that bright central bulge, day by day.

After a hundred and fifty days, Andromeda stopped receding altogether.

And by a hundred and sixty days, a hundred and seventy, it was obvious Andromeda was coming back for another pass.

By now Jophiel had done some studying; he understood that the whole system, the two bound galaxies, had lost a lot of gravitational potential energy to the great friction of the two structures tearing at each other. It was just as a bouncing rubber ball lost height with each impact with a hard pavement.

So here came the next bounce.

And, because of that loss of energy, the second collision would be nearly head on. This time the two massive cores would come much closer.

It happened at around two hundred days by Jophiel's clock. Four billion years outside. This time the two galaxies passed *through* each other, and the great wells of gas which populated the galaxies' spiral arms were mixed and compressed. All around the sky, in huge, glowing clouds of gas, massive stars were born. Many died quickly; supernovas flared and sparked in Jophiel's time-accelerated vision.

And Jophiel saw the heart of Andromeda, the great central bulge, pass beneath his horizon.

After that it got messy.

In the following days and weeks – for Jophiel, across hundreds of millions of years externally – the two systems underwent a whole series of collisions, short, shuddering bounces, each recoil less than the last. But the structures of both galaxies, at least away from their central bulges, became muddled, broken down.

Jophiel knew enough about the astrophysics by now to understand what was happening. By his two hundred and fiftieth day – about five billion years into this unanticipated future – the galaxies were merging into a new, single giant: elliptical, shapeless, rich with young stars. Their dense cores were coalescing into a single mass.

And, very soon, even the great black holes at the centres of the galaxies would merge – but since Andromeda's black hole was a monster that outmassed the Galaxy's by a factor of twenty thousand or more, it would be more a swallowing of Chandra than a merger. A swallowing of the object around which this Wheel orbited.

Yet, amid the destruction – the loss of the delicate beauty of two sets of spiral arms – there was creativity. Reservoirs of interstellar gas poured into the heart of the new giant galaxy; there was another rich wave of star-making, all across the sky.

He stared out, astonished, at the stars, bright, teeming, young. Detonating.

Memory flooded. And—

'I've seen this sky before,' he said to himself.

This was the bright young sky up at which he had stared, equally astonished, when he had reached the Eighth Room of the Xeelee Nest.

An alarm chimed.

His thousand years were almost up.

Jophiel, monitoring his instruments, saw that the disc-ships of the Wheel were stirring. Breaking free. Preparing to scatter – baby birds leaving an imperilled nest, he supposed.

'This is it,' he said to himself. 'Michael, you were right. This is what the Xeelee foresaw, and planned for. A sky full of young bright stars, created by the galaxy smash. New planets ripe for life and colonisation . . .'

That was when he heard a voice in his head.

Did you like the light show?

A voice he'd heard only a handful of times before.

Where I came from we called it the Formidable Caress.

A voice that was his own, and yet was not.

If I were you I'd activate your override. Wake your crewmates up a little early. Their disc-ship is going very soon. They won't want to miss the launch of their own lifeboat.

He complied immediately.

That voice—

Thanks to the merger, there will be a wave of star-making that should last for a hundred million years. Plenty of new worlds for your crewmates to fill up. And their lost children, the folk from the cupworld you called High Africa. You see, I've been watching.

'Is this what it's all been about? The Wheel has become a kind of ark after all, preserving life through the Andromeda collision? And this is what the Xeelee was waiting for? This new . . . arena for life?'

That was how it was all repurposed, yes. By the Xeelee, once it realised it had lost its chance of making it through Bolder's Ring before it was destroyed, thanks to the wounds your template inflicted.

'Bolder's Ring?'

The Great Attractor structure. The name – long story. Never mind.

Look, it might not have felt like it while the Xeelee was rampaging through your Solar System. But its basic motive, and that of its whole species, has always been to preserve life, baryonic life, and its diversity. That was even true when it tried to eliminate humanity, and created a new timeline in which we did not *extirpate half the Galaxy's inhabitants, and throw billions of our own children into a pointless war at the Core.*

'Yeah. Our own young people worked that out.'

Anyhow, once it was stuck here, the Xeelee started to work out what it could do to help baryonic life seed again, and survive in this *universe . . . That, and the dark-matter fauna too. And now do you see why I had you bring that pod full of photino birds from Goober's Star?*

'Fish. We called them photino fish. No, I don't see that. The dark-matter creatures were the deadly enemy of the Xeelee. What, are they just going to start their cosmic war all over again?'

Well, I hope not. We need them, in the end, you see, Jophiel. And they need us. The photino birds – fish, whatever – and their transgalactic parents that *you called Ancients. Just as they need us – though they don't know it yet. Even the Xeelee doesn't know that. Not yet. But it will. Anyhow you did a good job. But now it's done. What now for you, Jophiel?*

'I guess I'll speed back up. Rejoin the crew.'

You could do that. It would be fun to see what they make of all this, wouldn't it?

'Yeah. Michael building a world of his own. If that's not redemption for doesn't heal him, nothing will be. The crew who followed him all this way. Chinelo, the new generations. Susan Chen – I see her walking down a ramp, hand in hand with a knuckle-walker and a canopy-hanger from High Africa. Maybe relics of her own lost crew, after all.'

Fun, right? You could go down and join them.

'Or?'

The job's not done yet, Jophiel. It never is, in this universe. I could use some help.

'I . . . How do I find you?'

You know where.

So Jophiel sped back up to human pace. He left a farewell note for his waking crewmates. Left it clipped to the system files that stored his Virtual persona; Michael would find it, he would figure it all out – if he had time away from his own world-building, and personal healing. It didn't really matter.

Then Jophiel had himself projected back out to the Xeelee Nest, where the Virtual support systems he and his colleagues had left behind were still patiently functioning, a thousand years on.

Nothing had changed, as far as he could tell, from those hours of crisis a millennium ago. No weather, on the Wheel. But the Nest was empty now, so the remote sensors told him.

He spent a few minutes with Nicola, who stood as defiant as she had been in life.

Then he clambered back into the Xeelee habitat. Threaded his way through the tesseract.

Turned an impossible corner.

Found the Eighth Room. Passed through the last hatch.

And was back in the *Hermit Crab*, his first ship.

79

The lifedome – cramped compared to the *Cauchy*, just a hundred metres across – seemed as real as he was. He punched a console, kicked his chair; it kicked back. 'Embodied, at last! Ha ha! . . . Hm. Maybe I've spent too much time alone recently.

'And I've been dropped into the co-pilot seat. Typical. Good joke, Michael. I hope you're watching somewhere, Nicola.'

He swapped over to the left-hand seat, and checked out the status of his craft. There wasn't much to check. As far as he could tell there was no functional link between the lifedome and the rest of the *Hermit Crab*. None of his controls worked. Maybe that was beyond the scope of this simulation, or whatever it was.

So he had no motive power. In fact, no functioning GUTengine in the dome either. The power in the lifedome's internal cells might last – what, a few hours?

He didn't grouse about this, nor did he fear his future. Such as it was. After all, beyond the lifedome was the core of a new galaxy. What was there to fear in the face of that?

But Jophiel was alone. He could feel it.

He turned on lights, green, blue. The lifedome, partitioned into functional sectors, was a little bubble of Earth, isolated.

He got a meal together. The mundane chore, performed in a bright island of light around the lifedome's small galley, was oddly cheering. And there was a certain authenticity to the experience, to the texture of the food, the plates and cutlery, that he hadn't known he'd missed, ever since Michael Poole had had him spun off, a Galaxy's span and five billion years ago.

He carried the food to his couch, lay back with the plate balancing on one hand, and dimmed the dome lights. He finished his food and set the plate carefully on the floor. He drank a glass of clean water.

Then he went to the freefall shower and washed in a spray of hot water. Again, an authenticity he hadn't enjoyed for five billion years. He tried to open up his senses, to relish every particle of sensation. There was a last time for everything, for even the most mundane experiences. He considered finding some music to play. Somehow that might have seemed fitting.

The lights failed. Even the softscreens winked out.

Well, so much for music. By feel, he made his way back to his couch. Though the sky was bright, full of those young stars, the air in here quickly grew colder; he imagined the heat of the lifedome leaking out. What would get him first, the cold, or the failing air?

He wasn't afraid. Oddly, he felt renewed: young, for the first time in decades, the pressure of time no longer seeming to weigh on him.

He was sorry he would never know how his relationship with Nicola might have worked out. That could have been something. Or indeed Miriam Berg, in different circumstances. Or a different lifetime, which seemed to be an option if you were Michael Poole.

But he found, in the end, he was glad that he had lived long enough to see all he had.

And he wished his template, out on some new Earth, the best of luck.

He was beginning to shiver, the air sharp in his nostrils. He lay back in his couch and crossed his hands on his chest. He closed his eyes.

A shadow crossed his face.

He opened his eyes, looked up. There was a ship hanging over the lifedome.

Jophiel stared in wonder.

It was something like a sycamore seed wrought in jet black. Night-dark wings which must have spanned hundreds of kilometres loomed over the *Crab*, softly rippling.

That's the Xeelee. Emerging from its own cocoon on the Wheel. Recovered, as you can see, its ship rebuilt. Its nursery emptied, now: it is joined with its young. Restored, despite all the damage you did it.

Well. I suppose you're wondering why I asked you here today.

'I think I know who you are. At last. Slow on the uptake, aren't I? You're the original. From the timeline before—'

Yeah. That's the best explanation I have. I'm here. As much as I'm anywhere. But I'm not from here.

'How are you – here – at all?'

414

Ah. Because in my timeline I fulfilled one of your, Michael's, ambitions. I got to complete the Cauchy *project . . .*

The *Cauchy*, an interstellar exploration vessel turned into a ship of war after Cold Earth, had originally been designed for a stunt flight. The plan had been to drag a wormhole mouth on a circular tour hundreds of light years long, starting and ending at the Solar System. And by the time it got back – because of a complication of the relativistic time distortion that had, in the end, shaped most of Jophiel's own existence – the wormhole would have served as a functioning time machine.

'You did it. You sent a GUTship on a loop, to the stars and back. You opened up a time bridge between past and future. Wow. It worked?'

It worked. Well, we knew it would.

You know, we – I mean me, Harry, Miriam, Bill Dzik, the rest of the team – didn't pull that stunt with any particular purpose in mind. We did it just because we could.

Seemed like a good idea at the time.

Until an alien occupying force from the future came back in time through our wormhole bridge to attack us. Much as the Xeelee did to you, Jophiel.

'The Qax.'

You know some of this? Reality is leaky, isn't it? It should come with a warranty . . . Yes, the Qax. Well, I dealt with it. In our own era, we fought them off. Then I needed to cut that Lethe-spawned time bridge. So I fly into the wormhole, and start up a faster-than-light drive in there.

'Whoa. I need to unpack some of that. First of all, you got hold of an FTL drive? How did it work?'

Lethe knows. I just know how to turn it on. So I smash the wormhole. But I do a little more damage than I intended . . .

Ahead of me, spacetime cracks, opening up like branching tunnels, leading off to infinity. I start to wonder if it's a good plan after all.

And I fall into the future, Jophiel. Through a network of transient wormholes that collapse after me. My instruments are smashed, and I know my lifedome must be awash with high-energy particles and gravity waves. I'm as helpless as a new-hatched chick, fallen from the nest. I think I'm going to die. And I think I deserve it.

'Why?'

Because I built the bridge that brought the Qax to my era, my Earth.

'Hmm. We Pooles do carry a lot of guilt, don't we? Michael's tormented by it.'

Well, he shouldn't be. You can't be responsible for all of human history.

That's a fallacy of dictators, engineers and other lunatics. Even if Michael Poole had never been born the Ghosts or the Qax would have found us eventually, and we would have been drawn into the game. And don't disregard what Michael Poole did achieve. He built the wormhole network that dug us out of near-Earth space, at least. Without that we might have been even worse off when the aliens came. And in your timeline he saved the world, with the Displacement, the Cold Earth. Look – let him heal. He deserves it.

Anyhow, death doesn't always come along like some absolving priest. It didn't for me, when I fell through the wormholes. Because, then—

'Yes?'

I was a chick that fell out of the nest, remember? But this chick took flight.

The lifedome – fell away. I believe I became a construct of quantum functions. A tapestry of acausal and nonlocal effects . . . I don't pretend to understand it.

I fell across five million years.

Then I saw you.

'In the Eighth Room.'

And I started to take an interest.

'I first glimpsed you long before then . . . I guess cause and effect sequences aren't really the point now, are they?'

You're getting the idea.

I became . . . spread out, you see. In space as in time. And across realities, possibilities. For instance, one time, one place, I was drawn to another group – humans, fleeing out of my own universe in a Poole Industries starship called the Great Northern, *who actually made it to Bolder's Ring, and through it, to another universe. With a little help.*

And, in another part of the forest, I – or another part of me, a copy of me – was summoned. By a woman, an Ascendant, called Luru Parz. Smarter than you or I will ever be, my friend. And as ancient as the cosmos, or it felt like it. It was another time, another place, where human civilisation had survived for a million years – they called themselves the Transcendents – and was doomed. Well, Luru Parz tried to save Earth from the Xeelee. For, you see, in the final stages of our glorious Galactic war against the Xeelee, we were driven all the way back to the Solar System . . . What she did was to turn Earth into Old Earth, a jar of slow time stopped up to preserve its children.

And she threw me in there.

And she threw dark-matter creatures in there too, after the humans, after me. Made us cooperate – no, more than that. Made us symbiotes. That woman put me through a thousand lifetimes on that distorted world.

'Why you?'

Well, I really was a hero, Jophiel. Though I didn't deserve the tag. I think she imagined I'd fight my way back out.

'And you did.'

And I did. After those thousand lives. With the lessons she wanted me to learn.

Listen, Jophiel. You'd think a galaxy collision is drama enough. There's more to come. The universe is ageing, my friend. And faster than you might want to think . . . Have you heard of the Big Rip?

'The what?'

Actually our Uncle George Poole was the first of us to hear this bad news from the future. The cosmologists figured it out in his lifetime, you see.

The universe is full of stuff you can't see, Jophiel. The dark matter is just the start, and look how much trouble that *caused. But dark* energy *outweighs all of that, and it's far, far worse. Like an antigravity field that suffuses the whole universe.*

And, here's the kicker. It's getting stronger.

It's pulling everything apart.

It won't happen soon. It will make no difference to us, to planets and stars, for over two hundred billion years. But after that, this cosmic force will fold down to the scale of galaxy clusters – which it will pull apart. Then, galaxies, smashing apart like dropped glass bowls. A hundred and fifty million years later, even solar systems will be torn open – planets sent off into the dark. And then—

'What?

Well, the detail's not clear. Even stars may be disrupted. Even planets. But then it stops. The strength of the antigravity field starts to decline again.

But on the other side of that hill will be a very strange universe. Nothing left but thinly scattered red dwarf stars, lone planets – if we're lucky. Maybe nothing at all but us, and stuff the size of us, if we're unlucky, depending on the strength of the Rip. It's a new age coming, Jophiel. A very strange one. But new.

'Hmm. Asher Fennell told me that the Xeelee is a survivor of past cosmic ages. It lived through *them*. Cooperated with new kinds of creatures, so they could survive together.'

Right! You have it. And that is just what Luru Parz foresaw. If life is to survive in the new age, all of the inhabitants of this universe, in this previous age, will have to cooperate. Symbiosis, my friend.

And that means light-matter creatures like humans and Ghosts – why, the Ghosts even had prophecies about it. Which was why, incidentally, they experimented with human-Ghost symbiotes. Like your pal Nicola. Just as well you brought one along. The Xeelee, even if they tried to bail out of this cosmos altogether. And the dark-matter creatures too, as Luru Parz saw . . . All of us.

'Ah. And that's why we had to bring the photino fish in their box.'

Correct. So.

'So?'

So what's your choice?

'So I go out with the High Africans, and build a world with one copy of myself. Or I go save a universe with another?'

That's about the size of it. What do you think?

Jophiel Poole was born in a moment of doubt. He had no doubt now.

80

Timelike infinity

Even after the Xeelee had finally won their war against humanity, the stars continued to age, too rapidly. The Xeelee completed their great Projects and fled the cosmos.

Time unravelled. Dying galaxies collided like clapping hands. But even now the story was not yet done. The universe itself prepared for another convulsion, greater than any it had suffered before.

And then—

'Who are you?'

My name is Michael Poole.

'And I – I am Jophiel.'

Let's get to work.

Afterword

Work on this novel came at a difficult time in my personal life. I'm very grateful for the sympathy and support of the Gollancz team, especially Marcus Gipps and Craig Leyenaar, of my agent, Christopher Schelling of Selectric Artists, of Elizabeth Dobson for an excellent and invaluable copy-edit, and Paul McAuley for a discerning proof-read.

This novel and its prequel, *Vengeance*, are a pendant to my 'Xeelee Sequence' of stories and novels. The epigraphs to the sections are taken from earlier works.

My depiction of life in the Xeelee universe, with each cosmic age being as rich as any other from the Big Bang to the Big Rip, was originally inspired by Freeman Dyson's 'scaling hypothesis' ('Time Without End: Physics and Biology in an Open Universe', *Review of Modern Physics*, vol. 51, pp. 447–60, 1979), a paper which opened up the study of the far future of the universe – even if the modern view of that future looks quite different. More recently a suggestion that a 'Big Rip' might not after all be terminal for our universe was made by H. We *et al.* ('Quasi-Rip: A New Type of Rip Model without Cosmic Doomsday', *Physics Review D*, vol. 86, p. 083003, 2012).

'The Celestial View from a Relativistic Starship' was definitively analysed in a paper of that name by R. W. Stimets *et al.* in 1981 (*Journal of the British Interplanetary Society*, vol. 34, pp. 83–9). The idea of using millisecond pulsars as interstellar navigation beacons was suggested by Werner Becker *et al.* ('Autonomous Spacecraft Navigation Using Pulsars', *Acta Futura*, vol. 7, pp. 11–28, 2013).

Robin Hanson's *The Age of Em* (Oxford University Press, 2016) contains some fascinating speculations on a society of computer-emulated humans not unlike 'Virtuals', a long-standing feature of the Xeelee universe.

The planet Goober c was first mentioned in my first professionally published short story, 'The Xeelee Flower' (1987). A model of how a world like Goober c, at the limit of habitability – twice as far from its Sunlike star as Earth is from Sol – could bear life was studied by

Aomawa *et al.*, using the (real-life) exoplanet Kepler-62f as a model ('The Effect of Orbital Configuration on the Possible Climates and Habitability of Kepler-62f', *Astrobiology*, vol. 16, pp. 443–64, 2016). At the time of writing, this planet is seen as one of the three most promising candidates to host an environment of Earthlike habitability.

The notion of 'asteroengineering', adjusting the lifetime of a star, was studied by Martin Beech ('Aspects of an Asteroengineering Option', *Journal of the British Interplanetary Society*, vol. 46, pp. 317–22, 1993). While my own irresponsible speculations on structure and life in dark matter go back a couple of decades (*Ring*, 1994), scientific speculation that at least some dark matter might be self-interacting and so might contain complex structure has recently gained momentum (see *Dark Matter and the Dinosaurs* by Lisa Randall, Bodley Head, 2015). For a discussion on the dark-matter conquest of the universe I'm indebted to Stuart Armstrong and Anders Sandberg ('Eternity in Six Hours: Intergalactic Spreading of Intelligent Life and Sharpening the Fermi Paradox', *Acta Astronautica*, vol. 89, pp. 1–13, 2013).

The peculiar commonality of Earthlike gravity among the observed exoplanets was noted by F. Ballesteros *et al.* ('Walking on Exoplanets: Is *Star Wars* Right?', *Earth and Planetary Astrophysics*, vol. 16, pp. 325–7, 2016). A useful recent review of our understanding of galaxies is *Galaxy: Mapping the Cosmos* by James Geach (Reaktion Books, 2014). In the Xeelee universe the supermassive black hole at the centre of the Galaxy, known to the astronomers as Sagittarius A*, is called 'Chandra' – the Sanskrit word for 'luminous' – after the late astrophysicist and Nobel prize winner Subrahmanyan Chandrasekhar. My depiction of the collision of the Milky Way with the Andromeda Galaxy is based on such studies as John Dubinski's 'The Great Milky Way–Andromeda Collision', *Sky & Telescope*, October 2006, pp. 30–36.

Mark Maslin's *The Cradle of Humanity* (Oxford University Press, 2017) is a recent report on the 'pulsed climate variability' hypothesis, the latest variant of theories that the fluctuating climate of Africa has acted as a 'pump' for the evolution of successive types of humanity, or human precursors. My depiction of the nature of the Xeelee was inspired in part by speculations on the evolution of the octopus and other cephalopods, an entirely different evolutionary descent of brain and mind from the line that led to our own (see *Other Minds: The Octopus and the Evolution of Intelligent Life* by Peter Godfrey-Smith, William Collins, 2017).

As mentioned in the text my 'Wheel' stands on the metaphorical shoulders of previous giant structures as imagined by Banks, Niven and others. The engineering of ringworlds was studied by Forrest Bishop (1997, www.iase.cc/openair.htm). The so-called 'Ehrenfest Paradox', the idea that because of relativistic contraction a rapidly rotating disc would have a circumference larger than a stationary disc with the same radius – the principle on which the Xeelee Wheel is constructed – was indeed a valuable thought experiment for Einstein himself as he developed his theory of General Relativity (see G. Rizzi *et al.*, *Relativity in Rotating Frames*, Kluwer, 2004).

All errors and misapprehensions are of course my sole responsibility.

Stephen Baxter
Northumberland
February 2018

Stephen Baxter

FLOOD

Next year. Sea levels begin to rise. The change is far more rapid than any climate change predictions; metres a year. Within two years London, only 15 metres above the sea, is drowned. New York follows, the Pope gives his last address from the Vatican, Mecca disappears beneath the waves.

FLOOD tells the story of mankind's final years on earth. The stories of a small group of people caught up in the struggle to survive are woven into a tale of unimaginable global disaster. And the hope offered for a unlucky few by a second great ark . . .

ARK

As the waters rose in FLOOD, high in the Colorado mountains the US government was building an ark. Not an ark to ride the waves but an ark that would take a select few thousand people out into space to start a new future for mankind. Sent out into deep space on a journey lasting years, generations of crew members carry the hope of a new beginning on a new, incredibly distant, planet.

But as time passes knowledge and purpose is lost and division and madness grows. And back on earth life, and man, find a new way. This is the epic sequel to the acclaimed FLOOD; a stirring tale of what mankind will do to survive and the perfect introduction for new readers to one of SF's greatest tropes; the generation ship.

• • •

'Never has Baxter presented a more thrilling and moving glimpse of a possible future: ARK could well be his masterpiece' *Guardian*

PROXIMA-ULTIMA

Stephen Baxter

The very far future: the Galaxy is a drifting wreck of black holes, neutron stars, chill white dwarfs. The age of star formation is long past. Yet there is life here, feeding off the energies of the stellar remnants, and there is mind, a tremendous Galaxy-spanning intelligence each of whose thoughts lasts a hundred thousand years. And this mind cradles memories of a long-gone age when a more compact universe was full of light . . .

The 27th century: Proxima Centauri, an undistinguished red dwarf star, is the nearest star to our sun – and (in this fiction), the nearest to host a world, Proxima IV, habitable by humans. But Proxima IV is unlike Earth in many ways. Huddling close to the warmth, orbiting in weeks, it keeps one face to its parent star at all times. The 'substellar point', with the star forever overhead, is a blasted desert, and the 'antistellar point' on the far side is under an ice cap in perpetual darkness. How would it be to live on such a world?

Yuri Jones, with 1,000 others, is about to find out . . .

PROXIMA tells the amazing tale of how we colonise a harsh new eden, and the secret we find there that will change our role in the Universe for ever.

In ULTIMA the consequences of what we discovered make themselves felt. There are minds in the universe billions of years old and they have a plan for us. For some of us.

• • •

'[Stephen Baxter] is one of the few still producing massive, fastidiously textured SF epics that engage the intelligence of the reader. Ideas come thick and fast, and an exhilarating sense of wonder is guaranteed' *Independent*

'This is a hard SF novel that battles bravely with big ideas. With every passing year, the oft-made remark that Baxter is Arthur C. Clarke's heir seems more and more apt' *SFX*

ABOUT GOLLANCZ

Gollancz is the oldest SF publishing imprint in the world. Since being founded in 1927 Gollancz has continued to publish a focused selection of bestselling and award-winning authors. The front-list includes **Ben Aaronovitch**, **Joe Abercrombie**, **Charlaine Harris**, **Joanne Harris**, **Joe Hill**, **Alastair Reynolds**, **Patrick Rothfuss**, **Nalini Singh** and **Brandon Sanderson**.

As one of the largest Science Fiction and Fantasy imprints in the UK it is no surprise we have one of the most extensive backlists in the world. Find high-quality SF on Gateway written by such authors as **Philip K. Dick**, **Ursula Le Guin**, **Connie Willis**, **Sir Arthur C. Clarke**, **Pat Cadigan**, **Michael Moorcock** and **George R.R. Martin**.

We also have a strand of publishing in translation, which includes French, Polish and Russian authors. Gollancz is home to more award-winning authors than any other imprint, with names including **Aliette de Bodard**, **M. John Harrison**, **Paul McAuley**, **Sarah Pinborough**, **Pierre Pevel**, **Justina Robson** and many more.

The SF Gateway
More than 3,000 classic, rare and previously out-of-print SF novels at your fingertips.
www.sfgateway.com

The Gollancz Blog
Bringing you news from our worlds to yours. Stories, interviews, articles and exclusive extracts just for you!
www.gollancz.co.uk

GOLLANCZ
LONDON